dixi
books

Tadej Golob

Tadej Golob (1967, Slovenia) is a unique best-selling author with a thematically broad range of works, who put Slovene crime fiction on the map of world literature. He won the Slovene Novel of the Year Award for his debut, has written several biographies, two YA novels, and a book about the first person to ski from the summit of Mount Everest, also conquered by the author himself.

Gregor Timothy Čeh

Gregor Timothy Čeh was brought up in a bilingual family in Slovenia. He studied Archaeology and History of Art at UCL, taught English in Greece, returned to England to complete a Masters at Kent, and now lives in Cyprus. He translates contemporary Slovene literature for publishing houses and authors in Slovenia, with translations published in both the UK and US.

Tadej Golob

The Lake

translated from the Slovene by
Gregor Timothy Čeh

dixi
books

Dixi Books

The Lake
Tadej Golob
Original title: Jezero
Published by Založba Goga in 2018
Translator: Gregor Timothy Čeh
Editor: Katherine Boyle
Proofreading: Andrea Bailey
Designer: Pablo Ulyanov
Cover Design: Jurij Kocuvan

Co-funded by the
Creative Europe Programme
of the European Union

"The European Commission's support for the production of this publication does not constitute an endorsement of the contents, which reflect the views only of the authors, and the Commission cannot be held responsible for any use which may be made of the information contained therein."

II. Edition: **February 2022**
Library of Congress Cataloging-in Publication Data
Tadej Golob
ISBN: **978-1-913680-43-5**
1. Thriller 2. Crime 3. Detective 4. Slovenia

293 Green Lanes, Palmers Green, London, England, N13 4XS
info@dixibooks.com
www.dixibooks.com

Tadej Golob

The Lake

translated from the Slovene by
Gregor Timothy Čeh

dixi
books

The Voice of the New Age

Introduction

It started snowing at around midday, and when Joey, an impossible mongrel, a cross between a Doberman and a Schnauzer, rushed down the hill, only his black head with his droopy half-Doberman ears sticking out above the snow. Every time his head ploughed into the fresh snow he surprisedly and wistfully looked at his owner at the edge of the road and then continued to search for the yellow tennis ball. He was called Joey after Joey from *Friends*, the favourite character of the young woman standing at the roadside, laughing at the helpless dog. When the series first started on TV, Alina – that was the girl's name – was still at nursery school. She had only caught up with it in its final seasons and then also watched all the earlier episodes. Now, ten years later, she will still occasionally sit down and watch one. Whenever she feels melancholy and nostalgic. Melancholy and nostalgic at only twenty-five, she thought. What else is to come?

At the same time she couldn't actually explain why this soap was so dear to her. There are things that we like at certain times in our life and, when we come across them later on, we're surprised to discover that we don't really know what it was that made them our favourite books, films and TV series, for example. But with Friends it wasn't like that for Alina. Was it corny? Yes, certainly. Was Phoebe not a character who would not last three days in real life? Yes... although, she smiled, she does know a girl like her. And Joey... Joey Tribbiani.

"How you doin'?"

Though she would probably not admit it in company, at least not if everyone was sober, and although she has also in the meantime finished a degree in Anthropology, she still finds it sweetly amusing. If she did admit to it, she would add that Friends are her guilty pleasure. At least she doesn't listen to Bon Jovi.

Joey pushed through the snow. In five hours almost thirty centimetres had fallen. With his Schnauzer feet he trampled the cold white layer and when he reached the ball and grabbed it with his teeth, he didn't turn around and return to his mistress along the path he had made turned sharply and continued to plough afresh.

This was also kind of cutely funny. A short-legged Doberman with a yellow tennis ball in its mouth.

She grabbed the ball and, after a brief tugging, he let go. She pretended to throw it again but didn't let go of it, hiding it behind her back instead. The dog once more shot out into the snow, ran a few steps until he was stopped by the snow, and then, confused, first looked ahead and then back at his mistress.

"Oh, silly dog," she said, turned slightly to the left and threw the ball with all her strength down along the river bank as she always did on their regular walk – well, if we can say always on her third visit since they had arrived in Bohinj. The ball flew across the blanket of white and disappeared into the bushes. To the dog this seemed even more entertaining though Alina worried she might have thrown it too far and it could have fallen into the water.

"Joey, Joooeeey..."

The dog didn't listen, it never did. She could shout as much as she wanted – he was burrowing himself a new channel through the snow and disappeared into the bushes. Surely he won't go into the water if the ball has fallen in?

He barked. She waited for him to return with the ball in his pointy snout, but he didn't come. He barked again and she thought he must be barking at the ball as it flowed down river, but then there should be some movement through the bushes along the bank as he ran through them, but there was none. The bushes were calm and the dog was still barking.

"Joeeey!"

She could not be bothered to walk into the fresh snow. She was wearing waterproof Gore-Tex hiking shoes but they were only ankle-high and if snow sticks to your socks and then slowly drips into your shoes no Gore-Tex makes any difference.

"Joeeey!"

The dog appeared at the edge of the bushes, without the ball. She waved at him, calling him to join her, patting her thighs with her woollen gloves.

"Joey, Joey, come along, come to mummy..."

The dog barked sharply and disappeared into the thicket.

She sighed and left the road. The snow was almost knee high. She made herself step along one of the tracks the dog had made, just waiting for the dampness to reach her socks. It's almost half an hour's walk back to the apartments. Silly mutt!

She pushed through the branches, trying not to shake the snow off onto herself. From the edge of the bushes, the river was barely a few feet away. The dog saw her, barked, squealed, and wagged his tail, looking alternately at her and the river. The ball was beside him.

"What is it?"

She picked up the ball.

"Let's go, Joey..."

She looked up and glanced towards the water, frozen at the edges. There was something white sticking out of the ice which in the dusk appeared artificial, plastic, like the hand of a mannequin.

Who would throw a plastic mannequin into the river? she wondered.

Chapter 1.

Ukanc, Sunday, 31 December

"So you're a cop?" asked the woman around sixty clinging onto a glass of wine. In fact it sounded something like, "S…yur..hiccup…" Clearly she had already had a few. "How unusual!"

"Unusual?" he asked. "People usually find my name unusual, not my profession."

"Taras? Well, yes, Taras is a bit strange, but I do know a few, Gogol's Taras Bulba and... probably a few more, but a cop..."

She laughed as if she had just said something funny.

"He isn't a cop," said a woman who approached them and placed her hand on Taras' shoulder.

"He's an inspector."

She too stammered slightly, the r in inspector drooled on for a little too long, implying more than one glass of the mulled wine, Taras thought. She never could handle alcohol.

"Hang on, hang on… have you two not met?"

The older woman pouted like a teenager, and looked like... an older woman impersonating a teenager,

"No, my husband only ever introduces me to his... targets, never mine."

Taras smiled, trying not to make it look forced, and gave his hand to the older woman,

"Taras Birsa. If you ever get a parking ticket, do call me."

"Taras..."

"Don't interrupt him, Alenka," said the woman, still pulling faces as she extended her hand to him. "It's not every day a woman like me meets a charming policeman. I'm Karin. Karin Prelc, the wife of the gentleman shining over there…" she waved her hand pointing across towards the far end of the large living room. "He's your wife's partner. But you probably know that. What kind of a policeman would you be if you didn't?"

And she laughed again as if she had just said something very funny indeed. Taras made an effort to laugh too. Alenka clearly saw no need to.

"And Birsa? I don't know anyone called Birsa."

"Have you not heard of Valter Birsa?"

The woman shook her head.

"The footballer? On the national team?"

"Oh, I don't follow that kind of stuff. Not for me. How come," she turned to Taras' wife, "that you're not called Birsa when you're his wife?"

"Because we're not married, but I can't be bothered to explain to people that we're not. At our age I can hardly call him my boyfriend. But Karin, allow me to take him away for a while."

Karin pouted once again and Taras thought this really was unnecessary.

"Go ahead, Go ahead... so if he's not her husband, she's his... partner."

She paused before uttering the word partner.

"Pretend you are talking to me," Alenka said as she held Taras by the hand and escorted him to a larger group standing by a small bar on the other side of the room, clearly having fun.

"Why exactly am I doing this?"

"Because the old bat will devour you otherwise. You should thank me. By the way, why do you keep telling people that you are a cop?"

"Perhaps because I am?" he said with obvious irony. "You're not a doctor?"

"I am, but I am also a shareholder in the clinic. And you're a policeman, but most of all, you're an inspector, and that isn't the same. If you were still a policeman at your age, we'd probably not be together. Would you hitch up with, I don't know, some nurse?"

"Ugh, aren't we all high and mighty today."

"High and mighty or not, it doesn't change the facts, even if we try to deny them till we drop. People have ambitions in life. Some more, others less. Some stay policemen and some stay family doctors at some surgery somewhere in the back of beyond, but I'm not one of them, and you're not..."

Taras smiled.

"No need to mention a rich father, recently deceased," said Alenka and gave him a stern look.

"Did I?"

"Not so far today, thank you. But he was my father, thank God, and I am who I am and am not what I'm not. Why should I care what would be, whether it would be or whether it wouldn't be?"

Her slightly slurred words made it sound more as if she was babbling on about some watered, weathered and wooden bee. "I don't give a shit."

"Ouch?"

"Am I drunk?"

"How much have you had?"

"A glass of mulled wine and now this," she raised the stemmed glass she was holding.

"Then you're drunk," said Taras, Taras Birsa, police inspector, Birsa, as in the football player, and put his hands around her. "Let's drink to that."

He stepped to the drinks table with red and white wine and various kinds of spirits, and picked out a conspicuous glass of orange liquid.

"And what are we drinking to here?" A white-haired man with a tousled look and lensless glasses and a slight bristle, sporting a white jumper and white trousers approached them. Dr Prelc always reminded Taras of Richard Branson. Even his teeth were just as white.

"May I join you?"

He held a glass of wine in his hand. White wine. Had he chosen white to go with his jumper? Taras wondered.

"Well, what is it?"

"She's pregnant," said Taras.

"Taras! Of course I'm not," said Alenka. "He's joking."

"We're toasting our life's luck that we are among the one percent of the world population that is overloaded," Taras said and raised his glass.

"Well, of course. That's something to drink to," Dr Prelc said, joining in on the toast. He was no longer sober either.

"And Taras has a guilty conscience and is going on and on about it," said Alenka.

"No I'm not. It's just so I don't forget."

"Oh, don't be such a drag..."

She turned round to the food table, investigating the trays of canapés.

"Dinner is served in a quarter of an hour!" Dr Prelc - Branson shouted after her. Taras just dismissively waved his hand.

"Let her eat something, otherwise she'll feel sick."

"How much has she had? How long have you been here? A quarter of an hour."

Taras looked at his watch. A quarter to six.

"An hour, but it's not that. She can't handle it. Anyway, we dropped in unannounced and I don't want someone to go without dinner because of us."

"Do you think it might actually harm anyone in here if they went without dinner?"

Dr Prelc pointed with his hand towards the crowd in the room as he turned around and said again,

"Do you think it would harm anyone here?"

Around twenty people were gathered into the largest room on the ground floor of a weekend house that was big enough for them not to need remain a single crowd but could mingle in smaller groups. Including Alenka and himself, there were twenty-two, if he had not miscounted, and he was usually right in situations like this. By the looks of it, all older couples, and he usually assessed these things correctly as well. Part of his job.

Dr Prelc stared at his glass for a while as if deep in thought,

"Let's go for a cigarette?"

"You want me to come for a cigarette with you?"

"Yes, yes... I know you don't smoke. I go out for a cigarette and you go out to get some fresh air, plus my cigarette smoke, we both get something out of it. Come on, let's go..."

They made their way behind the other guests towards the door leading onto a small roofed terrace, big enough for a largish wooden table and a few chairs. Taras closed the door, pulled one of the chairs closer and sat on it. Two metres away the snow was still falling. Evenly and heavily. It wasn't even that cold. Around zero, Taras guessed.

"Nice, isn't it?"

Taras nodded.

"I've had this weekend house for thirty years. I was the first of all these doctors to build one. Well, many others have done so since and now we are a kind of *Hospital at the End of the City*."

He looked at Taras,

"Are you old enough to remember that? The Czech TV series?"

"The likes of Pane Sova?"

"That's the one..."

He seemed delighted, as if Taras had just said something brilliant. He took a sip of his drink and in his enthusiasm almost choked on it; most of it landed on the table in front of them.

"Shit, do you know when you're old? When you start telling jokes in a company and nobody else knows what you're talking about. You start telling a Mujo and Haso joke[1], and everyone just stares at you. Which Mujo? Who's Haso?"

He took another sip, carefully this time.

"And what's the snow like up on Vogel?"

"It only started snowing as we were leaving and there must be plenty now. But there was barely any before. You needed to watch out for rocks."

"Now there'll be enough for skiing down Žagarjev Graben," Dr Prelc said. "I love that. The last cable car up to Vogel, a quick shot of schnapps, and ski back home... for another shot of schnapps."

He laughed,

"Listen Taras, why don't you two stay the night here? You don't want to drive back home in this? Stay and we can get drunk like real people... animals always know when they've had enough..." and he laughed loudly again. "Well, at least the rest of us, you can sip on your apple juice."

1 Translator's note (all footnotes): Mujo and Haso were Bosnian joke characters used in (often racist) jokes throughout the former Yugoslavia.

Taras shook his head,

"Come on, we can go and have some fun in the snow tomorrow. I have an extra pair of cross-country skis and boots in the shed over there..."

He pointed to a shed about twenty metres away, barely visible in the dark,

"As far as that goes, it isn't a problem. In winter I always keep my cross-country skis and all the gear in the car."

From spring to autumn Taras kept everything he needed for running in the back of his Citroen, running shoes, socks, shorts, T-shirts, a towel. In the winter he changed it to his cross-country skiing gear.

"Our daughters said they'll come to our place after midnight and we'll all go for a walk around the old town. And if two twenty-year-olds who you otherwise never see promise that to their parents, then..."

"Then you have little choice," Dr Prelc said. "Are they both studying? Where are they?"

"Both in Vienna, both Microbiology."

"Well, then we really need to drink to high-flyers."

He raised his glass, they clinked and took a sip. Then from his trouser pocket Dr Prelc produced a cigarette packet that looked empty, and pulled out a ready joint.

"A gift from some students..."

He lit it, drew in deeply draw and leant back into the wooden chair. Taras could smell the smoke, which in the damp air rose up under the roof of the terrace in the shape of a small cloud.

"Oh, I hope you're fine with this. I keep forgetting that you're a..."

"Cop?"

"Well, yes, a detective. I mean the joint. Everyone uses it now anyway."

"I'm fine with it," said Taras. "I'm not at work anyway."

"Want some?"

Taras shook his head.

"And what do you think about this? Legalization and all that?"

"I don't care."

"You must have some opinion on it. It's your work."

He could not have cared less. If there was something that Taras had learned over almost quarter of a century on the job, it was that with matters he had no influence over – and there were certainly a huge number of such – he couldn't care less. Crime is a constant. A certain percentage of people will always hop onto the dark side. If you take away their dope, they will start trading in amphetamines, coke, heroin… amanita mushrooms. If everything is legalized, they will divert their attention to stealing from shops. There will always be something.

"I don't know," he said. "I really don't care. Besides, I deal with murders, Homicide and Sexual Offences Section, drugs come under another department. Organized Crime, Illicit Drug Section," he reeled off. "You're an abdominal expert, if I'm not mistaken?"

"Yes, intestines and stuff like that."

Dr Prelc laughed. Clearly the dope was having an effect.

"What do you know about lungs? Could you operate on lungs?"

"I don't know. I could cut a few bits off if needed. I do know that people shouldn't smoke."

He choked and he coughed for a while and then began to laugh. He laughed so much that tears rolled down his cheeks. He took off his glasses and wiped them away with the sleeve of his jumper. In fact, if it were up to him, thought Taras, he would keep marihuana illegal. With alcohol at least people become sociable. With two puffs of dope, they enter a world of their own. They laugh at their own jokes, for example.

"Your wife," Dr Prelc said, "Alenka, she's OK. I think she has always been OK, even as a student, and she still is. She's still great."

For which she can thank her genes, Taras thought. If he were as inactive as she is, he'd age in an instant, but she certainly looks much younger than her age.

Alenka was a beautiful woman, and still is at forty-five. When she steps into a room you can see all the men turning to her; women also, envious. Her friends, her generation, are either domesticated housewives with quite a few extra kilos or ardent sportswomen, fanatic followers of this or that way of life, vegetarianism, veganism, fanatical yoga... and too thin, all veins, skin and bones; as Dr Prelc would say, nothing to hold on to. Alenka had a good figure, a nice face with the right features and a slightly pointed nose at the centre, which should distract from this balanced beauty but did in fact enhance it with a cute attractiveness. And medium-long, fair hair, which turned almost blonde in the summer and now had the hues of a brunette. When Taras had first met her she wore her hair short, a bit like Pink in the days of her shortest hair. And for a long time he thought she dyed it blonde. For quite a while now, she had kept it much longer.

"Short haircuts are for twenty-year-olds," she said. "At forty it makes you look like an ageing lesbian."

Prelc took another deep draw and threw the rest into the darkness, into the snow.

"We did fuck a lot then, God did we fuck. You won't believe how quickly they offer themselves to a professor surgeon. It's something about the white robe."

"Butchers also wear one," Taras said.

"Butchers? Butchers?"

He laughed and, just as it seemed as if he had stopped, he laughed again, and again. He could not stop. Butchers, and ha, ha, ha and again, butchers, and ha ha ha...

"We annoy you, don't we, Taras?"

"Doctors?"

"Not just doctors," Prelc said laughing. "All of us high-flyers, the nouveau riche, the bourgeoisie. We do, don't we? It's pointless, Taras. We're here forever. This is because we aren't picky. We can make do with anything. We reproduce sexually, vegetatively, whatever works. That's why we need to recruit someone new every so often, new blood. You!"

He pointed at Taras with his finger and started laughing again. Clearly the joint was a good one, very strong.

"*Perhaps there will be a time,*" Dr Prelc said when he finally managed to calm down and Taras thought he was about to change the subject again, "when girls won't just offer themselves for a fuck to Rajko Prelc, perhaps, *but it is not now,*" he said and dramatically pointed his finger towards the sky, well, to the wooden roof above the terrace. "The hour of the wolves of impotence and a leaky prostate… *but it is not now*."

He exhaled the last smoke from his lungs.

"Do you know it?"

"Lord of the Rings?"

"Lord of fucking zilch," Dr Prelc said. "Hey, Taras?"

"Yes?"

"Why don't you stay tonight and we really can have a few drinks? There's a bunch of doctors of whatever in there, but I have nothing in common with them. They're all stuck behind the blinkers of their work, hidebound half-finished idiots. I'm fed up with them, they get on my nerves." He leaned towards Taras and whispered into his ear, "Do you know that I've fucked all their wives? Absolutely every one of them in there?"

He then slumped into his chair, continued mumbling, talking to himself or thinking aloud,

"Although, if I can be honest, and I suppose I can be because it's just me and you here; Fuck it, I'm sixty and the day is fast approaching. Some of these dumb students and nurses and all this clientele see me as some old lecher. I don't mind the second part because I've always been lecherous and always will be, but old… When I mount some of them, I feel like some pervert, seducing a child with some sweeties… perhaps I will somehow have to settle down…"

He picked up his glass and drank what wine was left in it.

"Settle down, Taras, eh?"

"Are you not yet settled?"

Dr Prelc snorted, as if he had gulped on spoilt wine.

"We're friends, aren't we Taras?"

Are we? Prelc was more than ten years his senior. Taras had met him when Alenka became co-owner of the clinic, so only a few years ago, four perhaps. He would see him regularly and they occasionally went on a bike ride around Ljubljana together, three or four times on longer trips… which is something you probably do with friends. Today he had even met his wife.

"Yes, of course."

"Seriously?"

"Seriously."

"Could you do me a favour? A kind of professional favour, as a friend, if I asked you for it?"

"What kind of a favour?"

Prelc stopped, looked at his empty glass and waved his hand dismissively.

"You've met my wife?"

"I have."

"Did you know she was at the Olympics. In Montreal 1976. The ones where Nadia Comăneci was awarded a perfect ten. The first ever. And Karin almost performed, had it not been for all the machinations in the Yugoslav national team. Like Jacky Stewart… Do you know who Jacky Stewart is?"

"I do. A seventies Formula One driver."

The door opened and Alenka stuck her head round the frame.

"Hey, you two, dinner is on the table."

Then she stepped out onto the terrace, gazing out into the darkness. The snow was getting heavier.

"Quite deep, isn't it," she said and shivered in the cold. She turned to Taras, "Taras, if we want to get home tonight, we'll have to hurry."

She seemed to have recovered. She opened the door back into the house and waited for Taras to join her. Dr Prelc followed close behind them.

"If I remember rightly, Balažič's wife is the only one I haven't fucked," he whispered and gestured with his hands towards a rather bulky woman across the room, "never had the stomach for that. Poor woman."

Chapter 2.

"Thighs on the table!"

Dr Prelc came laughing through the door to what seemed to be the kitchen and placed a large roasted turkey onto the dining table, made up of three smaller tables covered with a single tablecloth.

"I suggest that, as the expert in these matters, I dismember it and then you all just help yourselves with your fingers, we all feel at home here anyway... Well..." he paused, holding some large poultry shears in his hand. "...you probably don't know Mr Coolguy over there," he pointed at Taras. "And it's probably just as well you haven't met him anywhere else but here, because he's a cop, inspector at the department of... What was it again, Taras?"

"Homicide and Sexual Offences," Taras dutifully helped him out.

Everyone turned towards Taras. Taras was used to being the focus of attention in any new company for a while. Even just his name would warrant some intrigue, as would his abstinence, but when he added his profession... Very few of the people he met did not watch American crime series or films, crime and drama in which Hollywood superstars with three-day stubble and beautiful female assistants keep saving the world. Reality was unfortunately far more boring. There were no beauties, ever since Penca had died, he shared the office with two middle-aged men and the closest anyone got to beauty was Tatiana at human resources. Closest but still not particularly close...

"So you're a criminal investigator? Like..." and they would come up with the name of some actor, from Leonardo di Caprio to James Cagney, depending on the age of the person making the comment, though Taras could not recall James Cagney playing the policeman in any of the black and white films he had seen, usually he was more of a gangster.

Dr Prelc held the turkey thigh with the scissors and pressed hard until it cracked.

"That was right between the pubis and the ilium, and I probably cut right through the ischium. I hope there's no vet among us."

He placed the pieces of carved turkey onto a large plate and the pile grew for a while until, after his renewed prompting, the guests finally began helping themselves. Taras did not see Prelc's wife. She was probably still in the kitchen.

*

Taras discretely observed the other guests as he took a bite of the white meat. Alenka was to his right, to his left a rather stout woman - almost certainly poor Mrs Balažič. None other fitted the description. Next to her sat a man, tall, also quite fat, probably her husband.

"Interesting name," said Mrs Balažič, otherwise known as Irena. "I bet it was your mother who chose it, not your father."

Taras smiled,

"Why would you think that?"

"It is always the mothers who are responsible for unusual names. I work on the paediatric ward and some years ago when that series about Sandokan was first aired... Do you remember him? The Pirate of Malaysia?"

Taras nodded.

"Well, we had quite a few Sandokans around. More recently we have had a number of Justins... you know, Bieber? Heard of him?"

Taras nodded.

"Well, was it your mother?"

"I don't know," said Taras. "I never asked."

The man next to her cleared his throat and offered Taras his hand across his wife's plate.

"Balažič..."

He had not used Dr in front of his name, but it sounded as if he had. He was the first to reach for the turkey and the first to help himself to a second piece, now his beard glistened with grease. He would also probably be the first to say after dinner that he is getting fat on thin air, Taras thought. Something was tormenting him.

"You know what I want to know..." he began. "Well, of course you won't know, though... as a criminal investigator you might?"

He smiled and looked around to check how he was doing for an audience.

"What, if I've ever shot a person?"

"No, no... not that. Tell me whether or not there is such as thing as a perfect murder?"

"Where did you get that one from?" his wife asked.

The entire table fell silent and all heads turned to Taras.

"What do you mean?" asked Taras.

"Is there a way of killing a person without getting caught?"

"Good God," said Mrs Balažič. "You're not thinking of murdering anyone, are you?"

She laughed and a few people round the table joined her, but they all continued to stare with eager curiosity at Taras, the Inspector.

"There are quite a few unsolved cases. Is that what you're referring to?"

"No, no, I'm thinking of closed cases... Well, I don't know how to express myself, ones like those described by Agatha Christie. When at some gathering, like this one here today, someone poisons someone or something like that, and where you as the inspector perhaps even know the perpetrator but cannot prove it."

Balažič proudly glanced round the table.

"No," said Taras. "There aren't such murders."

"How come?" asked the man sitting opposite Taras. "Would you know if there was a murderer among us? If anyone at this table had already killed someone?"

Of course Taras could not know this.

"If I knew you were the murderer, they I would probably also know how to prove it."

Balažič shook his head, as if he was disappointed with the answer.

"And how do you, as an expert in the field, see Hollywood films?" asked a woman sitting at the far end of the table, some three chairs to the right. "If you watch them at all?"

"I do. Just movies. What you lot here do is also probably quite different to what Dr House does?"

"No," Dr Zgonc made himself heard. "There's no difference." They all laughed and a beaming Zgonc added,

"Well, apart from the fact that none of us work late into the night. I even think they must have filmed the series at our clinic because they needed the space and all the equipment and none of ours is being used in the afternoons. We even lent them our patients.

They all laughed again and Taras though that that would be the end of this and he would be able to concentrate on his piece of turkey again, but Balažič would not lay off,

"But..."

"But, dear Mitja," Alenka jumped in. "No, if you should wish to get rid of Irena, I don't recommend you do it when Taras is on duty. Everyone confesses to him. Even stuff they haven't done."

Another avalanche of laughter.

"Don't laugh. I was being serious. There's no keeping secrets from Taras. I am convinced that he already knows things about all of you here that you would not be happy were he to speak them out loud."

She appeared to be so convinced about what she was talking that the laughs were much shorter this time.

"Well, what do you know about me, for example?" asked Irena Balažič.

Taras looked at her with a smile that could be seen as polite.

"She's exaggerating, Alenka is exaggerating. How could he possibly know anything?"

"And besides," Dr Prelc spoke up and looked straight at Taras, conspiratorially. "We're all doctors here. As far as killing is concerned, Metod Trobec[2] is a complete amateur for us."

The laugher round the table turned into a guffaw. Mrs Prelc,

2 Metod Trobec was a Slovene serial killer convicted of killing at least five women in the late 1970s; He spent 27 years in prison before commiting suicide in 2006.

also a doctor, appeared at the kitchen door,

"Have I missed something?"

*

"Perhaps it really would be better if we actually stayed the night."

Alenka stared at the front windscreen. Taras kept switching between the low and high beams without much difference or success, especially since he recently, trying to change the bulbs in his headlamps, had managed to tear one of the wires keeping it in place. The bulb now hung loosely inside the headlamp and emitted the kind of diffused beam which made it look as if he was trying to use his Citroën to break the speed of light as shown in science fiction films. Well, at least in those which Taras still watched. Star Wars, for example.

"We promised the girls," he said.

"Yes, and when we get to Ljubljana, if we get to Ljubljana, we'll get a message saying, sorry, got held up somewhere..." Alenka fell silent and sighed. "God it's snowing hard. I can't remember when I last saw snow like this."

The road was empty. On the night of 31 December everyone is already where they intend to see in the New Year, especially in weather like this. He tried to recall whether it had been forecast, but all he could do was admit that he had only checked the morning weather when they were going to be on the ski slope, unconcerned at the time with what the evening would be like. There were already about four inches of fresh snow on the tarmac, unploughed and no tyre tracks visible at all. Had previously cleared snow not been stacked up in piles at the side of the road with the occasional red and yellow striped pole sticking out above it, driving would have been hopeless for the simple fact that it would have been impossible to locate the road. Fortunately his tyres were new but it was only because Alenka had threatened not to sit in the car again until he changed them. He would not have bothered himself, saying that winters were getting milder, and when he thought about how few times he went cross-country skiing last winter and even before, then it was probably true. And now this.

"Well, what *do* you know about them?"

She looked at him with an air of curiosity. He did not need to turn towards her, he could feel her gaze upon him.

"Know what, about whom?"

"What do you know about my doctor colleagues which they would not have liked you to mention in public? I saw you, Taras, when Balažič's wife asked you."

"Perhaps you should be the policeman, not me."

She continued to stare at him. She knew how to do that, pester him with her silence.

"All the women round the table apart from her have at some point had it off with Prelc."

Alenka laughed,

"Is that what he told you outside?"

He nodded.

"That's hardly a secret. Everyone knows that, even Karin." She fell silent for a moment and added, almost as if thinking to herself,

"Hmmm, so Irena actually hasn't?"

*

They drove for about fifteen minutes, leaving behind them the lights of the hotels in Ribčev Laz and were making their way in the darkness towards Laški Rovt, Polje, Kamnje... all the settlements before Bohinjska Bistrica where Taras hoped the road would improve. If they even reach the next village. The blizzard showed no sign of abating and so much snow had gathered under the wheels that Taras was waiting for them to begin spinning and for the car to get stuck in the white mantle. Would the batteries in the torch he kept in the glove compartment still last long enough for him to fit his snow chains? The journey was more and more like sailing though an endless whiteness which extended into dark shadows until, in this two-tone two-dimensionality, a blue flashing light appeared on the distant horizon, an oasis in the middle of a desert. It must be a Christmas tree, he thought, but only a few seconds later it turned out that the distance was strangely close and the blue flashing lights were those of a police car, inconsiderately parked too far into the driving lane for Taras to dare drive past it. A blue and white Skoda Octavia with its lights flashing and engine running. Taras swore and stopped.

"Well, here we go..." he said.

Alenka tried to look out of the window.

"There seems to be nobody around. You'd think it was some kind of accident, but where?"

He clearly won't avoid snow chains now, and why could he not at least once manage to fit the damn things without getting soaking wet. These two colleagues over there will need to have a pretty good reason for their behaviour. He opened the door and stepped out of the car which had only just warmed up enough to be pleasant, into the snow and the cold. He was about to march off towards the police car but realized it would not be that easy, so he opened the door again and reached to the back seat for his mountaineering anorak which he used for skiing.

"There's taste, there's bad taste, and then there is skiing equipment," he had once said to Alenka and stuck to using his rather worn black-grey Gore-Tex jacket instead of acquiring some fancy garish skiing outfit.

He closed the door quickly but not quickly enough for him not to get to sit on a dry seat when he would return to the wheel.

He pulled his hood over his head and looked across towards the police car. It appeared to be empty.

Chapter 3.

There was nobody in the car, at least not in the front. Surprised, he was about to walk round the car when he heard a bark coming from the back seat. He looked more closely through the glass and saw a girl holding a dog in her lap. He knocked on the window and opened the door. The girl was sitting in the corner as if she was trying to hide. The funny-looking dog in her lap almost made Taras laugh. He liked dogs, in fact he liked most animals. The mutt barked once more, in a good-tempered way, as if in greeting, as if it wanted, in its own canine way to say, "Hi, awful weather, isn't it?" Its head simply did not fit the rest of its body nor its character the face of the girl who was holding it. She was sitting in the darkness but Taras still noticed that she was shivering. As if she was cold, though the car was actually warm inside.

"Good evening. Sorry, but the car is blocking the road... Where are the policemen?"

The girl moved and Taras could see her more clearly. Young, around twenty-five, he thought. She clearly was not just a hitchhiker who the kind police officers had picked up at the side of the road in a snow blizzard.

She pointed somewhere outside with her finger.

"By the river."

Then she fell silent and squeezed further into the corner of the car. The dog was still excited, wagging its tail and trying to wriggle its way out of her grasp and run towards Taras. Taras thought it was hilarious and when the dog with its oversized head or too small legs jumped up and down restlessly in the girl's lap, he could barely contain his laughter.

He pulled his wallet out of his pocket and opened it to show the girl his work identification card, or rather its leather cover with his badge, a kind of star-shaped version of the state coat of arms with the sea and Mount Triglav with its two side peaks extended into Scales of Justice. The girl looked at it, then looked at him and stroked the dog on its head.

"I'm a policeman too. Here quite by chance, but I am a policeman."

She nodded.

"Someone is in the river. I found them when the dog was looking for its ball. I threw the ball for it to find, then he started barking..."

Taras nodded and the girl stopped.

"There's someone in the river, you said? Dead?"

The girl nodded again.

"And they just left you alone here?"

"Yes."

"I'll go and find them and will send one of them back here, alright?"

"Can you do that?" the girl smiled, or rather tried to.

Taras closed the door and looked down the short embankment along which the road was built. Footsteps, numerous footsteps, human and canine lead through the snow. It was all trampled. About twenty metres further ahead he could see two lights flashing among the branches. He sighed and set off into the snow.

*

By the time he reached the bushes, the snow had already gotten into his socks. It was not that the dampness in his shoes bothered him particularly, but he knew from previous experience that it could cause huge problems.

He moved some branches out of the way and ended up with one of the lights shining straight at him. He covered it with the palm of his hand and used the other to hold up his badge. The light beam pointed at it and then dropped to the ground.

"Good evening," said one of the men, the voice of a younger officer. "Goodness, we never thought you would come this quickly. We were told it would take a while with the road from Bled closed due to an overturned bus and problems on the road at three other points."

Standing before him was a cadet with a single white star on his shoulder, meaning he was not yet even a police officer, just a candidate for one, or whatever they were called. Because of the darkness he could not see the shoulder insignia on the other policeman but Taras assumed he at least had one or two more stars. Surely they hadn't sent a couple of students out alone?

"May I?" he said and without waiting for approval took the torch from the novice. He lifted it up to shine it on his partner who blinked nervously when the yellow beam hit his eyes and then stopped at his epaulette. Taras could not believe it – two recruits!

"What's this? So they send you out on your own now, do they?"

They stood in embarrassment and the one in the darkness tried to say something but Taras interrupted him. It was not their fault.

"Well, what's going on?"

"We called the station in Jesenice to send out a criminal investigator with a team and they said that they would send someone from Kranj. Are you not him?"

"No, I am a criminal investigator, bur without a team, on my way from one party to another, prevented by your car which is parked in the middle of the road with a girl and her dog sitting in it. Nobody called me, I'm here by chance."

"What?" the same policeman asked. "You've not come from Kranj?"

"Can we make something clear?" Taras said. "I'm the one asking the questions and you answer them, alright?"

The policemen both fell silent and stood before him like two schoolboys being told off by their teacher. In effect that was what they were.

"Let's start again. What's going on?"

"Have a look Chief Inspector, Sir," the one still holding his torch said and pointed it somewhere behind them. Taras stepped two paces forward so he could see across his shoulder. The wind whirling from the river current hit his face. He followed the light beam. There was something sticking out of the river, out of the ice that had formed along its edge encrusting the bushes on its bank, something white and smooth, as if it were made of marble. He stepped closer, squatted and turned the torch he was holding to get some more light onto the object.

Protruding out of the water was a hand, from the elbow upwards, almost at a right angle, bent at the wrist, fingers clenched. It was thin and tiny and at first he feared it might be a child, but the remnants of nail varnish pointed to the fact that it was in fact a woman. The ice surrounding the hand prevented him from seeing any more of the body. He stood up and turned to the policemen.

"One of you go back to the car, move it out of the way so we won't have to drag anyone else out of the ditch, and look after the girl."

"I'll go," the one with the torch said and nodded when Taras told him to only walk along a single one of the trails through the fresh snow. He disappeared, visibly relieved, before the other had a chance to protest.

"Well, now it's our turn," Taras tried to smile as he turned to the one who remained but would without doubt also have preferred to be looking after the girl.

He crouched down again and tried to remove the larger pieces of ice which prevented him from seeing under the surface. The ice was thin, it was easy to break up. He had to stop twice, the freezing cold biting at his fingers; eventually in the running, flowing darkness, a naked body appeared attached to the hand. It lay horizontally, its legs freely and steadily flowing with the current, the hand caught in the branches, and the shoulders below. The head was probably twisted backwards because it was not visible.

"Drowned, Sir?"

Taras did not answer.

"We did not want to just pull it out because we didn't know..." the young police officer fell silent.

"Didn't know what?"

Taras reached above the water and grabbed hold of the wrist. It was cold and hard. Like stone, like ice. She had not fallen into the water recently.

"We were not sure whether we were allowed to. Whether we could move her. Because if she drowned here, or whatever, then this is the scene of..."

Taras pulled on the arm and the branches surrounding the body lifted out above the water but they would not let go.

"She didn't drown here. The water is only a metre deep and anyway, I doubt she drowned. How many girls do you know who'd go swimming naked at minus five degrees? And I wouldn't want to risk the current carrying her downstream."

Even without this concern, Taras knew that, on a body that had been submerged in water for a long time, there would be nothing in terms of traces left that could be destroyed if they pulled it out onto the bank.

He broke up the last of the ice holding the body and the legs and the lower torso floated out of the water. The top was still entangled in a branch that had caught under the arm. Taras kneeled, trying not to let go of the hand and moving the branch out of the way. The top part of the body slowly floated to the surface.

"She didn't drown," Taras said, his voice changing as if he could not decide between tiredness and boredom.

Across his shoulder he glanced at the policeman shifting his weight nervously as if he was being examined.

"How do you know, Sir?"

"To drown, you first need to breathe. Help me please..."

The policeman eagerly, as if he had just woken from a stupor, jumped to Taras, held onto the leg and then, without letting go, turned away from the dead woman and Taras and collapsed into the snow. Taras patiently waited for him to get up again and without turning to look at the woman again, help him pull her body onto the shore. The young man then stood behind Taras' back, turned towards the car.

"...and in order to do that you need to have a head."

"I am sorry, I didn't..."

He fell silent and Taras could sense that he was shaking.

"It's alright. This is not exactly pleasant for me either."

In the snow before them lay the body of a young woman, a pale naked body, her skin almost without pigmentation, unpleasantly reminiscent of frozen carcasses hooked up in a meat storage cold room, especially the shoulders which joined into something that should have extended into a neck, but there was nothing there. There was no head. It had been, as Taras was able to quickly assess, cut cleanly off. Perhaps axed off? He flashed his light quickly along the entire body.

"Go and fetch me a bag," Taras said. "And bring me the portable radio station so I can talk to the guys in Kranj."

The body was frozen stiff and because of the hand that had been sticking out of the water at almost a right angle, Taras and the policeman had great difficulties in placing it into the black plastic bag.

"Should we carry her to the car?" the young policeman asked.

Taras shook his head.

"She'll wait here. Give me the radio."

The policeman handed him the radio transmitter that had been hanging from his belt. Taras pressed the button, introduced himself and waited for the voice at the other end to respond. The noise coming from the device had a calming effect. The sound of a police procedure of which most of the time the only point was to create a semblance of order in the midst of chaos. The responding voice, however, was barely comprehensible; the line was very bad, with lots of static interference.

It took Taras five minutes to explain who he was and how he came to be there and call for a team for investigating serious crime – a criminal investigator, forensics, a pathologist or doctor and an investigative magistrate. Because he was still not convinced of what they had in fact arranged after this painful 'do you understand?... can you hear me?... please repeat this?' conversation, he also tried to call from his own phone, but there was no coverage. He used the transmitter again and over the crackling noise tried to say a single sentence.

"Send a team, and a car, so your two guys here don't see in the New Year with a woman's..." He wanted to say headless body, but stopped.

Silence. Taras visualised the confusion coming from the silent transmitter.

"We don't have one," the device said suddenly with surprising clarity. "At this moment we don't have a single team on..." The connection was lost as if someone had cut the nonexistent wire.

"Well, when you can," Taras said into the transmitter in his hand. "I've done all I can here. All I can with what I have available."

He looked at the policeman who stood behind him so that the body bag was hidden from his view.

"Well, I bet you didn't expect to be spending New Year's Eve like this, were you?"

The policeman's sigh came out as a huge cloud of condensation in the cold air.

"Not in the least."

"No luck, boy. You'll need to wait. "If any wise guy tries to be clever," he said pointing to the ground behind his back, "tell him that I pulled her out. Taras Birsa, Chief Criminal Inspector at the Ljubljana Police Directorate. And I wish you a Happy New Year."

He handed the transmitter over to the policeman and made his way through the snow back towards the road.

He turned around after a few steps and glanced at the track through the snow, the bushes and the policeman, visible only as a silhouette. He was staring in Taras' direction. Although – perhaps he wasn't, perhaps he had just turned away from the body.

Chapter 4.

Alenka was sitting in the car, rummaging through the glove compartment to find a suitable CD. The music played on the radio on New Year's Eve was terrible, she agreed with Taras on this, just that Taras said it is terrible on ordinary days too and that she solved this with music she kept in the glove compartment whereas Taras, when he was not listening to the mawkishly sentimental station airing 1970s rock music, more and more often tuned into Radio Slovenia's Third Programme and classical music.

"Do you even know what you're listening to?" she sometimes asked him when some particularly 'heavy' piece came on.

"I'm not listening," he would say and really didn't now any more about classical music than she did.

She once mentioned that he did it to confuse his fellow passengers because deep within he is too much of a policeman and enjoyed watching people unable to fit him into a box, prevented from doing so by the fifty-fourth symphony of Hindeburg someone or other in xyz-minor about which he knew nothing more than anyone else.

"...except for perhaps some connoisseur with thick glasses who appears every so often from the radio archive and brushes the dust off the record on his way to the studio with a sadistic smirk on his face."

"I most often listen to classical music when I drive along alone."

"Then you're just trying to confuse yourself."

"Oh? And why would I be doing that?"

He listened to classical music because with it he could think if he wanted to and not if he didn't. The less known the piece, the less notable, Alenka would say lame and disastrous, the better when he needed to concentrate on something. True, he never remembered much of all this listening, never became a classical music expert, he barely got anything from it. He was familiar with classical music's greatest Schlager hits – another of Alenka's expressions – for example Bach's *Air on the G String* or Shostakovich's *Waltz* or something from Vivaldi, thought not necessarily only *The Four Seasons* and if he came across something like that he could not think. In such cases he would take a break and just enjoy the music, but this was rare. In fact there was just as much bad and unlistenable or at least bland classical music around than there was any other, just that in classical music there was less annoying singing and lyrics. At least he was spared things like *You Are the Flower of My Heart.*

"It's probably an age thing," Alenka made one last attempt at explaining. "I can't recall you getting high on classical music when we met."

He didn't and it was quite possible that it was an age thing.

She couldn't decide between Natalie Merchant and Shakira and eventually stuck Shakira into the CD-player, some old record when she still only sang in Spanish, before she hooked up with Messi, or whoever it was she hooked up with.

The snow was still falling, although it did appear to be thinning out and Alenka was able to look out through the side window. About fifteen minutes earlier, Taras had disappeared down the slope which led from the road towards the river and some bushes from where she could see flashes of what she assumed were torches. Then one of the lights began moving towards the road and the policeman – now she could see that that was what he was – opened the driver's side door and sat in the police car. Ten minutes later he was followed by another who reached the car without a light, opened the door and talked to the one inside for a while, took something out of the boot and returned to the bushes with it. This will take a while, she thought.

*

Taras stopped at the police car, opened the door and sat on the empty seat next to the driver. He informed him about the coroner, the criminal investigator and the investigative magistrate who were not available at the moment and told him they would have to wait, asking him whether he knew what he should do.

"Yes," said the policeman unconvincingly.

"Talk to the young lady here and prepare a report," Taras continued as if he had not heard the yes at all. "Then one of you can take her home... Do you live far?"

"The apartment complex in Ribčev Laz. A group of us came here to celebrate New Year."

"And cordon off the area, though in this weather and with all this snow it hardly makes a difference, but do it anyway. Once the young lady is back at home and all this is sorted, take turns in watching over the body. We wouldn't want the foxes to get to it, would we?"

"Will we take the body to Jesenice?"

"No," Taras said. "This won't be a sanitary case, it's a forensic one..." he avoided using the term *autopsy* and thought about the excitement this would cause at forensic pathology, how everyone would gather round the headless body. Dr Cvilak will have something on his slab with which he will be able to scare his students one last time before he retires.

"Is the road to Bled still closed?"

The policeman shrugged his shoulders.

"Last time we managed to get through it was, and they said it would take a while to clear it. The bus apparently overturned onto its side and the road is so icy they can't lift it."

Taras opened the door, said goodbye to the girl on the back seat and paused for a while. He glanced towards his car which was already covered in a thick blanket of snow, looked up at the sky, blinking when a few snowflakes fell into his eye, and instead of going back to his own car, sat back in the police car.

"Tell you what! I'll talk to the young lady here, and in the meantime, why don't you go over to my car and fit my snow chains for me, alright?"

He thought the young policeman would not object even if he dared to.

*

"In fact," he said when he had finished and handed over the log to the policeman who had already returned from fitting the snow chains. "I'll take the young lady back to her apartment myself. I am going to return to Ukanc anyway."

He introduced Alina to Alenka, then slowly turned the car around, careful not to drive any of his wheels off the side of the road.

"Change of plans," he told Alenka. "*Force majeure*."

"What happened?" Alenka asked Taras.

"The young lady found a body in the water."

"A body?"

She turned round towards the girl on the back seat.

"Joey… the dog found it. At first I thought it was a mannequin."

"Drowned?"

"Probably," said Taras and turned off the road at a sign that pointed to the apartment complex, found the right number and stopped. The holiday house was all lit up and rather noisy. The girl stepped out of the car.

"Thank you," said the girl as if she was not sure whether to say goodbye and walk off towards the house or return to the car.

"Will everything be alright?"

She nodded and turned towards the house with her dog in her arms.

*

"And a Happy New Year," said Taras as he sat back at the steering wheel.

"Poor girl, I don't know how I'd react if I came across anything like that."

"You're a doctor, you'd cope."

"A paediatrician. People come to see me alive and leave alive."

They drove along the road right next to the lake and whenever the trees thinned out a little they could see the water. Snow began to cover the thin sheet of ice that was forming on the surface. If someone had not known it was a lake, they could easily mistake it for a vast flat meadow. When Taras was a young boy he and his friends used to go ice skating on one of the reservoirs created in an attempt to dry out the marshy fields close to where he lived. The ice was usually covered with snow, but he did remember one dry winter when they skated on what looked like a huge black plate of glass. Although it was very cold, the sheet of ice appeared really thin and it was quite frightening skating across the small lake. You could virtually see the bottom under the ice, hear the slashes of the skates cutting through the surface, interrupted by the sound of the ice itself, the cracking noises as it expanded. As a child he would imagine that there might be dead bodies floating in the dark depths under the ice. However, even if there were, they never floated to the surface as they seemed to do here, from under this innocent white expanse. Where was the poor girl thrown into the lake? When? Clearly it was not yet frozen over then ...

Alenka called the girls to tell them that they would not be returning to Ljubljana that night.

"They didn't seem particularly bothered," she mumbled disappointedly.

Which twenty and eighteen-year-old would be? Taras thought. They appeared willing and that in itself was something.

"Was the body you found really a drowning, Taras?"

He smiled. He had often said that he could get her a job if things didn't go well with the clinic.

"What makes you wonder?"

"If there was at least a slight chance that the dead person had drowned, you would have said so. Because a drowned person means the least..." she was looking for the right word.

"Trouble?"

"No, excitement. The least excitement among people. Is your job not about setting people's minds at rest?"

"My work is to find the perpetrators of criminal offences." In fact his job was *to protect people's lives, their personal safety and property*. This was stated in the first of nine points in Article 3 of the Police Act of the Republic of Slovenia. The Act continues to say that a policeman's duty is *to prevent, detect and investigate criminal offences and misdemeanours, to detect and arrest perpetrators of criminal offences and misdemeanours*... and so on to the ninth point. There were times when Taras had known all the points off by heart, though there were not yet nine then.

"That too, but mainly it is to create a sense of safety. Just like my job. We heal, even though everyone dies in the end. Many before the age given by statistics to reassure them, even everyone is convinced that they're entitled to at least eighty. Many of those who spoil the statistics are your cases."

It slowly stopped snowing and at least he could see the road, though driving, sliding along, was still just as difficult, despite the snow chains. Another kilometre and they would reach safety. He would spend New Year's Eve with people who will keep asking him about his work.

"Well, that's also a way of looking at it. Or you can just say that my job is going to work and getting paid for it."

"Oh, not you, Taras. Perhaps you're able to fool others with your indifference, unfortunately also when a new star needs to be added to your uniform, but you can't fool me. If I ever happen to end up in some stream like the poor... You never told me – was it a man or a woman?"

"A woman."

She sighed as if the revelation made it worse.

"Well, if I were in her place I'd want you to be the one looking for the person who dumped me in the water. And do you know why?"

"Because I'm a good detective?"

"Because you take it personally. You're angry with..."

"People who kill other people? Is that not normal?"

"No, not that. You're angry because you feel that they are just vexing you. If they weren't killing themselves and weren't being killed, you could be home by eleven a.m. You make fun of us doctors but we in fact have to be at the surgery between eight and two, even if there is nothing to do. You'd go crazy if you had to be somewhere only because that's what it said on your door."

"Have you ever thought that with me it could be a case of work ethic? Satisfaction with a job well done?"

She stroked his head.

"Taras, I'm your wife. Keep this for one of your commissions."

Shakira was singing away, *Dónde están los ladrones*. Perhaps this song should be adopted as the international police anthem, he thought. He knew some Italian only, but *ladro* in Italian and *ladron* in Spanish are probably the same thing.

"That's not what I was asking you."

"What then?"

"Was I right? She didn't drown, this alleged drowning, did she?"

"Even if your were right, darling, I couldn't tell you."

"Well, I'll just have to read it in the papers tomorrow," she said and sounded more fed up than offended. She never found anything out from Taras.

"Tomorrow is a holiday."

"The Internet works on holidays as well."

As they turned into the drive leading to the weekend house, Taras was grateful to the young policeman for fitting the snow chains. The tracks they had left when they left only a couple of hours ago were barely visible and their Citroen C8 ploughed through the fresh powder snow. The noise from the party could be heard coming from the house. The jolly crowd had probably each had on average half a litre of wine more in their stomachs than when Taras and Alenka had left. When Taras stepped out of the car he thought that it would at least be warm inside the house and he would be able to dry off his socks, as he had no spare ones with him.

A few firecrackers went off closely.

Yes, these people got on his nerves.

Chapter 5.

Monday, 1 January

It was a cold morning. There was about thirty centimetres of fresh snow. If the temperatures remained this low, it would stay powdery for a while, Taras thought when he stepped out onto the terrace where he had and Prelc had talked the night before. He could see the lake through the branches, or rather sense it was there beyond the mists that covered it. With this much snow here, imagine how much must have fallen higher up, in Rateče, on Pokljuka and on Rogla... No sound came through the trees and the mists and he wished he would have enough time to check the conditions on the loipe from Ribčev Laz to Bohinjska Bistrica. Had the groomers already set the track? On the morning of New Year's Day? Then he remembered the young woman they had pulled out of the water and felt ashamed, almost guilty. When he was younger he had thought that with time, over the years, he would eventually get over this feeling of regret and a guilty conscience with people who were, as Alenka called them, his patients, or at least manage to numb it, but it was still there. He turned around and opened the door just as Alenka came down the stairs.

"Hey? Have you been outside already?"

She was still in the same clothes she had been wearing last night, apart from their skiing outfits, the only ones that they had brought with them. Jeans and a tight white t-shirt, sports underwear in fact. She appeared younger than her peers anyway, but in the company of the women at last night's party who were all ten years older than her and wore excessive makeup, Alenka looked almost like a teenager. In a number of aspects Taras was a happy husband.

"Just as far as the terrace."

"Are our hosts not up yet?"

He shook his head.

Alenka checked the time.

"Well, never mind, we can't wait for them now. We're meeting the kids in just over two hours' time.

They had quick breakfast, picked up their things – they only had their wallets and mobile phones anyway – and walked out to the car. Taras was glad Prelc wasn't around and even happier that he didn't have to speak to his wife. In the mornings, before he 'gets the machine going', as he called it, he liked some peace, and after the previous night even more so.

The lock was frozen and it took some effort to open the door, especially because the rubber moulding around it seemed to have frozen onto the chassis of the car, and when he pulled the door, the rubber came loose, hanging limply mid-air like a lose string on a bow. He straightened it against the door by kneading it against the metal, as if wanting to paste it back in place. In the heat of the summer this might have worked but not at minus something degrees Celsius. He gave up and sat in the driver's seat, carefully closing the door to try and get the moulding to stay in place and at least partly fill in the gap.

He drove down the drive and, after a hundred metres or so, stopped in front of a huge mountain of snow. A snowplough seemed to have cleared the main road but at the same time blocked the access to it. Taras stepped out, looked at the pile and kicked it angrily. What now? He carefully drove back, trying to keep to his own tracks, not a simple task with his back window covered in a crust of snow and ice.

"Did you notice a shovel anywhere?" he asked Alenka.

She shook her head and they spent a while trying to find one. There didn't seem to be one around the house. Taras glanced towards the wooden shed at the far side of the yard, looked at the deep snow between it and the house, then at the car, sighed and began walking. By the time he reached the shed his socks were wet again and it was locked anyway. Not wanting to wake up the Prelcs, he gestured to Alenka that he needed a key. She disappeared into the house and a while later returned with a bunch of keys. He retraced his own tracks to reach her.

"I found them on the wall behind the door. Check to see if any of them fits."

He looked at the lock, chose three possible keys and was lucky with the first. The door opened outwards and he barely managed to push through, trying to figure out whether the shed had a light or not. With his hand he felt around the wall and found a large switch, one of those massive ones you need to hold with two fingers and turn hard. The light it switched on was surprisingly low, as if some of the famous local frugal way of life and stinginess had rubbed off on Prelc. It barely managed to light up the tiny space where everything was very tidy. Two bicycles on stands, some skis, a rubber dinghy by the back wall, some tools and a snow shovel among them. He picked it up and walked straight to the road. When he had finished and Alenka had returned the key, the Prelcs were still fast asleep.

It was cold in the car and because he had to drive slowly, the diesel engine took a long time to warm up. It was also cold because he had to keep the airflow on so the windscreen would not keep fogging and freezing up. The aircon was useless, so he had to have the window open slightly. Only after about fifteen minutes did the car heat up enough for it to be bearable and he could properly see the road in front.

"Don't you think it's about time we got something better? We can certainly afford it," said Alenka, trying to keep her hands warm under her arms.

Taras shrugged his shoulders and waved his right hand above the steering wheel, smiling to himself. If someone he was questioning had answered a question in the way he had just done, he would have repeated the question.

So where do say you were on Thursday between twelve noon and five p.m.?

"Why are you so reluctant? What worries you?"

"Nothing worries me."

"We have money and we only have one life. We're old enough and have been through enough to be able treat ourselves now."

"We're going skiing in Austria in just over a week's time."

"Are we really going to manage it? Until now, something has always come up."

"This time we'll go, no matter what."

She took her hands from under her arms and tried to heat them by blowing into them.

"We pay Unicef to sponsor some impoverished child in this country and one in Africa, and we drive around in a car with this rubber hanging off the door, and a turbine, or whatever it is that keeps lagging. Whoosh and then nothing and only then whoooosh… what is it?"

"The clutch, I think. I will take it to the garage."

"You will, yes. I hope it will be this year, not next."

"But this year has only just started."

She didn't laugh.

"I have a clinic Taras, which lays golden eggs. And it always will because people will always be having children. I try to charge the minimum, but it is still more than enough. Why could we not indulge if we can?"

"Have you ever sat in a new, large, expensive car?"

She rolled her eyes. Just like Anja and Mojca used to at the height of their teenage years. They got that from Alenka, even though it was she who got worked up the most when they did it.

"Don't you go rolling your eyes at me, you brat!" she would bark at them at the end of an argument before Taras intervened.

"I've sat in new, large and expensive cars. Well, until I met you. You have me sitting in a large, old and cheap one."

"Sorry, I keep forgetting."

Taras had only been in such a car once. The murders in Petačev Graben had brought him momentary media fame and a car magazine had called him…

"Yes, I know, and you were given that Merc or whatever it was. That barge of a car."

"Yes. S Class. For three days, so I could write something about it."

He smiled and waited as if he was thinking about whether to tell her or not.

"They sure found the right person to give it to."

"Exactly. Doors that close automatically at the touch of a

finger, a self-fastening seatbelt, it all works, assistance this, assistance that… A nice car for invalids. Rich invalids. That was what I thought when I first sat in it and I was ashamed to drive around town in it. By the third day I felt as if the car belonged to me, that I had earned it. With all the useless shit it offers."

"But it wasn't yours."

"I know, but it still felt as if I had deserved it because I was better, cleverer, better in goodness knows what than others. I remember seeing my own face reflected in a shop window where I had parked."

"And?"

"I had this idiotic expression on my face. This… I don't know how to explain. A face that goes with expensive cars."

Alenka rolled her eyes again.

"I think it's a kind of automatism which you can't avoid. You need to keep things on a tight leash."

"And that's why you don't have the clutch fixed?"

He had to admit that this really would not be a good enough excuse.

"You know, I remember having that idiotic expression all those years when I shuffled the bills from the left pile to the right. Or when I dreamed of holidays that never were, and I would want to forget about all that now. Sometimes I feel that we've thrown away fifteen years of our life. Those between twenty-five and forty. This damn car reminds me of it."

They reached the spot where the police car had blocked the road the previous night. It was not difficult to notice the only point on the road towards Bled where there were numerous tracks from the road to the river.

"Can you tell me any more than you could yesterday with all those people around?"

*

They had returned to the Prelcs place half an hour before midnight and walked into the house to a loud cheer of people he had barely met only an hour earlier but were now behaving as if they had known him forever. They were drunk, of course, and the average must have been quite a lot more than half a litre. Just because they were doctors didn't mean they drank any less.

"Shhhh," Prelc shouted. "Shhh, hush, let's listen to what he has to tell us!" And when they all fell silent, Prelc tried to order Taras a glass of wine, as if he had forgotten Taras did not drink. "Well, Taras, don't disappoint us. The TV programme was shit."

They all laughed. The TV programme probably was shit, but at his weekend house, at least in the large room where the party was in full swing, Prelc didn't have a TV anyway.

"I'm afraid I will. All I can say is that we found the body of a dead woman in the river. Why she died and who she was... I do not know, and even if I did I wouldn't be allowed to tell you."

"It took half an hour of questioning for him to even tell me that it was a woman," said Alenka, sounding very disappointed.

Despite this they kept asking him, again and again, as if he might be able to tell them more individually than he could in front of everybody. This went on until about four or half past four in the morning when they all dispersed to their nearby weekend houses.

"She didn't drown," Alenka repeated later as they lay on the pull-out bed which took up almost the entire guest room on the first floor. She repeated the sentence again a few hours later as they were driving from Bohinjska Bistrica towards Bled.

Taras switched the radio to Radio Three and some xth string concert in yz-minor. Alenka rolled her eyes.

"Damn classical stuff. First Mother with her piano, now you."

The motorway was almost totally cleared and Taras turned into the first petrol station to remove his snow chains. He had problems with this because the young policeman had clearly wanted to do a thorough job and tightened them really hard. His fingers were already numb with the cold by the time he had taken the first chain off. Rubbing his hands to warm up, he glanced towards the petrol station and swore loudly. If there was one thing he hated whenever he went climbing, it was his fingers numbing with the cold. That and getting up early to go on a trip. It took forever to get the fingers warm again. Just as he managed to take off the other chain, Alenka rolled down the window and waved at him with the phone. It was Marn, criminal technician, part of Taras' wider work group. What did he want now? For a moment he thought about not taking the call. He was not on call and they knew he would not be in Ljubljana... He sighed and pressed the green button on the device.

"Taras, a Happy New Year and all that. Should I start without you?"

"Start what?"

"Processing what arrived today at... hang on... at four in the morning at the IFM. Apparently you sent the package?"

"Who? What did I send?"

Marn's voice acquired a tired tone. As if he had used up all his cheerfulness in the address.

"The evidence receiving report..." he said slowly and it sounded as if he was looking though the page to find the right sentence, "...for a female body minus head says. It says here that the criminal investigation officer responsible for it is called Taras Birsa. How many Taras Birsas are there in Slovenia?"

Chapter 6.

Sitting at the reception of the Medical Faculty, which on its third floor houses the IFM, the Institute of Forensic Medicine, was someone who had to work on New Year's Day. With a faint sense of sympathy towards a person in the same situation as himself, Taras knocked on the glass above the closed service window. The man behind the glass was on the phone, and had their back turned to the counter and any possible visitors, probably unexpected on New Year's Day. He turned slightly in his seat so Taras could see that he was probably a student covering for the regular porter. He pointed to the phone in his hand and smiled immediately afterwards, though the smile was not intended for Taras but for the phone, or rather the person he was talking to on the phone. Then he turned his back towards Taras again. Taras stepped to the door of his booth and calmly, carefully, but also forcefully, took the man's phone. The expression on his face was no longer kind.

"Professor Cvilak? Where?"

The student stared at Taras in surprise as if he could not decide how to react. Taras recognized some teenage defiance in his gaze but was not particularly good at handling it even with his own daughters, so much less so with an apparent adult.

"Cvilak. Up? Down?"

"Down..." the student or whatever he was responded in time and this unwittingly saved his... whatever.

"Thank you."

Taras turned round and went into the first basement which is not really a basement but the ground floor with large refrigerators along one side of the corridor, some fixed, some movable, and another one, a large black box which was morbid just to look at in itself, used for 'bulk cargo', as they called the remnants of bodies after serious accidents, explosions etc. Refrigeration was open for vehicle access on one side; bodies were delivered in dark blue vans. On the other side it was connected or rather crossed by a corridor, beyond which was another space, just as grim, the dissecting room. Taras noticed a few people standing in the corridor between refrigeration and dissection and when he got closer he noticed two other people smoking outside. Among those inside he recognized Dr Cvilak, the Head of the Institute, Šparovec, also from the Institute, and a younger man he knew was the radiographer from the University Medical Centre, though he could not remember his name. The Hatlak woman, the photographer was also there, and Majda the typist. There was also a younger man he did not recognize... Basically, even a less dedicated observer would recognize the post-mortem team and they seemed to be waiting for someone. Cvilak was nervously shifting his weight from one foot to the other.

"Good morning," said Taras. "What's on today?"

They all remained silent and Cvilak shifted his weight once more. At that moment the door to the dissecting room opened and out walked Marn, pushing in front of him the trolley with his equipment. He nodded at Taras.

"Well, we've finished with her. She's all yours."

Behind him Taras briefly saw the table with the body lain on it, a naked female body with it's feet turned towards him and an unnatural void at the upper part where the head should have been. Although the door had only been open for a few seconds, the stench of rotting flesh came rolling out of the room.

"For fuck's sake, Taras, where have you been?" said Cvilak and before Taras had a chance to ask him what he was referring to with this "for fuck's sake", the young man next to Cvilak also spoke.

"I'm relatively new here, I admit..." he began, "...and I know I'll need to get used to operating between how things look on paper and how these things are actually handled, but haven't we gone over the edge here, New Year's Day or not?"

He didn't look wasted and he must have plucked up quite

some courage to start having a go at a senior criminologist in front of everyone. Perhaps he was just dumb but he didn't look it.

"And you are?" Taras asked, looking calmly straight into the man's eyes, confusing him so he looked towards the others, none of which came to his aid. Like Taras, they too were called in suddenly, and all the younger man got from them was a glare saying: Settle this so we can get it over with and get out of here.

"Marjan Doles," he eventually mustered. "The investigating magistrate in this case, and I have to say that something like this, and I'm not being clever here… this should not have happened…"

Of course Taras, even though he did not know the man, knew who he was after the first sentence. Even before that. Investigating magistrates were required by law to be present with crimes such as those he dealt with, he was obliged to cooperate with them and on paper they were even in charge of the process, in charge of inspection, and they were supposed to direct the investigation, though most of the time this was limited to following the work of criminologists and forensics. When they were at the scene of the crime, then the inspection was legally and formally not questionable in court. It generally worked, as long as they were not some cocky youth who took their job description too literarily and did little more than interfere, so they, as Brajc once said, had to be kicked out of the way.

"Listen, it's the first of January, I intended to go for a walk around town with my daughters who I rarely see and I will do so. I don't have much time. Can you tell me in brief what this is about, otherwise I will leave."

He pulled his phone out of his pocket and glanced at the screen,

"In fact I'm already late."

"Are you or are you not the Inspector assigned to this thing over there?"

The young investigating magistrate shouted and was totally red in the face. Everyone else, from Cvilak to the typist, stared at the floor.

"No," said Taras. "I'm not."

"But how?"

He repeated the 'how' once more and looked at everyone else gathered. They were still staring at the floor and the walls and Taras could see, in all their apparent disinterest, that they did not believe him.

"Right, it's my day off. Yesterday, as I was returning from a ski-trip to Vogel, I came across a police patrol car, two cadets with single white stars on their shoulders, who found this woman. And I helped them. That's all."

"How? Did you not order the body to be pulled out of the river, you conducted the conversation with the witness who found the body, you ordered her to be sent home, your name is on the report... And as if that was not enough, when we got there the area was not even suitably secured... We didn't even have forensics with us because we were told this was supposed to be a drowning. Nobody told us that the woman was without a head!"

"Didn't tell you?"

Taras sighed and smiled. Should he ever want to get rid of anyone he would do so on New Year's Eve.

"Clearly there's some mistake. I don't know how it happened, but briefly; I was driving back from skiing on Vogel, found a police car in the middle of the road, found the policemen who were dealing with the body in the water, helped them pull the body out of the river and sort it out in as much as that was possible, that was all. In any case, it is the Kranj Police Directorate which is responsible for problems in Bohinj, not us."

Cvilak nodded. Taras pointed to the door to the dissecting room behind the magistrate.

"Then I did indeed conduct the interview with the lucky finder and told the policemen to send her home, in fact my wife and I even drove her there. And that's all. This is not my case. Beside, I told the people in Kranj loudly and clearly that this was not a natural death. And that is why she ended up here."

He didn't mention that he did some of this in return for the policeman fitting his snow chains. There was awkward silence, then everyone looked up at the investigating magistrate who was now even redder in the face than before.

"But how? How? When they called us they said that the

criminal investigator had already been at the scene and the Ljubljana Police Directorate has taken on the case. That is why we went there with the coroner. We found two policemen who told us that the criminal investigator had been, done his stuff and left."

"That is what they said?"

"Well... that you had been there."

"May I," Cvilak intervened. Everyone, Taras, the investigating magistrate and everyone else turned towards him. "Over there we have a body which is surprisingly fresh for one that has been in the water, estimating off the top of my head, for over a week, yet is still doesn't exactly smell nice. And worse than that, out there is a world that will wake up tomorrow and realize that the police and the IFM have started the new year with a total fiasco. So I suggest that we first get down to doing our work as if we had actually agreed and arranged it all properly, and then you two sit down somewhere and sort everything out in retrospect. I only have a few months left to retirement, so they can't do anything to me, you two probably have quite a lot more."

He looked at Doles who turned bright red again. Taras waited a few moments, then shook his head.

"Cvilak, this is not my case. If I get involved now, there's no way I'll be able to get out of it, and that's not what I want.

"And why don't you want that?" Cvilak was surprised.

Taras shook his head.

"I just don't."

What was he supposed to say? That he had promised Alenka a week's skiing in Austria which he had always been able to avoid but if this woman is assigned to him, Alenka will never believe that he had not taken on the case deliberately.

"Couldn't you just come in with us so we won't waste our entire New Year's Day waiting for them to find someone who will sign the damn report? Have some pity on us!"

He gestured with his hand towards all who were gathered and inadvertently followed it with his gaze. A row of sour faces.

He sighed, took his phone from his pocket and walked through refrigeration to the glass door which opened automatically, out into the open. He nodded at the two men smoking there and checked whether he had a signal on his phone. When he returned, the team was still standing outside the dissection room. Taras offered Doles his hand.

"Taras Birsa, Senior Investigator from the Ljubljana Police Directorate… *When* I'm on duty."

Doles gratefully shook it and smiled.

"I don't know, it suddenly seems that I messed things up here… although we *did* get a message from Kranj that the criminal inspector was there and that we should take over because they had their hands full with road accidents… and then this."

*

An hour later Taras and Cvilak sat in Cvilak's office on the third floor of the Faculty of Medicine, drinking coffee from a vending machine. Cvilak looked tired.

"I'm too old for this shit, Taras, you know that?"

"That's why you're about to retire, isn't it?"

Cvilak pulled a face,

"I expected you to say something like: no one is old enough to retire."

He looked at Taras and then his gaze turned out of the window of the third floor of the Faculty of Medicine.

"No, really. Over the years… for a while it looks as if you'll cope. You start and you really aren't prepared for some things. They shock you and you feel awful. Then it becomes less terrible every time because you've already seen it all before. You wash your hands, lock the office and go home, saying to yourself, Now I'll have something to eat, drink a glass of wine and pull the wife's panties off in the evening… and it doesn't bother you that you've only just cut open the body of a twenty-year old girl from the neck to the symphysis, basically to the groin. You work mechanically, or at least think that you're working mechanically. You saw this today? Freshly shaved cunt, she went somewhere for a fuck, and someone goes and cuts off her head. For fuck's sake…"

He opened the drawer to his desk and pulled out a bottle.

"Don't you have a problem with this?"

"No."

Cvilak held the bottle in front of his eyes.

"Whisky. Irish, supposed to be one of the better ones, a little softer than Scotch."

"I know it, Bushmills. We visited the distillery with Alenka two or three years ago."

The guided tour had first taken them to the coast, to the peninsula with the Giant's Causeway, the famous octagonal basalt columns, then to the distillery where they were given a talk about the angel's share during ageing. After the tour they bought a litre of special blend, something with a black label, though Taras knew that he would not even try it. So much for them never treating themselves to anything.

"So many pathologists are alcoholics. Did you know Breznik?"

Taras nodded.

"He had the habit of keeping his drinks cool in the refrigerator with the corpses. Then he drank the stuff and offered it around. 'Want a rotten shot?' he would say. An annoying man. Long dead now, his own rotten shots got the better of him. I'm not, but that's only because I didn't drink. Never at work and no spirits before eight o'clock at home. It's only because of these rules that I didn't become a drunkard. I got this bottle for my fiftieth birthday, now I am sixty-five and still haven't opened it. I always said I would do so on some special occasion or something..."

He unscrewed the top.

"Well, now I have six months to retirement. Surely I won't become an alcoholic in six months, so... Besides, the special occasion was here all the time, it was just that I never saw it. I'm alive, she isn't. None of my clients are. May God let them... rest in peace. As if that isn't a special enough occasion... Well, I don't have any glasses."

He took a swig from the bottle.

"You still don't drink?"

Taras shook his head.

"Does it still affect you?"

"It did the last time I tried."

Cvilak gave him an inquisitive look.

"Five years ago. A single glass."

"You don't want to try again now? You might be over it."

"It wasn't pleasant last time. It's not far from here to A&E of course, but I don't get pleasure from drinking with all this in my head. I'm not used to it."

Cvilak tilted the bottle again, took a sip, licked his lips and placed the bottle on the table.

"But would you if you could?"

"If my stomach could take it or if it wasn't harmful in general?"

"Both."

"I'd be drunk all the time."

Cvilak laughed, looked at the bottle, screwed on the top and put it back in the drawer.

"No you wouldn't Taras, not you... Fifteen years waiting for this? Whoosh..."

They sat in silence for a few moments, Cvilak with his hands in his white hair.

"What have you found instead?"

"What should I have found?"

"Surely you had to find something," Cvilak said. "Nobody can handle this life the way it is. Do you smoke at all? Like kids?"

"You're the second person to ask me that in two days. No, I don't smoke."

"What then?"

"Nothing."

Cvilak shook his head in disbelief. Strong disbelief.

"Well, I do go running, and the gym and stuff like that."

"And it helps?"

Taras shrugged his shoulders.

"Do you play around?"

"Play... where?"

"With women?"

Taras laughed. Cvilak shook his head, opened the drawer and took out the bottle again. He unscrewed the top.

"You never were particularly talkative. I've observed you all these years. I could see what is bothering you, I'm not crazy and I'm not from Ljubljana either."

"What's that got to do with it?"

Cvilak smiled.

"You work and you try to catch up with everyone else who keeps going to mummy's mountain weekend houses in Trenta, and daddy's seaside home down in Portorož. You work, put up with all this human trash, and you don't have anything while they all go off skiing in Austria. Don't tell me that all that doesn't get you pissed off."

"Well, I have it all now," said Taras. "And in a week's time Alenka and I are going on a skiing holiday. Guess where."

"But the damage has been done, hasn't it?"

"Bad Klein..." He had to repeat the Klein in order to get through Kleinkirchheim. "To an eight-hundred-euro-per-day apartment. With a jacuzzi and a view of the ski slope."

"You know best."

Taras smiled. What was he supposed to say? That he was right? That he wasn't? That he would have been pissed off even without the twenty years of what Cvilak had described?

"It's not that," he said eventually.

"I'm telling you this because I consider you a friend, even if we do only meet rarely and like this most of the time... You've always been quiet, and I apologize if I'm badgering you."

"People change."

"No," Cvilak mumbled, trying to swallow his drink and interrupt at the same time. "We don't change." He choked and had to cough. "We don't change, we just become grumpier."

He put the bottle on the table and looked Taras in the eyes.

"What do we have this time, Taras?"

Taras shook his head.

"This isn't my case. Even if I wanted to take it on, it will never be mine. Tomorrow when they wake up after their New Year parties, the General Directorate will take over because the Kranj Directorate is too busy and too small, because we're not responsible for corpses north of Medvode, and also because you don't get a headless corpse on your slab every day."

Cvilak continued as if he hadn't heard him.

"Who would cut the head off a woman, a girl?"

He looked at the bottle.

"Was she still alive?"

Cvilak shook his head, held the bottle and pushed it away.

"No, she didn't bleed. That means her heart was already dead."

"But you don't know what she died of?"

Cvilak shook his head again.

"I took samples for histological tests, but at the moment it seems NAF. I sampled the blood and a piece of flesh for DNA profiling. Your guys will get the results and you'll be able to check your databases. All else was, as you yourself assumed, washed away by the river."

"What about tools?"

Cvilak pretended to look surprised and then looked at the bottle as if it was glowing on the table in front of him.

"Perhaps it should be chilled. Pouring it into you warm like this must be a waste."

Taras smiled.

"What are you smiling for?" Cvilak asked.

Taras will miss him when he leaves the Institute. First Penca and soon Cvilak. A grey-haired gentleman, a great expert who has seen in his life and on his table everything a person could and should not see, who, with his serenity and refinement, managed to give this task – cutting dead people up into pieces – a purpose and dignity. And he could also take a joke.

"I came to the Institute by chance," Cvilak had once explained to Taras. "As a young doctor I worked at the clinic in Moste where we had four old hags in charge. It was still a time of collective professional decision-making and they kept sending us here and there, to stitch minor hand wounds, handle the A&E department and all kinds of things. Then I saw Dr Milčinski was advertising for an assistant at the Institute and I applied. I thought I didn't have a chance because the listing said it would be recommended if candidates had a Master's degree or were at least working towards one. I didn't have one, of course, but then I got an invitation to the interview and my colleagues said I should go, that it was not a good idea to get on the wrong side of the old man. So I went. I got to his office; the old man was sitting there, smoking a cigar, and he said,

'Well, colleague, tell me your anamnesis.'

'Dr Milčinski, Sir, I come from the countryside and...' I began and the old man shouted out,

'You'll do!'

Then I went back to the clinic to terminate my work contract there and Dr Vodeb, that was what one of the four was called, wouldn't let me go until I told her I was going to work with Milčinski, and then she had to. Well, I did an autopsy on Dr Vodeb myself some ten years later."

It was because of Cvilak that going into the dissecting room was much easier for Taras. It was the only place he knew where everything, every object, every item, was there purely because of its basic function. No décor, nothing that would make the square space of what was in effect a slightly larger consulting room more human. A waist-high steel sink with outlets for blood and other liquids to drain away dominated the centre of the room. It had fittings for the metal bed with the body that would be brought from refrigeration, avoiding the need for moving or lifting of the corpse. All other work spaces Taras could think of had something, at least some little, trivial thing which was not there because it was absolutely essential, some superfluous decoration, a tool which was only half a tool, or some picture drawn by someone's four year old daughter, a paperweight that nobody really needed... On Taras' desk it was a Cartman from South Park, a present; or all other desks were at least untidy, full of papers with coffee marks, as with Taras', or greasy marks from sandwiches with Brajc; even Osterc's pedantically organised workplace, where every last paper was in place, was still nothing like this room. Penca is also no more, he too came onto the slab, in the room where, amidst all this sterility, Cvilak reigned like some kind of sun above Mount Everest. At least in brightness, if not the warmth.

Just over an hour ago Taras had stepped to the table where the headless body lay and looked at it for the first time in a light brighter than a pocket torch. The body of a mid-sized woman without any particular features at first sight, slim, small breasts, shaven pubic hair. For a moment he once more thought she could be a girl.

"Well, let's see then what we have here," Cvilak had said,

approaching the corpse with gloves on his hands.

"Why do you care how they cut off her head if this isn't your case?"

Taras waited patiently, staring at the bottle on Cvilak's desk. He always liked the idea, the image of whiskey. The colour of the bottle, a simple label, all the blah blah about malt, single malt, double malt, maturing in some kind of brandy or port casks, the angel's share and blah blah... But when he tried it, when he still drank, all this disappeared, it just tasted like spirit made out of fermented grain. This at least was one thing he did not miss at all in his forced abstinence.

"A knife, a large and quite sharp knife, judging by the cut. Between the third and fourth vertebra. Smooth and decisive, without making much of a mess."

Chapter 7.

When Anja was born Taras was still an ordinary policeman with a single yellow star on his shoulder. He was twenty-two. Alenka was in the fourth of six years at medical school in Ljubljana. When she found out she was pregnant she first cried her eyes out and then called Taras to tell him she would have an abortion. Taras was in Nepal at the time on a police expedition to the Himalayan eight-thousander Dhaulagiri and it took her a week to muster the courage to tell him, then another week to coordinate setting up the telephone satellite links with Taras' absences from base camp when he was up on the mountain. Despite the expedition being called a police expedition, Taras was in fact the only policeman on it; all the others were sportsmen employed by the police force, students, and sponsored climbers. He would throw that at them when they teased him about parking tickets, fines, jokes about policemen and similar stuff. On the twenty-first of May at ten in the morning Slovene time and three and three quarter hours later according to Nepalese time, Taras, who had returned from the mountain the previous day and had a free day, found out that a few months after returning home, he would become a father. He sat on a pile of stones, below him the tents fastened on the shelves cut into the ice, above him the glacier and the mountain rising almost four kilometres above all this, pressing the satellite phone against his ear, being told that the *Clearblue* result was a plus, but that he shouldn't worry because she would go and have an abortion.

"OK," he said and then the line was cut because the satellite responsible for it working had disappeared somewhere behind Annapurna. If he went out of his tent in the middle of the night for a piss, he could watch them fly above them, yellow dots that were not stars and were far too fast to be airplanes.

He had a two-day break, then it was his trio's turn to climb to the top. In those two days three people died, a French woman with her Sherpa who had set herself the task of climbing all fourteen eight-thousanders and a day later a Greek climber. When a Russian freight helicopter picked up the remainder of the Greek team, Taras stepped to the leader of his expedition and asked whether he could jump the phone queue because he had something urgent.

"Keep it," he said to Alenka.

"Are you sure?"

"Yes. We'll manage somehow."

All he could do was hope that she actually heard this last part, because the echo was so strong that is sounded as if he was talking to himself. When, a month later, in mid-June, he arrived at Ljubljana airport, he was met by a girl in a summer dress with a visibly rounded belly.

On the twenty-sixth of May Taras stood at the summit of his fist and – though he didn't know this at the time – only eight-thousander. Had he known, he would probably have tried to stay at the top longer than just the fifteen minutes he had done, but he remembers these fifteen minutes as one of the rare moments of complete joy, hard to compare with anything before or after. In terms of intensity, the closest to it was Anja's birth and two years later Mojca's. But it was still not the same.

After he returned, Alenka moved in with him, into his rented studio flat in Koseze. Her father, a representative of a foreign multinational corporation which supplied medical equipment, sent her a letter in which he informed her that he was renouncing her and that she should 'never contact him again.' They did not speak for the next fifteen years and, in these fifteen years, Taras and Alenka managed, with a mortgage and for quite a long time a single salary, Taras', to move from a rented studio into their own, one-and-a-half-room flat. Her old man only got in touch again when he fell ill with prostate cancer and decided that he would correct his errors over the last fifteen years in 'looking after her,' as he said. He bought her a share in Dr Prelc's clinic, which was having financial difficulties. It was initially set up as a general internal medicine clinic but, when Alenka joined it, it also began working in paediatrics. This meant old people with intestinal problems and children who had caught a cold all came to the same clinic, albeit to separate waiting rooms. Just before her father died, he asked Alenka about Taras. Alenka mentioned it to him and Taras even thought about visiting him in hospital but he died before he had a chance to do so. He went to the funeral because of Alenka. Anja and Mojca also went, both still teenagers at the time, Anja in the last year of primary school.[3] They even cried.

The sisters could not have been more different. Anja was tall, dark, had chocolate eyes and black hair and when she was a little girl, she was a copy of her father as he was on the only photograph he had of himself at that age, just that she was also beautiful and elegant. Mojca was five centimetres shorter, blonde and blue eyed like Alenka, and she also had her temperament. In fact in terms of character, they had both inherited things from both of them and when they were teenagers, things were often quite lively at home. They had had problems particularly with Mojca, ones that Taras would now not be able to explain precisely, and if he tried they would sound banal. Now the arguments they had at the time seem silly, but he knows they were unavoidable. Did he really have to have nervous breakdowns because Mojca would not roll her sleeves up when washing her hands? At least she slept, something which Anja didn't for the first few years of her life. As a baby she would wake up every two hours on a good night, on bad ones she would stay awake all night, sit in her bed and scream if they didn't entertain her. Taras, who was at the time the only one with a job and also doing extra training to become a criminal investigator, spent quite a few nights sleeping in the bathroom, with a choice of having his head next to the toilet or the drain – both stank. The two girls, Anja as well as Mojca, were incredibly beautiful, although Taras allowed for the possibility that they seemed so to him because they were his daughters. They were now twenty and eighteen years old; the same girls who stood up in the cot at three in the morning expecting to be entertained, whose nappies he'd changed, who

3 Primary schooling in Slovenia lasts until the age of 15

went to the first day of school with a yellow neckerchief[4] round their neck and a fluffy bunny toy in their hand, who he enrolled in gymnastics, and then basketball… On his desk at work Taras had a photo of Anja on her first day at school. She is biting her lip with her top teeth of which one is missing, to her right, slightly out of focus, is Mojca who with Taras and Alenka walked her to school that day; behind Anja is Tinkara, Anja's best friend at nursery school, eating a poppy roll. What happened to her?

"*Grüß Gott*," said Anja when he caught up with them at the Triple Bridge which, at two in the afternoon on the fist day of the new year was rather empty, not counting the municipal garbage collectors picking up the litter left by the revellers on the previous night. She always teased Taras with *Grüß Gott* because she knew how Austrians got on his nerves.

"She'll go there," he had said when Anja expressed her wishes to go and study in Vienna, "meet some Austrian bloke, and then you'll have grandchildren who speak with Austrian accents."

At the time he still believed that a father was allowed a few prejudices when it came to his daughter's boyfriends, though in fact Austrians didn't get on his nerves any more that Slovenes or anyone else.

The four of them walked through town, across the Tripe Bridge, to the Robba Fountain, left across Cyril and Methodius Square and in front of the Puppet Theatre turned into the narrow lane leading up to the castle. Taras had lived in Ljubljana for thirty years but still had problems with street names. He knew the town like the back of his hand, of course, but if he had to name a street that was not one of the main throughways or one close to the police station where he worked, then he needed to consult Google. It was the same with the new holidays in the new country. He knew all the old ones, but since independence there have been quite a few changes, many of the old holidays abandoned and many new ones added… What came first? Independence Day or Statehood Day?

He mostly listened. Anja and Mojca talked, Alenka asked

4 Yellow neckerchiefs are given to first year primary school children as a newcomers to traffic, a warning to drivers and others of the extra caution needed around very young children.

questions, and as they walked like this with the two young women, for young women they had become, without Taras realizing when, they didn't appear that much younger than Alenka and himself. Alenka laughed along with them, just as vivaciously and youthfully, Taras also didn't drag his feet, wrapped in his grey coat, he was still fit. If this was the criterion, he said to himself, it was probably the lowest possible one. They both had local boyfriends, both students, pharmaceutics and architecture, a little bland for Taras' tastes but this too probably comes with age, younger people getting on your nerves, especially when they are your daughters' boyfriends. They were still asleep now, of course.

"And you old-timer?" Anja said. "You seem a little quiet."

"I'm pondering on the incomprehensibility of life."

"What was so urgent that you had to go to the station?"

He explained briefly where he had been and why, without getting into details, especially not the one about the head.

"Can you now tell us whether she drowned? He never tells me anything," Alenka said and laughed. Taras probably felt she should be more serious about the matter.

"She didn't drown. She was murdered. Barely much older than Anja and Mojca."

When they were still young he sometimes panicked at night, thinking about all the things that could happen to them. A road accident, a careless driver driving over the pedestrian crossing, headphones over the ears, phone in hand at a level crossing without a barrier... A million possible dangers. He tried to calm down by thinking of the thousands of dangers that he had somehow survived but then immediately thought about how many others hadn't.

"Really? So how did she die?" Mojca asked, still sounding a bit too curious.

"I'm not in the mood right now, OK?"

He understood that she did not have the same image in her mind. To her the dead girl was merely an association of two words, there was no image behind them. There was no headless corpse lying on the table in front of which even Dr Cvilak with his scalpel paused briefly, almost as if even he was baffled.

"I usually begin at the head, but since there is none..."

And he made the incision from the neck downwards...

When Anja was six years old she decided she would not eat meat because she did not want to kill animals. Taras wasn't happy about it, but there was nothing he could do. Had she said that she didn't like the taste, he would not have allowed her to get away with it, but was powerless in the case of conscientious objection. Within a month Mojca also decided she would do the same. In their family album, volume one, there is still a photograph taken on a seaside holiday with both girls, one dark, the other blonde, leaning with their elbows on the wooden table, each holding a huge Wiener Schnitzel. It was the only evidence Taras had that they ever ate meat. And if he had said he had been at the autopsy of a horse whose head someone had cut the head off, they would have been shocked and upset enough.

"Sorry, it probably wasn't pleasant?"

"Eh, well... it never is. And it wasn't even my case. A misunderstanding."

Seen from above, Ljubljana appeared sleepy. There was far less snow than in Upper Carniola, ten centimetres, perhaps just a little more. The mountains in the distance were hidden behind low-lying clouds and all that could be seen from the castle walls were three or four shades of grey through which the Christmas lights shone softly.

"Let's go down to Trnovo for a coffee? You two tell us what's new in the Imperial City instead."

They walked down the steep path, gravel at first, then asphalt, to the Church of Saint James and from there to the River Ljubljanica, across the Hradecky Bridge to Trnovo where, a little out of the town centre, are four joints – cafés, inns, pizza parlours – which, even in summer only the most persistent tourists ever come across. Anja and Mojca talked about their studies and Taras tried to listen, but soon his thoughts wondered off. He simply wasn't interested. Even when they were young, in primary school, it was Alenka who took exclusive care of their education, Taras would take them to the playground and play basketball with them. Alenka kept reminding him how at the end of ninth grade, the last grade of primary school, Anja once mentioned some Mrs Petrič and Taras asked who she was.

"Don't you know? She's only been my form teacher from fifth grade onwards!"

He only once went to a PTA meeting and was so bored listening to the discussion on whether mobile phones should be allowed on school trips or not, that he never went again. If it were up to him their use should be banned, not only in primary school, but for everyone on the entire planet.

"You should have had a son," Alenka said sometimes and perhaps she was right. Both girls played basketball at primary school and Taras and Alenka attended their matches and cheered them on, even though they all knew it wasn't leading anywhere. That they would stop one day and start doing cleverer things. When Anja was fifteen, in the last grade of primary school, she found a farm where they had some retired horses in the stables, close to the home of one of her friends. They were looked after by a girl a little older than herself. She began going there, helping with the work and also riding occasionally, when the only mare in the stable that could still be ridden was not injured. Mojca soon followed her. That was the end of basketball. Taras could still precisely recall the change. He had gone to collect them from the farm to take them to their training session and found them teasing Norda, or whatever the mare who could still be ridden was called, by passing the apple to each other, throwing it at some strange angles so the animal could not reach it.

"Give the poor animal the apple," he said, only to be told that they were doing stretching exercises with the horse.

"One of the really good exercises for a horse is if you pull its tail, but we don't dare do that yet," said Mojca, born and bread a town girl, whereas Taras who grew up in the countryside had problems even just stroking the horse on the head.

They never went back to training and when, about a year later, they needed to choose what they would study, they both, the eldest first and then the youngest, chose veterinary science or, after thinking things over together for a long time, biology. After all, apart from a small part of it, veterinary science is in fact preparing animals for the journey onto our plates, quite the opposite of what Anja and Mojca had imagined. The first year of their studies in Vienna was paid for by their grandfather whom they had met when he was already in hospital, after that it was Alenka's clinic.

"My father," said Alenka and Taras thought about how quickly she had forgotten the fifteen years in which her father hadn't been her father, "would like to provide for their studies somewhere abroad and I said I needed to ask you first..."

What should he have said? No, I'll pay for it? No, studying in Ljubljana is just as good...

Dhaulagiri was his last Himalayan expedition. The December after his return Anja was born and over the next few years Taras had dealt with getting by on a daily basis, combining his efforts for furthering his qualifications and regularly paying the bills and the mortgage, and was also forced to adopt a life without mountaineering. And since a person without motivation achieves very little, and motivation spurns from emotions not reason, he chose anger as a means of handling it all. He would show the old man.

It was not easy. At twenty-five he began living a life for which his current colleagues, at least behind his back, called him a robot. Work at seven, work, work, coffee break, work and work, then home, busy with his daughters, running, boxing at the gym, and only later, when Alenka eventually got a job in the clinic in Moste, they also managed the occasional cinema or theatre or foreign language course... He stopped going out drinking with friends, and by the time his stomach problems forced him to total abstinence he had already been a moderate drinker for ten years. His fellow climbers in the meanwhile went on trips to the Himalayas, Patagonia, Kyrgyzstan, South America, Lofoten, or at least to Chamonix. Without wanting to, since he avoided mountaineering news, Taras still found out about their feats. Unfortunately also deaths. At about the time his father-in-law reappeared with cancer, Taras counted the victims and realized that thirteen of his former mountaineering friends were dead. All but one in the mountains.

Should he have thanked the old man that he was alive? That he had begun behaving responsibly early on in his life? To thank him for, fifteen years later, taking matters over? Should he have been angry with Alenka for taking his gift almost for granted? Should he thank her for not giving him the chance to reject it?

They walked around town for a couple of hours. In Trnovo they had some mulled wine and Taras drank tea, then they went for a pizza and when he and Alenka returned home a little after three in the afternoon, they collapsed onto the sofa in front of the TV. The film they had began watching had long finished when they both woke up and it was already dark outside.

"I should have gone for a run," Taras sighed. "I hope that the saying that you'll do all year what you do on New Year's Day isn't true. I wouldn't like to sleep though the entire year."

While Alenka went to the bathroom he found a bottle of wine in the refrigerator, filled a glass for her and made himself some black tea. He won't go running. It will be *dolce far niente* for today. He looked at his cup and felt silly. Once again and still.

"Congratulations for the New Year, or whatever it is they say," he intercepted her as she went naked towards the bedroom.

They laughed, she drank a sip, he embraced her and when he held her in his arms he remembered the headless girl in the refrigerator at the Institute of Forensic Medicine, he remembered his colleagues who were also dead... He stroked her bottom with his hand, then moved it up her back and turned towards her breasts. He caressed the nipple on one and then the other breast, leaned closer and touched it with his tongue.

Fear of death is the best aphrodisiac. Besides, in an hour's time or so the girls would be home and they needed to utilize the time they had.

Chapter 8.

Tuesday, 2 January

"Drvarič is waiting for you in his office," said Pavlica, the man sitting at reception.

"What does he want?"

"I don't know. He said I should intercept you and send you straight to him."

Taras was always the first to get to work. Not among the first, but the first. If you are first nobody knows when you arrived and nobody can accuse you of leaving early, Taras believed and a couple of times a week he wickedly sent an email to Drvarič, his immediate boss, as soon as he arrived at work, asking him things he knew he would not know the answer to. It was not that he hated his work, it was just that after twenty years he no longer enjoyed it so much that he would, on days when it was not necessary, spend more than six hours at it. Six hours was of course less than the mandatory eight, but Taras had no guilty conscience over this. In six hours of uninterrupted work, without a lunch break or sitting round having coffees, he did what three others did in their combined twenty-four. But since results are not everything, he always made sure that when he raised anchor, as he called it, he had some papers in his hand with which he was supposedly going somewhere or which he would sort out in the evening. Even if it meant returning to the office in the evening, he preferred it to wasting the entire day there. The tactic was successful and it was these split working hours which brought him the fame of an orderly workaholic.

Being the first at work meant a quarter to seven. That was the time he stepped into the small kitchenette to make himself a coffee and until seven he browsed the Internet, reading the web pages of the daily newspapers. Then he would send his question to Drvarič and begin work. By the time Brajc and Osterc arrived between eight and half past, he had a precious hour's advantage. His most productive hour that he used for the usual nonsense, as he called it, meaning writing reports, notes and records. Unlike most others he knew, he needed more peace and quiet for this work than any other. Of course there were exceptions, days when he appeared at the office at the same time as everyone else, and this second of January was one such day. He parked his car at half past eight and set off for his office.

There was a woman, still almost a girl, sitting outside Drvarič's office and when Taras approached the door she quickly stood up and greeted him. Taras returned the greeting, slightly bewildered, and waited for a moment to see whether she would speak to him. When she didn't, he knocked on the door and entered without waiting for a response. Sitting with Drvarič in the office was Kristan, the Head of the General Police Directorate. Kristan nodded when Taras entered, Taras shook his hand and sat on the only empty chair available.

"Taras, damn it, we need to sort this out urgently," Drvarič began, and when Taras did not return the ball he had sent into his court, he continued. "This stuff with the headless girl. This stuff we messed up in Bohinj."

Of course Taras knew what it was about, he knew the instant Pavlica sent him here. Just as well that he had said 'we messed up', Taras thought, though not that good that he had said 'we messed up in Bohinj.' He too had been in Bohinj, in fact of the three of them *only* he had been in Bohinj.

"We already discussed this with some young colleague from the courts," said Taras trying to remember his surname – what was it again? Dolenc? No, Doles. "I thought we'd sorted it out."

He once more went over the events and when he finished Drvarič and Kristan looked at each other.

"Well, it's not important now how it happened. The problem is that in half an hour's time we will have five journalists at the General Police Directorate who have of course found out more than we know and then I will have to pretend that everything is clear to me."

"I must say that I don't see any problem," Taras said. "Yesterday we pulled a body of a young woman out of the water and we are trying to establish her identity. If you didn't send a competent team to investigate, that's not my fault, but you can still do so. Even if everything hadn't been all trampled over at the site, you would not have found anything there. She did not die in the bushes where we pulled her out of the water. And that is about it. Why don't we know who she is? Because she had been in the water for some time without any identifying items of clothing. That's what we tell them. We do not have to mention the missing head unless those two cadets already let it slip."

The Head of the Ljubljana Directorate and the Head of the General Directorate looked at each other again, then Kristan stood up, shook Drvarič's hand first and then turned to Taras. As he shook his hand he said,

"And good luck. We'll intervene if necessary."

"Why, is this my case, or what?" Taras asked when Kristan had left and shut the door behind him.

Drvarič nodded.

"How come? How come the federal investigators have relinquished a treat like this?"

"Upon my request."

He fell silent and when Taras showed no sign of making his performance easier, he continued somewhat disappointedly,

"Taras, things are getting complicated. We get a certain amount of money from the budget of our wonderful country..."

Taras hated it when he spoke to him as if he was a school kid.

"...for which we have to do a certain amount of work. In our case..."

"I know what that means in our case," said Taras. "You can skip that part."

Drvarič paused as if he had to decide whether to ignore him or not.

"What cases are you currently working on?"

He was younger than Taras and not very good as a criminal investigator. With him Taras often thought about how unfair it was that someone who is useless at their basic job is promoted simply in order not to do damage. They become the director. Of course a person like that is needed, they need someone who can take instructions and delegate them, which was in essence what Drvarič did, but it would have been more appropriate if the job was called 'administrator' for example, and came with a salary a couple of grades lower than people working out in the field. If you are a good investigator you will probably remain one, if you are a bad one, you will sooner or later be promoted. No matter how bad the investigator, when they are put in charge they begin to flatter themselves that they were promoted because they know and are capable of something more. Taras had to be impudent with Drvarič if he wanted to be left alone.

"Three," said Taras and listed them.

All this was easier since Alenka had the golden-egg-laying clinic. Drvarič knew how to be very respectful towards people who were higher up on the social ladder, something which doctors, owners of private clinics and also their partners certainly were. He was more polite towards Taras than with others and politeness was basically all that Taras expected. That and his salary, though thanks to his deceased father-in-law, even that was not as essential.

"How far are you with them?" Drvarič asked even though he knew the answer.

"They're at court."

"It means that as far as you're concerned..."

"Yes, three testimonies if they will ask for them, and that's it."

Drvarič feigned surprise. Taras had to admit that he had some acting talent.

"Why then are you reluctant to take on this case? It's not every day that you come across a female corpse without a head, not even in this job. Perhaps never."

"I don't think I have any problems in fulfilling the quotas."

"No of course not, but I still don't understand how come you're prepared to decline a treat like this, as you called it yourself."

"Because I promised Alenka I would take her skiing in Bad Kleinkirchheim."

Let him know.

"Oh, you're going to Bad… For a long time?"

It sounded as if he was there every day.

"A week."

"A week," Drvarič repeated and paused as if wanting to process the information in his mind. "That would be fine. I still can't see any reason why our PD couldn't take on this case."

He stared at Taras.

"You mean, why I couldn't take on his case?"

Drvarič nodded.

"You and your guys, Brajc, Osterc and…"

He stopped and looked at Taras who made him wait for a while and then couldn't be bothered to play this game,

"Penca has been dead for quite some time now."

Drvarič shook his head.

"I didn't mean him."

He stood up, stepped to the door, opened it and half stepped into the corridor.

"That's why…"

When he returned to the room, the woman who had previously greeted Taras outside the door followed him into the office and now also nodded.

"This is Tina Lanc, a qualified psychologist and at the same time, or in addition to this, also a graduate of the Faculty of Computing. Did I get the order right?"

"Well, in fact it's the other way round," said the girl with embarrassment.

"Whatever, our new colleague and the new member of your team, Taras."

The girl offered Taras her hand and he automatically responded.

"Tina," she repeated.

Taras nodded, let go of her hand and turned towards Drvarič who clearly wasn't expecting the reaction he could discern from Taras' face.

"Thank you Bojan," Drvarič pointed to himself with all ten fingers, "thank you for rising the aesthetic average of my group and also taking into account all the professional and educational criteria..."

Taras interrupted him.

"Can I speak without..."

He waved around with his hands, looking for the right word.

"Politeness?" Drvarič asked.

"Restraints. If I understand you correctly, the young lady is here in Milan's place?"

"Penca? Yes. Do you know, I forgot that his name was Milan. I don't think I ever called him Milan."

Doesn't matter, Taras thought, he too had forgotten that Drvarič's first name was Bojan.

"Milan was my mentor, even though he was only three years older than me, but he was with the criminal investigation department from the beginning," said Taras and turned so that it was not obvious whether he was talking to Drvarič or the girl. "He worked as an investigator for thirty years. And for this case I would certainly need someone with experience, we're not dealing here with some drunk son stabbing his father, or something like that..."

The girl nodded. Clearly she had been informed about the case. And, it seems, even before Taras knew that the case was his.

"Someone with experience. And, I am sorry, but that is not you, is it?"

"No," said the girl, "I have no experience."

Taras shrugged his shoulders and had already turned towards Drvarič when the girl continued,

"But you too were not experienced in the Varta case and still it was you who solved it, not the two groups of experienced colleagues who had been dealing with it before you."

Taras looked at her in surprise. Varta, how long ago was that?

"I was lucky," he said.

"You were lucky because you had a good mentor," said Drvarič. "And our young colleague is not here because she's pretty, but because among all the candidates for this post, she was best qualified. She holds degrees from two faculties, Taras, Psychology and Computing, and a course in criminal investigation with marks that I would rather not compare to yours. And how many such candidates do you think were prepared to come here?"

"The fact that the colleague is pretty is something you keep pointing out, twice so far already. I don't care what she looks like, what I do have a problem with is that she is inexperienced and that she will need to be trained, something that we cannot afford to do in the case awaiting us."

He took a better look at the girl. Drvarič won't have to work with her directly. To him she is just a decorative plant in the office.

She had her long black hair tied back in a ponytail. Very black. Dyed? Considering her dark complexion, probably not. Around five foot seven in height, dressed in a dark blue jumper and a skirt that reached above her knees. At least now that she was sitting down. Despite the snow outside, she was wearing shoes that Taras would call stilettos. Other female colleagues Taras knew, forensics and other female staff, all wore trousers to work and when at some party or on other occasions they wore slightly more feminine shoes, they looked unnatural and awkward, or at leas that was what they seemed like to Taras who was not used to seeing them dressed up like that. Tina Lanc, who after shaking his hand put hers behind her back in embarrassment, was sitting in Drvarič's office as if she was at an audition for a hostess at some motorcar show. Pretty? The first thing he noticed were her eyes, which were a little too large, like in those Japanese comics, manga, and to him it made her look almost comical.

"I don't mean to say that you're not pretty... or that you are, or anything in this sense."

What was it he wanted to say? Whatever it was, it made her blush.

"So you did notice? Excuse us, miss, we will try to watch what we say, but this is still predominantly a male occupation."

"You were twenty-seven when you started on criminal investigation. I'm twenty-nine."

She smiled. She was certainly prettier than Penca.

"I didn't turn up in a mini."

"Taras!" Drvarič almost shouted.

"In an hour's time my team will go out on fieldwork in Bohinj, if I correctly recall the first part of our conversation. There is a metre of snow there now. High heels won't do."

He thought of how Brajc and Osterc will drool when he introduces her.

"And if I'll have to work with... Excuse me, what was it again?"

"Tina," she helped him. "Tina Lanc."

"Taras, can't you handle a joke? I told you that the young lady has all the necessary qualifications and is the best we can get, and if she happens to be prettier than any of the other mugs in your group, what's wrong with that?"

Taras turned to the novice who looked at him, appearing not to be put off at all. In her place about twenty years ago, Taras would have pissed his pants.

"As far as fieldwork is concerned," she said, "I live in Cankar Street, just five minutes walk from here and I can go home and change into a burka if you want me to."

Drvarič laughed, Taras somehow managed to control himself.

"And I do indeed have a couple of mini skirts at home, but this one," and she flirtingly grabbed the edge of her skirt and rolled it up a centimetre or so, "isn't from that drawer."

Now Taras too couldn't help it and smiled sourly. For the second time he thought about how he would have pissed his pants had Penca had a go at him like this over two decades ago. He looked at Drvarič.

"I really would need someone who has done some of this stuff before."

"No," said Drvarič. "She's yours."

Chapter 9.

Two minutes later Taras was walking down the corridor towards his office with the new girl. The corridor was long because Taras deliberately chose the office that was the furthest possible distance from Drvarič's, even though he wasn't doing himself any favours by this. He stayed silent until they walked the entire length of the corridor and stopped only when they reached his door, turning towards her,

"Are you related to him?"

"To whom? Drvarič? No."

"Any other connection..."

She shook her head pulling a face.

"With Kristan?"

She rolled her oversized eyes.

"Just asking," he said and opened the door. "I want to know where I stand."

He shared the office with his other two colleagues who were, when needed, also members of his team. They were both sitting at their computers and Taras would bet they were not looking through work-related emails on the second of January. Brajc was probably on some trash news site, looking at articles about Tiger Woods' and Lindsey Vonn's break-up or something similar. And Osterc is getting ready to check on e-bay whether he can find the rear right light for his Opel Omega, but was for now still bending over the keyboard with a straightened paper clip, trying to fish out the large flakes of dust that had accumulated between the keys. When they noticed Taras they gave him a barely visible nod and would have gotten back to their tasks uninterrupted had something new not appeared behind him. Osterc remained in his previous position with the metal wire above the keyboard, and merely raised his eyebrows. Brajc swivelled round in his chair, placed his hand on the back of his neck and leaned on the backrest,

"Woo-hoo, and what do we have here?"

Taras did not respond. He sat at his computer, pressed the button, and patiently watched the screen as something began stirring somewhere in the guts of the machine and took a while for the window demanding his password to appear. Tina stood indecisively in the middle of the room and looked towards Taras who was still staring at the screen in front of him. Brajc shrugged his shoulders at Osterc, then stood up and stepped towards Tina. Floated might be a more accurate description. With the huge saggy belly he pushed in front of him, his movement reminded Taras of a tanker trying to sail into port.

"I'm Pavle, if I may be of assistance," he offered her his hand. Tina shook hands with him.

"Tina Lanc, your new colleague. Apparently..."

She looked at Taras again who lifted his head above the screen and without as much as a nod, looked back down at it.

"Well, I *am* pleased to meet you," Brajc interrupted and repeated the sentence again, looking like some old man in retirement who dropped a Viagra into his tea by mistake. As he repeated how pleased he was, his chin wobbled. And this man is younger than me, Taras thought in horror. Brajc eventually passed her on to Osterc who briefly shook her hand and, as he did so, he stared at her sideways and close up to her face. Taras wondered whether Osterc had already been to the dentists to have his rotten lower right six fixed or whether his breath still stank today, and, without wanting to, even felt responsible for it. He looked across his desk and picked up a paper cup with some dried up remnants of coffee in it and was about to throw it in the waste paper bin, but changed his mind and defiantly put it back.

"Ms Lanc is here instead of Penca," he said and observed the effect his words had on his colleagues' faces. They nodded. Was it only he who found it strange that instead of an experienced criminal investigator, they were sending him a computer graduate with a degree in psychology?

"That's his desk over there, and his computer, but his stuff is still here..."

When Penca died at the beginning of autumn, he left behind drawers full of papers in his desk. At the gathering after the funeral Taras informed his son of this and he had said he would call round. He never did and now, almost half a year later, Penca's place looked just as used as Taras', perhaps a little tidier, as if its occupant had gone on an extended holiday.

"What will we do with all this now?"

"I'll find a box and clear it all out," Tina said.

"The password for his computer is..."

"No need. They've already created an account for me on the network and I'll log in with my own."

"If you're looking for a box," Brajc spoke again. "Go and see Marjana in accounts. They are always getting stuff delivered to them and are sure to have some boxes around. Tell her I sent you."

She smiled at him. He stepped to the door with her and showed her where she had to go. He came back tapping his feet.

"Hey, Taras, what's this you brought us today?"

"Drvarič, not I."

"Wow, what a rocket!"

He patted his belly with both his hands, a gesture which Taras, however much he tried, could not understand. Did he intend to eat her? He looked at Osterc who was now already typing away on his cleaned keyboard, looking like he had swallowed a stake, his elbows glued to his torso.

They were both peculiar guys, Pavle Brajc and Zoran Osterc, Brajc and Osterc, for they never used each other's first names. Only Taras was always Taras and never Birsa, perhaps because his name sounded like a surname anyway. Someone who didn't know them would never guess that they were good criminal investigators. The same way that you'd never guess that the Rolling Stones were a great band just by seeing them. Nothing special individually but nicely complementing each other. Osterc bony with thinning hair, a wizard when it came to technical matters in a kind of practical car-mechanic-type way. Whenever Taras was buying a car he turned to him. All his cars, including the current one, were second hand, and Osterc always went with him to the dealer and negotiated the price. He was about ten years younger than Taras, five younger than Brajc and his two children were still at primary school. Brajc's only boy was finishing secondary school and he saw him every second week. That was the arrangement made with his former wife and in as much as Taras knew people and knew Brajc, he could confidently say that there was no one else in Brajc's life after her. He still had her photo on his desk with the excuse that the son was also in it. Taras doubted that he didn't have a single photograph of the son without the mother. Brajc was already totally grey, fat, and when he wasn't gorging on sandwiches he was stuffing himself with anti-cholesterol tablets provided by the public health system as well as green coffee extract pills and similar stuff which Osterc found for him on the web in an attempt to lose weight and lower his blood sugar enough to go for his meniscus repair surgery before it totally gave in. Both he and Osterc had a way with people and whenever they appeared at a scene, people accepted them as their own kind. Much more than Taras who did not, like Osterc, wear oversized patterned jumpers out of fashion some thirty years ago – this was more thanks to Alenka than his own initiative – nor did he, like Brajc, come limping along, one eye constantly on the lookout for anything he could eat. In fact one of the reasons they were so successful was because they were so very different. But until now it had been the three of them. A woman could substantially complicate things.

"Osterc, do you too find her attractive?"

"She's alright," said Osterc without moving his eyes off the screen.

"Just alright, or attractive?"

"Both."

Taras looked at Brajc who shrugged his shoulders as if to say, that's Osterc for you.

"Idiot," said Brajc, "not only is she attractive, she's a real rocket!" he shouted and looked at Taras who nodded simply for the sake of peace and quiet.

Tina returned with a large cardboard box, opened the drawers and, without showing any sentiment over the contents, began emptying them. This is all that is left of a person after thirty years, Taras thought. A drawer full of office supplies – biros, pencils, a rubber, a stapler… – another drawer full of documents and documentation that the dead person no longer needs, and a tape or some other sound and picture storage device from which you would need to go to great lengths to find equipment which could actually still read it. They had been wondering what to do with all this stuff for half a year, and now along comes this girl and tidies it all away in half an hour.

"Where should I put it?" she asked when she had finished.

"I'll take it," said Taras.

He would call Penca's son again and, if he doesn't turn up, he will store it in the basement. Perhaps he will once even find some time to look through it himself. Tina sat at the computer, cleaning the screen and the keyboard with some liquid and a sponge that she must have acquired when she went to find the box. For the first time since he had been here, and that was at least twenty years, Taras looked at his own keyboard.

"Oh, what an old box!" she said as she waited for the computer to respond.

It was as if Osterc was waiting for such a comment and for five minutes he went on about things which Taras didn't understand or care to, Brajc clearly also not. They got on his nerves. He tapped his pencil on the desk so all three turned towards him.

"Now that we've all got to know each other, a word or two about our future tasks. You two don't yet know that we are to start the year with a new case..."

Once again, for the third or fourth time in two days he told the story. When he finished there was silence in the office.

"At around twelve we can expect the report from the IFM. Fingerprints and DNA..." he said and stopped when he realized he was already talking to Tina. Brajc and Osterc knew these things anyway. In fact she should too. What is he supposed to call her? Lanc, like Brajc and Osterc and not Tina as in Pavle and Zoran? Will Brajc continue to tell the dirtiest, raciest jokes he can find on the Internet over morning coffee? Well, that's one thing he wouldn't miss.

"In an hour's time Drvarič will inform the public about the body. He'll say that it had been in the water for so long that identification was not possible. He won't mention the head and that means we are also not to mention it, not even during informative conversations. Be careful not to let it slip."

Brajc and Osterc didn't even nod, but this last part was not intended for them anyway.

"Any ideas yet?" Osterc asked. "I mean, is this all you know?"

"Yes."

Taras stepped to the board which he had had fixed to the wall. Two, in fact, one was a cork bulletin board that he could pin things to, the other a whiteboard where he could write and erase things with a marker pen. He used it to note down guesses and assumptions which, once confirmed, travelled to the pinboard. He picked up the eraser and wiped off all previous notes, leaving it clean and white before starting to write afresh, speaking out aloud. He was not talking to them, Brajc and Osterc knew that, he was talking to himself, and he would not change his habits because of the newcomer.

"One. We will send forensics to the site where the body was found, let them check whether there is anything I missed yesterday, or the day before. Considering the circumstances I could have done, but I don't expect they'll find anything."

He wrote a number one and next to it *site inspection*, dash, *forensics*.

"Two – information gathering conversations with villagers in what is luckily more or less the only village upstream from the site, Ribčev Laz, and then interviews with owners of weekend houses in Ukanc. We'll also check how things are with guests at the hotels by the lake. Whether anyone is missing from around the time we believe the crime happened. She could only have gotten into the river from the lake, which means that the crime must most likely have occurred somewhere close to its shore. And three..."

He paused and thought for a while...

"What are experts on water called? Hydrologists?"

He did not wait for an answer but wrote *hydrologist* next to number three.

"There probably isn't much point, but let's try."

He took a step backwards and looked at the board again, then turned to the trio behind his back.

"I will go to the SEA and see a hydrologist, Brajc, you call Golob and send his team to Bohinj. Tell them we'll meet them in Bohinjska Bistrica and to call me if they get there before I do.

You two wait for the report and bring it there."

"And Tina?" Brajc asked. "Is she coming with us?"

Taras looked at Tina who was sitting at the computer and looked a little puzzled when their eyes met. She glanced at Brajc and then looked at Taras again. She looked so young with her helpless gaze, she reminded Taras of his daughters.

"She can go with you or she can come with me. You'll need some time to get used to us."

And it will take us even longer to get used to her, he said to himself. Her confused glances kept shooting between Taras and the other two.

"In fact... You can come with me. You said you could get ready quickly, didn't you?"

She nodded emphatically.

"I'll be back in fifteen minutes."

"We could go on the way. I can wait for you in the car."

"I see, so we're asserting our *jus primae noctis* are we? Nice, nice..." Brajc couldn't help himself.

Brajc, you really will never get another woman, Taras thought, and let him get it off his chest.

"And one more thing. Things were pretty informal in here with the three of us, so no Misters and Mses if that's alright Tina, if you think you can handle an ageing gentleman like Brajc?"

Brajc snorted angrily,

"Elderly? Look who's talking!"

Ten minutes later Taras stopped his car at the taxi rank on Cankar Street and while Tina went to her flat, he filled out the travel order. He utilized her absence to get through the boxes that had to be ticked and the vague numbers he had to fill out and thought that in fact from now on Tina could do this. When he would go out into the field with Penca, he was thc one to fill out the forms even though he was driving; now that he had been alone for a while the same, of course. And no, he hid the fact that he needed reading glasses from Brajc and Osterc as well, so this wasn't about the fact that he would have a younger woman sitting next to him when Tina returned. And an attractive one, at least that seemed to be what everyone thought.

Chapter 10.

"If I understand you correctly..." said the man with a neat trimmed beard which, with its defining line between the hairy and shaved parts of his skin, seemed to frame his face, even more so because he was rather pale, "...you want to find out how long it would take for a body thrown into Lake Bohinj to float to here..."

He put his finger on a map on the desk in front of him.

"... about three kilometres from Ribčev Laz?"

Taras looked at the map, found the section of the road where he had encountered the police car and nodded.

"I'm afraid I cannot help you on that."

"Because?" Taras queried.

"I haven't a clue how fast water carries bodies. Whether they stay on the surface or sink... All these are things beyond my knowledge."

He glanced at Tina, not for the first time.

"In fact I didn't expect you to tell me where the body was thrown into the water, but rather where it wasn't."

"What do you mean?"

"According to the experts from forensic medicine, the girl was killed about a week ago and that is also the time the body has been in the water. Within that time, could the water have brought it from any part of the lake?"

The hydrologist smiled.

"No, I don't think so. Lake Bohinj does in fact have quite a current. But the entire body of water in it is replaced at a rate of only three times a year. If a body was thrown into the lake in its north-western side, somewhere near Ukanc, it would most probably still be there a week later."

"Does that mean that it must have happened closer to the lake's outflow into the Sava Bohinjka?"

"The Jezernica. The stream flowing out of the lake is called Jezernica and it only becomes the Sava Bohinjka when, after about a hundred metres or so, it merges with another stream called Mostnica."

"OK, the Jezernica."

The hydrologist was getting on his nerves and clearly he got on his as well.

"Yes, probably. Why don't you go to the lake and throw a lump of wood into it and watch what happens to it?"

"I thought that in the twenty-first century we would have had some more advanced methods," said Taras without even trying not to sound sarcastic.

*

"Well, we tried," Taras mumbled more or less to himself when they sat back in the car and drove towards the bypass. The roads had been cleared of the worst and the snow at the sides was already grey-black. Taras always thought snow in town was not beautiful, and didn't mind if it rained all winter in Ljubljana as long as there was a metre of snow on Pokljuka where he went cross-country skiing.

For a while they drove in silence and Taras realized with embarrassment that the radio was sending something classical but dull through the loudspeakers. Let it play, he thought to himself, but a minute later switched it to a rock channel. Deep Purple's *Child in Time* blasted away and he was about to press the button to switch to the next channel but stopped mid-gesture. What was he doing? It wasn't him singing, after all.

"So, what brought you our way?"

It sounded like a question Cvilak would ask, a man just before retirement.

"Me?" Tina asked as if there was someone else in the car, and smiled. "Do I have to?"

"No, not if it's some kind of secret."

"Oh no, it isn't. If you are interested Mr…"

"Just Taras."

"Sorry, I'll get used to it. No, it isn't a secret. Boredom. That's the answer. I had other goals and wishes in life but for my parents' sake I forgot about them and enrolled in computing and data processing and, to please them, also completed my studies, even though I knew that I was not really interested in it."

"What were those wishes?"

She smiled.

"You'll laugh... When I was a little girl I'd play in the sandpit and imagine that I was an archaeologist or something like that, a palaeontologist, even before I knew that such a thing existed. Other girls played with dolls, I played with a spade."

"And the psychology?"

"I though that that would be it. Or at least be better. Or... Oh, I don't know what I thought. At the same time I kept reading crime fiction and watched a lot of American crime drama series. I know it's silly and childish, but I wanted to be part of a crime investigation team which solves riddles."

"Why would it be silly? That is in fact what we do."

She fell silent for a moment and then smiled hesitantly.

"Well, in fact *you* are in part responsible for me being here today."

"Me?"

"Yes, the Varta case. It was one of the cases discussed on my psychology course. Was it really just luck?"

"Luck is always part of it as well. How come you discussed this Varta case?"

"In the third year, in psychopathology and social psychology, we looked at crime."

He bit his lip not to say anything. Instead of someone who had some hands-on experience of criminal investigation, he has been sent an expert on psychopathology, social psychology and Facebook. Is this what they call modern times? Who will replace him? Will it still be a person, or some computer program?

"Varta was my first case. I mean, my... the first case in which I was involved."

A month after he had finished his course in criminal investigation and had also completed the required weeks of practical training, he was assigned to Penca's team investigating the disappearances of some people who were initially believed to have disappeared to avoid creditors, the taxman, their wives; then some chance walkers, mushroom gatherers, found the first body in the forest. A Varta battery was found at the scene and that is how the case got its name.

Was Penca at the time also put out by his arrival? He certainly didn't show it.

The investigation had been dragging on and was going nowhere. Lack of any concrete evidence made them try bluffing. They arrested the first person who appeared to be involved in a network of vague associations with the three known victims and turned on him with all their arsenal. Based on vague hints that were not even clues, they first detained him for twenty-four hours, and then, based on even weaker evidence which had the investigating judge simply shaking his head, managed to extend his detention for a further forty-eight hours with a court order. They were unable to find out anything. When they despaired, Penca sent Taras to the man. Let the kid try. Taras sat before the fat, cocky man who was later identified as the leader of a murderous organization, and the man gazed at him arrogantly and began complaining about how the police were treating him and how they kept pestering him even though he had an alibi for all the things they were accusing him of.

"That's why fings are as they are in 'r country," he hissed, "People from down south are all protected, aren't they, but you don't fink twice 'bout havin' a go at an honest man..."

"I completely understand," Taras lied though his teeth. "All we need to do is a kind of summary of what you told my colleagues and you are free."

He nodded and nodded for an hour and a half, for as long as the conversation lasted. It was more or less a monologue by the suspect and Taras didn't find out anything his colleagues had not heard before him. He only persisted because Penca had ordered him not to reappear from the booth in sooner than two hours.

"So, I'll tell you too where I was at the time you're badgering me about..."

He gave him a list of alibis without Taras even asking him to.

"When Slonjak disappeared..." he had been in such and such a place, "when Brajnik was taken away... and Kovač... and

Markež..."

Four – for three bodies. They had not even found the fourth one yet, they had not known about him at all. Even Taras almost overlooked this.

They pressured him and although he then didn't say anything else, the rest was pretty straightforward. When you know, when you are convinced about what you need to be looking for, then you'll find it, Penca used to say. He could have easily had taken credit for solving the case and anyone else in his place would have done.

Taras has never forgotten this 'when you know what to look for, you'll find it."

Half a year ago Penca died of lung cancer, twelve years after lighting his last cigarette and six months before retirement. When Taras last visited him, a week before he died, they walked to Štorklja at the far end of Zaloška Street and had a coffee. Well, Taras did. Penca could no longer handle anything that might irritate his stomach and had ordered a mint tea but left most of that.

"I read somewhere that in fourteen years your body restores itself entirely," he had said. "I was two years short."

He was a tiny man anyway and was now only half of what he had been. He had to tie his trousers, blue and white stripy pyjamas, into a knot at the waist, otherwise they would not stay up.

"Had I known," he said regretfully, "I wouldn't have taken that much care over these years. When I closed my eyes in the evening, or in the day sometimes, I could feel it... you know, that sensation when you blow the smoke out of your lungs. What a pleasure! I'd given it up for twelve years, but it's not something you forget. Goddamit!"

He took a sip of his tea, which made him cough and rasp for a long time, then Taras escorted him back, supporting him to the pedestrian crossing and across the road to the oncology department and his room.

"Can I give you some advice, Taras? My last..."

"Come on, Penca..."

"You come on. Listen to me..."

He had indicated with his finger for him to draw closer, as if he didn't want his roommates who both observed his arrival apathetically from their beds, to hear what he was saying.

"Indulge. Get up every morning, step out onto the balcony, look at the sun and say 'Wow!' out loud. Every morning, Taras. What if it's your last?"

As a mountain climber Taras had seen many a sun, watching it rise from his sleeping bag. In the months since the funeral he often wondered whether, without meaning to, it was these suns that Penca had been describing. Suns you don't forget, whatever happens, just as smokers don't forget cigarettes.

A day after Taras' visit Penca fell into a coma from which he never awoke. And now this attractive young girl Drvarič has brought in, has tidied away the last remaining physical evidence of his existence. Worse, he thought, it's all just getting worse.

Chapter 11.

"So that's what happened?" said Tina, sounding almost a little disappointed. "The case was presented to us at university as a crown example of how a ruthless investigator can, with suitable tactics, make the accused person talk."

"There were no tactics involved, and if there were, they were Penca's, not mine."

He began regretting that he had taken her with him. He was used to driving along alone and all this talking, this enthusiasm in the passenger seat was a nuisance.

"We had a professor who I think must have been a criminal investigator manqué," Tina continued, obviously not picking up on Taras' mood. "Half his lectures were on stuff like this. Maybe it's also thanks to him that I'm here now. Perhaps I feared that I would spend my life talking about things I would have wanted to have done, but never would."

She was wearing jeans and hiking boots and when she sat in the car she put a pair of gaiters on the back seat, and not some kind of touristy ones you might use to go on a family walk up Šmarna Gora. She saw that he had noticed.

"There's one thing I don't get. The case got its name from the battery found at the first body. What happened to that?"

"The battery? Nothing. I spent a week asking sellers in shops and at newspaper stands whether they could recall if anyone had bought a Varta battery, but came up with nothing. Everyone was buying batteries then. For hand-held torches, CD players, whatever. It's possible that the battery ended up there by chance, that it was there before."

"You wasted a week's work?"

"Yes... and in a way no. Depends how you see it."

He smiled. He had never told this to anyone, not even Penca, not even when he was in hospital and it no longer mattered. Had he been more experienced and had he known what he knows now, they could have caught them earlier. When he asked people about this battery, everybody immediately knew what it was about. The case had attracted attention even then and somehow they knew about it and talked. Nonsense, various theories, but he blindly continued looking for the buyer of the unfortunate battery who could have been some forest ranger or a hunter, at least that was what they assumed at the time, and was blind to... let's say, the wider picture.

"A woman at a kiosk in Škofja Loka explained to me how the murdered man had recently bought a new car and that someone surely and clearly – I can recall those were the exact words she used, surely and clearly – could not handle that. In the end it really was about greed and envy. The leader of the gang was his former business partner, a neighbour who had given up his share of the company and opened an inn, which wasn't doing very well... From his closed inn he had to watch his neighbour thrive and when the neighbour bought a new car, it was indeed more than he could handle. Disappointed?"

She shrugged her shoulders.

"Not exactly Kevin Spacey in Seven."

"Don't overestimate criminal investigators. They're often even dumber than cops."

She laughed.

"Have you had a case like this before?"

"Like what?"

"Like..."

"You mean decapitated?"

He wanted to say that he did not distinguish his cases according to which part of the body was damaged or removed, but the question was clear and there was no need for him to try and be clever about it.

"No, at least not one where criminal investigators needed to be involved. When I was still a policeman I was in on a case where someone accidentally cut off their own head when using a pressure gun. You probably didn't mean that kind of thing?"

She shook her head.

"No."

He had had bodies in water before. Among them was a body of a man in the River Sava without any documents who nobody was missing. Not at home and, as an extensive search of databases in other countries should, at least in those where such databases exist, also not outside Slovenia.

"And what are your thoughts on it so far?"

"I don't know."

He didn't have any thoughts.

"First we need to establish who this woman is. That's a start."

If there are no problems with this, then it is more likely that things will go smoothly afterwards as well. A name, then a motive, which will lead them to some husband or former husband or lover. It's usually the case. And if that is so, they will have the name and the motive today and when you know these you also know who the murderer is. Then all that is needed is to prove it, which is not always easy, but they usually break when you get close to them.

"The thing is..."

He fell silent as if he wasn't certain whether to tell her what was going on in his head.

"Is?"

"Nothing, we'll find out today who the poor wretch who ended up in the water is, a day or two later, who had a motive for her murder and then we'll slowly and persistently, mathematically deal with gathering evidence. That's how things usually are and I can't see why they should be different this time."

The thing is, he thought, that if this was a case of a raging husband who attacked his wife in an outburst, this would have been a butchery. But here they have a girl whose head someone cut off with a knife...

What was it Cvilak had said?

"...with a knife, a large and quite sharp knife, judging by the cut. Between the third and fourth vertebra. Smooth and decisive, without making much of a mess of it."

The thing is that, if you want to cut off someone's head, you need the space and the tools to do it, something you do not have if you are acting in an outburst of rage.

The other thing is that in all this time someone should have begun missing her, but clearly nobody had.

Tina laughed.

"And I thought that you'd be thrilled; that criminal investigators are happy when they get something like this to work on."

"Why would that be?"

"Because this isn't a case like all the others."

He looked at her and she smiled with embarrassment.

"I mean, isn't this better than chasing after chicken thieves? You know what I mean."

For a while now Taras had perceived his profession as a job. Clearly it was useful, for he was being paid for it; it wasn't the worst job in the world, but if he could, he would probably be doing something else. What? He didn't know, and occasionally he worried that he was becoming like most Slovenes who preferred certainty, reliability and staying put, part of which meant a standard, forty-hour week. People who go to work as if it is their second home, perhaps even prefer it to their first because it does not include the wife and children, who always expect, question and demand things... How often had Taras, when he returned to the office in the afternoon or even evening because there was no way of avoiding it or he had forgotten something there, come across Brajc or Osterc, sitting at the computer, browsing through whatever it was. And it was always the same,

"Oh, is it that late already? I really need to wrap things up then..."

And Osterc or Brajc would switch off the computer and, as if they had been caught doing something illegal, set off home.

"Chicken thieves don't kill people."

"Not the best of metaphors, I admit, but you know what I meant."

Chicken thieves never stole his evenings, not even his afternoons.

He nodded. It was easier that way.

"But, why the cut off head?" Tina continued. "That must say

something."

He wished he could just suggest they changed the subject. He was not in the mood. Somewhere he had read that when American marines were waiting to disembark after their long journey to Tokyo, it was only the novices who talked about the battles, the experienced soldiers not at all.

"You tell me. Your degree is fresher than mine."

She paused for a moment, as if she had to think about it because much would depend on the answer she would give.

"An organized murderer – and the fact that he bothered to cut off the head, points to a degree or organization unnecessary for achieving the basic goal which is to kill someone – well, someone like that plans the event, controls themselves in the act, usually murders the victim at a hidden location and disposes of the corpse in another," she deliberated, staring out of the front window. "This points to a professional, and such murderers are usually of above average intelligence who chose the ideal type of victim, usually meaning that though the victims are not known to them, that they share some common external characteristics. Why the head? Maybe he wanted to hide her identity, and has so far been successful. It is characteristic of murderers like this that they know the limits of forensics and thus often burn the body or, as in our case, dispose of it in water."

She stopped, as if she had gotten carried away.

"You said – victims."

"Yes?"

"We only have one."

"Oh, yes..."

She thought for a while, as if she had just received a missing piece of information.

"Of course. I don't know why I even thought about a serial killer."

"Careful with words," Taras interrupted her. "We only had one serial killer in this country and he only succeed because he attacked women from the very lowest level of society whom nobody missed. Had he tried with a single one with a home, one who had someone waiting for her, he would not have reached the numbers to qualify for the club."

How come nobody was missing the girl in refrigeration at the Institute for Forensic Medicine? He turned off the motorway onto the main road and at the roundabout with a concrete accordion in the middle took the turning towards Bled.

"Well, what about the cut off head?" he asked her after about a minute of silence.

She looked at Taras and smiled, slightly embarrassed. For the first time he lingered on her face for a moment longer that he would normally. She might be going on thirty, but she looked younger, and for the second time that day he wondered whether she would be the right person for the job. Until now this had been a male domain and even women who had worked with him had had to go through a kind of unique re-training. Brajc liked to tell a story about a colleague who once bedded one of these women – though it was possible that the story, which had become a sort of internal legend, was in fact totally made up – and complained to her that she was biting him... Apparently she looked up and said,

"Are you gonna teach me how to give a blowjob?"

In more raunchy versions of the story, Brajc himself replaced the colleague.

"Then we're dealing with specific hatred," Tina said. "You need to hate someone a lot to cut off their head."

"And what do you do with the head?"

"Perhaps it's still in the stream, but we just haven't found it yet."

Taras shook his head.

"I don't believe that. There's no logic in going to these ends to cut someone's head off and then throwing it into the same lake. The head's a trophy."

"Like with IS?"

"Sort of."

"Is it possible that it was IS?"

He shook his head again.

"I don't believe that. Anything is possible, of course, but it's not likely. And if, in a week's time we'll be investigating whether it is a case of IS, then we're in trouble."

"So?"

"I don't know. If the victim is local there should not be any trouble. Sooner or later someone will miss her. If she is a foreigner... Let's say she is a prostitute who John X from Jesenice fell in love with. He visited her for a while as a client, then tried to persuade her to stop being a prostitute, she refused, then he catches he with some other man..."

"And where's the head in this case?"

"I don't know. But even if it's roughly what happened, there shouldn't be any major troubles. The average John X would, when he sobered up, jump into the lake after her."

"Why do you think she might be a prostitute?"

"I don't think she was, I'm supposing she could be."

"*Shaved pubic area,*" Cvilak had dictated to the typist at the autopsy before he cut into it. "*All pubic hair removed apart from a narrow strip above the clitoris, one centimetre wide and four centimetres long...*"

"That doesn't mean that she was a prostitute."

"No, but there's definitely a greater possibility that she went to Bohinj..."

How should he say this?

"For some fun," she said instead of him.

"So to say. Thank you... Well, or at least she thought that this was a possibility. You women usually don't trim your styles every day."

She laughed.

"Each to his own. And... Taras?"

"What?"

"I'm quite old enough to be able to handle words like fuck and others."

"I'm glad to hear that," he said and wondered whether he should tell her Brajc's story. He probably wouldn't have done, but the phone rang anyway. Taras pressed the button and listened for a while.

"It was Brajc," he said when he placed the mobile into the compartment on the car door. "As I thought. Whoever our guy was, he was most probably right-handed. There's little else in terms of information that could be useful. No other traces. I was not expecting fingerprints anyway, perhaps a few traces under the nails, but there's nothing. Nothing. No victim's fingerprints in the database, at least not ours. The DNA neither; we're waiting for the results from other countries, and also for the toxicology tests from the IFM. Basically, for now, zilch."

*

Half an hour later, having driven in silence, listening to the rock and roll hits of the seventies and eighties, Taras parked the car outside the log cabin pub in Bohinjska Bistrica where a car with the markings of the National Forensic Laboratory was already parked. The parking area outside the premises was barely cleared of snow and Taras had trouble fitting his car between the wooden fence and the pile of snow under which must have been a car. In an otherwise empty pub sat Golob with two colleagues wearing jackets clearly displaying their police badges and when Taras approached their table he also noticed they were wearing green work overalls. He would have preferred them all to have still been in plain clothes but had forgotten to tell them. He sat on the only empty chair and almost at the same time another chair appeared from the next table along for Tina. He introduced her, they shook hands and Taras received a few meaningful, not exactly discreet looks, the meaning of which he never understood. Did they really believe that women would fall for or even react to this? To: Oh, hi there… a handshake and a glance at Taras?

Whether she noticed it or not, Tina managed to ignore it. They sat down and Taras briefly repeated the story about the female body in the river. He told them how the body had been caught in some bushes and that it had been snowing heavily at the time…

"Well, que será, será," said Golob. "There's always something to find, though snow just creates problems. Had she been killed where you found her, it would have been different, but this way… We'll try hard, but in your shoes I wouldn't expect much."

"I'm not," said Taras.

"We called a diver who will be at the site in an hour's time. Just in case there was something of use in the water," said Golob and checked his watch. "He should be there at one."

Taras nodded. He called Brajc and found out that he and

Osterc were only about a kilometre away from Bohinjska Bistrica, so he told them to go straight to the site. He could imagine Brajc's disappointed face when he said "yes, OK," after a pause, realizing that he was not going to be offered a coffee and croissant before starting work. He'll make up for it, for sure.

Before leaving, Taras stepped to the bar, paid the waitress, and pretended to be asking indifferently,

"Apparently they found some woman in the river, or what?"

"Yes, she drowned. That's what they say."

"Who is she? Do you know anything?"

"Not one of ours."

Taras looked at her inquisitively. The woman returned his change and gave him the receipt.

"We'd know if she was one of ours. We don't really care about others."

There was so little space next to the snow-covered car that Tina had to wait for Taras to squeeze into it. The wheels skidded on the ice which had formed in the tracks and he had difficulty getting it to the cleared part of the parking lot. He waited for Tina to get in and set off.

"I have the feeling," he said when they drove off towards the lake, "that this time we'll be happy to find anything at all, even if it's just an old battery."

Chapter 12.

Taras stopped at the side of the road and took care to leave enough space for two more cars. He stepped out of the car and waited for the forensics to put their plastic protective white Tyvek suits over their overalls. The suits were more or less the kind anyone can buy in any DIY store if they need protective clothing when painting their walls. Then he took them along the deepest track to the river and showed them the bushes from which he and the policeman had retrieved the body. Tina went with them, Brajc and Osterc stayed at the car.

"As I thought," said Golob. His gaze moved along the river and the bank, and Taras knew that despite his grumbling, he could rely on him. If there is anything under the snow, he will find it. "We'll check everything, but it will be hard. If I had to choose between fire and snow, I would always choose fire. With snow you're quick to mess things up when you try to remove it. When the diver arrives with his boat, we'll go up the river to the lake."

"Will the other two not take a look?" Tina asked as they were returning to the car.

"They would just trample over what hasn't been trampled yet, and besides, it's sometimes better if each person does their thing and does it well. You know what it is like if everyone does a bit of everything..."

They reached the road and Taras turned towards the river. Now, during the day, it was visible through the bushes, also because some of the snow had already fallen off the branches. The men in white were carefully moving through the bushes.

Brajc and Osterc were leaning on their work Renault Laguna which already had almost five hundred thousand kilometres on the clock. Brajc was smoking, of course.

"Hey Boss, I need a coffee," he said. "I know you've already had yours, but at least let me have mine."

Taras nodded benevolently and told them to follow him in their car. Ten minutes later they were sitting in Hotel Jezero in Ribčev Laz and Brajc was sipping his cappuccino and nibbling on a croissant.

"I'll never understand who decorates these places," Tina said. She pointed at the bar and the dining area with two long rows of tables that had not been set yet.

"What's wrong with it?" said Osterc.

"The colours, the shapes," said Tina and Taras had to smile.

"I think it's fine," said Osterc and shrugged his shoulders. "It's clean."

"The hospital is clean too," said Taras. "But you wouldn't go there for a coffee."

Brajc nodded, his mouth full, and Taras could just imagine him, sitting at the tables of farmhouses that he and Osterc will visit, asking questions, munching away on *potica* and washing it down with a plum brandy or two. Osterc is the driver anyway. He told him about the "We'd know if she was one of ours..." comment.

"Well, in that case this thing today will be more like an outing," said Brajc as he wiped the crumbs from the corners of his mouth with a napkin. "Right, Taras?"

"We'll see. It would be nice if we found out today who our client is."

Brajc laughed and Taras regretted putting it this way.

"Our young girl is."

Taras went to the counter and settled this bill too, though Brajc was shouting across the room for him to wait, pulling his wallet out of his pocket. At least he wasn't stingy like Osterc. Osterc was one for the books. Whenever it was time to settle the bill, he was quite capable of sitting stone-faced, as if it had nothing to do with him. Taras waved his hand to say it was OK, and pulled his police ID from his pocket and showed it to the waiter.

"Is this about that woman in Bistrica?"

Taras nodded.

"First I'd like to talk to the hotel manager. Is he still... already here?"

"Yes. I'll call him."

The waiter dialled a number, told them that the police were here and then waited on the line for long enough for Taras to beckon to him, and when he appeared to waver, almost pull the receiver from his hand.

"Hello. My name is Taras Birsa, criminal investigator. My colleagues and I are on a murder case and we'd like to talk to you. Where can we see you?"

A moment of silence.

"You can see me, Mr Birsa, but right now I have..."

"We don't seem to be understanding each other here," Mr Birsa said with his most monotone, stern voice. Why does it always have to be like this? "A couple of days ago a body of a woman was found in the river very close to your hotel and I need to talk to you urgently. *Where* will we do so?"

He waited for the response and, without a greeting, put down the receiver and thanked the waiter.

*

"You must excuse me," the hotel manager said as he introduced himself and Taras jotted his name in his notebook. "The New Year celebrations are over, it was a madhouse round here, and we're only just recovering. I understand, of course I understand, the dead have priority. Please, do tell me what you need... Can we also offer you a drink or something?

The manager's office was a tiny room at the back of the hotel, looking out onto the forest and not the lake. They probably kept the best for the guests, Taras thought. Under an oil painting of a landscape, Lake Bohinj, of course, sat a tiny man, bald and podgy, his shirt tucked into his trousers and his belt pulled too high. When, after the initial shaking of hands, he sat back down at his desk, it seemed as if he had fallen off the chair and was now crouching behind it.

"Well, then, we have a body of a woman which we found the day before yesterday in the river about three, four kilometres along the road towards Bohinjska Bistrica. A young woman whose identity we're trying to establish. We hope that you'll be able to help us."

The manager opened his arms and looked even more like a curious child.

"Anything within my powers."

"You and your staff."

"Certainly, certainly... Can you give me some kind of photograph?"

He sounded curious. Taras felt he wasn't taking it seriously enough.

"It wouldn't help you. The animals... have done their part..."

The hotel manager flinched.

"The woman died about a week before the New Year. How booked was the hotel then?"

The director nodded.

"Oh... well... considering that there was no snow yet and that, apart from around Christmas and New Year, the end of December is not really our season, just enough for us not to be making a loss. Well, we did have a few guests and this year we were saved by the meeting of some chemists or biologists. They were here for three days. About the time when... when it happened, as you say."

"Chemists?"

"Biologists, I think they were from the university in Ljubljana. Pharmacists in fact. From some of those institutes in Ljubljana and elsewhere. I'll check to see what exactly it was called. Although Mr Mihelič also came along to see them..."

"Mihelič? The Director of Salubris?"

"Yes. He was here for the full three days."

He waved his arms though the air and gave Taras a conspiratory smile.

"As I said, there were some individual guests as well, but only a few. I'd need to check."

"Would you be so kind to get me a list of all your guests between the twentieth and twenty-fifth of December? With their dates of birth and phone numbers if they gave you one."

The manager was now nodding so fast, with such brief intervals, that Taras knew that a question would follow.

"But can I give you this information? You see, these are

delicate matters. Not everyone comes here..."

"With their family?"

"Right, right... exactly that."

"Look, if you want I can get you a court order, but it's just a waste of time which I'm short of. You find me the information and I can promise you that I'll handle it like..."

Taras' turn to give the manager a conspiratory look.

"...a very good manager. All I want to do is check that everyone on the list is still alive."

The gnome under the oil painting of *Lake Bohinj Before a Summer Storm* – that was what it said at the bottom of the frame – nodded.

"Yes, you do understand my concern, don't you?"

Slightly embarrassed, he glanced at Tina who smiled kindly.

"First I would like to talk to everyone who was working at the hotel at the time. Right away."

The manager picked up the phone and when he finished turned to Taras with a whisper.

"Was she killed?"

Taras nodded.

"Ooooh..."

"I would also like to ask some questions," said Tina and Taras had to control himself not to show his surprise. Of course, let her...

"Please, go ahead..."

"If the victim wasn't a local girl, and many things point to the possibility that she was not... Do you have any idea who she might have been? Is there anyone missing in even the most obscure sense of the word?"

"Any of the guests, you mean?"

"Guests, staff, people you or your guests know..."

The manager shook his head.

"No, not that I know of."

"If you had to guess, what would you say, who could this woman be? Young, as far as we can say, fairly attractive, and, let us assume that she was not from around here?"

The manager shook his head again.

"Could she have been a prostitute?"

The manager flinched as if he had been caught with his fingers in the pie.

"Excuse me, but here we don't deal with..."

"Nobody is saying that you deal with anything," said Tina as if she was chatting with a seller at a stall in the market. "But surely you must get a few come this way. You are a hotel, aren't you?"

"This is a very family scene. People come here on skiing holidays, many with their children, with Vogel a kind of family ski slope. Short pistes, not too steep, you know..."

"I do know," said Tina. "But at the same time there must be some guests who... how did we out it before... don't come with their family."

"Yes, of course, we get a mixture of people, but we don't ask them what they do for a living."

"Basically, all the guests who registered with you, also signed out?"

"Yes."

Tina fell silent and looked at Taras.

"Well," he said. "You were not a great deal of help to us, but still."

The manager spread his arms in embarrassment.

"No, no... If you don't know, you don't know. But you can help me with one thing."

The manager nodded and Taras pulled out his notebook, found a clean page and placed a biro on it.

"I would ask you for a list of hotels by the lake, just so we don't miss any."

"Oh, you won't have any problems with that."

Taras gave him a puzzled look.

"They were all closed from November until Christmas. As I said, most of December is a dead season. Some years ago we agreed that one hotel would remain open, kind of hold the fort, and absorb the losses of this part of the season, while others would do all their inventories and things like that during this time. This year it was our turn to stay on call."

"What about the apartments outside Ribčev Laz?"

"The same. They're closed the week before Christmas, so

they can get ready because it gets very busy afterwards."

*

A number of the hotel staff were already waiting in the conference room. With their help Taras first created a list of all who had been here during the week when the murder probably took place and then Tina and he went through the list interviewing people. They spoke to everyone on the list apart from a cleaning lady who was due to come in that afternoon, and the male receptionist who had gone on holiday after the New Year. Nobody knew anything, nobody had seen anything unusual. All guests had registered and all guests had signed out, no member of staff was missing. Basically nothing.

"Here is the guest list," the manager said and held the page in his hand for a moment before passing it to Taras."

"No worries, I'll call them during work hours."

He took his leave and when he was already by the door, Taras remembered something and turned around again. He gave the manager his visiting card.

"Two members of your staff were not here today. A cleaning lady and the guy from reception. Can you please tell them to contact me as soon as they come in?"

The manager took his card and looked at it carefully, perhaps only out of politeness.

"By the way, the cleaning lady, how old is she?"

"Oh, hard to say," said the manager and thought for a while. "Well over forty, going on for fifty, I'd say. Why do you want to know?"

Chapter 13.

"I hope I didn't mess things up," Tina said as they drove alongside the lake and Taras was silent.

"What with?"

"Cutting in like that with the manager."

Taras shook his head.

"No, just let me first finish my stuff. I use some kind of system… Intuition, then you can try. At least until we get used to each other. But I'm afraid," he continued as they drove past the Vogel cable car station, "there won't be many more opportunities for such coordination today. The owners of the weekend houses in Ukanc are almost certainly all back in Ljubljana. Well, at least the ones I know."

He stopped by the side of the road in an area which was barely cleared of snow, just enough for two or three vehicles to park. From there you could sense rather than see the nearest house. Only a narrow track led from there on down the snowed-over side road which about a hundred metres further along led to a group of weekend houses. A single other vehicle was parked in this siding, still covered in a thick blanket of New Year snow. As the drive towards the first house was not cleared, Taras would have gone past it had it not been for the light shining in the living room. Before they even reached the door it opened and an old lady with a white cat and a mongrel dog at her feet stood at the threshold. The witch from Hansel and Gretel.

"Hello," she said inquisitively.

"Hello," Taras greeted her and pulled his police ID from his pocket. "Senior Inspector Taras Birsa and my colleague Tina Lanc. We're gathering information for a case we are working on and would be very appreciative if you could give us some of your time."

"Is this about the body in the Sava?" the old woman asked immediately, her eyes glistening.

This one won't be a problem, Taras thought and, indeed, a minute later Tina and he were sitting on the L-shaped bench in corner behind a table which had a single chair at it in what was clearly the only large room in the small house which extended into the attic. A plate with a piece of *potica* appeared before them and the old lady was fiddling around the stove. The dog wound its way around the table legs and Taras stroked it on the neck.

"Would you like coffee, tea?"

"In fact we're in a bit of a hurry. We need to speak to all the other weekend house owners around here."

"Oh, then you're not in a hurry," she sung. "There's nobody here today... Apart from one house. Well, you do need to see them."

She looked at Taras across her shoulder, as if she had just entrusted him with a secret. Then she put the pot of water to boil and sat at the table.

"She was murdered, wasn't she?"

"Yes," said Taras and continued before the old lady had a chance to ask how. "We are now trying to establish her identity, and I wonder whether you might be able to help us."

The cat jumped onto the bench next to him and stared at him intensely with its emerald green eyes

"Oh my," the old lady called out. "Oki, what is it with you? She's never done anything like this before. You must have some strange energy."

Taras smiled and was about to stroke the cat but it hissed at him and didn't move even when he moved his palm above its head. It was still hissing when he slowly pulled his hand back and found his notebook in his jacket. Then it settled on the bench and stared at him motionlessly with its glassy green gaze.

"Can I have your name please?"

"Marija Stropnik. Stropnik is from my husband, though he's deceased."

"How often do you come here Mrs Stropnik."

The old lady laughed and Taras decided he liked her.

"I don't come here, I live here. This is my home. When my husband was still alive we used this place as a weekend house, but then I came here permanently. I won't leave until they carry me away in a box."

"So you know the neighbours?"

"I know everyone. You see, I'm the only person here all the time, so we have a kind of arrangement that I keep an eye on their houses, and that I call them if anything is wrong. Not that there ever is, but you never know."

"And you have their phone numbers?"

"I do," said the old lady and popped to the stove where the water was boiling. She took the pot off the heat and sprinkled some dried flowers into it.

"Home brew, I collected the flowers myself."

"Smells nice," said Tina.

"Peppermint, chamomile, willow bark and a few other things which are my secret. It is good for a cold and even helps get rid of headaches."

"Can you give me a list of the neighbours and their phone numbers?" Taras asked.

"Absolutely, absolutely..."

She put the box with the tea back in the cupboard and opened another drawer from which she produced a notebook she placed on the table in front of Taras. She opened a page and showed Taras a list of names with phone numbers neatly written out in pencil.

"Can you copy it out," Taras turned to Tina who nodded, produced a mobile phone from her jacket pocket and clicked the camera icon a few times.

There was a loud bang outside, somewhere close, and the dog ran squealing from under the table to the basket near the wardrobe. The cat hissed.

"Well, they are the only ones I don't know," said the old lady. "Some new people. I've already tried talking to them about these firecrackers but to no avail."

"How new are they?" Taras asked.

"Today is the ninth day they are here. It first banged when they arrived. Just before Christmas, but then it was only once or twice, and I didn't know what is was about, but on New Year's Eve it was as if we were on the battlefront. Young people, but they're here all the time. Don't know what kind of work they do."

"We'll go and visit them and mention that using firecrackers in the Triglav National Park is forbidden."

The old lady gave him a thankful smile.

"But tell me please, have you have seen anything unusual recently?"

"Unusual?"

She furrowed her brow and thought for a while.

"It depends what you consider unusual."

"Something which is different from how it is normally."

"The Markolis have a new car. That's probably not what you mean."

Taras shrugged his shoulders.

"What happened with the old one?"

"The daughter has it. Yes, before they had..."

And she told him the make of the car they had before and the one they have now. Taras listened calmly but was no longer taking notes.

"Oh yes!" she almost yelled. "And Balažič's boat got stolen!"

"We're talking about Dr Balažič? A large man, slightly overweight?"

The old woman nodded.

"A boat?"

"Yes, a wooden boat. Nothing special. Though it is possible," she said in almost a whisper, "that it just wasn't properly tethered and drifted away on the water."

"When was it stolen?"

"About a week ago."

"And did he report it to the police?"

"I don't know. Probably not. It was only an old, rather battered, wooden boat."

She jumped to her feet and went to the stove, strained the tea and poured it into two mugs. Taras' had *Home Sweet Home* written on it.

"And you haven't heard about anybody missing of the people you know?"

"No," she said and shook her head, almost with regret. "They went back to Ljubljana on the first of January. They all came to have a cup of tea with me before they left. No one missing. Well, at least the regulars who come. A large grey car drove past here early on New Year's Day morning. That one I had never seen before."

"It was mine. I spent New Year's Eve at Dr Prelc's place."

"Oh, yours."

"Everyone has to drive past your house anyway if they want to get to their weekend houses?" Taras asked. The old lady nodded. "Then you will probably know who was here around the twenty-second, twenty-third of December?"

She furrowed her brow, then shook her head.

"Normally I would know. But I was in bed on those days. I had a fever, and were it not for those firecrackers, I would not have known anyone was at the lake at all. The only person to stop by was Milan... Milan Balažič, that is. He went abroad for Christmas and New Year with his family and just came by to check how things were at the weekend house. That was when he noticed that the boat was gone. He called me first to ask me whether I could come over to his place, but I couldn't."

"When was that?"

"Hang on, let me think... Milan called when I'd been in bed for two days. I was in bed for four all together. I went out for the first time on Christmas Day, which means that..."

"The twenty-second?"

"Yes, it must have been then."

Taras stood up from the table and was about to say goodbye when he remembered the snowed-in car.

"Is that your car?"

"Which car?"

He told her about the snowed-in car by the main road.

"Do you know, I don't know whose it is. I rarely go onto the main road. If I have to go to the village I take the route on the far side of the lake, it's a much nicer walk. There is nothing on the road of interest to me."

As they left the old lady stood on the doorstep waving at them, the dog and the cat both at her feet. Before driving off,

Taras carefully noted the registration number of the snowed-in car, its make and colour in his notebook. By the time he had finished his hands were freezing and he had to blow on them as he sat at the driving wheel.

*

They looked at each house and all they came across were locked doors and closed shutters. The Prelcs house was like that too.

"This is where I celebrated at New Year."

"You don't say..." said Tina and then became serious. "And where were you the previous week?"

She laughed and at that moment there was another loud bang, another firecracker. A brief pause and then another, two, five.

"It's time we did the work of the Bohinjska Bistrica police station," said Taras and drove the car along the road that was already turning round the far north-western part of the lake. He arrived outside a large weekend house where two cars were parked outside, both urban crossovers, and a group of four young people, aged between twenty and thirty, two couples, stood around a large snowman. They were passing a bottle around and one of them, a man with a beard, was kneeling down in front of the snowman, trying to attach to it an elongated snowball which was supposed to represent a penis. When Taras stepped out of the car, the man stood up and turned to him aggressively.

"What d'you want?!" he shouted.

Slowly, as if he had all the time in the world, Taras pulled out his police ID and waved it in the air. This didn't stop the loudest of them all.

"Only if you have a search warrant... otherwise you can just fuck off."

The girls behind him giggled.

In the meantime Tina also stepped out of the car.

"Hey, hey, what do we have here? A police... cunt? In fact we have two..." he turned towards his chorus and shouted. "Two police cunts. One to fuck and the other to fuck off."

They laughed as if what their colleague was doing was

something quite usual. The police could do nothing to them on their land. Tina stood at the door and looked at him queryingly. Taras approached the one who was shouting. The man stopped laughing, frowned and tried to entrench himself in the snow with both his feet, but swayed and wavered as he did so.

"We just want to talk," said Taras, calmly as if he had not heard the man's shouting.

"What could *you* possibly talk to *me* about?" his opposite shouted and swung his hand. It wasn't much of punch, more a drunken sway than a real threat and it was easy for Taras to move out of the way, grab the man's arm, pull him closer, turn him round and twist his arm up his back. He cried out and fell to his knees.

"Tina, there are some handcuffs in the car."

"Fuck you..."

He tried to wriggle free, but Taras twisted his arm further, the man howled and cried out when Taras tightened his grip, and then stopped. The other three friends, the guy and the two girls, also paused. Taras calmly observed them as he waited for Tina to bring the handcuffs from the car.

"What, are you just going to lock him up?" one of the girls asked.

Taras didn't reply. He handcuffed him, pushed him towards the car, and made him sit on the back sear. He locked the car and turned towards the remaining three.

"Now where were we? Oh, yes..."

He showed them his police ID again.

"Taras Birsa, Senior Criminal Investigator. Can you spare five minutes?"

They looked at each other in confusion and then the girl who had spoken before nodded.

"Alright then. Should we go into the warm?"

Taras pointed to the house; the three looked at each other again and then turned towards the door.

The living room in the house, reached via a small hallway, was in chaos with the aftermath of a party. Items of clothing everywhere, empty and half-empty bottles on the table, glasses, some tipped over. Taras, without waiting for an invitation, sat at a small table with a glass surface, indicated at the chairs around it. Tina stood behind his back.

"We'd like to conduct an investigative interview about the case which you have probably already heard about..."

"Now hold your horses here for a minute," said the man, around thirty, who was sitting between the two girls. "I've studied law for long enough to know that we're not obliged to agree to investigative interviews."

He looked around to seek confirmation. It seemed he didn't get any but he still continued.

"Am I right? And if I am..."

He pointed towards the door with his hand.

"If you're right I'll get the narcotics department here in half an hour," said Taras and ran his finger across the remnants of white powder on the table. "And I will stay in the house to make sure nothing ends up in the lake. So shut it."

He pulled his notebook out of his pocket and looked at the first girl. Ten minutes later he had their names, addresses, phone numbers and occupations – all were students. They had been here ten days and were going to stay another three. The four of them, nobody else. They did not miss anyone and had not seen anyone...

"Did you lot steal Balažič's boat?"

They looked at each other.

"Well, we did in fact go for a boat trip on the lake," said the girl who had clearly taken over the role of leader.

"And?"

"Well, we used it for two or three days, I can't really remember. But we never stole it from anyone. We just found it on the shore. Then we tried to return it where we found it but couldn't find the exact spot, so we tied it to some stake on the shore."

"Stake?"

"A mooring," said the young man. "We certainly returned it... to someone."

"Could you find the spot?"

The girl nodded.

"There at the first crossroads which takes you to the main

road, you turn towards the lake and when you reach the shore it should be there somewhere, a hundred metres left or right. Can't remember exactly."

"You can show my colleague, right?"

The girl looked at Tina as if it was the first time she noticed her.

"But we can't get there by car now."

"We'll take a walk," said Tina and pointed to the door. "After you..."

*

Taras sat in silence with the remaining pair. He observed them and waited. He didn't have to wait for long.

"Are we under suspicion at all?" said the girl.

"You mean apart from attacking a police officer, drug abuse and stealing a boat?"

Both flinched.

"Didn't you say..."

"What?"

"That you would ignore this?"

She pointed at the table with her hand.

"I did," said Taras. "And I will keep to my word if you help me a little."

They both obediently leaned towards him.

"A girl, about your age, probably not from around here, just like you two, was, about a week ago while you lot were partying here, rather brutally murdered by someone. Pick those brains of yours and tell me... Anything."

"What?" asked the girl.

"Anything," Taras repeated and stared at the man.

"She was a rather attractive girl. A girl that men would remember. Give me ten women you noticed around here – on the ski slope, at the hotel, wherever..."

The guy shrugged his shoulders.

"I don't know... I saw a group of English girls up on Vogel."

Taras nodded.

"I remember them because I think it must have been the first time they had stood on skis."

Taras nodded.

"I saw a waitress at the hotel..."

"Tall, hair dyed blonde?"

"Yes, her."

Taras had her in his notebook.

The guy shrugged his shoulders.

"I dunno. We're... kind of isolated here, and anyway..."

Taras nodded. Yes, and they were here as couples.

"And you?" he turned to the girl.

"Me?"

"Mmmm."

"I don't really look at women... Well, I don't know, there's nobody here anyway. I too noticed those English girls on the slope, I can't recall the waitress, then there were some young girls there at the hotel. Remember how we took the piss that they were..."

"Pickarels," said the man.

"Apart from that... I don't know any more."

"Do ghosts count?" the guy asked.

"Ghosts?"

"About three or four days ago we drove to Bled one day because we wanted to find a few firecrackers or fireworks for New Year's Eve. On our way back, when it was already dark, we almost knocked over a woman about a kilometre from the lake. She was walking along the road in a dark coat and had no lights on her at all."

"Had you run out?"

"Of what?"

"Firecrackers?"

"Oh no... Tilen, the guy you have in the car, had forgotten them in Ljubljana and we had to go to Bled. They hadn't arrived there yet, so we ended up having to drive to Radovljica to collect them."

Taras nodded,

"And this woman? Did she have a dog?"

"Yes, indeed."

"A small thing with a large head?"

"I don't know. It was certainly close to the ground."

*

"The boat is there," said Tina. "At the mooring outside the weekend house."

"I told you it was, but that was not where we took it from."

"Nothing," said Taras and stood up from the sofa chair. "Thank you very much for your time. Before we leave we would ask you to hand over any remaining firecrackers, and as far as the boat is concerned... here's the phone number of its owner..."

He tore out a page from his notepad and placed it on the table.

"I will call them tomorrow morning to tell them what had happened with it. I hope that they will already be informed by then."

Taras opened the car door and placed the box of firecrackers between the two front seats. Then he turned to the back seat.

"You'll pay for this, you wanker," the handcuffed guy said, Tilen apparently.

Tina sat on the passenger seat and looked at Taras.

"You and this bitch of yours. When my old man gets his hands on you, you'll both be sacked, I can guarantee that."

Before he returned to the car, Taras had intended to release the guy. It would be crazy to want to pile on more work for himself with this spoilt brat and even now, as he and Tina were being showered with insults, he was considering removing the handcuffs, kicking him into the snow and driving off. For a moment he paused with the open door.

"Do you know who I am? Do you fucking police bastards know what my surname is?"

Taras stepped out of the car, opened the back door, pulled the guy who began shouting "help, help, the police are beating me up..." out in front of the car, kneeled on his back and pushed his head into the snow.

His shouting muffled, he began gasping for air and wiggling wildly.

"You're crazy," the guy shouted when Taras allowed him to take a breath. "You're..."

He didn't finish the sentence because his face was buried in the snow again. This time Taras pushed him even further than the first time.

He no longer shouted. When Taras allowed him to move his head he tried to turn towards him, but Taras would not let him. He counted his jerky gasps, attempts at filling his lungs and when he reached five, he pushed his head back into the snow.

"Taras..." said Tina.

He counted in his mind. One, two...

"Taras!"

...seven, eight...

"Taras!"

...nine, ten.

He stood up and took a step back. The body under him twitched its head and lifted it above the snow, turning onto the side. Saliva mixed with puke ran out of his mouth. Taras stepped behind him and removed the handcuffs. He took them back to the boot of the car and returned to the front where the man was trying to rise.

"Was that enough?" Taras asked.

On his knees, he looked at Taras with bulging eyes.

"You pissed yourself."

As they drove off he was still kneeling in the snow, staring in the direction of the car.

"Remind me please," said Tina when they reached the asphalt. "Not to argue with you if I ever get the urge, right?"

They checked the other houses in Ukanc, but there was nobody there. All of them were locked up. Tina was silent the whole time.

Well Tina, here's your sandpit, Taras thought.

Chapter 14.

Both Brajc and Osterc liked working in the field. Taras also preferred fieldwork to sitting in the office, waiting for something to happen, not to mention meetings with his superiors, but Brajc and Osterc really only came alive when they went out to work with people. Osterc too, not only Brajc whose motives were chiefly oenological-culinary. Osterc, though he didn't show it at first sight, liked to chat just as much as Brajc liked to eat. At least when the conversation brought up things he was interested in. Out among country folk, such as where they were now after having driven for barely a minute or two from the hotel by the lake in Stara Fužina, a typical alpine village, there were plenty topics of conversation which interested him. From the best building materials for building extensions, to spare parts for anything on wheels, even small tractors, though a small lawnmower would be more than enough for cultivating whatever grew around his small prefab metal house just outside Horjul.

He was quite capable of starting a conversation with, "A fine hay loader you have in the yard. One with thirty three knives is it?"

And would go all soft when he was told that it had a renovated clutch and drive shaft.

"This'll be a nice trip," Brajc repeated with satisfaction as they parked the car outside the Mihovc Inn with an inscription on its outside wall announcing that it has been in this business since eighteen eighty-eight. Guests may also read in tourist guidebooks, that they also house one of the village attractions, an *orchestrion*, a kind of cupboard-size musical box originally from Bohemia.

"Wanna bet that I know their menu off by heart?" said Brajc as they were getting out of the car.

Osterc didn't reply. For a start he knew that Brajc was not expecting a reply, and he also had no doubt that Brajc did indeed know the menu off by heart.

"Beef soup, pork roast, sautéed potatoes, mixed salad and sweet *štruklji*," Brajc reeled off anyway. "That's the first option, then there's beef soup, chicken steak in a wild mushroom sauce, sautéed potatoes again, and mixed salad and sweet *štruklji*. There, that's the second one, and the third is vegetable soup, fried cheese, sautéed potatoes, mixed salad and sweet *štruklji*. That's the vegetarian one," he finished.

Osterc didn't comment but Brajc thought he was listening anyway.

"You're right, basically they just change the meat. Chicken instead of pork and then fried cheese. Simple, isn't it? That's the trick. Instead of fussing around with some fancy stuff, some sixteen types of some ravioli stuffed with goose turds, you put something straightforward, home-made and fresh on the table.

"Where will we start?" Osterc asked. "The inn?"

"That's the foundation of everything," Brajc continued, ignoring Osterc's question. "The world is constantly changing and in order for it not to get carried off into space somewhere, there have to be some foundations. Pork roast is one such foundation. Have you ever heard of molecular gastronomy? Well, that's one such change. Is it OK, or is it just plain shit? Who knows, and for as long as there are places like Mihovc with their pork roast, nicely prepared in the oven, it's not important. If someone prefers to eat ants with chopsticks instead, why should I care as long as there's something like pork roast somewhere in the world. Now, however, if they cancel all this and we're left with molecular ants, then that would be the end of the world on a par with some cataclysmic event such as war or a natural catastrophe such as, I dunno, a large comet hitting Earth."

A few days earlier Brajc had watched the umpteenth repeat of *Armageddon* with Bruce Willis on TV and now that the conversation took them to comets, he was, in the back of his brain, looking for the name used for a comet which obliterates all life on Earth.

"*Global destroyer*, is what they call such a comet," he eventually remembered though he was not entirely certain. Osterc didn't have a clue anyway. "It's quite possible that at this very moment there's one lurking somewhere round the corner and..."

"*Global killer*," Osterc corrected him, clearly having watched the same film.

"...might come flying at my pork roast and transform it into molecules."

Irritated, he looked at Osterc.

"No, we won't start at the inn, that's where we can work towards," he said and pointed to the road along which they had just driven. "That end, and, nicely, one by one, we work our way back to Mihovc and pork roast."

Two hours later they really had reached the inn again and a satisfied Brajc reached for the door handle. Satisfied because they had completed their task, satisfied because, as he had predicted, this task was unnecessary, for they hadn't found out anything that could be useful for their case, and nothing that could help further their investigation, and satisfied because at some house he had come across some excellent *sadjevec* and bought two litres of the stuff, and satisfied because his mouth watered just at the thought of the pork roast and sautéed potatoes. He was hungry enough to eat the entire pig, as he said, and Osterc, though he didn't say anything, didn't doubt he would, were he given the chance.

Brajc pushed open the wooden door with an opaque yellow glass inlay and loudly greeted the waitress who was standing at the bar washing glasses. He then just as loudly extended the greeting to the few guests sitting in the middle of the dining room. An older couple who spoke with a Styrian accent who Brajc connected to the grey Skoda Fabia with a Maribor number plate parked outside. The other three guests were locals, two seemed to be farmers who had come for a glass of wine instead of lunch, and the other the village idiot who sat at the bar. The Styrian couple returned his greeting, the other three didn't bother.

"What can we bring you?" asked the waitress, a girl in her mid-twenties, dressed in a floral skirt, grey pleated blouse and a waistcoat of the same colour over that.

"Number one for me!" Brajc called out as if he was saying something important, accentuating his order by hitting his fist on the table.

"Roast, potatoes and salad, then?" said the girl, in no sense sharing his enthusiasm. "And you?"

"I'd like the roast too, but is it possible to get chips instead of sautéed potatoes?"

"Chips?!" Brajc shouted. "Who eats chips with pork roast?"

According to the information given by the Statistical Office of the Republic of Slovenia, the website of which Osterc was checking on his phone as he and Brajc were walking to the first house they were planning to visit, reading out the data to an uninterested Brajc, Stara Fužina has a population of five hundred and seventy-six, of which two hundred and seventy-nine are men and two hundred and ninety-seven are women, forming one hundred and sixty families or two hundred and nine households and live in two hundred and ninety-one abodes of which all are in houses with steep roofs, huddled between the Mostnica stream and the steep hills which surround it. The latter is not on the official site, but they could see if for themselves.

"If we check every tenth house, then we are done in three hours," Brajc estimated and rang the bell at the last house on the northern edge of the village. It was twelve forty-five when Osterc and Brajc entered the house and twelve fifty-two when Brajc had drunk his first *šnops*, two minutes later by the time Osterc had downed his. There had been times when Brajc envied his Styrian or Littoral colleagues for the wine they were offered and also given to take home, but since then wine production has also progressed in Lower Carniola, covered by the Ljubljana Police Directorate, and he also became used to the *sadjevec* and other spirits. Now he didn't regret anything.

"Spirits are better than beer anyway," he decided. "At least you don't have to keep going for a piss."

Brajc was an alcoholic of course. He satisfied most expert criteria – from longing for a drink to the physical consequences, which in his case manifested themselves as neglect – though not to the degree where his immediate environment would not be surprised by such a suggestion and defend him saying that he just liked to have a drink or two when in company. When his wife left, clearly not agreeing with the rest of his immediate environment, he became really drunk and came to work in a terrible state, collapsing onto his desk after having puked all over it first. It was only thanks to Osterc that he found his way back home. Taras said nothing that day, but the following morning he went to Brajc's house at seven in the morning, rang the bell and allowed the crushed Brajc to make him a coffee before explaining with an unusually relaxed voice, as if commenting on yesterday's weather, that this was the last time Brajc did this if he wanted to continue to work in the civil service.

"OK?"

"OK," said Brajc.

"You'll still get an official pre-dismissal written warning, just so you don't think that I'm kidding."

Brajc nodded. Taras finished his coffee and took his leave,

"See you in an hour's time."

Brajc nodded once again, and was left sitting at the table, his head emptied of thoughts. When they returned it occurred to him that, with all the other problems in life, abstinence was definitely not an option. He went to the cellar, found a rope which, in some happier times, builders had used for pulleying buckets of mortar to the top floor, and tried to find a suitable place to attach it in order to hang himself. He couldn't think of anywhere suitable and automatically thought of calling Osterc, but by then the idea of suicide had already abated and it was only as he was driving to work that he remembered that he could have shot himself with his work Beretta M92FS. His stomach churned and he had to stop at the first bus stop where, in front of a bunch of people waiting for the number six, he threw up into a small litter bin.

"For God's sake, someone call the police!" he heard someone say.

He threw up another two times before reaching work and decided that suicide was also not an option. From then on he protected himself by never drinking alone, not even a single glass. He kept a few bottles of wine and a crate of beer in the cellar, tonight he would add to this the two bottles of fruit brandy he had bought, but all this would wait until one of the dinners or picnics he would organize. On such occasions he was usually no more drunk than everyone else, also because nobody else could eat as much as he could. He discovered that if he ate, he could drink, if he stuffed himself with food, he could hold his drink.

Fieldwork was sort of in the middle, a grey zone between being alone, work and having company, and he would take the opportunity to drink in quantities he could control, albeit with difficulty, and of course when Taras wasn't around. A glass or two were enough for his mind to thaw pleasantly and even start working better than before, shutting out external distractions, then a short break, a house or two where he even managed to decline what was offered, just enough for the effect to abate, then another glass, and so on until the imperative grub, as he called it, which usually almost sobered him up, so that if he had to go back to the station he appeared slightly tired but composed. Osterc was the driver anyway. He was not a teetotaller and would accept the offered beer at Brajc's picnics but only sipped on it to keep on top of his thirst; in fact liked it less than any other drink. He had only ever been drunk once in his life and when, as is common the first time one gets drunk, he felt sick, he realized in his practical head that alcohol was not his thing, in the same way he knew, for example, that any oil other than ELF was out of the question for Taras' Citroen.

People in Upper Carniola generally don't like to be disturbed in the middle of their work or at least in the middle of that part of the day intended for work. They also don't like to be visited by the police and are in this respect no different to people in other parts of Slovenia, but this time the curiosity caused by the news that a woman's body had been found in the river not far away, prevailed over the usual reserve. They did not, as they would were some other state official to appear before them, just shrug their shoulders and say that they minded their own business and were not interested in anything else, but, would, as a popular announcement of some radio programme says, *stop working for a moment and listen*[5]. Unfortunately there was not much Brajc and Osterc could do with their answers.

"Who could she be?" they would respond to a question with a question. "You know wot, I don't 'ave a clue. If she were from around 'ere, summon'd 'ave said summit..." Or, "If she were one of ours, we'd know. No one missing 'ere..." And wherever there was a man present, especially a retired man, a bottle with a cork top would soon find its way to the table.

"It's from that *tepka*[6] outside the house. Made it meself, y' know. Will y' try some?"

It is in this light that Brajc's affected enthusiasm in ordering menu number one should be understood.

It took fifteen minutes for what they had ordered to arrive at their table. It might have taken less had Osterc not complicated matters by requesting chips which was the only food that had to be prepared afresh. Brajc dug into the food and for a while Osterc was spared any thoughts longer than "this ain't bad," or "nothing like home cooking" or "pork really is the best meat"... But when Brajc took the first deep breath and wanted to say something more profound or at least more extensive, Osterc got there first,

"Do you think we should go through a few more? Just so Taras won't say we didn't..."

Brajc put his fork down on the plate, which – considering that the plate was not yet empty – meant that Osterc's question had irritated him greatly.

"He can go and collect this census information himself," he almost shouted so that everyone in the inn turned to look at him. "It's all pointless anyway, nobody knows anything and nobody is missing anyone."

Osterc nodded and looked a little like one of those nodding figurines with heads on springs, popular for a while when people placed them on the back shelves of cars, various dogs and penguins sent into a nodding frenzy by the movement of the vehicle. Osterc only stopped nodding and shook his head when

5 An iconic phrase from Radio Maribor's s Sunday lunchtime musical requests and greetings programme Želeli ste, poslušajte (You Requested, Listen)

6 a traditional variety of pear

Brajc picked up his fork again. Then he tried again,

"Still, we only have ten..."

This time Brajc would not be distracted, forking a piece of meat and pushing some potatoes onto the fork with his knife, he put it all in his mouth, chewed it slowly, then carefully placed the knife and fork on the plate in a way that if the waitress turned up she would see that he had not finished and would not take away his plate by mistake. He wiped the corners of his mouth with his napkin and asked,

"Well, how many do you think is enough?"

"At least around fifteen."

Brajc swallowed what he was chewing, looked around the inn, cut another piece off the pork roast, stuffed another helping of potatoes into his mouth and mumbled,

"Fourteen will be quite enough."

Chapter 15.

Wednesday, 3 January

A list of hotel guests lay on Taras' desk. Fourteen people in fifteen rooms. He had rather hoped there wouldn't be any foreigners among them, but, of course, there were. Well, only one couple who had signed out of room 212 on the twenty-third of December. Lise *und* Hans Hahn *aus* Fürstenfeldbruck, which is – he typed the name into the browser – a few kilometres west of Munich, outskirst to the left, in as far as he could see on the map. Good, clearly there will be no problem with them.

He then brought up his favourite translation app and jotted an outline of a conversation onto a piece of paper. It was time he tried out his German.

"Were there foreigners?" Tina asked as she hung up her coat.

"Two."

"That means we'll need to get some international legal advice through the Ministry for Justice..."

"No," he interrupted her. "Let's not complicate matters."

He dialled a phone number which began with 49 for Germany and 89 for Munich and waited for a few *"Guten Tag, darf ich mit Herrn* Oliver Scholz *sprechen, bitte. Mein Name ist..."*

He worried that the female voice at the other end would tell him that Mr Scholz was already retired, but apparently he wasn't.

"A colleague," he explained to Tina when he finished and put the phone down with relief. Only a month ago he would not have dared speak German. Three years of courses were finally starting to produce results.

With a little luck Scholz, whom he had met on a training

course in Munich where he had been sent with three other Slovene criminal investigators, when Taras still didn't dare venture beyond the relatively safe English he knew, would hopefully tell him even as early as today whether *alles was in Ordnung mit Frau und Herr Hahn* and he would be able to concentrate on the attendees of the seminar organized by the Biotechnical Faculty from Ljubljana and for a start, look up what the Internet has to say about the meeting.

He could not find anything on the Internet, which struck him as odd. If you are not on the Internet, you don't exist, but this meeting had clearly taken place. An overview of the work done over the last year and an informal gathering, was what he kept getting. Everyone called it 'informal gathering' and nobody called it a party. Is that how these generations talk? And if it was all so ordinary and normal, why did he detect a slight embarrassment with everyone he spoke to? And why were they all saying the same thing, as if they had been told what to say? He called the faculty office and demanded to speak to the dean who was apparently the organizer of this informal whatever, but he was unavailable. He was about to argue with the secretary who managed to explain in time that she has been trying to contact him for the last half hour and his phone is telling her his number is unavailable. Please try... He told her to get him to call him back as soon as she finds him.

The Director of Salubris was also unavailable. Somewhere mid-air between Ljubljana and Moscow. He would get in touch as soon as he was able.

"Upon landing," Taras demanded.

"As soon as he will be able to," a female voice at the other end of the line insisted.

"He will call me immediately because I'd like to ask him about the woman who was with him in Bohinj and who registered at the hotel as his wife."

Silence.

"Do you understand?"

"Yes," the voice at the other end said, still curt but with a shade of alarm.

"For a person using the name Antonija Mihelič – that was the name she had registered in – was, according to the information I have gathered, celebrating her eighteenth birthday on the twenty-third of December in Bohinj. Surely you understand that I need to verify this information and I would like to talk to Mr Mihelič first, before I dial the number I have for his wife, who I assume is not eighteen years old."

"Mr Mihelič will call as soon as he lands at Sheremet-yevo," the female voice said, this time without a pause.

"And when will that be?"

"He lands at three, then it will take another fifteen minutes or so. Can we arrange a call for half past?"

"Fine. I would also like the phone number of the eighteen-year old Antonija, because I would like to ask her a few questions too."

He was given it and her name was Barbara.

At the next desk, Tina was trying to find the owners of the weekend houses. With a little more success but with similarly unhelpful answers. Nobody amiss, nobody missing, and "was she really killed?" "We're unable to say anything at the moment Mr, Mrs… and thank you for your time and kindness."

Brajc and Osterc sat at their desks writing their reports. They were putting down on paper what he already knew and what Brajc summarized in a single sentence,

"We found out shit all."

It will take them all day to type up their notes from the interviews conducted with the villagers of Stara Fužina, especially because they both typed with one finger. Taras used a kind of almost-ten-finger, almost-blind typing, for which he had to thank Penca, who sent him on a typing course as soon as he joined his group.

"It's too late for us," he had said at the time. "For you, though, it will be valuable to learn the most useful police skill – fast typing."

At the time he was scornful, although he didn't show it, now he was grateful. In fact he used nine fingers, the little finger on the right hand stayed mid-air all the time and he often moved his right hand onto the left part of the keyboard.

"Taras…"

He turned towards Tina who was covering the phone receiver with her hand.

"It's someone called Prelc and he says he knows you..."

Taras nodded and stepped to her desk.

"I can put him through to you," she said, but Taras was already holding the phone.

"Hi Taras, how's it going, fucking are we, fucking?"

"More by the day," Taras said, not without feeling unease.

"Hey, this girl of yours was asking me where I was the week before Christmas. I was in Switzerland on a course, you know that."

"I know, but she's in charge of Ukanc, so I didn't interfere."

"Alright, no problem. There wasn't anyone in our house at the time. As far as I know Karin also didn't go there. Do you know who the unfortunate girl is yet?"

"No."

"How come?"

Taras smiled. It was the question he feared. He will be asked this question at least once more today, by Drvarič, and probably by others as well.

"Unfortunately nature has taken its toll," he said. "And it seems nobody's missing her."

There was a moment of silence at the end of the line, as if Prelc was processing 'nature has taken its toll' or 'nobody is missing her' in his mind.

"Oh, so that's it then," he said. "There isn't much we can do, is there Taras? We all carry our own cross."

"The owner of the weekend house where I spent New Year's Eve," Taras explained to Tina who inadvertently listened to the conversation.

"So I don't need to call the wife then?"

"Call her," said Taras. "We need to tick her off as well."

"Meeting," he said at two o'clock and pointed at the whiteboard. Brajc and Osterc looked up and pushed their chairs slightly from their desks. Tina half stood up, gave an embarrassed smile and sat back down again.

"Did you think we were going to some conference hall?" said Brajc and grinned. Osterc giggled and Taras smiled.

He stepped up to the whiteboard and wiped off all the points he had written on it the day before. Carefully until the whole surface was clean.

"What do we have?"

He looked towards Brajc and Osterc.

"Well," said Brajc and picked up a piece of paper from the desk in front of him. "We conducted investigative interviews in Stara Fužina..."

The phone on Taras' desk began to ring. He beckoned to Tina to pick it up and continued to listen to Brajc who was saying that...

"...with fourteen people in as many houses, meaning households or addresses. The result, in as far as our victim is directly concerned, is zero..."

Tina covered the received with her hand and beckoned to Taras. Brajc paused.

"Hleb from the Biotechnical Faculty."

Taras moved over and took the phone.

"Hello, this is Senior Criminal Investigator Taras Birsa..."

He explained what it was all about and asked a few questions, similar to what he had been asking others. The voice at the other end of the line was reserved, only giving brief answers, but then that was how everyone else he had spoken to had reacted. Nothing, he had seen nothing, everyone he knew who came to the seminar had also gone home, nobody missing.

"Tell me," said Taras, "what was the purpose of this seminar?"

"What do you mean?"

"Why were you there for three days?"

The voice at the other end was even more reluctant.

"In fact it was not as much a seminar as it was a work meeting," he said after a brief pause. "A gathering."

"Informal?" Taras asked.

"...Also."

"Is it usual for your meetings to also be attended by the director of Salubris? And for the full three days?"

Another brief pause.

"We train future researchers, you see. Cadre which might well be useful to Mr Mihelič."

"A working and informal gathering..." he looked at the list before him, "of four students, a faculty dean and the director of a pharmaceutical company with his companion?"

He could sense the unease at the other end.

"The best students. There are usually not many of these. Four who cooperate with Salubris."

Taras made him wait a second,

"I don't know why, but I have the feeling that we will talk again."

Hleb did not respond immediately and when he did his voice showed no alarm.

"That, you see is not something I'd know, Inspector."

Taras coldly said goodbye and put down the receiver. He looked at Brajc who continued,

"Meaning that nobody knows of any missing woman, all the home sheep are accounted for, and there's no talk of any tourists, not to mention prostitutes. 'No, you won't find the likes of 'em here!'" Brajc put on a silly voice. "'We're all honest folk 'ere in the village!' We also tried finding out whether there was anyone messing around and with whom, but nothing specific came up, the only thing that did was thirty years old. There are a lot of old people in the village."

"Well, our girl, the one on ice, is thirty years old."

Brajc stared at Osterc, then looked at Taras, and sighed,

"I knew you'd say that. Indeed we came across some thirty-year old fling out there among all those honest folk."

"Well, you go ahead and start if you've finished," Brajc beckoned to Osterc who had emptied his plate. He pointed to the two farmers sitting at the next table, "Before they get away."

Without saying a word, Osterc stood up and approached the pair who were sitting at the table closest to the door. He cleared his throat when he stepped in front of them. They looked at him suspiciously and then stared at his police badge he held up for them.

"Can I join you?"

He sat down without waiting for a response and placed his note pad and biro on the table.

"Is this about the woman in the water?" asked the man in

a red-blue chequered shirt sitting opposite Osterc. Apparing to take the lead, he was the more nervous of the two.

"Yes," said Osterc, explaining that he and his colleague over there – he pointed at Brajc who was quite peacefully with a slightly sad expression on his face, handling the last piece of pork roast – were conducting investigative interviews which is basically collecting information, and that, if they so wish, they do have the right to refuse such an interview...

For a moment it seemed as if they were considering this option.

...but that it would certainly be better for everyone if they didn't.

They both quickly nodded.

"But what do we know about it?" the man in the check shirt asked. "D'y' know anyfink Bogdan?"

Bogdan shook his head and ten minutes later Osterc placed his biro on the table.

"How are things otherwise?" he asked.

"What d'y' mean?" the man in the check shirt asked.

"Has anything similar ever happened in your village?"

"Not that I know of," the other man said after a pause which seemed slightly too long to Osterc.

"You sure?"

"We're all good folk, round 'ere," the man in the chequered shirt added.

As soon as Osterc had finished with them, the men stood up, paid and left.

"What did you do to them to frighten them away?" Brajc asked, munching away on some *štruklji*. He'd chosen those with a walnut filling.

In the meantime the couple from Styria also paid and said goodbye.

"I'll also go and see the waitress, now that she's free," said Osterc and Brajc nodded magnanimously.

He returned ten minutes later to a rather sullen-looking Brajc staring at his empty plate. They would have to leave soon.

"Well, let's do one more," Brajc mumbled and called out to the grubby-looking guy at the bar, "Hey, mate, can you come here?!"

"Osterc, have you written that part up already?"

Osterc nodded and checked his papers, pulled out a page, glanced at it and summarized,

"At the Bučar farm, that's how it's locally known, at some point in the early 1980s, they apparently had a child without a father, we were told."

He put the page down on his desk and looked at Taras.

"Right, and?"

"Nothing, that's what we were told."

If he hadn't known Osterc all this time, he would sometimes think that he was dumb.

"Told by whom?"

The man at the bar with a thick black beard, peppered with grey, wearing his grey hunting jacket which he didn't take off despite the fact that the inn was heated, pointed at himself and Brajc nodded. He slowly and cautiously stood up, looked around the inn as if he was looking for some help, which of course he could not find. Meekly he approached and stood in front of Brajc who was mopping his chin with the linen napkin. He put down his napkin, indicating the empty chair.

"We're from the police," said Brajc and Osterc once again produced his badge. Brajc couldn't be bothered with these things.

"And who are you?"

"Anton Štefe," the petrified creature said. "They call me Tona."

"The person is... is what you might call a farmhand..." Osterc checked his list. "On the Oblak farm, more or less for as long as he can remember. He knew nothing about who the woman in the water might be, but after a long questioning he told us about..."

"Look, Tona," said Brajc after about ten minutes of questioning to which the repetitive answer was always, 'Well, I wouldn't know 'bout that,' "Why don't you tell us what you do know then."

The farmhand must have been around sixty and Brajc included in his estimate years of hard work and regular drinking. The tan on his face covered some of the alcoholic redness and broken capillaries. Otherwise he was thin and stringy and didn't stink as badly as he had expected him to.

"What d'y' mean, Sir?"

He had two bottom teeth missing.

"I have a nagging boss back in Ljubljana," said Brajc and thought of Taras who really could be nagging sometimes. "Give me a present for him."

Tina coughed and the three men turned towards her.

"Yes?" said Brajc.

"Nothing, I just coughed. You go on."

Taras smiled to himself. It would take a while to get used to her. She sat at poor Penca's old desk. His computer was gone and instead she had her laptop on what now looked like a spacious desk. Taras, Brajc and Osterc were each working on their own old buckets, and Osterc, who often complained about his equipment, was astounded to see Tina's device.

"I could have done that too," he said and looked at Taras who could not have cared less. At home he used a laptop and its delicate keyboard got on his nerves so much that when he worked on it he used a second, external keyboard which he could at least bash away on and which responded with a plain old pleasant click sound rather than the rolling rrrs and tutting ttts of the laptop.

Tina was in the same jumper and jeans she had been wearing the previous day and Taras found himself glancing at the jeans when she walked through the desks or bent down to pick something that had fallen on the floor. Brajc, and even Osterc gave him a knowing glance.

Osterc picked up the page again and read from it,

"The pregnant girl was apparently Dijana Baloh, daughter of Milan Baloh… who is the owner of the Bučar farm. According to what this Tona said, she was pregnant, and then she suddenly wasn't pregnant one day and there was no sign of the child."

"Did you not investigate further?"

"Yes, of course," said Brajc. "We paid for his next drink…" And you joined in as well, Taras thought to himself.

"…and a week after her belly disappeared, she vanished."

"Taken by the water," Osterc said. "She'd taken a boat and

threw herself into the lake. She was only found a week later and they had great difficulties fishing her out. Officially it was supposed to be an accident."

Taras took the marker and wrote on the board: Dijana Baloh, Stara Fužina, illegitimate child and a question mark next to it. At least it won't stay empty.

"Look further into this."

"However..." said Brajc and raised his hand with his finger extended as if trying to catch the teacher's attention in class. "You should know something about our source. He's a little crazy."

"How crazy?"

"Crazy enough to go fishing for catfish in Lake Bohinj."

"And?" Taras asked.

"Don't take him seriously," the waitress had said when Tona left the inn after talking to Brajc. "He's not all alright up there, you known. He's been secretly fishing for catfish in the lake for twenty years."

"And?" Brajc had asked.

"There are no catfish in Lake Bohinj."

"Crazy or not. You two check the situation with this drowned woman, and then we'll see if there's anything tangible there or not," said Taras.

He looked at the whiteboard.

"Anything more recent? From this millennium? Anything at all?"

"Someone had burnt the boat of a certain..." Brajc shuffled his papers, "Janez Bertoncelj. He used to keep it on the shore a little further along from the beach." He looked up from the paper. "He reported it to the police who went to investigate and concluded that it had been burnt deliberately, because someone had doused it in petrol. Well, I don't see how else you could burn a boat on the shore of a lake. It probably wouldn't just burn on its own."

"Did he say whether he suspected anyone, this Bertocelj of yours?"

"Yes, he did." He looked at the paper again. "A certain Marjan Magušar, a neighbour of course, with whom they've had some differences over some plot of land since… forever, probably."

"Clarify this as well," said Taras. "We also have a boat, stolen and then returned in our case."

He turned to Tina who smiled and tidied the pages in front of her. The sun shining through one of the two windows into their office gave her hair, still tied in a ponytail, a metallic shine. *Rabenschwartz* is what the Germans call it, Taras thought, crow-black… and they use another word connected with this *raben*, raven. *Rabenmutter*, cruel mother… Was this Baloh woman, one such *rabenmutter*?

Tina gave him a questioning look. He had totally forgotten that he was staring at her. He shook his head as if to say, it's nothing, and looked away. It really will all be different. Brajc and Osterc could have a supernova shining on them and Taras still wouldn't know how to describe the colour of their hair, or what was left of it.

"Well…" said Tina when Brajc fell silent and Taras showed no sign of intending to speak. "I spoke with all the owners of weekend houses in Ukanc apart from two who I have been unable to find. There's twelve of them. I think the results are fairly similar to what Zoran and Pavle got…"

She looked at them and Taras could almost swear that they blushed. When was the last time a beautiful young woman called them by their first names? In the last twenty years? Ever?

"…basically, nobody is missing anyone, nobody saw or heard anything, and, in fact, most of them were not even there at the time of the murder."

She told them about the old lady at the lake and the four students who were celebrating and extended New Year in Ukanc and were at the time of the murder…

"…in as far as we know, other than the old lady and Balažič, Milan Balažič, the only people there for a time."

She did not mention the incident with one of the students.

"And yes, the boat. I spoke to Balažič about it, he had reported that the boat was missing to the police… On the twenty-second, when he was on his way back from Ukanc. Apart from New Year's Eve he's not been back to Bohinj since, but this morning he got a call from his new neighbour, who we…"

She looked at Taras and, so he thought, gave him a barely noticeable smile.

"...visited yesterday, and was informed that they had borrowed the boat and also returned it. I was able to confirm that the boat really is tied at the mooring in front of his weekend house."

She pushed away the papers on the desk and moved back slightly.

"For which he thanked me and asked whether he needed to inform the police. And that's it."

Taras looked at the whiteboard. He very much wished he could add something, but there was nothing to add. At the time of the murder, the only people at the weekend house settlement were the old lady lying in bed with fever, four idiots who were capable of many things, but, unless they were helped by some fierce drug, probably not of killing a woman, cutting off her head, and continuing to behave as if nothing had happened, and this Balažič who probably would not have been going round police stations after a murder to report a stolen boat. Or would he?

"Did you ask Balažič whether he saw anyone else when he was there?"

"I did, and no, he saw no one. Apparently he only came briefly, for half an hour. He came, checked that everything was closed, switched off the electricity and the water, visited Mrs Stropnik, something she also confirmed, and drove off to the police station to report the theft."

He removed the lid from his felt-tip pen and, after brief deliberation, wrote *boat* with *2x* in parenthesis next to Stara Fužina and illegitimate child. What is it they say, *the universe is rarely so lazy for coincidence*. He fell silent, moved two paces backwards and looked at the whiteboard. A regular procedure in which he never really looked at what was written on the board. When he will give Brajc, Osterc and Tina his own report, he will also add *Biotechnical Faculty seminar* to the board. It is not every day that the director of the largest pharmaceutical company in the country attends such a seminar with a prostitute who celebrates her eighteenth birthday there. But not yet. He glanced again at what was written, deleted the *2x* by the boat, and put *3x*.

He checked the time on his phone.

"Drvarič will be calling shortly," he said. "Whoever answers the phone, please let him know that I am somewhere out in the field without a signal, and that I'll be back here at around four."

He switched off his phone and took his jacket from the coat hanger.

"See you."

Chapter 16.

Taras was home at half past one. Five minutes later he had changed into his running trousers, a thick vest and an anorak and stood at the door in his trainers, holding a banana in his hand. He set off for the Trail of Remembrance and Comradeship[7] along which an alleyway of trees was planted when the president of the now long defunct Yugoslavia died; eighty-eight lime trees, one for each year of his life, which in the summer created wonderful shade. On ran through a green tunnel. But now, instead of a leafy canopy, the bare branches reached up towards the sky, and the ground was covered in trodden but not yet well-compacted powdery snow, which was impossible to run on, providing no footing. In any case, a run for which he barely had enough time, certainly not enough to warm up and stretch properly for, was not Taras' idea of fun, but he knew that if he had things to do in the evening, impositions, as he called them, he would be impossible if he didn't go for at least a short run. It took him around fifty minutes to complete his route, never measured, but around seven kilometres long and do some quick exercises; he then showered, dressed, grabbed a sandwich he had prepared in the morning and left in the fridge, warmed up some tea he had also brewed in the morning and was back at the parking lot outside his work by three. Three minutes later he was in the office, still flushed from the running. All three of his colleagues were there, sitting at their computers. He hung his jacket on the hanger, sat at his desk and switched on his computer.

"Did he call?"

7 A 33 km trail around Ljubljana, a kind of recreational greenbelt along what was, during the Italian occupation of Ljubljana in the Second World War, the barbed wire fence which surrounded the city.

"He did," said Tina.

"And, did he want to know why we still don't know who the murdered girl is?"

She shook her head.

"You should be in his office tomorrow morning at nine. Someone called Petan would like to talk to you. I'm to come as well."

He smiled. What a loser, who would have thought. Brajc and Osterc both stopped typing.

"Did he say why?"

"No, nor did he say who this Petan was."

"I know who he is," said Taras and smiled. She looked at him, baffled, then she understood.

"Oh, him?"

"What does that queer have against you?" Brajc asked.

"Oh that Petan, the lawyer...?" Tina asked.

"Yes," said Brajc, "Lawyer of the Year and all that. And more... Should I tell her?"

"Tell her," said Taras even though Brajc would have said what he wanted to say even without this affirmation.

"When I was still at Narcotics, we had a boss who took no shit from anyone. Tiselj, Taras, you knew him..."

He always began the story this way and, like now, Taras always nodded.

"... Well, our investigations into some of these cocaine cases brought us to a bunch of high-society lawyers, businessmen and politicians, who organized cocaine orgies at a well-known mansion down on the coast, right on the Italian border. A mixed band, international, Balkan-Italian, mixed also in terms of sexual orientation. All kinds, all very democratic. We got one of our guys in as a waiter and he recorded them so we knew what we were going into. God knows by what miracle we managed to get a warrant and by some even greater miracle nobody let it leak, so we got quite a show when we raided."

He made a lengthy pause which Taras also knew was coming.

"Hey Osterc, where were you then... Well, basically, there were fifteen girls, all naked, all with the same haircut, dyed blonde, with shaven fannies, none older than twenty. None were underage, we checked that of course, all of them either 'in the act' or sniffing coke, both, in many cases. Well, we didn't find our Petan there. We caught him in a private booth with two guys. He was sucking coke off their cocks. Depilated, mind you, just in case the gentleman were to choke on a pube."

Taras wasn't looking at Bajc but at Tina. When Brajc began talking about Petan she grimaced briefly, then she looked at Taras.

"Are you kidding me?"

Taras shook his head. She looked at Brajc.

"Wish we were. It still makes me want to throw up today just thinking about it. I mean two male dolls with hard-ons and the potbellied Petan slurp, slurp..."

He pulled a face and Taras had to smile. Whatever his flaws, Petan certainly didn't have a larger belly than Brajc.

"And when was this?" Tina asked.

"It's not important," said Brajc. "Never. Officially it never happened. We herded them all together, noted everything, collected just under a kilo of coke, but when we got to work the following day, we had the financial police on our back, Tiselj was dismissed over some pointless shit, and our case was dropped."

"What do you mean dropped?"

"Because, supposedly due to a procedural flaw, the case would have been unsuccessful in court. We had a warrant for searching the restaurant facility but not those booths, which were part of the private area. Apparently we only found cocaine there, which isn't true, of course. It was everywhere."

Tina looked at Taras again.

"And what does this man want from you?"

"Oh," said Taras, "there's always someone."

At a quarter to four Mihelič called.

"This is Mihelič," he said in a deep, almost solemn voice. "I was told you wished to talk to me."

Taras introduced himself, repeated what he had said at least thirty times that day...

"I'm afraid I can't help you..."

And as he began explaining how he did not know anything about the case and had not seen anything, Taras thought whether he should ask him what the director of the largest pharmaceutical company was doing at some chemists gathering for three days, but then decided on a different approach.

"Your companion..." he began.

"Yes?" came from the end of the line.

"She's a prostitute, isn't she?"

A silence which lasted five or six seconds. Not just at the end of the line, also in the room around Taras.

"Have you ever heard of tactfulness, Mr Birsa?"

"Unfortunately I don't have time for it."

Silence again, a little shorter this time.

"I prefer to use the term companion, but have it your way, and to simplify things, yes, a prostitute."

"Was she the only prostitute you had dealings with during those three days?"

Laughter.

"My dear Inspector, it's true that our company is a leading producer of generic Viagra, but despite this, I *am* nearly seventy!"

"Meaning yes?"

"Yes, the only one."

"Well, then I thank you for your time."

"Mr Birsa?"

Taras knew what was coming.

"I suppose I can count on your discretion."

"Of course," said Taras. "Anyone can."

For the second time that day Taras dialled the phone number of Barbara, Mihelič's companion, and her automatic answering machine said the number was not available.

*

At eight Bojan and Anže, Anja's and Mojca's boyfriends, the pharmacist and the architect arrived. Alenka was busy with the cooking which she didn't like doing and was all worked up. Also because she wanted to make a good impression on both boyfriends. Taras tried to help and hide his indifference. If there was one thing he didn't like, it was the fuss people made over food. He was once a guest on an evening chat show where there was discussion about working irregular hours and, as he sat in makeup, the host asked him whether he watched any reality shows.

"No," he said.

"Yes, they really are terrible," said the host. "Well surely at least some cooking programme?"

"Especially not those."

It wasn't just food, he had little understanding for most modern things. Taras was a man from a different era, an analogue era. He was not too stupid or too old to understand what smart phones or social networks, or eBay purchases were about, he just didn't care for all that.

"You're the only person on planet Earth not to have taken a selfie," Anja had discovered at some point about two years ago. He still hadn't.

Bojan and Anže were digital types. When Taras was twenty-two, he was a confused creature. He knew what he would like to do in life, and knew he would have to do something he preferred not to think about in case he were to realize that that was not what he really wanted. Then he met Alenka, fell madly in love, they had a child neither had planned, but now it was here... Chaos. But when you are just over twenty, that's how things ought to be, isn't it?

At their twenty something, Taras thought Anže and Bojan were more like sixty. Everything was planned, everything sorted, every act thought through, they knew how to use chopsticks, knew all the streets in Vienna and Paris, and were Taras to drop them from a helicopter somewhere on the slopes of Triglav and tell them to find their own way home, they would, without a phone with which to call mountain rescue, die of hunger. They did *do* sports, in fact more than one, whatever was fashionable at the time, and they dropped it as soon as some new fad appeared. With their solidly planned life line, Taras sometimes wondered whether they would have even been interested in his daughters were it not for Alenka's clinic, if they had just been the daughters of a criminal investigator, albeit a senior one. Did Anja and Mojca also fit into their business plan?

On their first visit they stopped at the photograph of Taras on the top of Dhaulagiri. In it he is kneeling in the snow, putting his gloves back on. He can no longer remember why he had taken them off. Next to him is Janez, now dead, and the shot was taken by Dare, also already deceased...

"Nice," one of them, or even both, had said.

Nice?

"So this is from your wild period, is it?"

Period?

Unfortunately they were probably right and it really was just a period, one they unfortunately never had themselves. When he poured them out a glass of wine and they all toasted, Taras with a coke, they took the obligatory sip and then barely touched the drink for the rest of the evening. They knew more about wine than he did, for he knew nothing, but they clearly didn't drink it.

"Nobody will ever be good enough for you," Alenka said when he tried to discuss it with her. "You wouldn't like it even if a pair of heavy metal guys from your Prekmurje would call in."

"Firstly, Motörhead are not heavy metal, and secondly Prkekija is not Prekmurje."

And thirdly, he had listened to Motörhead when they had met and he still climbed. Ace of Spades before his ascents to perk himself up, fill up with energy and determination. For going to work and what he has been doing for the last twenty years, he didn't need it.

They had chicken with rice and Taras thought it was very tasty, though of course he was not a measure. Basically they ate what was served. Alenka finished off her glass of wine and felt at ease. She brought out the family photo albums. She would always carefully arrange the photos taken by Taras. At first with an analogue Canon camera he bought in New Road in Kathmandu, then with a digital equivalent. A holiday with the local sports club camp somewhere in Istria, a holiday in Greece which they had driven to in their rather battered, old, dark-blue Skoda, climbing Triglav where Taras took them all when Mojca was barely six years old. They had slept overnight in a stony hollow under Kredarica. On that day veterans of the Independence War happened to have a gathering there and Taras had almost been involved in a fight that afternoon because one waitress was not enough for the inebriated crowd and they had begun shouting at Alenka.

"What do we have here?" said Anja and pulled a worn notebook from the album drawer. It contained Alenka's photos from before she knew Taras. Taras had never seen it. When they had begun dating, she had once started to say something about one of her exes and he stopped her,

"I don't want to know, alright. And if you still keep their photos or anything, you can do so, just don't show them to me."

So when Anja produced this album, he stood up and switched on the TV, as if he wanted to see the news, which he normally never did.

At half past ten the youngsters went out for a drink, probably with relief... and although they kept inviting them to come along, Taras and Alenka chose not to. Alenka had a quick shower and Taras cleared the table. After he had stacked all the plates and cutlery in the dishwasher, all that was left on the table was the worn notebook. He thought about leaving it there, sat on the sofa in front of the TV, stood up again, sat at the table, opened it and listened out for the sound of running water in the bathroom. He looked through it. Alenka's birth, school, a confirmation photo in which she holds a large red candle, family photos, Alenka as a teenager, a teenager at the seaside, a few empty slots, Alenka as a student, and on some trip with her fellow students from the Medical School. She stood in the middle of the third row, smiling into the camera. She had a beautiful smile even though she said herself that she always looked terrible in photos... And there, at the end, in the second row, stood the familiar face of Dr Prelc, the charming lecturer with a dandy beard and slightly wavy light, almost platinum blond hair who was not looking at the camera like everyone else but upwards to the left. It didn't take a criminologist to realize what he was looking at and why.

Chapter 17.

Thursday, 4 January

Taras arrived at work at seven and the first thing he did was try once again to call Barbara, Mihelič's companion. Once again she was not available. Then he spent some time sorting out the reports on the investigative interviews and when he finished he opened his notebook and carefully checked what he had written in it. He went through all his notes and when he came to the end, closed the notebook and placed it on the table but then immediately opened it again, found something he had scribbled in it, used his other hand to find a page from the pile of reports and stared at both for a while, then put them back on the desk and leaned back in his chair. He sat like this for a while, shrugged his shoulders and stepped to the whiteboard and wrote something on it.

At eight he called the secretary at Salubris and was surprised when she answered.

"Oh, Inspector, you're early," she said. Clearly the conversation with the Director had done its work, at least the promise of discretion. Secretaries are always good indicators.

He thanked her for passing on the message…

"I can't seem to find your Barbara."

An uneasiness on the other end of the line, a few seconds of silence, as if the secretary was not able to decide.

"We can't either," she eventually uttered. "Number unavailable, isn't it?"

"Yes."

"Can you give me an hour, please? I'll try another way."

He agreed. Let them think they are allies. Nothing wrong

with that for as long as they can be useful.

"What number can she reach you on?"

He gave her his mobile number and greeted her. Then he checked the time and rang another number. It rang for a while before anyone answered.

"Goodness Taras, just because you can't sleep it doesn't mean everyone else has problems doing so."

"Good morning Mr Cvilak. For someone about to retire, you sleep surprisingly well and long."

"What do you want?"

"This Jane Doe of ours..."

"You still don't know who she is?"

"No, that's why I'm calling. You said she must be around thirty?"

"Yes, about that."

"Is there any chance that she might be younger, around twenty, let's say?"

"No, no chance."

Taras sighed and although Cvilak probably heard him, he showed no compassion.

"Is that all?"

"Cvilak, give me something. Anything. Profession, hobbies, bad habits... Deformations which show that, I don't know, she used a bobbin to make lace, whatever, anything."

"You got the results, so you know she had only haemoglobin in her blood, nothing else, no drugs, no alcohol. There are also no external signs of any kind of drug related activities in the recent past, talking about the veins... Her internal organs also all fine, the X-rays of the skeleton shown no deformity that might suggest anything different. Basically she didn't work in a foundry or down a mine, and if she pursued any sport, it was at a recreational level... There's nothing on the skeleton that would suggest... anything. What the hell got you thinking about bobbins and lacemaking?"

He might not have wanted it to come across that way, but it sounded as if his anger was abating. Taras listened in silence and didn't say anything even when Cvilak finished. He waved at Tina who stepped into the room, and, not really knowing why, looked at the clock on the wall. She noticed this and quickly took off her coat, hung it up, and with it with a small satchel she had brought along. She was wearing a skirt shorter than the one she wore at their first meeting. Did this one qualify as a mini?

"By the sounds of it you're stuck, Taras," said Cvilak.

"Yes."

"Sooner or later someone will come along who knew her or will miss her. It's only been three days."

"Ten."

"Well, maybe they won't. I thought that at your age you'd be over, how can I put it, taking cases personally."

"Me too," said Taras.

Perhaps Alenka was right.

"Hi," said Tina when he put down the phone. "Am I late?"

He shook his head.

"No, no… quite the opposite."

She looked at him in surprise.

"I'll explain," he said, stood up and put on his jacket. "But now I need to do something first."

"Nine o'clock at Drvarič, Taras, that's still on?"

"I'll be a little late," he said, already in the door. He quickly went down the long corridor towards the exit where the secretary caught him just as he was going out.

"Where are you off to? Don't you have a meeting with Drvarič at nine?"

Some years ago she had whispered into his ear on a union outing that she was not one to wreck families…

"…if you know what I mean?"

She had been slightly drunk already and squeezed up to Taras who was sitting at the table drinking his juice.

"Well, that's the point… Me neither," he had said regretfuly. He sometimes wondered what his answer might have been if he too had been drinking.

"I might be a little late."

"Oh… And what am I supposed to tell him?"

"That I might be a little late."

"As you wish, Mister. By the way, this arrived for you."

She gave him the sheet of paper. It was a fax. He thanked

her for it and without looking at it, in case he were to meet Drvarič or Petan on the corridor, leapt out of the main door of the Ljubljana Police Directorate building. Drvarič might be his boss, but he would deliberately not be there at nine.

This was how, five minutes before the meeting was due, Taras was sitting drinking coffee in Maxi, observing the clientele. He knew the waiter who had previously worked at other nearby joints, and now landed among the pensioners who came here for tea and cakes, and MPs who came here for the convenience of it being located just across the road from the Parliament.

"Do you have *čebelji pik*?" an elderly lady in the company of two others asked.

"*Čebelji pik*?" Marjan the waiter queried.

"Yes, *čebelji pik*," the lady insisted and began explaining to her friends what it was[8] and how well they used to make them in Styria.

"Can I get you anything else instead?" Marjan asked, annoyed by the waiting.

"Then I'd like... Are you sure you don't have it?"

Taras read the fax which was from Scholz, informing him that Lise *und* Hans Hahn were *noch am Leben* and asked him *wie geht es dir...*

A fax? He tried to recall whether some protocol existed about sending messages like this via email that he had forgotten, but he couldn't think of one.

Ten minutes past nine he left and went to the meeting. At nine sixteen, he opened the door to Drvarič's office.

"I apologize, work."

Neither Drvarič nor Petan greeted him. He sat next to Tina who breathed a sigh of relief when she saw him, at least that was what it looked like to him.

"What's up?"

"Drvarič indicated with his hand to Petan to explain.

"I'm Boris Petan," he began and Taras interrupted him.

"I know who you are. Greetings from Brajc."

"Brajc?"

8 a less known fruit and cream filled sponge cake with a layer of pastry on top, a version of the German *Bienenstich*

"Brajc, the policeman who arrested you that time at that hacienda down on the coast."

"Oh, I see..." said Petan and Taras had to congratulate him for not even blushing. "Well, whatever, I'm here as the lawyer for Mr Rezman, whom you have probably heard of..."

"I have," said Taras and turned towards Drvarič. "He's the crook who got out of going to jail by confessing and is now under house arrest." And turned to Petan again. "What was it about again? Drugs, cocaine...?"

"It was about completely legal trade in food supplements..."

"Oh, you're right, that's it, steroids. I'd forgotten. The cocaine just happened to be among them, or what?"

"Mr Petan is here to complain about your treatment of his client's son," Drvarič spoke.

"And where am I supposed to have had the honour of meeting his son?"

"Yesterday in Ukanc by Lake Bohinj," said Petan and carefully watched Taras' face.

Taras shrugged his shoulders.

"Help me a little. I spoke to quite a few people in Bohinj yesterday."

"In Ukanc, when you arrested him for inappropriate behaviour towards an officer of the law, something we do not deny, you drove him away in your car..." he pulled a page from the folder in his lap. "I quote: 'Through the forest for about a hundred metres away from the holiday home belonging to his father, pulled him out of the car and pushed his head into the snow three times for so long that he almost fainted, and the third instance caused him vomiting and involuntary passage of water..."

"It caused him what?" Taras asked.

Petan fidgeted with the page uneasily.

"What kind of water passage was caused?"

"He peed himself," Petan finally said and blushed.

"Oh..."

"This caused him bodily and psychological pain and harm as has been recorded. Here..."

He showed Taras another piece of paper. The letters blurred

before his eyes as he tried to hide that he had to hold the page far from his eyes if he wanted to read it.

"This says, that he vomited and that this caused him..."

The report included a medical phrase that Taras could not for the life of him make out.

"Oesophageal rupture, a tear in the throat," said Petan.

Taras handed back the page to him and smiled.

"What you mention is probably caused by the cocaine I noticed when I visited the premises you referred to."

"That won't be true..." Petan began, but Taras interrupted him.

"You don't have a case. Now, if you'll allow me, I'll take my leave because some of us in this institution actually have work to do."

He stood up and turned towards the door.

"We have a witness."

Taras turned round.

"Your colleague," said Petan and pointed at Tina.

Without intending to Taras looked at her and noticed her calmness, almost a kind of ridicule on her face. Surely she didn't? What was there in it for her? All kinds of possibilities went through his mind at that moment. Penca wouldn't have. Brajc and Osterc wouldn't have, nobody he knew would have. But her he didn't know. He knows her generation, twenty years younger... and she's a woman. What does he know about women? He has never worked with one. What if she's one of those ambitious people who walk over dead bodies? What about Drvarič? Was it him? Did he put her up to this?

"Tina, speak," said Drvarič.

"From where on?"

"Tell us what happened."

"Well, so, what Mr Petan said is of course true..."

Taras felt as if someone had just struck him across the face. He felt like someone at a party probably feels when, after flirting with a girl they realize, once sober, that she had been their daughter's school friend. Twenty years of detective work, developing an instinct for people, for their intentions, behaviour, characters... all gone up in smoke when a girl in a short skirt appears. Oh dear, Taras...

"...is of course true," she repeated, "when he described the events outside the weekend house. After that they diverge considerably from the truth. It's true that my colleague detained the person concerned for attacking him while carrying out his duties, but when the person concerned had calmed down – indeed that was some hundred metres away from the premises referred to – my colleague released him. There was no – what did you call it...?"

Petan did not respond. He observed Tina motionlessly.

"well, there was no violence involved. We parted quite calmly if I ignore the shouting and swearing of your protégé."

Petan pouted and reminded Taras of a giant toad.

"Until that moment he had not yet peed in his pants. I think that he called me a police cunt and mentioned fucking."

The pout turned into a grimace.

"Have you really though this through? Misjudgement in these things could cost you dearly."

"Misjudgement? What's that supposed to mean?" Tina was surprised.

"Judging when to tell the truth. I think we all here know what actually happened in Bohinj."

Taras stood up and walked to the door. Drvarič stared at him without giving any indication of what was going on in his head. When he opened the door, he turned over his shoulder and said,

"Tina, when you're finished here, I'd ask you to come and see me."

He was about to close the door when Drvarič finally spoke.

"Taras, when I'm done with Mr Petan I would like to speak to you."

"You know where to find me."

When he got back to the office Brajc and Osterc were already there, sitting at their computers. It was probably obvious from the expression on his face that he wanted to shove another head into the snow, because they both gave him an inquisitive look.

"Nothing to tell. This piece of shit always knows how to piss me off, and he did it this time too."

"What did he want?" Osterc asked.

Taras waved his hand dismissively,

"Oh nothing... no point in bothering about it."

Clicking on the keyboard the screen switched itself on, he then checked the headlines of the online newspapers. He realized, in fact he had been realizing it for the last year, that he was less and less interested in it. Peter Prevc was winning the New Year Four Hills Tournament. Great for him. If things go one like this he himself will be sitting in his room at sixty staring at an imaginary point on a white wall. He tried to read the entire article to kill time until Tina returned and he could thank her and find out how Drvarič and Petan handled her after he left.

"Hey, Taras, this isn't looking good," said Osterc and pointed at the whiteboard. "What's that you wrote on there? Firecrackers? What Firecrackers?"

Taras looked at the board almost as if it was the first time he was seeing it.

"Nothing..." he said. "Just a note, so I don't forget."

Chapter 18.

Unborn, illegitimate, disappeared child, boat, first or second or third, pharmacists' meeting and firecrackers. He had written on the board anything that seemed out of the ordinary, anything that rippled the surface… of the lake.

"Brajc, can you call social services… Who's in charge of Bohinj?"

"No idea."

"Probably Jesenice," said Taras. "Well, call them and speak to someone who's been there since the early eighties. If not, they should give us the phone number of anyone who used to work there and has retired."

"It's been thirty years…" Brajc tried but fell silent because in the meantime Tina had walked into the office. She greeted Brajc and Osterc and sat at her, well Penca's desk. The three of them turned towards her. She lifted the flap on her laptop, switched it on, fixed her ponytail, and, as if she had only just noticed them…

"Oh, what is it?"

"What did they want from you?" Taras asked.

Absorbed with the screen, she pressed a few keys…

"Just a moment…"

A few more clicks and,

"There…"

Only then did she look up.

"Sorry, what was that?"

"What did they want from you?"

"Oh, that. Nothing special. I had to listen to a lecture about all the bad things that could happen if I hide the wrongdoings of my senior colleagues."

"Whose lecture?"

"Mostly Petan's. Drvarič merely added that in these cases it's essential to speak the truth and that he hoped I had done. I didn't get the feeling he wanted to get you into trouble. I think he just wanted to get through this in a way that there'd be no resentment on Petan's behalf."

"Are the two of us missing something here?" Brajc asked and Tina obligingly explained why Petan had called in and accused Taras of whatever he accused him of supposedly having done. When she finished she looked at Taras and smiled.

"What's funny?"

"You thought for a moment that I'd blow the whistle, eh?"

"Perhaps I did," said Taras.

"He pissed himself?" Brajc asked enthusiastically and then shrugged his shoulders in disbelief. "What's the world coming to? You used to at least punch a scoundrel and the arsehole knew why he'd got them, at least they were that honest. And today – it's the same at school. Can't do this, can't do that. I remember when my Blaž was at school and kept getting into trouble, I went to the teacher and told her, reassured her that I for one wouldn't protest if she were to give him a slap. Do you know what she said? I thought it would be, oh, no, we don't do things like that because it's not educational. She actually said, well, you might not, but what about your wife?"

Only Tina was listening to him. Taras and Osterc had already heard the story which actually had a continuation which was now not going to happen because someone knocked at the door and opened it at the same time. Drvarič.

"Taras, do you have a minute?"

"I do."

Drvarič stepped into the office. He seemed to be looking for an empty chair but there was none. He stopped in front of the whiteboard and looked at the points.

"How are you getting on?"

"We're not," said Taras.

"And this?"

"These are just strands of straw we are holding onto."

"Do you know who the body is?"

"No."

Drvarič sighed, but didn't seem particularly bothered.

"You'll get there... What I in fact came to say is, this Petan who came here today... Don't let him lead you along because with what he's got he can't get anywhere along official routes. He knows that. He tried with your young colleague..." and he pointed at Tina, "but he could have spared himself that too. Here we don't tell, do we?"

"Of course, especially if there's nothing to tell."

He nodded.

"Of course. What I wanted to tell you is that he won't leave you alone. The guy he works for, besides dealing in food supplements, is also the co-owner of one of the TV stations, about three radio stations as well as a few newspapers and magazines. Expect malevolence."

Was he wrong about Drvarič? So what if he was a bad investigator and threw himself into being the director, a position where every so often you needed to digest some of the dregs and delegate stuff downwards. So what if, as time went on, he occasionally forgot about how he was well aware that it took much longer for his dead to receive justice than for those Taras was responsible for. Would he have wanted to be in Drvarič's position? Would he want, for a mere hundred euros more a month, to spend his days in the office, at meetings and sucking up to x, y or z? Was he nagging him more than any other boss would?

"He can do what he wants. I'm not hiding any spectacular skeletons in the closet."

"In fact we should all be prepared for under the belt attacks. We should bear these things in mind."

He turned to the door, stopped in front of Tina and asked her what her new job was like and before he left they exchanged a few words of politeness.

"Skeletons?" Brajc was perplexed when Drvarič disappeared. "What kind of skeletons were you thinking of?"

Taras did not reply. He looked at the board and the points written on it as someone who has managed to put three pieces of an unknown puzzle together and is trying to figure out what image they hide.

In vain. Three pieces of a puzzle of goodness knows how many pieces and nobody even knows whether they are even part of the same, relevant image.

"There, Taras, at last!" said Osterc from behind his screen. "Got it. Five hundred and ninety euros, clutch and flywheel. We'll see about the work."

*

At twelve they went for lunch in the canteen at Maximarket. There were times when even this was too expensive for Taras and his lunch consisted of homemade sandwiches, yoghurts with bananas and similar substitutes. If he ever went there for a pot of stew he almost had a guilty conscience and even now, when he could easily afford more respectable restaurants, where he could enjoy the company of the likes of Petan, he preferred to eat at student and workers' joints. He chose the chicken with rice, Tina had the same, Brajc and Osterc took the goulash with polenta.

They sat down and Brajc began going on about how the best goulash is at food banks because... Taras wasn't listening. He sat opposite Tina.

"Taras, why did you write firecrackers on the board?" she asked.

Taras had just taken a bite of his chicken and was trying not to swallow it too fast. Ever since his daughters were born and there was not enough time for anything, he had had problems with eating food too quickly and the food wedged in his windpipe and now, when there was no need for gulping down his food, the problem remained. He managed to control it this time.

"Do you remember what the old lady with the cat and the dog said?"

"About the firecrackers?"

"Yes."

"She said the bangs began when those four arrived."

"No, that's not what she said."

Tina gave him a puzzled look.

"She said that it first banged when they arrived. And that she was not even sure that they were firecrackers at the time until they began using them before New Year. When I talked to the other two while you went to check the boat, they told me that they had bought the firecrackers only a day or two before New Year's Eve. One of them had forgotten them in Ljubljana and they had to drive to Radovljica to get them.

Tina placed her knife and fork on the empty plate and pushed it away slightly. Taras' plate was also already empty.

"What does that tell us?"

"It tells us that that firecracker on the twenty-third was thrown by someone else. Someone whom our informant must have missed. If indeed it was a firecracker."

"Is this our Varta?"

She looked at him curiously. Brajc and Osterc were still fully occupied with their goulash. Osterc was, not exactly discreetly, in a kind of halftime break between two attacks on the plate, picking pieces of meat from the gaps in his teeth. Brajc was tearing up some bread and mopping up the sauce with the pieces... If they ever possessed such a thing as professional curiosity, they had long lost it. This was not necessarily a bad thing. A case can drag on, and if you throw yourself at it like Tina seemed to have done, you will not last until the forty-second kilometre. He looked at Brajc who had a drop of goulash running from his bottom lip down his chin... Well, the comparison with a marathon was not the most appropriate in his case.

"I hope it's something," he replied. "Anything is better than nothing."

*

When they returned to the office, Taras' phone was ringing. He had forgotten it on his desk and it stopped ringing before he could answer it. A Celje number. He called back and Mihelič's secretary answered it.

"Mr Birsa?"

"How can I help you?"

"Please write down this phone number. I told her you would be calling."

He jotted it on a piece of paper, thanked her, and was about to hang up when the secretary interrupted,

"And Mr Mihelič would also like to talk to you. Just a moment..."

He waited a few seconds for Mihelič to pick up the receiver. No greeting, a person who does not need to deal with daily politeness, he got straight to the point.

"Inspector, I can't prevent you from looking into things which are totally unrelated to your problem, I don't even want to make it difficult for you. That's also why we gave you the number of our... how can I put it, friend. But because there are big things in the game here –you're certainly right about that – and it was also the reason I stayed in Bohinj for the full three days – I could, if you wish, explain."

"Please do."

"I can't on the phone. Would it be too much trouble for you to come and visit us at Salubris, in Slovenske Konjice? Let's say the day after tomorrow at eleven?"

"Just let me check..."

He moved the phone away from his ear, shuffled some random papers on his desk, waited a little while longer, and replied.

"Yes, that would be fine."

He said goodbye, put down the phone and, looking up, caught Tina trying to hide a smile.

"What?"

"Nothing, nothing..."

"What is it?"

"Did you shuffle the pages to make it sound as if you're looking for one of those diary things... what do they call it?"

"What, a schedule planner, is that what you're thinking of?"

"Yes, probably. Does anyone still use schedule planners these days?"

She picked up her mobile and swiped the screen with her finger a few times. No noise whatsoever, of course.

"You won't believe it but I was talking to a person older than me."

He stuck his tongue out at her and caught Osterc' surprised look. He was just finishing a phone call.

"Social Services in Jesenice. I've arranged a visit."

Taras nodded.

"And there's something you can do..."

He turned towards Tina and handed her the phone number he had just noted.

"... this is Mihelič's companion. Meet up with her and try to find out anything useful. First of all whether she's still alive."

She held the paper between her thumb and index finger, eagerly, almost flirtatiously. For the first time since he had met her, the proportions of her face seemed balanced. In fact those oversized eyes gave her face a sort of unique cuteness.

Chapter 19.

At half past nine in the evening Taras was lying in a pool of his own sweat on the floor of the gym at the primary school at the centre of Ljubljana, gathering the strength to open his eyes. He was glad the session was over. He could congratulate himself for getting through it, for getting through the circuit training, all the stages, including the incredibly difficult one where you had to jump off the wall bars onto a large mattress with a somersault and then a double leg hop over four hurdles. Every time he said to himself that he would leave this stage out, but he never had. Until he tears some ligament in the knee. People much younger than he have done so and if that happens, he thought, then he will stop. In younger people such tears can be repaired with an operation, with him probably not. He picked himself up from the floor and placed the mattress onto the pile with all the others.

"Coming for a drink, Taras?" Jasnič, head of a private security company asked. He used to be a competent middleweight boxer; now, like Taras, he went to the gym three times a week and never pushed himself nearly as hard as Taras did. He would warm up, hang up his bag and punch at it in two-minute intervals. Ten times with a minute's break between the intervals, then twenty push-ups and stretching. And while by the end of training Taras was soaked, Jasnič barely sweated enough for his t-shirt to darken slightly round the neck. Despite this Taras had no illusions. He would have no chance opposite him in a ring.

"I can't..."

It seems that the punches in Jasnič's career had also taken their toll on his abilities to remember and whenever they did manage to go for a drink, he was always surprised that Taras didn't drink alcohol. He had to explain every time why he stuck to coke. And every time their conversation on the subject finished with Jasnič asking,

"Can't you fix it in any way?"

Every time Taras patiently shook his head.

"Just a beer?"

"I have work."

He went to the *burek* shop on Miklošič Street.

"A coke for you Inspector?"

"Yep."

The Albanian gave him a half-litre plastic bottle of coke and when Taras counted out the euro and a half, he grinned.

"I'll give you a *burek* with that."

"If you do, I'll pay for it."

The seller smiled and shook his head.

"No you won't. We good folk should help each other."

"I'm not from the sanitary inspection."

"I know you're not. That's not the point."

He had almost finished the *burek* by the time he got to the car. No, he had nothing to do, the only thing was that he had promised Alenka they would watch a film she's brought from the library together.

"You two still borrow films?" Anja asked when she first came home from Vienna. As if in the two months she had been away everything should have changed.

"I'm still a police officer and it's still illegal," said Taras – who had still not learnt how to download films. In fact he had never tried.

"It's real simple..." Anja told him and Taras believed her, but he could not be bothered and this time it would not have been relevant anyway because the film Alenka had brought from the library was Turkish, a masterpiece apparently, which won some award at Cannes. He could not handle watching Turkish dialogue with English subtitles. If things have to be lost in translation, at least they can be lost in Slovene. Although it was probably translated from the English anyway.

"It's three hours long," said Taras when he took the disk from the sleeve.

"Three hours?"

They decided that they would watch half tonight and the rest tomorrow and Taras reckoned that Alenka would be fast asleep after twenty minutes and he would switch to Southampton vs. Bolton or some other lame match. He was so tired that he was not sure he could follow the plot in an Anatolian village or whether he could be bothered to watch the story of Aydın, some former actor who now runs a small hotel in a remote village somewhere in the middle of Anatolia, and in his spare time writes a column for a local newspaper and plans to write a book on Turkish theatre, as the sleeve said.

"Taras, can I ask you something?" said Alenka, absorbed in thought.

"Will it help if I say no?"

She wasn't biting.

"Go ahead."

"Is something wrong?"

She sat in her corner of the orange sofa they had bought... oh, ages ago. Taras could not remember when but it was probably one of the first things they bought together. Good quality. Survived all these years, but at the same time very uncomfortable. At least once a day Taras would complain about it when he sat down in it and say he would get rid of it. Quite a few contortionist skills were needed for someone to find at least a modestly comfortable position.

"What do you mean?"

"You're quiet, absorbed in thought... Some things, some people, get on your nerves more that usual..."

"Who?"

"Doctors, my colleagues, for example."

"They always got on my nerves."

"More than usual."

"Since when is this more?"

"For the last six months or so."

"They used to get on your nerves too."

He paused the DVD and sat on the orange torture device. He somehow discovered that the best position if he was watching TV or reading was to place both his legs on a kitchen chair and press his pelvis against the edge of the sofa, lying down like formula-one drivers do in their cars.

"Not that much."

"What's wrong? Nothing is wrong..."

He raised the remote control.

"Should I start it...?"

"Do you have someone else?"

"I do, one without a head."

She didn't smile and as soon as he said it, it didn't sound funny to him either.

"I'm being serious, Taras."

"Where is this coming from? Have I said something... in my sleep, or what?"

"No, I just want to know. I thought it could be that."

"Who could it be? I don't know anyone."

She stared at him for a moment in the way Taras used to stare at people across the table in the room with a mirror.

"That's not true, that you don't know anyone. What about this new girl at work?"

"I've known her for three days, apparently I've been strange for six months."

Alenka dismissively waved her hand, as if to say, what's the point in arguing.

"I didn't say you had something going on with her, just that it's not true that you don't know anyone."

Taras pressed play.

"What then?"

The trailers for other films appeared and he used the remote to fast-forward through them until he got to the warnings about copying being a crime, just like theft, showing a shot of a young man trying to break into a car. To be precise, Taras had once said to Alenka when this shot appeared, they should have sent the thief to the car factory, not to a car. People who download film from the Internet are stealing from the source, not from individuals.

"Nothing, everything is fine."

What could it be? A number of things. How can he tell her that he feels kind of... empty. Why had he abandoned climbing, why had he pushed himself all these years if in the end everything is as it should be thanks to her old man? Get up, work, cope with the kids, one at first, then two, pay the bills, pay off the mortgage, find an alternative to climbing, something that is not so dangerous and would not waste so much time and money, running, cycling, recreational boxing, and push, push, push, so that in the end it will all seem the same… And keep saying to yourself that you have no choice, that this is what it's like and that it isn't that bad after all. Despite everything, millions of people would swap with him. Billions.

Once he had met his father-in-law in the supermarket by chance. The only time in all these years that he saw him. Taras was holding a shopping basket in his hand, there was no need for a trolley. The old man didn't even greet him and glanced at the contents of the basket,

"Managing are you?"

"I don't understand you Taras," said Alenka without looking at the screen where an elderly man was walking across a field and the camera moved out to reveal the sandstone pillars of Anatolia, or Cappadocia, or wherever. "I don't understand. After all these years we finally have the money so we could have everything we previously could not afford, and you go into depression. Sometimes I think you're really asking for it."

The old man reached a small house, a hotel, and stepped behind a kind of reception counter. Clearly he was the owner.

"No thanks to me."

"What?"

"The fact that we can afford things. It's no thanks to me."

She looked at him as if he was saying something unimaginable.

"Does it matter?"

"If that doesn't, then what does?"

"What does it matter what you do with the lottery ticket you've got? Besides, if that's how you want it, you won, my father admitted…"

"I won? What did he admit? He was just afraid of death, not me. And even then he didn't ask me, just did things his own way. Besides, it's not about that, I wasn't competing with him…"

Although he probably was.

"Things are great now, but not because of me. Not because of my work. Not because I pissed blood for twenty years, for twenty years I didn't go anywhere, I mean into the mountains… Why? Why, so that he can just… like that, in a second."

"You could have said you didn't want his help."

He shook his head.

"If I could, we would still be there..." he pointed to the table. "Counting the bills. Perhaps I'm depressive, but I'm not mad. And he was dying, in a way he owed it to me. He owed you and because we never had separate accounts, he owed me too. So..." He looked at her with probably a slightly more accusatory look than he intended. "Anyway, I didn't take anything, you did."

She rolled her eyes.

"Is that where we are? If you had wanted to count every cent before paying things for the rest of your life, then..."

"Let's stop this," he interrupted her. "It isn't leading anywhere. I don't resent anything, and even if you had asked me I would have said yes."

"What then is the problem?"

"There isn't one."

The problem was that even now, after twenty years, in fact now more often than before, he remembered things like the evening meal they had in a home in the village of Tukuche where the last houses before the trek to base camp are. The owner, a Nepalese lady from the Gurung people, had roasted two chickens upon their request. They had waited for the food all evening until eventually two trays appeared with everything chopped up, heads and claws included, all hard, burnt and inedible.

"They were old chickens," she said as an excuse.

But they ate it all. Does he remember what he had to eat last night?

"I don't know," he said hesitantly. "I have the feeling I've not given enough time to mountains, that's it."

"Then go climbing. Call one of your mates from those days and go, you're probably fitter than you were then anyway."

Taras laughed.

"Thanks, but I'm not."

Besides, he had recently made a list in his head of his permanent, occasional and one-time fellow climbers. Twenty names of which thirteen were dead. One had cancer, all the others had died in the mountains.

"Who is there to call?"

And yet... When he thought about them, these twelve too, news about whom inevitably reached him over the years, he, though he didn't want to, felt envious. Silly, but yes.

"Taras, you're not quite with it, do you realize that? And what you're saying is not exactly a compliment to me. To any of us. You envy the dead?"

"I envy them that they lived as they wanted to live. I would not like to be dead, of course, but still. They lived life to the full, but I..."

He ran the Ljubljana marathon. With millions of others. Thank God for Anja and Mojca, but they have left now, have their own lives...

"And when I listen to you, I thank fate that we had girls. If you'd have had a son, God knows what you'd have made of him."

"What would I have made of him? What do you mean? That I'd gave dragged him off climbing?"

Alenka stayed silent.

"And besides, I don't know if it's even about climbing. If I think that I'd have to wake up at four in the morning, drive somewhere for two hours and then slog it off somewhere for two days, freezing half way up some rock face... Perhaps I'm just nostalgic for the days when I could be bothered to do such a thing... Do you understand?"

"You're having a mid-life crisis," said Alenka. She sounded relieved.

"Yes, probably that's what it is. And what now?"

They fell silent and Taras remembered that they were supposed to be watching the film. On screen the hotel proprietor was arguing with a woman, a much younger one. His daughter or wife?

"Should I rewind it?" he asked because the plot had already progressed, Alenka had not even looked at it once and he too had not followed what it was about.

"Don't you think that something similar would bother you in any case? Even if you hadn't given up climbing?"

"Or I would have been among those twelve and your old man did in fact save my life... He arranged everything so it worked out well."

Alenka stared at the blank screen.

"And what's this new girl like, what's her name again... Tina?"

"I have nothing going on with her."

"I know. I'm just asking."

"Young and beautiful," said Taras. "At least that's what they all say."

"And you?"

He shrugged his shoulders.

"You know Osterc and Brajc. To them every girl is beautiful. I don't think she's anything special."

He took the film back to the beginning, once more pressed the *Play* button, having gone just too far, so they had to watch the clip about illegal copying. For the second time, the man with a grey beard walked along the misty path among the sandstone pillars of Cappadocia into which people had carved out their homes... It has been more than twenty years since he had last properly gripped a rock the way rocks should be gripped, and still he thought of climbing with every rock formation he saw.

"Can I ask you something?"

"Sure, what?"

"Why did your old man pull Prelc out of the mud?"

"How do you mean?"

He stared at the screen where whatever it was that was happening was happening very slowly, and waited for her to speak.

"As far as I know they weren't mates. There was no real need or purpose in merging paediatrics with a gastrological clinic."

"I don't know," she said. "He must have had his reasons. Does every why need its because? Why do you want to know that now?"

He waved his hand.

"Professional deformation. It just happened to come to mind."

Twenty minutes later she was asleep and Taras was about to switch to a sports channel, picked up the remote, but then put it back down again and watched the slow, difficult tale about the relationship of an older man and a younger wife to the end, until half past one in the morning. And he found that, as he watched it, his thoughts kept returning to the case they were solving. He thought of boats, firecrackers, Mihelič and his eighteen year old prostitute, the pregnant girl from Stara Fužina from thirty years ago, IS, the lake, Tina more than Brajc and Osterc... And yes, every why does need its because, as an investigator he knew that.

Though he dozed off a couple of times during the film, he was wide awake at the end of it. An opportunity to look at today from a distance, he said to himself, with different eyes. He stood up and began pacing up and down the room in order to get the blood flowing and hopefully deliver an extra molecule or two of oxygen to the brain. He sat and picked up some bill or whatever it was, and sketched the lake and the places surrounding it, Ukanc, Stara Fužina, the river that flows from it and after about a hundred metres becomes the Sava Bohinjka, whereas before it was... now what was that...? Under his sketch he wrote, boat, child and meeting of students from the Biotechnical Faculty. He stared at what he had written for a while.

Maybe there was nothing he could have overlooked because there was nothing there. He wished there would be, but in reality... He crumpled up the page and threw it at the TV which had the Sony sign flashing on a black screen, He switched off the DVD and then the TV and sat on the sofa, as if he couldn't decide whether to get up or lean back and try to find that balanced position. It had been four days since they found the body, eleven since someone cut off the girl's head, and they still don't even know her name.

He took the remote to the cupboard under the TV set and on the way picked up the crumpled paper, checking what was on the back of it. In case it was something important. It was the bill for the car repairs which Osterc had arranged for him. Clutch, flywheel, plus labour – eight hundred and seventy euros. He put it on the table. He'd deal with it tomorrow... or whenever.

Then he remembered, it kind of clicked what he might have overlooked and was almost disappointed. This? Was this it? He found his grey notepad and flicked through it until he found what he was looking for. It might not be anything, he said to himself, but there usually really is a because to every why.

Chapter 20.

Friday, 5 January

Mihelič's office was as could be expected for the office of a director of a pharmaceutical company. An old-school director. His desk with a leather sofa and a watercolour on the wall behind it. An ebony African sculpture on the desk and next to it a similarly sized babushka. About a metre in front of it a round coffee table with two slightly less imposing sofas either side and a little further away a large oval table with seven chairs around it, the walls above this conference table covered with all the awards and certificates the company had received and, central position on this wall, a large colour photograph of Mihelič with Marshal Tito. Based on Tito, Taras reckoned it was from the late seventies, a year or so before his death. There were a few cupboards with glass doors containing what were probably decorative books that nobody had looked through in a long time, if ever. When the secretary escorted Taras into the room, Mihelič stood up and in surprisingly lively steps for a man over seventy, intercepted Taras as if he wanted to prevent him from reaching his desk.

"Good morning, good morning, Inspector!"

Taras greeted him and Mihelič beckoned to the secretary. Taras ordered a coffee, Mihelič water and a juice.

"Where should we sit?"

Mihelič looked around the room as if it was the first time he was seeing it.

"What about there?" he pointed to the small round coffee table.

Taras nodded and chose a seat.

"The weekend?"

"Fine."

"I heard you were a sportsman?"

"How do you know that?"

He listed some of Taras' mountaineering achievements, uncomfortably in the same sentence as his later recreational activities, though Taras never saw himself as a marathon runner or cross-country skier. Mihelič was using a page on the table to help him.

"I prepare myself for..."

He frowned and then made a blowing sound as if he had just messed something up,

"I meant to say, I prepare myself for business, but then this isn't business, is it?"

"Not as far as I'm concerned," said Taras. "An investigative interview is what we call it in the police."

The secretary brought their drinks and offered Taras sugar and milk which he declined. Mihelič took a sip of juice and rinsed his mouth with water, leaned back in his sofa chair and waited for Taras to take a sip of his coffee.

"So, what is it you want to know, Inspector?"

"Well, in fact it was you who asked me to call in on you. Supposedly you have something to tell me."

Mihelič smiled.

"You're right. Indeed I did request this meeting."

He interlaced his fingers, thumbs touching on top.

"The reason is that I'd like to ask you to handle this matter discretely. Not only because I was in Bohinj with... a friend, no, no, that's not really some huge news. A week or so of sulking at home, but I'm on the road a lot anyway. Don't you read the tabloid shit?"

"If I have to."

"Yes, you're right. I don't either. But it's a different matter if... Do you have the time for a slightly longer explanation, Mr Birsa?"

Taras nodded.

"It almost has to be slightly longer because... There are such high investments in the game, that it would be irresponsible of me, because of the investigation which you are of course obliged to carry out… to keep silent about this. So…"

He raised his hands, his open palms turned towards Taras,

"… and so, the truth and nothing but the truth. So let's go. From Adam. Are you at all interested in medicine? You'd better be, otherwise the next five minutes will be extremely boring."

He did not wait for an answer, took another quick sip, juice and then water, leaned back and, eyes half closed, began,

"You see, humanity…" he smiled and briefly opened his eyes again, just enough to add, "I did say – from Adam." He closed them again and continued, "Well, humanity, you see, has many problems, health problems, which we can, in terms of intensity, imagine on a kind of graphic representation. On this graph you have a small group of very serious problems, then the intensity of the problems drops and we have a long tail of problems which become more serious over time. I'm talking of the rise of pathogens which, due to globalization, are now carried more rapidly around the world. Ebola for example. If winters here become warmer such viruses will survive and spread without any problem. They had cases of it in the United Kingdom, so it's just as likely we could have cases here. Then we also have viruses which have always been in forests where there were not great numbers of people, now people are moving there…"

"HIV?" Taras asked.

"Yes, HIV was one of the first such viruses. At some point a group of people come into some specific part of the world, they have numerous offspring who move around the world. Can you imagine? Something new comes into the forest where there has been nothing new since time immemorial, imagine the feast the bugs and parasites have? What an opportunity for a quick leap of illnesses which before didn't even exist for humans and for which we don't even know what they cause. Something similar happened recently in Brazil where they cleared the forest, built towns and then suddenly found that they had a terrible disease attacking their offspring, their children. What was happening? The mother is bitten by a mosquito, which infects her with a virus, which is upon conception transferred to the embryo and begins multiplying inside its brain. Children are born, if they even survive, with totally atrophic brains. This is one example of an illness from the tail of this graph."

"You're talking about the Zika virus?"

"Of course."

He paused briefly, as if wanting to allow Taras time to think, to process what he had said.

"And these minor problems to which nobody pays attention are like the toads which develop. If you don't deal with the soup of tadpoles at the beginning when they're still small, you end up with a roomful of bufonids."

He looked at Taras as a lecturer might look at a student to figure out whether he was following the lesson.

"But the tadpoles I mentioned are not important for our story."

"The toads are," said Taras.

"Yes, the toads. The problems are at the other end of the graph."

Mihelič smiled and then turned serious, continuing at a much faster pace, almost spewing out his words,

"The second acute health problems of humanity are antibiotics, more specifically resistance to them. This is not a problem from the tail because it concerns the masses. In the western world the population is getting older and in the last fifty years there has been no decent flu epidemic which would kill off most of the population older than sixty-five, seventy. In Japan, for example, almost sixty percent of the population is over fifty. The greatest proportion of money is spent on keeping this section of the population healthy."

He shook his head.

"Meaning my contemporaries. From cholesterol medication and chemotherapy to Viagra. All these are medications which you yourself will not need for some time yet,"

"Thank you," said Taras and thought of his doctor who during his last obligatory visit to get a health certificate for work had made him take a blood test.

"Your cholesterol level is high," he had muttered. "But knowing your life style I don't think there's much point in bothering you with pills."

"I wouldn't take them," Taras had said.

"Did you know," Mihelič continued, "that most health money that the state spends on each person coincides with the last year of life?"

Taras didn't know that.

"If I exaggerate a little, with men this means that they are, as far as the health budget is concerned, more or less healthy from birth until they are about seventy-seven, and in that last year when they fall ill, they use up to eighty, in some cases ninety percent of the money spent on health during their entire life. A large part of this is for pain management, then there is direct cancer treatment and infections come in a close third. Gastric infections, infections of the respiratory organs, skin, urinary, and post-operative infections. Basically bacteria."

He fell silent, stared Taras straight in the eye for a few moments.

"And this is where we step into the story."

He finished off the juice and once again rinsed his mouth with water.

"Antibiotics. For treating these infections we use huge quantities of antibiotics, the effectiveness of which is declining fast. There are more and more strains resistant to antibiotics. In hospitals we have strains which are more or less resistant to everything apart from one, which is hugely expensive and is only produced by some obscure company which sells it for vast amounts of money and it is only given to patients after considering the value of their future life, the cost of therapy... Basically, if you're over seventy and the senior doctor who decides these matters does not happen to be a friend of yours, then don't expect to be treated with it. Then there's another group of antibiotic users that I have forgotten to mention. Because of an ever-greater degeneration of the population in the western world, because there's no longer any natural selection, there are kids with cystic fibrosis and similar problems, who need antibiotics all the time. A lifelong course of antibiotics, they don't stop taking them. And all these and millions, billions of others, all of us, if you want... live an antibiotic away from death."

Taras had read something about this but had believed it was just journalistic exaggeration.

"Why aren't there any new antibiotics? Why aren't there any if such an antibiotic could be worth millions? Because their development is even more expensive, gruesomely expensive – I'm talking of tens of billions of dollars or euros. For something, the patent of which expires within ten years. Ten years after you have used tonnes of money, the generics, such as ourselves, cut in. On the thirty first of the twelfth at twenty-three hours fifty-nine minutes and fifty-nine seconds the lorries are waiting down there," and he pointed through the window, "filled with the medication and all the documentation, ready, engines running at the gate, and at midnight – hop!"

"You're talking about generics?" Taras asked.

"Yes, generics. These aren't difficult to manufacture once you have the original on the table. But the original, that's a different story and in this I back the state. This is the point of the state, it finances things that the private sector never could, science among others, and they then sell the parents to industry so they can make radios, TVs, iPhones, Gore-Tex, titanium hips and knees, or antibiotics. If we had to wait for the much-praised private sector, nothing would ever come of it, because the numbers just don't add up. Do you know Novartis?"

"The people who bought Lek Pharmaceutics and are your rival?"

"Not only our rival. His turnover is around sixty billion US dollars. But Novartis is also a generics company. You wouldn't think so, would you?"

He stopped as if he had said something he ought not to have.

"I'm an old guard communist, as you can see." He pointed to the photograph of himself with Tito on the wall. "The Communist Party is no more, nor is communism, but I'm still what you might call 'red'. Democracy? Come on… Our firm supports an entire region, half the country. Do you think it would do so if the workers were to choose the director themselves? And why could the state if a company can't."

He waved his hand through the air.

"Well, let's return to our issue. Can you imagine the scene;

lorries waiting at the gate in the middle of the night? This is no metaphor, they really do wait there and countdown."

"Sort of."

"Well, and now from the general to the specific. What I'm telling you is no secret. Everyone knows it, governments included, and recently there's been a lot of talk on initiatives for developing new antibiotics, but, you know how these things go – slowly. Despite this, the pharmaceutical industry has begun to stir. Not too much and not particularly ambitiously. Let's say we've begun clearing out before we renovate our home. In view of this we at Salubris a while ago, about a year ago, to be precise, decided to revive some of our older strains, kept cryodesiccated at minus eighty degrees in chest freezers..."

Taras of course didn't have a clue what 'cryodesiccated' meant, but Mihelič hadn't said it for Taras to understand.

"...and allow students of microbiology and biotechnology to handle them. What for? To revive strains of bacteria and get them going, testing growth media, testing our measuring equipment, checking whether the cells still produce the basic natural substances... Basically the preparatory work, without any expectations, nothing special."

Taras finished his coffee and shook his head when Mihelič asked him whether he wanted another.

"So we called the University and they sent us the four students. We pushed a non-disclosure agreement into their hands and sent them to our storage. Do you know what such an agreement means?"

"That the results of your cooperation remain confidential," said Taras.

"Yes, which means – ours. Just in case. Are you interested in chemistry, Inspector?"

"At this moment or in general?"

The old man smiled and nodded.

"What you will be interested in and the reason I invited you here..."

He took a felt-tip pen and underlined something on a piece of paper and turned it towards Taras,

"...is this."

Before him appeared a marked line of numbers and letters connected with dashes, hyphens and brackets. For a second or two only, then Mihelič put it back on the table.

"I hope you don't have a photographic memory, because in that case I would need to have you killed."

He laughed and stopped when he saw Taras was not joining in.

"I apologize, an inappropriate joke."

"This is a formula for a new antibiotic, if I understood correctly?"

Mihelič nodded.

"Not just for some new antibiotic, but for the most effective new antibiotic on the planet."

He fell silent and watched Taras.

"Well, at least we think it could be the strongest."

"I assume you didn't discover it in Bohinj?"

"No, no… Just a little more patience please. Then all will become clear, the entire picture you need to know in order to understand why I'm asking you not to poke into a subject which is greater than anything in your, my, or anyone's life."

He knocked on the table with his knuckles, then intertwined his fingers and looked at Taras.

"Do you believe in miracles, Mr Birsa?"

Taras shook his head.

"Coincidences at best."

"And how many such coincidences would constitute a miracle?"

Taras didn't reply and Mihelič produced another piece of paper from a drawer and placed it on the table before continuing, looking alternately at the page and at Taras.

"What happens if you close four students in a lab who eventually become four exhausted students. One of them is cultivating strand XPZ79.1989.FTC14 on plates of culture medium A and can filter out the cells where the antibiotic is apparently after reception linked to the baculovirus within the cells…"

He spoke so fast, without pauses or accentuations, like some TV advert for medication where the actor reading it tries to roll off the 'consult your doctor or pharmacist' phrase prescribed by law in the shortest possible time.

"... he contained the remainder of the culture medium in a Schott bottle intended for destruction. Until that point the bottle was beyond the line which separates used from fresh mediums. He didn't mark it, and its colour is exactly the same as those containing the fresh medium. In the night someone, almost certainly the cleaning lady – the lady who ten years ago worked in Germany and learnt how to keep things tidy – wiped the surface of the counter and, as she did so, neatly moved the unmarked bottle from the used medium A across the line to the other bottles."

He smiled.

"The poor lady had worked in Germany for ten years until her visa was cancelled and she had to return back south. And if she herself hadn't asked, a day or two later, whether she's also supposed to clean the lab counters, we'd probably never have found out. Well, the second student, according to protocol, picked up this bottle with the used medium A in an unmarked bottle, and planted in it his own strain. The result: rapid growth at thirty seven degrees Celsius without mixing in microaerobic conditions and when he measured the production of the substance with HPLC, the chromatograph showed four extra peaks which shouldn't have been there."

He leaned towards Taras and whispered,

"To put it plainly, he fucked up the experiment!"

Then he straightened up and continued at the same rapid pace as before,

"The continuation of this story is at least as much a crime investigation as it is microbiology or chemistry. What does someone do when they make a mistake? They can admit it, or they can try and roll the blame onto someone else. Our student harvested the cells which had grown because it was the last vial and the cells needed to be harvested. At least he had revived them, even if the experiment failed. At least that. And what's more essential here is that he couldn't just dispose of the twice used medium A with the three basic peaks and the additional four because that's not SOP in pharmacopoeia, and he could not just return it because everyone knew that he was handling it, so he poured it into the bottle of a third student whose task was to change the components grown in the medium by adding enzymes. Thus the third student, when he appeared at the lab on the following Monday, exposed the concentrated fraction in his own bottle to an enzyme reaction in a test tube, but because he made a mistake and didn't properly dilute the basic solution which was ten times stronger than..."

He looked up and, with embarrassment, said the next few words at a normal pace.

"It wasn't really his fault. They had supplied him with a cheap mix of the solution he was supposed to be working on. The original pure version is around four thousand five hundred euros, whereas the two hundred milligrams he got from us cost only one hundred and fifty four. You know how it is, it'll do for student research."

Then he switched to the faster pace again.

"During the reaction he got a green tinted product from the medium of his strand, whereas it should have been slightly yellow. In panic he threw the test tube into a water bath at forty-five degrees."

"In panic?" Taras asked.

"It's what people do," Mihelič said. "It isn't logical, but that's how it is. We burn so we get rid of the evidence. Well, but when he put this thing into hot water, he realized that he'd not achieved anything by doing so. So he fished out the test tube and when he had retrieved it the contents were pink. Now no longer green, but pink. So what now? He couldn't pour it out because all test tubes are noted and besides, there are no drains in the lab. Because of its colour he couldn't just place it onto the test indicator strains, because everyone would notice it. So what does he go and do? Before putting on the hazmat suit and going into the lab, he called student number four and asked him whether he could use some of his extra unmarked plates onto which he'd put drops of water. There would thus return no results, and he would clean the pink plates secretly in the autoclave, and all would be fine and dandy. And, had the student been able to do that, our story would have ended there and you'd not be dealing with us at all."

Taras waited patiently.

"But because this student had just been for an operation for a herniated disk..."

He laughed,

"... well, you see, there are also some who decide to use a little more of their medical budget before the age of seventy-eight. And because they also had hospital infections at the orthopaedic clinic where he was kept for a few days, he, as a microbiologist, took samples from a few door handles and his own hand, and then in Lab number four, without the knowledge of his superior, tried to check what he would cultivate from these swabs on the growing agent. Among other things, to make it short, also *necrotizing fasciitis,* basically a flesh-eating bacterial disease and *neisseria gonorrhoeae*.... all of them superbugs which he exposed overnight to the pink solution. Out of curiosity. And when he came to check it the following day..."

He looked up and put down the page he was holding.

"... it was, if we drop the professional terminology here, all dead."

He fell silent, as if the explanation had exhausted him, leaned back onto the leather seat.

"It took us half a year to decode the experiment and repeat it."

"And what were you doing in Bohinj? Surely not cooking pink soup?"

Mihelič smiled.

"No, we were there to discuss the terms of the non-disclosure agreement."

"Money?"

"Not really, that was the least of it. There'll be plenty if there isn't envy. We talked about who gets the credit and how to present the story. It will, of course, not be the same as the one I've just entrusted you with. You know, something along the lines of... After many years of cooperation between... and blah, blah, blah."

"Hmmm..."

"Precisely, Mr Birsa, hmmm!"

"Still, what kind of money are we talking about?"

"If the clinical study produces the same results, and we have almost no doubt that it will, and after all the international tests and licences... Around a hundred billion euros to start with."

"A hundred billion?"

"At least. With negligible costs – free enzymes, free used procedures, free production procedures, and high efficiency. For the next ten years, until we get copied."

"A hundred billion?"

"I know what you're thinking about inspector."

"You do?"

"Yes. You're thinking that a human life, if it trips on money like that, doesn't really have much of a chance, does it?"

"In fact I've not got that far yet. But yes... especially if it has photographic memory?"

"A bad joke, I told you and I apologize again. But well done, I'd already forgotten it..."

He sighed, supported his elbows on the table and leaned towards Taras.

"You would be a dangerous rival, Inspector. I wouldn't like to have you on the opposite side. But the truth is I don't now whose body you have in Ljubljana, what I do know is that it has nothing to do with us."

As he took his leave, a bag awaited Taras with the secretary.

"A small gift," said Mihelič.

"You know I can't accept this?"

"It is nothing special. Just a few sports supplements and lotions we produce. For the knees and things like that."

"Thank you," said Taras and set off down the corridor towards the lift.

"One more thing..." Mihelič called out and caught up with him in the corridor. "I'll walk you out."

He called the lift and when it appeared and the door opened, Mihelič pressed the hold button. He moved his hand from the panel and stood briefly as if arranging his thoughts before uttering the next sentence.

"Two things... Firstly, you do believe me that I have nothing to do with this dead girl?"

"You should ask me instead what I'm thinking, not what I believe. I cannot afford the luxury of believing in my line of work."

Mihelič laughed heartily.

"Unfortunately," he said as he finished, "this is where we're very much alike. I cannot afford that either. I can hope that you might stop poking into this dead end, but I cannot believe it, can I?"

"Sort of," said Taras.

He peered across his shoulder as if to check whether they are still alone in the corridor.

"One more thing. Do you have children, Mr Birsa?"

"You haven't checked this?"

Mihelič smiled slyly.

"Of course we have. Two daughters, twenty and eighteen."

And then in an instant the expression on his face changed. From cunning to frank.

"You probably condemn my behaviour?"

He did not wait for Taras' response.

"But you see, I never paid the poor girl who was with me in Bohinj to be with me. You don't believe me? I mean in money. But I will arrange things for her. Apparently she wants to be a singer. And she will become one. She won't leave me any more sullied than she came."

"I don't care," said Taras.

"Really?" Mihelič smiled.

"Yes, really. As long as the eighteen-year-old is not my daughter."

He stepped into the lift and pressed the button. Someone had called it whilst it was on hold so it went up instead of down, but when it stopped, there was nobody waiting for it. Just a little longer, he thought as he was going back down, another year or so of working, and he won't have to care at all about things even more important than what rich horny old men drool over.

Mihelič went back to his office and sat there for a while, his elbows on the desk and hands interlocked. Slowly he then unclasped his hands and picked up the page on the paper and stared at the formula on it.

"Simona!" he shouted and when there was no response shouted again.

"Yes?" the secretary appeared at the door.

"Call Predalič for me."

"Our Predalič? Predalič from Human Resources?"

"Who? No, what use is he to me? Predalič from the Ministry of Finance."

The secretary disappeared to her office and Mihelič stared once again at the page in front of him. Words and numbers he had scribbled on the paper five minutes before Taras arrived. He was not nuts enough to risk the chance of him actually having a photographic memory.

Chapter 21.

Tina was expecting something else. A fake blonde with lots of make-up. Or a dark-haired singer with lots of make-up. Somebody with lots of make-up... Somebody who would, from across the road look, like girls who sell themselves for money in films. A whore, basically, though she had not really seen many in her life. Of course she had been to Amsterdam and visited the red light district, in Paris she had even gone with her friends for a night walk through Pigalle... Well, that was about all. She would not know where to look for prostitutes in Ljubljana and there were certainly none like those she had seen in Holland and France at this joint.

In the bar where she had arranged to meet Barbara sat a tiny creature, blonde, natural blonde, in an unimposing light blue jumper and a mug of cocoa in front of her. She looked even younger than the eighteen she had only just turned. Tina checked three times whether there were other possibilities but the only other people there were two couples at two of the five or six tables in the room.

"Barbara," she asked with uncertainty.

The girl smiled, stood up and offered her her hand. Tina waited for the waiter to take her order and bring what she had ordered. Then she stopped talking about the weather and winter.

"Do you know why we've met?" she asked and tried to sound as indifferent as possible, realizing she had not managed to sound like that. She sounded more like a teacher. Barbara seemed not to notice or was used to it.

"Not really. Brane said the police wanted to talk to me. Nothing special, that I should go and talk to you."

"Brane?"

"Mr Mihelič."

"Oh..."

"It confuses you because everyone else calls him Mr Mihelič?"

Tina nodded.

"How long have you known each other?"

The girl furrowed her brow and after a short deliberation said,

"About half a year, I think. Only recently as Brane."

"Well, that's what I want to know," said Tina. "What's your relationship with Mr Mihelič?"

"What do you mean, relationship?"

Her astonishment seemed genuine and for the first time Tina recognized the wide vowels of Lower Carniola in her speech.

"You were registered in the same room at the hotel for three days. What would you call this relationship?"

"He's my patron," said the girl with relief, as if Tina's elaboration on the question genuinely helped her to the right answer. "He will sort my things out. I want to be a singer."

She smiled sweetly and Tina pictured the Mihelič she knew from the newspapers and TV, grey hair, styled in the fashion of God knows which era, combed back across his scalp, his skin full of grey patches and wrinkles, a double chin, always wearing a suit and tie, usually light grey with a blue tie. The image of a neat old man, but still an old man. She nodded so as not to betray what she was thinking.

"I think that in the long term I'd like to be a nursery school teacher. I'm studying, here at the Faculty of Education," she said and pointed behind her, probably in the direction of the faculty. "I'd like to work with children. They're so cute."

"And what kind of music do you sing?"

"Oh, I don't. I would like to. I don't mind what, something... Something along the lines of Modrijani or Jan Plestenjak[9], I'd like that. Do you like Plestenjak?"

"Yes, a lot," said Tina.

"Well, you see! I don't know any girl who doesn't. Which

9 pop musicians, Modrijani are a group, Jan Plestenjak is one of Slovenia's most sucessful pop-singers

song of his do you like? No, no, let me guess…"

She began singing and Tina had to admit that her voice wasn't bad.

"In room one-o-two, he stole my broken heart, in room one-o-two he set me apart…" she sang. "This one?"

"Indeed. And Mr Mihelič offered to arrange all that is necessary?"

"Yes, exactly."

"And how will you repay him for this help?"

"Oh, I won't repay him. I don't have any money, you see."

She giggled as if she had said something funny, picked up the biscuit that came with her cocoa, dipped it in, carried it to her mouth and bit off the tiniest possible piece.

"I would like to know," said Tina who was no longer embarrassed at all, "if in exchange you offered him sexual favours? I ask you to tell me the truth because we will also talk to him about it, and besides, anything you say is strictly confidential."

"Oh that," she cried out as if she had only just understood the question. She took another tiny bite of her biscuit. "Yes, well, yes."

"I see," said Tina.

"But not before I was eighteen. The first time we did it was in Bohinj. I didn't even know it, but Mr Mihelič said it was illegal before the age of eighteen."

"Not quite," said Tina.

"Isn't it?"

"No, it's illegal if the underage person is less than fifteen…"

"Really?"

"Or if the other person, the adult, is much older. Then it's eighteen. Like in your case."

The girl bit her biscuit again and, so it seemed, became engrossed in a brief deliberation,

"Well, then it's just as well we didn't do it before?"

"Yes."

She gave Tina the look of a child who had just found out that eating the biscuits out of the cupboard was not going to get her into trouble. Tina smiled and thought that she now knew why

Taras had sent her here. Her own world and that of this girl were so infinitely far apart.

"And you are fine with this?"

"I told you, I don't have any money. It doesn't cost me to give him a little love."

Love? She wanted to say, but bit her tongue. It's none of her business.

"OK, let's forget that," she said. "That's not what we called you for. Did you know that we found a body of a young woman in the lake, or rather in the river that flows from it…?"

"Really?"

"Yes."

Was it possible that she didn't know? Tina stayed silent, waiting for her to betray in some way that she knew something about it but there was nothing. She bit off the next piece of biscuit, swallowed it, smacking her lips slightly as she did so. Without wanting to, Tina thought of oral sex, those very tiny lips…

"I didn't know, I really didn't. Nobody mentioned it to me."

"It was in all the newspapers and on TV."

"You see, I don't watch TV at all," she said and when Tina gave her a querying look, she almost apologetically added, "I read books."

They discussed books for a few minutes and she mentioned writers Tina had never heard of.

"Romance novels," Barbara explained, blushing slightly.

And no, she had no idea who this girl could be, and yes, she was the only one in the hotel for those three days who wasn't part of the group from the Biotechnical Faculty.

"To be honest, I was slightly bored there," she said when Tina pulled out her wallet to settle the bill. "Brane was with them all day and even afterwards, you see…" she confidentially leaned towards Tina, trusting her, woman to woman, "…there wasn't much he could do." She raised her tiny fist, extended her little finger and wiggling it made it subside. "He didn't dare take those tablets. Blood pressure…"

*

Tina walked back to the bus stop on Prešeren Street. She

tried to think like a policewoman. Did the fact that the eighteen year old rolled around in bed with an old man have anything to do with the body in the water? How old is Mihelič? Sixty-five? More? He was no longer young even as the girl was born.

Her phone rang. She fished it out of her bag. Taras.

"Hi," he said. "Where are you?"

She explained that she had met the girl and was on her way back to the station.

"And?"

"Nothing," she said. Nothing that she thought might be useful. He didn't let her finish.

"Yes, I thought that would be the case. Can you check a number plate when you get to the office?"

She found a pen and noted it down.

"Whose car is this supposed to be?" she asked, but he had clearly already put the phone down but had forgotten to hang up. All she could hear was music. Was that Bon Jovi?

He was in a good mood even though there was no real reason for it.

"So we've ticked this one off as well," he tried to sing to the tune of *Bed of Roses*.

He waited for the song to finish, then he found the button for changing the radio stations below the steering wheel, pressed it a few times so from rock hits on the private radio station, he switched to the third programme of state radio, listened to a few notes of the classical music, enough to decide he didn't want it right now, and switched back to the rock hits. Just as Alice Cooper with *Poison* came on his phone rang and without looking at who was calling, and without lowering the volume, he pressed the button to accept the call.

"Yo ..."

"Taras..." came from the handsfree device. It was Alenka, her voice such that he was instantly sorry about the yo and playing Alice Cooper at full blast. "Have you heard?"

He switched off the music.

"Heard what?"

Whenever she called him with a voice like this, three, until now maybe four times, he worried something was wrong with their daughters.

He also always said to himself that if something was wrong with their daughters she would not begin the sentence with 'have you heard,' but it still didn't help.

"Heard what?" he repeated impatiently before she could actually have said anything.

"Prelc has had a stroke."

It wasn't nice, but he was relieved.

"Half an hour ago, while he was at work."

"Is it bad?" he asked.

"A brain haemorrhage. I called Balažič... Remember him? He's at the neurological department and didn't want to say much more than that things weren't looking good."

They hung up just before Trojane and Taras reckoned he had another twenty minutes drive and was still in a good mood. He increased the volume on the radio and someone was singing *Hot in the city, hot in the city tonight*... which was strangely in contrast with the snowy landscape through which he was travelling.

Chapter 22.

When Brajc and Osterc walked into the office, Taras and Tina were both at Tina's computer... In fact Tina was sitting at the computer, typing away, and Taras was looking at the screen over her shoulder. Osterc who was the first to come in just caught Taras saying,

"...not a money collector. Tell her to come here."

Tina typed something and pressed the send button. They didn't have to wait long for a response.

Taras nodded and Tina wrote something else and they both waited. Only when the new response came, and was clearly satisfactory, did Taras turn to his colleagues,

"Hello."

When Taras had arrived back at the office Tina was not there. There was a piece of paper on his desk with the Ljubljana car registration number he had asked her to check and under it, in letters so small that Taras had to hold it as far away as his arm could stretch in order to read it, the name, Iva Paska. A funny surname he thought and just as he placed the paper back on the desk, Tina walked through the door, drying her hands with a paper towel.

"Hi," she said.

He returned the greeting and lifted the piece of paper again.

"Yes, I called her home address and couldn't find her, then her mobile, and I kept getting the message that the number is not available, then I called her work..." she shuffled some papers on the desk, "in Hyrdotechnica, a water management company in Ljubljana, where..."

"You didn't find her," said Taras.

"No, she wasn't there," Tina nodded. "They did, once I used

your tactics, give me her mail and said she was on holiday in Thailand and was in fact on her way back from there, and they were expecting her back at work tomorrow."

"My tactics?"

"I was rude," she said, "and, if I remember correctly, threatened them with some kind of inspection."

"Clever girl," he muttered and he thought she blushed, but he could not check because she sat at the computer and typed something on the keyboard.

"I sent her a message five minutes ago…"

"And there was no answer, of course."

"Well, in fact…"

Taras jumped to her chair and looked over her shoulder. The screen in front of Tina said,

"@ Frankfurt Airport, on way back from holiday today. Is it urgent?"

Taras sighed and Tina looked at him with surprise.

"She should have been dead," he explained. "This, what's she called…"

"Iva Paska?"

"Whatever… I thought she was our Jane Doe."

He fell silent and paused, his hand on the back of Tina's chair.

"What should I tell her?"

"That I'm sorry she's alive."

She looked at him over her shoulder.

"Tell her," he said slowly, "That we need to urgently talk to her. Tomorrow morning at eight, let's say…"

"At her home, at work?"

"No, I've had enough of this. I'm a police officer investigating a murder, not a money collector. Tell her to come here."

Friday was not the right day for visiting Simona Natek, Head of Social Services in Jesenice. Not because she didn't have office hours on Friday but because she was overwhelmed with work. We deal with people from birth to the grave, she would sometimes say when people asked her what social workers actually do, and as if this was not a long enough period, the social services departments had recently also been made responsible for sorting out funeral expenses on behalf of the state. This meant that even the dead were now coming to them from beyond the grave, through their relatives who came to collect money for their funerals. This was on top of all the problems they had with child and family protection, mental health of the socially most disadvantaged population, and their financial problems which were often the cause of their mental health problems in the first place.

Jesenice was, as far as her work was concerned, a very unique place. The area her department covered reached from Žirovnica all the way to the Austrian and Italian borders. Their coordinator of community treatment – an euphemism for handling mental health problems – covered an even wider area that in other aspects came under the social services departments of Radovljica and Tržič. Jesenice was a unique place, firstly because of its steelworks, which brought in people from less developed areas of the former Yugoslavia in order to cover its workforce needs and did not care what would happen with these people at the end of their working lives and whose burden they would become. The factory was so large and needed so many workers, that today the original inhabitants of the town, locals with roots in the area, represent barely a third of the population. And when, within a generation or two, the newcomers became settled into the community, new foreigners began to arrive, migrants from Kosovo, Albania, Macedonia... Because of these people, many of whom spoke only Albanian, a part-time interpreter in charge of communicating with them had to be employed at the Centre. At this rate, the Head had said at the last board meeting, the interpreter's position would soon become a full-time permanent post.

"At least something useful from all this," she said to everyone at the meeting, all of them women, in her office on the second floor of a reddish-brown building which the Ministry had recently bought from the Ironworks.

She was not pessimistic by nature but she sometimes couldn't help it as she sat at her desk unsure where to begin. Problems with retired factory workers who had to live off a miserly pension and often have to support other members of their family, or the programme for the quality parenting group, which was one of seventeen they organized on top of their regular work. From a group aiding the integration of foreign women, to a group providing free bread and a warm meal for the most needy, usually elderly men without any relatives...

She sighed and decided that dysfunctional families had priority this time. Families who find it difficult to raise their children, don't know how to deal with money, do not posses basic social skills and will have to be taught all these things. Then the phone rang. She would not have been happy about the call, regardless of who it would be.

"They say they're from the police," said the girl from reception.

"Did you ask them what this was about?"

"They say they need to speak to you personally."

She sighed once more and told the receptionist to send them up. What could this be about? She could not think of anything specific although there were of course endless possibilities; visits from the police were common.

"Good morning Mrs Natek," said Brajc.

"Good morning," she said reservedly. Had she not been told they were policemen, she would have thought that he was one of her clients, one of those from the lone elderly men category.

"Good morning," Osterc also greeted her.

"May we take a seat?" Brajc asked as he looked around the office.

She pointed to a table with two chairs. The investigators sat at the table, she stayed at her desk.

"Of course, you must want to know, what this is about?" Brajc asked and when there was no response, he, slightly agitated, began telling the story anyway.

"...and we thought we could ask the Social Services Centre which covers that area..."

"We don't cover it," she said.

"How come? Who does?"

"Radovljica. Radovljica is responsible for Bohinj."

"Radovljica?"

She nodded.

Cursing Taras in his mind, Brajc looked at Osterc who

shrugged his shoulders. Who's responsible for Bohinj? Jesenice? He stood up and made his way to the door. Osterc reluctantly rose and remained at the table, as if he was uncertain whether to follow him or not. Brajc was already holding the door handle when he turned round to say goodbye, surprised to see that Osterc was not following him.

"So this means," said Osterc, looking alternately at Brajc and the Head, "that you can't help us at all?"

She smiled. If there was one thing she had learnt in her work it was to keep her cool. People came to her with unsolvable problems and still expected, even demanded, that they solved them. Everyone lost their nerve, cried, pleaded, threatened... not her.

"That is not what I said, Inspector," and Brajc noted that she had called Osterc Inspector whereas she hadn't called him anything. "All I said is that Radovljica covers Bohinj, not Jesenice."

She looked at Brajc.

"Are you going to take a seat?"

"I thought I was going to knock the bloody woman's head off, but somehow I managed to hold back," Brajc said. "And then she tells us that she had a case at some point at the end of the eighties, which she worked on personally. And that some woman rushed into the hospital in Jesenice at the last minute, gave birth, and disappeared the following morning."

"Disappeared?"

"Yes, disappeared into the mist. She had registered in what proved to be a non-existent name and she just picked up her stuff and left."

"And the child?"

"Children. There were two. Twins. A boy and a girl. The boy didn't survive, the girl was put up for adoption."

Taras scratched his head.

"Did you..."

"Of course we did. She was adopted by an elderly couple, both of whom died last year. A straight forward death, nothing suspicious, and after that..."

"...the girl visited the Centre," the Head had told them. "We keep track of our children, you know, and usually these children have a good relationship with us, even if they move to other parts of the country, they still turn to us when they need advice or assistance. I think that we social workers are important people in their lives."

"That was the last time you saw her?" Osterc asked. She nodded.

"And when was that?"

"At some point in early autumn. End of September, I think."

"We got her address, her phone number, called her, visited her in Koroška Bela, right next to Jesenice... and nothing."

Taras waited patiently for Brajc to finish.

"The parents' house, the adoptive parents' house has been sold. The guy we spoke to told us he had bought it from a young woman who said she was going abroad."

"And does this woman, this girl, have a name?"

"Of course. Ana Zvonar. Zvonar from her adoptive parents."

"And where is this Ana now?"

Brajc laughed.

"You see, this we don't know. We know she worked at the nursery school in Jesenice where she was a teacher and handed in her notice last September. We also know she was the quiet kind and that when she visited the Social Services Centre she asked the Head there about her birth parents... Of course she was unable to help her."

"And her phone?"

"A non-existent number."

Taras tapped on the desk in front of the keyboard, then moved his hand to his head and continued to tap in rhythm, indeterminate at first, but which after a second or two did sound like some well-known tune in the making, though it was still not enough for anyone to guess which one.

"Check her in the register," he said eventually.

"And as far as what you asked us to check out," Brajc continued, "point one, you were right, the car is still there and is still covered in snow..."

"I wasn't right," said Taras.

"But how, if it is still...?"

"OK, forget it. Point two?"

"Yes, we went to the hotel... what was it again?"

"Jezero," Taras helped him.

"Yes. And there we checked for the guy from reception and the cleaning lady. The cleaning lady didn't have a clue. She kept repeating that she only cleans there and for a pittance as well..."

"And?"

"Well, the receptionist was a different story. Here..."

He flicked through his notebook.

"What did the receptionist say?" Taras asked.

"Getting there... He says he noticed this microbiologist, this boss of theirs or whoever he is..."

"The Dean?" Tina asked.

"That's the one. He saw him in the morning, the day before he went on holiday, that was on the twenty-second of December, talking to a young woman who was not from the hotel, but he, the receptionist, thought that she looked familiar."

"How familiar? As a guest, as a local, or what?"

"He didn't know. I asked him the same thing and he said she looked strangely familiar. That was the word he used. He wasn't sure where he knew her from. And I asked him whether he had seen her before, perhaps as a skier, a regular guest, a whore, anything, but he didn't know. All he knew was that she looked familiar. And, you know what Taras...?"

"I know. She corresponds, in as much as she can correspond, to the girl we have on ice."

"How do you know?"

Taras didn't answer. He stepped to his desk and drummed his fingers on it.

"Finally," he said and pulled out his notebook, checked through it until he found what he was looking for, picked up the phone on his desk and dialled the number. It rang for a while before anyone answered it.

"Biotechnical Faculty, this is the Dean's office, how can I help you," came from the end of the line, almost as if uttered by a machine.

Taras explained who he was and stressed the 'Senior Criminal Investigator' part, but it seemed to make little impression on the lady at the end of the line.

"He's not here," she said.

"He has to be," said Taras. "This is a murder investigation with which he may be able to help us. Where is he?"

"At his weekend house in Bala," the voice at the other end said, with slight embarrassment this time. "He will stay there until Sunday because he's working on a project for which he needs peace and quiet. He goes there when he needs to work. I can give you his mobile phone..."

"Yes?"

"...but there's no signal where he is. I'll give it to you anyway and perhaps you'll be lucky if the Dean happens to pop into Bovec or somewhere closer to the valley."

The secretary gave him the number and Taras also asked her for the address of the weekend house which she gave him. He dialled the number as soon as he hung up.

"The number you have dialled is currently unavailable..."

He looked at Brajc and then Osterc who froze,

"Taras, I need to collect my kid from school. Don't drop this on me right now..." he squeaked.

Brajc didn't say anything. There was no need. Taras understood even without this. He had had a couple of drinks in Jesenice, and no clever boss would send him on a journey in his state.

"Surely you weren't thinking of today?" he asked relaxedly as if Osterc had already dealt with the matter.

He turned towards Tina who smiled and pointed at herself. She might not be a true beauty, or at least a true beauty at first sight, but she had a nice smile. Not just her smile. She is one of those women, he thought, who you overlook when there are two dolls in hotpants at the next table, but when they leave and she's the only one left in the room, you realize that she outshines them in every aspect. Perhaps it's that, perhaps it's also that these are not things he sees. Drvarič and both his asexual colleagues put her in the beauty compartment, in fact rocket compartment, as soon as they met her.

"Yes, Taras?" she asked and it didn't sound at all like Brajc's 'surely you weren't...'

"Do you like the unspoilt nature of our most beautiful alpine valley?"

"Are you inviting me on a trip to… Where in fact?" said Tina.

He checked the time on his phone and nodded.

"To Bala. Yes, but not today. Today I have something I'd avoid if only I could. Tomorrow, when we've finished with our…" he looked at the paper on the desk, "… LJ OB-073, then we take a trip to Trenta, OK?"

"Right," she said and of course Brajc began going on about how he always had to go out in the field with Osterc, only him, always him and never anyone younger – as if there were more of them and as if there had been others before Tina. Taras looked at Tina who shrugged her shoulders.

Chapter 23.

He was reluctant to step into the room. He was not afraid of the dead, but the suffering of the living got to him. When he was still a boy, the family that looked after him took him to see an aunt who wasn't his aunt, they just called her that. She had had a stroke. The old woman lay in bed and the only thing she could move were her lips, even those silently. He could only assume that she was praying, her eyes wide open, full of the silent dread of a person who wants everything to be over the soonest possible. There was nothing to show that the people around her bed were making it any easier or whether they, all still able to move and talk, were simply causing her further distress. "I beg you, fulfil my prayer..." he heard those mute lips say and even though forty years have passed since then, they were still vivid in his memory.

If Prelc had been lying there dead, he would have to make an effort to show compassion and sadness on his face. This was nothing to do with Alenka, whether he had anything with her or not. He just didn't fit into some circle of people without which he could not live – there were only three in that group. He would cry over them, not for Prelc. He was not a member of his pack, had never been at the other end of the rope or shared a tent with him, torn apart by hurricane winds at minus ten degrees, threatening to be thrown five thousand metres down into the Kali Gandaki.

The first thing he saw when he opened the door was Prelc's wife. Karin, if he remembered correctly. He stepped silently into the room, closed the door behind him and discretely cleared his throat. She turned around, saw him and smiled, or rather tried to smile. Her face had mascara running where her tears had melted it away and when she smiled it was a grotesque mask.

He reciprocated with a smile and when he stepped closer he saw that she was holding with both hands her husband's limp, motionless hand. He looked as if he was asleep, not asleep, but dead. She then let go of it, stood up and gave Taras a hug. Taras patted her back, slightly embarrassed as one is when hugged by a woman he had only ever met once before, whatever the circumstances.

When he looked over her shoulder, he saw Prelc's face, so different from the face he had last seen that he almost didn't recognize him. The healthy Prelc had been tanned, full of energy, an old playboy with light grey, almost white, and for his age still surprisingly abundant hair, the one here in front of him was ash grey, as if all the blood had drained from his body, so grey there was almost no difference between skin and the hair that now seemed crumpled and creased, stuck to his skull. The worst thing was that in the middle of this face which could well belong to a corpse, was a pair of eyes which were lively, lively as always, even more so for being caught in the dead body surrounding them. They followed Taras when he patted Karin on the shoulder and she cried,

"Did you see, Taras, did you see?"

That was all she kept repeating,

"Did you see, did you see...?"

When she eventually let go of him and collapsed into the chair, he was left standing there and realized that it would have almost been better if she hadn't. Standing next to the bed, he didn't know what to do. If he looked at Prelc's face he met his ghastly eyes, if he looked away, he was instantly embarrassed.

"How bad is it?" he asked and received more sobbing in reply.

"Silly question, yes, I can see..."

Karin found some paper tissues on the table next to the bed, pulled one out of the plastic packet and wiped her eyes, smearing her mascara further. He did not know whether to tell her or not.

"They don't know," she said. "They say they don't know yet. That it's too early. Either they don't know, or they don't want to tell. That's what doctors are like."

Taras managed to control himself and was now looking into

the sick man's eyes. Prelc could not move his eyelids, at least that's what Taras assumed, as they seemed to be open all the time and there was a bottle of eye drops on the table next to the bed that Karin had clearly forgotten about.

"Are those his eye drops...?"

"Yes, yes..." she said and picked up the solution to moisten his eyes.

His eyelids didn't move.

"This isn't right," Karin complained. "This isn't right... for forty years I waited, all...

all my life, that he would... and this isn't right... why did it happen to him... all my life..."

It was stuffy in the room. The smell of medication mixed with the stench of bodily excretions, sweat and urine. Being winter, the only window was closed, of course.

"Alenka said she was coming," said Taras when she had stopped. "In fact I don't know why she isn't here yet. We were supposed to come together, then, you know, she had to arrange things at the clinic, now that... Well, you know..."

He fell silent and Karin didn't say anything either. He stood by the bed looking the motionless Prelc into the eyes that stared back at him. Only a few days ago they had sat on the terrace, Prelc smoking a joint and talking about his bedroom successes and still being alive. He could walk, run, talk, and wipe his own arse... He could drink wine which Taras couldn't. And now – none of this. And Taras didn't need a doctor to explain that he never would again. Can he think? Is he watching him at this moment and feels terrible because he sees from his face how hopeless it all is? Can a person who is unable to control even his eyelids think about these things? Does he wish that Taras, like in some film, would pull out his Beretta from an inside jacket pocket and fire a mercy shot in the head?

Karin sat holding his hand between her palms and every so often dripped water into his eyes. Time dragged on and when Alenka finally stepped into the room, Taras was exhausted as if he had... In fact he could not compare it to anything.

The women hugged and all the sobbing and groaning repeated itself, so similar to before that Taras unwittingly wondered whether her sadness was an act, and as soon as he thought it felt guilty for doing so. Alenka began crying as soon as she walked in and a continuous stream of tears rolled across her cheek and dripped to the floor. And however sad and painful the meeting of the desperate women was, it brought some relief to Taras. Like the protagonist in a play when for a moment a minor character takes the spotlight off him, enabling him to rest in the shadows at the edge of the stage before a new performance. Then he looked at Prelc and winced.

His eyes... His eyes were gazing straight at him, so it seemed, with an unhuman exertion they stared straight at Taras. Droplets of sweat appeared on his forehead and the motionless surface of the skin on his face seemed to tighten, as if the muscles beneath were trying to find a connection with the brain and ran out of steam just before they found it. Taras leaned over him while Karin continued to sob and Alenka patted her on her shoulders and back, saying,

"It'll be alright, Karin, it'll be alright..."

She produced some tissues from her handbag and mopped the tears on the broken woman's face, though she didn't look much better herself.

Taras held Prelc's hand and stroked it...

"How're things, old man?" he said gently and quietly so that only Prelc could hear him if indeed he could hear at all. He leaned across him as if expecting a whispering response...

"Glllhhh..." came from Prelc's mouth, a kind of "glllhhh"... and Taras reflexively jumped away.

"Did you hear that?" he asked although he didn't have to. Karin jumped past him, pushed him out of the way and embraced her husband round the neck.

"Rajko! What was that? What are you saying?"

She embraced him so forcefully, shaking his head so hard that Taras worried she might cause him harm. It was as if she was trying to shake the words out of him.

"Tell me, tell me..." she kept repeating deliriously and Taras tapped her lightly on the shoulder.

"Karin, gently, gently..."

Alenka stood behind her and was now no longer the

distraught friend but a doctor. Taras knew this sudden transformation and the nicest thing about her was that it didn't make the previous Alenka seem any less sincere. She beckoned to him and stepped back a little.

"What happened?"

"He said something, or rather tried to say something."

"Are you sure?"

He nodded.

"I'll go and find the doctor," she said and with her finger and lips, without a sound coming from them, indicated he should keep an eye on Karin.

She needn't have done so. When she left Taras turned around and Karin was once more sitting calmly at the bedside, holding her husband's hand, just as she had been when he entered the room. And Prelc lay motionless, just as his face was motionless. Whatever it was he wanted to say... The wires just didn't connect.

"How is he?" Alenka asked when Balažič came out of the room.

Balažič, fat old Balažič, whose wife was the only one Prelc hadn't been with, if he was to be believed, shook his head. When Alenka brought him into the room he encouragingly nodded at Taras and if Taras had to choose a doctor whom he found most agreeable among those at the New Year's Eve party, he would have chosen him.

"Milan, tell us," Alenka said. "You didn't study seven years just to shake your head."

Balažič sighed and began talking, hiding behind medical mumbo jumbo. Taras didn't understand half of it, but knew that it didn't bear well.

"Intercerebral bleeding..." he said. "...hypertension... aneurysm... thalamus.... Vascular malformation..." or something like that, "...vascular fistula..."

When he finished he seemed exhausted. Both he and Alenka seemed exhausted. They stayed silent for a while, then Balažič spoke again, looking at Taras,

"Whatever it was that he wanted to say, you were the last person to hear his voice."

"He won't be able to talk any more or...?"

"Prelc is dead," said Alenka. "Today, tomorrow, in a year's time..."

She was crying again.

Balažič nodded and sighed,

"More likely tomorrow than in a year's time. And to be honest if anything similar happened to me, I'd just beg for it to finish me off. I wouldn't wish upon anyone what has happened to poor Rajko."

He patted Alenka on the back, shook Taras' hand and began walking down the corridor before turning round a few steps later,

"I know, Inspector, that this isn't really the right moment... But have you found out who killed that woman?"

"No," said Taras.

"Well, good luck."

They collapsed into the seats in the hospital corridor and a few seconds later, after Balažič's steps died down, all that could be heard was Alenka's sobbing and sniffling. Taras waited for her to stop and offered her a paper tissue.

"Your makeup is all smudged round the eyes."

Gratefully she took it and wiped away as much of the running make-up as she could.

"About that skiing trip, we'll have to..." she began.

"It's fine, I understand," said Taras.

"No, we won't cancel it. We will go this year, no matter what. We can just shorten it, right?"

He nodded. At least that.

"Do you know where it happened?" he asked.

"At work apparently. I don't know, in his office or somewhere... I don't know."

"I didn't understand what Balažič was saying. Why did it happen?"

She sighed. She was back in control.

"They don't know. A ruptured artery. Why? A thousand reasons."

She stood up and looked at him.

"Let's go and say goodbye to Karin?"

Chapter 24.

Monday, 8 January

Taras skipped browsing the newspapers and typed up the report on his meeting with Mihelič. He summarized his long explanation into a few sentences, printed it out and re-read what he had written, then sat for a while behind the desk, massaging his forehead and the edge of his scalp with his fingers. This was how Tina found him just before half past seven.

"And what do the little grey cells say today?" she asked in place of a greeting.

"Have you been reading Agatha Christie?" Taras asked instead of an answer.

"I have read all of them. From Agatha to these modern Scandinavians, Jo Nesbø and the likes of."

"And?"

"What, what I liked best?"

Taras nodded.

She furrowed her brow, moved her head left and right, trying to decide…

"What I think is the best, or what I like most?"

"Like."

"Nesbø," she said and immediately explained. "Yes, I know, this Harry of his, or whatever he's called, is superman, incredibly dedicated to his work, and at the same time an alcoholic who manages to bed every one of his female police assistants or at least make them fall in love with him…Why are you smiling?"

"I'm not," said Taras and really wasn't.

"Well, basically, if I had to choose a crime novel to take on holiday, I'd take him. Besides, his books are much fatter than Agatha Christie's. It can be pretty boring on the beach sometimes. And you, have your read them?"

"I did read some Agatha Christie in my time, and my little grey cells are telling me that our balloon has fortunately begun inflating and will have to burst sooner or later."

She gave him a puzzled look.

"I mean our case."

Iva Praska was on time, in fact the porter called Tina in the office at around two minutes before eight. She went to find her and returned in the company of a dark haired, tanned, slightly overweight woman in her mid thirties. Taras greeted her, shook her hand and offered her a chair at his desk. She sat down, crossed her legs and looked at Taras with an expectant unease.

"You don't know why you're here?" Taras asked.

She shook her head and, in case this was not enough, added after a considerable pause,

"No, I don't. I really don't."

"Are you the owner of the vehicle with the registration number..." he read it from his notes.

"No," she said and after a while remembered to shake her head.

"What do you mean no?"

"Well... I'm not... I mean, I am no longer, and I thought that had all been sorted out, but I'm afraid, as I see... What has he done now?"

"Let's slow down," said Taras as it seemed she was about to burst into tears. "Nice and slowly, tell me what this is about. Nobody has done anything, we just found a car, abandoned, with a number plate which is registered in your name. That's all."

He managed to calm her, or at least that was what it looked like for a second or two, then, almost in an instant, her fear was replaced by anger.

"Fucking bas...! I'm sorry."

She had had a boyfriend who moved in with her a month after they started seeing each other and for a while all was fine, then one fine day the police knocked on her door with a warrant to search her flat. They had found drugs in their, her bedroom, in the cupboard he had chosen for himself. Heroin, cocaine, marihuana, various kinds of pills… everything. She had had to go to the police station with him where they questioned her, but not in an ordinary office, in a special room. They noted everything, kept her in for twenty-four hours and only released her when a lawyer her mother had arranged for her appeared.

"Do you know how they stared at me at work? Even now I can hear them whisper behind my back as I walk down the corridor, 'there goes the drug princess.' But I knew nothing, really absolutely nothing about it. I also didn't tell anyone I had to call in at the police station today. Everyone thinks I'm at home with the flu."

It took half a year and fortunately ended with the boyfriend getting a conviction, a conditional sentence, apparently, and the case against her was dropped due to lack of evidence. She demanded that he moved out, he left but took the car they had supposedly bought jointly during their relationship.

"It wasn't even true. It was mine, I bought it, but Mother said, let him have it, as long as he leaves."

"And when was that?"

"Oh, it must be… almost a year now. In February I would need to get the road tax renewed."

She burst into tears and Taras hoped it wasn't about the car.

"What has he done again?"

Tina offered her a handkerchief and she took it.

"Do you know who your then boyfriend was distributing drugs for?"

She shook her head.

"And what he might be doing in Bohinj?"

The same reaction.

They released her at half past eight and when Tina escorted her to the front door, she had to reassure her three times that, despite the car being registered in her name, she would not be in trouble, whatever her former boyfriend who was called Robi Lap had done. When she returned to the office, Taras was on the phone.

At nine they were in the police Skoda and drove out of Ljubljana towards Upper Carniola.

"Are we going across Vršič?" Tina asked.

"Across Predel. There's snow on Vršič and I can't be bothered to plough through it with snow chains.

It was a sunny day and Taras imagined how nice it would be on Pokljuka or even better in Tamar, which he preferred when it came to cross-country ski runs. On Pokljuka the track went through a forest of thick fir trees. They were beautiful enough, but ten kilometres of just fir trees...

It could be worse. In two hours time he will have an answer, the name of the body that has been lying in refrigeration at the Institute for Forensic Medicine for ten days and all they know about it is that it is that of a woman, around thirty years old, and nothing else. In fact he was not even sure why he thought that the conversation he was hoping to have would give him the answer. After all, it could have been some chance acquaintance who Hleb briefly met at the hotel and did not think worth mentioning simply because she was still alive and well, but... Someone must have seen something and there had been too many coincidences in this story already and something told him that today was about time that the ball began to unravel. Or was it just a wish? Frustration that, despite the mountain of notes which he had had to compile, he still had nothing specific to go by. Because he had a new colleague on the team who had learnt about him at university, and now this.

"What is this Lap's involvement in all this?"

"I don't know. And because I don't know and we still have nothing concrete to deal with, no track, no suspect, no motive, we're looking for curves, things that deviate from what they should be like. The car of a small-time drug dealer from Ljubljana some ninety kilometres from his usual field of activity is one such point. Where is he and why has he left the car behind?"

Would he talk to Brajc and Osterc about graphs, curves and points? Of course he wouldn't. Nor would he mention it to just any apprentice.

"Who did you call?"

"A colleague from the narcotics department. I wanted to find out who he worked for."

The ski slopes in Kranjska Gora were, judging by the numerous dots moving down the hillside, very full. Taras tried to remember whether it was the winter break time for primary schools, but decided it was too close to the New Year for that.

"Do you ski?" he asked.

"Yes, of course," she said.

*

They drove past Rateče and the former border post with Italy and just before Tarvisio turned towards Sella Nevea and Predel.

"I've never come to Trenta across this way," Tina said when they drove past the abandoned border posts, first on the Slovenian side, then the Italian. Taras still remembered the days when one would have to show a passport every time. "Have you?"

"Yes."

As a mountaineer he must have driven the road across Predel in his old Renault 5 at least a hundred times. Daytime, night-time, on his way there trying to wake up, on the way back trying not to fall asleep with exhaustion, when sometimes only the thought of a beer at the first petrol station, back in Jesenice, was what kept him awake. That ended when the Restrictions on the Use of Alcohol Act came into force and the refrigerators containing beer were covered over with a kind of tarpaulin cover at nine o'clock when Taras and whoever happened to be with him were still on their descent from the southern slopes of the mountain. If he was lucky. Then he had to swig on some cheap Red Bull imitation all the way to Ljubljana.

They drove past Cave del Predil, an abandoned Italian mining town which, over the last decades after the closure of the mine, has attempted to recover, and four bends later up Predel from where the road drops steeply into Log pod Mangartom, all the time driving under the majestic rock face of one of the least known precipices in Slovenia.

"I've never been here before," Tina said. "I didn't even know it existed."

She didn't say what she was thinking. About the rock face on the other side of the narrow valley, the road or everything together.

"Did you know that it was here, above Strmec, that they

filmed one of the Kekec films?" Taras asked and wondered if she even knew who Kekec was[10].

"Really, I thought it was supposed to be happening around Vršič or somewhere above Kranjska Gora."

"Yes, the stories are set there, and some of the films were filmed there too, but they used this area in the second film."

They drove through the village of Log pod Mangartom, past the inn where Taras used to celebrate his victories, and try to find solace for his failures or would just spend a rainy day. Now there was a sign hanging on the door with large letters announcing the place was CLOSED, and it looked as if nobody had served anyone there for a long time. They continued down the road to the Austro-Hungarian fortress Kluže at the confluence of the Koritnica and Bavščica streams where Taras turned left onto a narrow asphalt road under the rocky face of the eastern edge of Loška Stena, drove towards their destination, the closed, true back of beyond Bala, forgotten by God, but not by weekend house owners. He drove to the corner where a decade or so a large portion of rock had fallen from a hundred-metre face above and its largest piece, a massive rectangular slab, landed right next to the road. In the cliff above you could still see a pale yellow wound where it broke off.

"When this came tumbling down I was close to here," said Taras and he had barely finished the sentence when a dark green Hyundai urban 4x4 came speeding round the corner and Taras was only able to avoid it by turning right and crashing with the nose of his car into the wall of snow left by the snowplough, getting stuck in it. He swore and looked across his shoulder. The green Hyundai was already gone.

"Did you see the number plate?"

"Only enough to see it was a Gorica number," Tina said. "When he appeared I was looking up at the rocks."

Taras got his phone and tried to call the operative communication centre and send them after the dark green

10 Kekec is a fictional character created by Josip Vandot. He is a brave young boy who has adventures in the mountains above Kranjska Gora and is something of a cultural icon in Slovenia. Jože Gale made three films based on the character (1951,1963 & 1968) The second film, *Good Luck, Kekec,* was largely filmed in the Bovec area.

Hyundai, but there was no signal. He reached for the police communication radio and switched it on but only got a crackling sound in response.

"Well, great!" he said and got out of the car to check the front wheels. They had dug a deep channel into the soft pile of snow. He swore again and kicked the tyre. He would probably have continued doing so had Tina not stepped out of the car and come to see the damage for herself.

It took him half an hour to break off enough branches from the bushes by the road, place them under the wheels and with a slipping clutch that stank terribly, finally get the car back on the road. Two hairpin bends later, they drove through forest into a clearing, and what was for this area an unusually wide and straight valley opened up before them. Taras checked for the signal on his phone again, thought about calling in about that Hyundai for a moment, dismissively waved his hand and put the phone away again.

"He's probably miles away by now."

They drove along slowly, looking out for the signs at the edge that pointed to the side, usually to the right, where the road widened.

"There it is," he said and was not surprised that the road to the weekend house was cleared just as well as the one they had come on. They parked by a huge white Toyota and Taras was about to comment on how some people are doing well for themselves, but then remembered he had recently fallen into that same category.

They stepped out of the car, Tina immediately put on her coat. Taras in his jumper set off for the house which was nothing like the size of a hut he had expected but a former farmhouse with a satellite dish on the roof.

Even without it, it would be obvious that the renovated and neat building no longer functioned for its original purpose. They probably pulled down the old building and built a new one in its place based on the original plan. There were too many straight, right angled and parallel lines, too much symmetry for it to be of any venerable age. He stepped to the front door, surprised to find it was not even closed properly, and knocked.

Nothing.

He knocked harder and when there was no response, stepped into the hallway that looked nothing like the outside of the house. This, however, was not what caught Taras' attention. There was a smell inside which was familiar to Taras. He beckoned to Tina to move away and he went out of the house, ran to the car, opened the glove compartment and took out his gun.

"Wait until I call you!" he whispered to Tina.

The hallway led through a half-open door into a lighter larger space, converted into a living room where the fire in the fireplace was dying down. Taras hesitantly stepped in and stopped. He tried not to start coughing when the smell of gunpowder filled his lungs. He noticed Tina in the doorway behind him and raised his palm to show her to stop and wait there. Why did she not listen in the first place?

Cautiously he turned round the large sofa which partially obscured the view towards the fireplace and there, between the sofa and the hearth, he saw the body of a man lying on his back. He was probably the Dean of the Biotechnical Faculty in Ljubljana, Professor Hleb, whose students' lucky mistakes might have meant that he would have soon been all over the media. Now he will still get his five minutes, Taras thought.

The body lay straight with its hands down at the side and the blood on the white carpet seemed to be fresh, as if it had only just stopped flowing from the wound. He could only assume that the man on the carpet was Hleb in as much as he remembered him from the photographs of the faculty web site, but he could not be entirely certain. The bullet which must have hit him in the back of the head and exited somewhere at the height of the eyes had left the face in a mess.

So much for the balloon which would imminently burst.

Chapter 25.

Taras beckoned to Tina to come closer and was already dialling the number of the head office in Ljubljana. There was no signal inside the house so he had to go right out to the road where the signal was still weak but enough for him to order police patrols to stop a dark green Hyundai 4x4 with Gorica number plates which could be driving from Rateče towards Ljubljana or from Bovec down the Soča valley and added they should take precautions because the driver is suspected of murder and is armed.

"Have we clearly understood each other?" he repeated. "Particularly this last point?"

"Armed, you said?"

"With one of the highest calibres available."

Then he returned to the house and the room with the murdered man. Tina stood there looking pale. She stared at the body as if she could not take her eyes off it even though the sight of it was shocking.

"Go out to get some air," he told her but she just stood there as if she hadn't heard him.

The shot had taken off all of Hleb's lower brow facially, together with the eyes and nose. One of the eyes was missing entirely, imploded by the shot, the other hung on a thread of nerve from the remaining corner of the right eye. The hole in the middle was oozing the grey-white tissue of the brain mixed with blood. The metallic smell of blood mixed with the stench of gunpowder and burnt flesh.

"Taras, I don't know if I will..." she said, grabbed her mouth and ran outside.

Taras never threw up. Not because of things like this.

He checked the house. The living room connected to the kitchen which was also the dining area, one door led onto a small corridor off which was a bathroom and slightly further along a staircase leading to the upper level. The attic was converted into a separate flat with a small bathroom of its own and a large space with a double bed and a work area with a desk where the laptop computer was still switched on, but when Taras used the tip of his ballpoint pen to touch the keyboard, it requested a password. He returned to the ground floor. Tina was clearly still outside.

He crouched down next to the body to take a closer look. Apart from the blood around his head, there were no other traces of blood in the room, on the furniture, walls or even on the floor outside this pool. It seems, Taras thought, that the killer forced him to kneel down or even more likely lie down on the floor and then shot him through the head at point blank range. And since the bullet had entered the head from the back, he must have also turned the body over after shooting him. Why? Did he want to make sure he was really dead? Take pride in the deed? Taras touched the wrist. It was still soft, still almost warm.

Tina was sitting in the driver's seat of their car with her legs outside on the thin layer of snow which had not been cleared from the asphalt, her elbows on her knees, holding her head in her hands. She was breathing shallowly.

"I'm sorry..." she whispered, trying not to throw up again.

Taras took his phone from his pocket again and walked to the road to call Golob at National Forensics.

"What's up?" Golob asked.

"Another body, this time shot at close range. Still warm. It must have happened about an hour ago."

"Where?" Golob asked and it took Taras a while to explain how to get to Bavščica and when Golob had almost understood, Taras stopped,

"Tell you what. Take your team to Brnik Airport and demand a helicopter. This can't wait for two hours."

When he returned Tina was standing up. Still pale, but at least she could stand without support.

"Once again, I'm sorry..." she began but he stopped her. He

went to the back of the car and found a pair of latex gloves in the case he kept there.

"Here... along the corridor and up the stairs you'll reach the attic. That's where his computer is. Can you take a look?"

She nodded gratefully and when she disappeared into the house, Taras sat in the same seat she had sat in, only that he placed his legs under the steering wheel, lowered the seat into a lounge position and lay down. Two minutes, just that, two minutes to compose himself.

"It needs a password..." said Tina when she returned and Taras nodded impatiently. "I can break it but not here with what I have. Well, I don't have anything anyway..."

She appeared much better. Her face was no longer colourless and she was breathing normally. She even smiled slightly at the last sentence.

"If we get a chance," Taras said.

She gave him a confused look.

"This is now our second body and we still don't even know who the first one is. Tomorrow morning at nine o'clock I will be in Drvarič's office and if, as I assume they will, they'll put pressure on him from above because they will fear a media outrage, this will..." he pointed to the house, "and the one back home on ice, will all get passed on to the GPD. That's why I want you to check the computer now. Can you do it without anything disappearing in this digital void?"

"Yes, indeed... But..." she began and stopped.

"But what?"

"Have we done anything wrong?"

"No, but sometimes that's not enough."

"Aren't you considered to be the best criminal investigator in the country?"

She was clearly much better.

"That was how Drvarič talked about you. 'Well, dear young colleague, I'll send you to Taras, he's the best we have...' he had said."

"Even so," said Taras. "That was before. There are a number of poor sods in Ljubljana waiting for me to fail."

He unplugged the computer and handed it to Tina.

"Can you check tonight?"

"Yes."

"And make a copy. Of everything it has on it. OK?"

She nodded.

Golob with his assistants came, or rather flew in two hours later. In the meantime Taras checked outside the house where there were no tracks at all, fresh snow. He took a photograph of the tyre marks that he and Tina had not driven over and compared them to the tyres of the parked Toyota, though he knew that Golob would do the same. It was obviously not the same. He did not go back into the room with the body.

"Now feel free," said Golob as he took off his gloves and plastic cover. Behind his back his assistants were carrying a metal crate out of the house. The sun had already set behind the nearby peaks and once the valley was in shadow, it became much colder. Only then did Taras realize how hungry he was.

"Listen, Taras. Up in his study there's a printer, but no computer. How's that?"

"You'll get it tomorrow morning."

"Why the mistrust? This is certainly not according to protocol."

Taras patted him on the shoulder.

"You know why. Nothing against you and your team."

Golob sighed and shook his head. He was a man of rules, but at the same time trusted Taras. How is he to coordinate this? He noticed a patch in the snow in front of them.

"Is this ours?" he asked and pointed to the pool of vomit in the fresh snow about two metres from the car.

"It's mine, I'm afraid," said Tina.

He gave her a compassionate look and turned to Taras.

"You'll get the report tomorrow around midday. For now..."

"You know, tell me something I don't know."

"Then we can be brief, Taras. Your theory about how events unfolded is probably right. The weapon also, probably a rifle or a handgun, calibre unknown for the time being, but in any case unusually high."

"Forty five?" Taras asked.

"11 millimetre, let's stick with our measurements. Probably.

There will be a few problems with this because the bullet shattered when it entered the skull and that's how it hit the floor. We had to cut out a whole square metre of flooring so we can study it back at the lab. We have taken fingerprint samples, picked up whatever we could and will sort it all out tonight… Basically, the man is dead and was killed…"

"What I don't know," said Taras. "Only what I don't know."

"We have lots of finger prints this time."

Taras waited for the helicopter to leave and then went back into the house. He walked through the rooms, looked at the wardrobes, books on the shelves, glanced at the stain on the living room carpet and then at Tina who was also staring expressionlessly at the stain. Once more he went into every single room in the house. There was nothing one wouldn't expect to find in a dwelling belonging to the Dean of the Biotechnical Faculty. Even all the books on the shelves were scientific, the only literary volume he noticed was Joseph Heller's *Catch 22*. He did not try to understand why. His stomach was rumbling badly.

"Are you hungry," he asked Tina.

"I don't know… Yes, but I don't know if I can eat anything."

Twenty minutes later they were wandering around Bovec, trying to get food in two places where they just stared at them and said that in the winter season they only sell drinks and the occasional sandwich. They were also told that they were the only tourists in town and that this is how it has been since a wire on a cable car failed and the thing had crashed to the ground with two skiers inside. Eventually they found a place serving pizza. Tina ordered only a piece of apple strudel and a glass of water.

They sat in silence for a while.

"A hard day," Taras then said.

"Yes, it was…" she said with a bitter smile, staring for a while at the vase with plastic flowers in front of her and then looked at Taras. "My first body."

The waiter brought the pizza to the table and Taras had to control himself not to leap at it. He was famished and the pizza looked good. It was what a pizza should be. The crust just the right thickness, well baked, tomatoes, mushrooms, sweet corn, peppers… all out of a tin of course, but still. Not even he could handle ham right now.

"Not bad," he said, his mouth full. "Want a piece?"

Tina smiled and shook her head. The waiter clearly intended to bring her the strudel once Taras had finished with the pizza, but she showed no sign of impatience or desire for food.

He ate in silence.

"Do you have a theory yet after all this?" Tina asked.

He shook his head.

"Penca, the ghost whose desk you had to clear out, taught me many things. One was not to develop theories and not to deal with them until absolutely necessary. There's always a victim, a motive, an opportunity and there is material and other evidence. That's all. The theory will take care of itself."

Tina's strudel eventually arrived and she ate in small bites, but at least she was able to eat.

"What does your guy do?" he asked her, not really knowing why.

"My guy? You mean work?"

"Is he in computers as well? Did you meet at university?"

She gave him a tired look of surprise. Picking up the glass of water, she took a sip, put it back down and used her finger to wipe away the few drops the glass had left in its previous position.

"Third year of my computing degree. Then I went on to psychology and he went into marketing. In fact he still hasn't finished his studies."

"And what does he think about you being a criminal investigator?"

"I don't know..."

He is fine with it. He thinks it's sexy, he had once said. He thinks it's cool to be going out with a forensic investigator or a police psychologist like out of some TV series, though she was neither. What was she in fact? A woman who throws up when she sees a dead person?

"You don't have to," she said. "We can talk about the case."

"I thought you'd had enough of it for today."

"I'm just thinking about how the man might still be alive if we'd arrived a little earlier."

"Or not. And we might also be dead now."

He recalled the mess made of Hleb's head by the bullet. What chance did he have with his nine-millimetre Beretta in the glove compartment? Where was his sixth sense when he stepped into the house?

"This time we at least know who the victim is," he said and wiped his mouth with a paper napkin. "At least I think we know, because Golob needs to first confirm that it really is Hleb."

She put down the fork with which she had been eating the strudel.

"Sorry, I forgot."

"No, I can't anyway."

"Look, as far as my theory goes... We're looking for the owner of the green Hyundai who we also hope is the driver of the car which forced us off the road into the snow, and must almost certainly be connected to the murder. Where else would the murderer disappear to in this valley with a single road leading out of it? When we get them, and we will, even if we have to arrest all the owners of green Hyundais with Gorica number plates, we will see what next. Theories are for crime novel writers, I'm not a writer. If I had to think of myself as something ... and I'm not at an age when this is recommended..."

She smiled.

"...it won't sound particularly appealing, but I would say I was just an official with particular know-how. An employee who follows protocol and occasionally improvises a little when necessary. Within the limits of what's possible."

He finished his mineral water, called the waiter and ordered a coffee. Tina just shook her head.

"And you? Do you think the murders are related?" he asked her.

"Are officials allowed to think?"

She was cute when she smiled. Of course this is all it would ever be, a discussion about their work out in the field, but that was fine. At least she is not like Brajc whom he would have to urge to get on with it and stop pestering the waiter for the recipe for sour turnip and ribs stew with *budelj* dumplings.

"Hleb was present in the place where the first victim died,

and himself died after we tried to talk to him about this victim, and both were murdered in a brutal manner..."

She looked up at Taras.

"Do you know what I felt when I saw the body, what it was that made me have to go outside. Not the actual scene itself, at least I think not, or at least not only that. It wasn't nice but I could probably have handled that. At least I think... Hatred, it was the hatred that must have driven someone to do such a thing that made my stomach churn. And how he must have hated the girl, if it was the same person."

"No murder is a pretty sight and there's always hatred somewhere in the background."

"What about..."

She stopped as if she was not entirely sure whether to say it or not.

"Go ahead."

"What about the thirty year old story from Stara Fužina or the pharmaceutical meeting for billions of dollars or the drug dealer's snowed in car?"

"I don't know. Blind leads. At least I hope..."

They got back to Ljubljana at ten in the evening. Alenka was with Karin and Taras sat on the sofa in the living room, staring for a while at the screen of the switched off TV. He thought about how another woman today must be in a terrible state, the wife of this Hleb, whose first name he could not remember at all. He almost hoped that she had been less attached to her husband than Karin had been to her Rajko.

He switched on the TV and switched it off again before anything had a chance to appear on the screen. Prelc and Hleb were dead, well, one less, the other more, but he wasn't. He stood up, changed into his tracksuit, picked up his head torch and went for his night run on Rožnik.

Chapter 26.

Tuesday, 9 January

Taras was wrong. The meeting in Drvarič's office was not at nine but at eleven and they were all invited to it, not just him. He was at work by half past seven, a few minutes before Tina. Minutes in which he was able to switch on the computer and check through the morning's news. Dean of Biotech Faculty Murdered, it said in big letters, bigger than those informing him of a new wave of refugees on the southern border. A contract killing? one of the subtitles suggested.

He read the article which was full of suppositions and very few facts but among the three or four possible reasons mentioned which, however improbable, Taras wrote out onto a piece of paper, he also came across one which suggested the answer might be related to some recent discovery at the Biotechnical Faculty which would rock the established relations between important players in the pharmaceutical industry. It also ended with the information that the first person at the scene was Inspector Taras Birsa, the very inspector in charge of the mysterious body from the Sava Bohinjka.

"Clearly the most powerful weapon of the Ljubljana Police Directorate continues to plod around in the dark," the writer ended his thoughts, with 'most powerful weapon' in inverted commas.

Tina stepped into the office and instead of greeting Taras placed in front of him a brown envelope with around thirty pages in it.

"Read this," she said, clearly tired and lacking sleep. Next to the envelope she placed Hleb's laptop. "Everything on there I also have here," she waved in front of him something flat the size of a smart phone.

He took the pages out of the envelope and began reading the first on which some matej.verbic@gmail.com – he looked through the other pages, it was always this same matej.verbic – wrote,

I'm sitting here thinking about things and I believe in God. God is great and is the reason for everything and everything is the instrument of God. You are his instrument and I am his instrument and His will be done. In this light I understand that your will is His will and your acts are His acts and my affliction. Was I worthy? Was I sent into this world for something great or was my only worth the life of an ant? Was I less than you? Is it possible that a pig like you is worth more in His eyes than me? Your eyes! I want to throw up when I think of your eyes. You think that you can sack me? You? Don't act nice, because your eyes betray you. Your own eyes tell more about you than all this babble. You are nothing but a pig and if God is your creator he made a mistake. Anyone can make a mistake. You are nothing but a plain old slut who deserves no bread, no water, no anything. If I were God I would admit that you are a mistake and make amends. I would send locusts onto your eyes, to devour them, and flies and wild boars...

Taras greeted Brajc and Osterc who entered the room, both at once, as usual, almost always, even though they didn't live close to each other, use the same buses or anything like that. They both drove in with their cars.

Two sides of single spacing, including five lines of animals which should eat away at his eyes – eighteen different ones, Taras counted them – and all the letters ended with a quote from the Bible, at least that was what Taras assumed it was. The last time he had read parts of the Bible was some thirty-five years ago.

For of this you can be sure: No immoral, impure or greedy person-such a person is an idolater-has any inheritance in the kingdom of Christ and of God.

"That's the last one," said Tina. "There was no further correspondence after that."

"Perhaps Hleb deleted it."

"No, he didn't delete anything, he archived all these mails. I found them in a separate folder."

"Osterc, do you recall this Hleb reporting any harassment, threats or anything similar?"

"When?"

He checked the printouts. The mails began on the twenty-second of November and the last one was sent on the twenty-second of December.

"I can't recall any such report but I can check," said Osterc.

"Do so, then we can all go and discuss and arrange things further over a coffee."

Why had Hleb not mentioned anything when he's spoken to him?

Five minutes later he had the information. If Hleb had anything to complain about he did not do it at their police directorate.

"I called the GPD. They said they would check and let me know."

The coffee shop on the corner of Prešeren Street was almost empty at this time of day. Too late for the regular customers from the nearby Foreign Ministry and the teachers from the Economics Secondary School, too early for students from the Art Academy. Their arrival confused the waitress. Usually, as soon as she saw them, she started making two coffees, a black one for Taras and a cappuccino for Brajc, and a mint tea for Osterc, but this time there was a young woman with them, almost a girl, who somehow didn't fit into the group. She stood at the bar, confused with two coffee cups in one hand, a teacup in the other and beckoned to Taras.

"What do you want?" Taras asked Tina.

"Want?"

"To drink, what do you want to drink?"

She chose a black coffee. Taras didn't know many women who had their coffee without any form of milk, none in fact before Tina.

"How come you take your coffee black?"

"I don't like milk."

He waited for Silva, the waitress, a lady of around sixty, to bring what they had ordered and then briefly, in as few words as possible, summarized what had happened the previous day, told them what Tina had found on Hleb's computer and waited for half a minute so that his colleagues could process what they had been told.

"So then this… what's he called, Verbič, is the person we're looking for?"

"I don't know," said Taras. "You tell me."

He looked at Brajc, Osterc and finally Tina. In fact he did not need their thoughts, just a voice. Only a spoken stupidity becomes a stupidity, for as long as it is inside the head it seems entirely plausible.

"Just now Golob also sent me a confirmation that what we found yesterday near Bovec was indeed the Dean of the Biotechnical Faculty, Drago Hleb."

He finally managed to remember his name.

"If it looks like an elephant," Brajc began, "and stinks like an elephant, and shits like an elephant, then it probably is an elephant."

"Everything fits in," said Osterc and removed the teabag from his cup. He wound the string around his spoon – a gesture which, due to the total concentration and dedication with which he set about doing it, Taras found mildly annoying. He squeezed the last drop of water out of it and placed it on the saucer. Clearly this was all he was going to say because he then began sipping on the tea and pulled a face because it was too hot. He always did this.

Taras turned to Tina who looked at her older colleagues, wanting to make sure they had finished.

"He fits the profile. The hatred that the messages emit also corresponds to the way the last victim was attacked. Clearly he had a motive there…"

"Where's that?" Brajc asked.

"With the last victim, Hleb, I mean. From his letters we can assume he blamed Hleb for losing his job and he…"

She spoke of the letters which Taras already knew. Perhaps it was that, perhaps the tiredness accumulating over the last few days as he stayed at work for longer than usual and came to his running, boxing or any other form of recreation later, and slept less... perhaps that was why he was staring at the cleavage of the white blouse she was wearing for a moment longer than was discrete, even though it revealed almost nothing. Barely the beginning of the cleft between her breasts but in combination with her face which he forgot that he only a week ago thought of as interesting at most... He sighed and nodded to her to continue because she clearly thought that his resigned gaze was intended for what she was saying... Great, now he can stare as much as he wants, clearly no longer among those who could be credited with sexual motives.

"...stopped sending mails on December twenty-second, a day before the murder of our unknown girl..."

"The twenty-third is only the assumed day of her death," Taras said. "It could have been a day earlier or a day later."

And even if he could? If he got the chance? She was almost twenty years younger than him. Almost as young as Anja. Well, not quite, but certainly closer to her age than his.

"...who was murdered in a similarly brutal way. What if Hleb and the first victim were lovers and he wanted to punish him with her murder but when he didn't succeed or when that didn't seem enough, he killed him as well?"

"Why had Hleb not reported it when we asked him about it? Surely this would not be something he would fail to mention?" Taras finally stopped thinking about the cleavage.

"Was he married?" she asked.

"Probably," said Taras. "I don't know."

Like him. In a formal legal manner yes, but actually not? What if he was divorced, like Brajc, for example? Probably the former.

"Well, she's not only good looking, she's also clever," said Brajc and had clearly also noticed the unbuttoned blouse.

She smiled politely but somewhat wearily. Would she have done so if he had said the sentence? Would it not be better if he was thinking about the two bodies at the IFM for which he is responsible? He shook his head and they gave him a quizzical look.

"Just some thought stuck in my head."

"And what next?" Tina asked.

"We shall all go to the meeting," Taras drank the last sip of his long-cold coffee and when he moved his gaze up from the cup glanced for the last time at the gap in the blouse which offered nothing, or almost nothing, and it was perhaps this nothing which made it so tempting. Less often *is* more. "We'll go to the meeting and see what they have to say."

Drvarič was waiting for them in his office which Taras would swear was more tidy than usual. By the small table where there was room for two chairs there were now five, huddled in two semi-circles, and there were even flowers on the table. Something growing from some bulbs which had not properly blossomed yet. Kristan from the GPD was sitting on one of the five chairs with Drvarič at his desk. When they knocked and entered the office he did not greet them and Taras assumed, not assumed but knew, that something was wrong. People like Drvarič were very suited to letting you know how happy, or rather how unhappy people higher up are with you. Kristan's face, as usual, did not reveal anything, but even just his presence spoke in itself.

When they settled down Drvarič looked at Kristan and, when he received a sign only he saw and recognised, he began,

"It's no good! It's no good at all! It hasn't been good from the very start, and what begins in this way, inevitably doesn't end well."

"What are talking about?" Taras asked.

"I'm talking about the fact..." Drvarič, who had never liked Taras' tone of voice but usually tolerated it, spoke aggressively. It appeared he would not do so today. Enough time had passed since they had been equals, enough for him to forget what an average criminal investigator he was when he still was one. "I'm talking about the fact," he said again, "that the first body has been with us for long enough that we could find out who she is. I'm talking about the fact that we now have another, clearly connected to the first, and please, enlighten me – do we at least know how they are connected, apart from geographically?"

He leaned towards Taras and the fact that Taras didn't move back, look away or do anything similar appropriate to his lower status, worked him up even more.

"We don't know!" he almost shouted. "And why don't we know? Because instead of investigating the crime, instead of doing what we're paid to do, we dig into people's private lives as if we were some kind of moral police. Well, we're not!"

Taras smiled and did not try to hide it either. So this is what it is!

"Yesterday Mr Kristan here had a visit from the Minister. Not the Minister for the Interior who's responsible for us, though that in itself would have been bad enough. No, he had a visit from the Minister of *Finance*!"

He stressed the word as if that would make a greater impression on Taras and his team. Taras didn't react. He looked at Kristan who showed no sign of perhaps having instructed Drvarič to directly have a go at Taras in front of his colleagues. They had probably at least discussed it before, otherwise Drvarič would not be foaming at the mouth and Kristan would not be calmly waiting for the outcome of the duel.

"What are you actually interested in?" Taras turned to Drvarič again.

"As your boss, if you happened to have missed the sign on the door, I'm interested in who murdered our unknown girl and Dr Hleb who had, if the weekend newspaper supplements are to be believed, become the new hope of science in the heart of Slovenes, or could have become, had you acted in time."

"Oh, that," Taras said sarcastically. "Tina, what's his name again...?"

"Matej Verbič," she helped him and he will have to congratulate her on her cool, indifferent voice. It was like some answering machine.

"And this is why the GPD will take over this case. And what this means for you and your three colleagues here, we'll discuss later."

Everyone in the office apart from Drvarič looked at each other and even Drvarič noticed that he had probably made some mistake somewhere. He peered at each one of them in confusion and finally looked towards Kristan who ignored him.

"Taras, are you saying that you have a suspect?" Kristan asked.

Taras shrugged his shoulders.

"Yes, that is what I'm trying to say. If of course it's what you're interested in. For a moment I thought we are here because of my visit to Mr Mihelič"

He looked at Drvarič who turned to Kristan, confused. He slowly, barely noticeably shook his head.

"Believing that in this country we are, at least in the eyes of the law, all still equal..."

"The suspect, Taras," Kristan sounded reconciliatory and impatient at the same time.

"Tina found him."

"Nice... and?"

"We extracted some threatening letters from Hleb's computer by a certain Matej Verbič, apparently a former employee at the Biotechnical Faculty whom Hleb had sacked. We're still unsure what connection he had with the fist victim, but we suspect that, Hleb at least knew her and also met her in Bohinj."

"Well...!" Drvarič shouted but Kristan stopped him with a hand gesture.

"Go on!" he told Taras.

And Taras told him what he knew; about the receptionist who spotted Hleb talking to an unknown woman at the hotel and about their trip to Trenta – he said Trenta because he could not be bothered to explain where Bavščica is every time – about the car which came driving down the road, about the still warm body...

"...and because I do not believe that there's some conspiracy by the pharmaceutical lobby behind all this, or because I don't wish for such a development any more than anyone else in this country, even though Mihelič seems to be trying his best to convince me of the opposite..."

This actually made Kristan laugh.

"...I'd be very happy if it emerged that our suspect is guilty. It would be best for all of us this way. If this Verbič turns out to own a dark green Hyundai crossover, I would almost bet on it."

"Nicely put. Have you asked for a warrant?" Kristan asked.

Taras shook his head.

"I sent out an order yesterday for the car to be found, but I didn't have his name or number plate then. What I have just told you is entirely fresh."

"Well, ask for one. Go to the Faculty and find out about him. The secretary, colleagues, someone will know, then let me know and we'll send Special Forces to pick him up."

And you'll go with them of course, Taras thought. Followed by a camera crew from the national TV station and two private channels in the background.

"I thought that the GPD was taking this over."

Kristan laughed wholeheartedly again.

"We're not that wicked, Taras, and this here is a good opportunity to demonstrate to the fourth estate that we're not divided. We'll carry out the arrest, you'll do the rest, we all get the credit."

Kristan stood up, shook Taras' hand, and Tina's, Brajc's and Osterc's, in that order. When shaking Tina's hand he added a brief "well done, colleague," in the charming voice of an ageing playboy, waved at Drvarič who stood feeling betrayed at his desk, and opened the door. As he stepped out he turned back briefly towards Taras,

"And give my greetings to Alenka."

"Will do," Taras said.

He waited for Kristan to leave and then turned towards a baffled Drvarič who was only a moment earlier still considering whether to tell Taras that there are limits to his patience.

"She is his grandchildren's paediatrician."

As Taras left the office, his team behind him, Drvarič continued to sit at his desk, trying to figure out how to digest this information. Whatever happens, he should probably be a little more careful with Taras in the future.

Chapter 27.

"Got him!" Osterc cried out. He was looking for Verbič in the central population register, an old system but still surprisingly usable and updated system. To find a person all he needed was a name and if you entered one and twenty names come up or, with some common names probably even more, then you added a year of birth or some other known piece of information and the system would narrow down the list to the image of the person wanted, to all their addresses, children, even cars they have ever registered, who they bought them from and to whom they sold them.

"Matej Verbič, Gorica Street 12, Ajdovščina."

"Ajdovščina? I was in a restaurant there once, what was it called..." Brajc said lost in thought. "Oh the food..." he stopped when he met Taras' gaze.

"Taras, guess what car our man drives?" said Osterc, and without waiting for an answer added, "he drives a car with the number plate GO U2-17P which is, bingo – a Hyundai, 2016 model..."

He looked at Brajc who was already filling out an arrest warrant and added with envy,

"Not bad for someone working in the public sector. Brajc, when did you last buy a new car?"

Half an hour later Taras was parking his work Skoda in the parking lot of the Biotechnical Faculty, past which he regularly ran whenever he did his longer eleven-kilometre run. His short run avoided it and with a slightly guilty conscience he thought about how he had not panted past here in a while. Perhaps this evening when the slush that accumulated over the day will freeze over a little. Or tomorrow during the day if it turns out they will finish their job today.

A black flag was hanging from the mast next to the building.

"Aren't you happy you're about to solve your first case?" he asked Tina as they walked across the bridge towards the path leading across the Glinščica stream towards the entrance into the circular glass and metal building.

She shook her head.

"A little disappointed, to be honest."

He gave her a questioning look. She smiled.

"Perhaps I've seen too many TV series. I don't know what I was expecting, but certainly not some plain old madman."

"Don't expect anything and you will be spared many things in life."

She laughed and Taras did too. He was satisfied that the trail was leading to the mad Verbič rather than to Mihelič or to a thirty year old case. At least things were less complicated this way. With a lone madman there is far less work than with a conspiracy.

They showed their ID cards and asked how to get to the Secretariat. They did not say what they were here for but there was no need. Taras could sense curious eyes following him along the long corridor.

The secretary was an elderly lady, around sixty. Taras recognized her voice when she responded to their knocking by shouting 'come in.' He showed her his ID too and then looked around the office and pointed to a table with two chairs in the corner.

"Can we talk?"

The secretary stood up from her desk and sat on the chair Taras had pointed to without taking her eyes off him for a moment.

"As you probably know, we are here because of the murder of Professor Hleb..."

Of course she knew about the murder. The flag outside the building, the newspaper articles, the news was probably all over the TV news which Taras didn't see, but he didn't finish his sentence. The woman burst into tears and couldn't stop. Taras was happy that Tina was with him when she produced some paper tissues from the pocket of her jacket and passed them to the secretary. He waited for it to be over with a mixture of satisfaction that he is used to such things, and only ever has a real problem when similar news must be given to a wife or god forbid children. Regret, almost nostalgia for the times when he would have been the one to have to mop the tears of this secretary and show compassion. He waited for her to calm down.

She put down the wet tissues and gave him a look of hate.

"I told you it would come to this. I told you. And what did you do? Nothing!"

She burst into tears again but this time Taras didn't wait for her to stop.

"Who did you tell what?"

The secretary almost grabbed a new tissue from Tina's hands and wiped her tears.

"After those first threats began arriving I called the police and told them about it. They told me to send them the messages and I did. When they stopped arriving I thought they had sorted it out, but they hadn't."

"Who did you call? Where did you send the messages?"

She stood up and went to her desk, checked something on the computer, clicked on the mouse and a moment later the printer made noise. She waited for a page to print out, picked it up and returned to Taras.

"Here, Inspector, this is where I sent them."

Taras looked at the header of the official letter. Republic of Slovenia, Ministry for Interior, Štefanova 2, Ljubljana... He turned towards Tina.

"The GPD, she sent it to the GPD."

Gorica Street is the main road through Ajdovščina towards Italy and, as the name suggests, towards Gorica. There were two companies registered at number twelve, a geodetic surveying company and a tile fitter, both at ground level, above these was the private flat of Matej Verbič. At two in the afternoon three police vehicles, an unmarked white van with tinted windows, and, as Taras had predicted, vans from three different TV stations, all arrived at a nearby parking lot. The journalist from the national TV station flirted with two female colleagues, waiting for some attention from Kristan who was in charge of the operation. Kristan was an old acquaintance of the media and the journalist seemed to consider him his personal friend with whom he was on first-name terms and every time he called him Andrej he was merely trying to display their familiarity. After all, he said to the two female journalists who he called 'girls,' it was journalists like him he had to thank for his career. When the policeman eventually approached them, the journalist affected a slightly offended face,

"Andrej, I thought you'd forgotten about us," he said. Kristan, like the unit waiting by the white van, was in full gear, including a Heckler machine gun and helmet, even though there was no need for it, for he was not about to participate in the attack about to be carried out by the six members of the special forces. For what he was about to do the black panther symbol of the security forces on the sleeve of his black uniform would have been more than enough.

"Let's get the job done first," Kristan said and smiled vaguely at the journalist. He knew how to handle these things. Unlike his predecessors who would break out in cold sweat at the mere mention of a camera, Kristan adored them. Not only because he very early on realized that they could help his career. People have a limited capacity for remembering, so they simplify things in their memory. He had once read somewhere that if a hundred random people anywhere in the world were asked to name a single physicist, all hundred would respond by saying Einstein. Half would also know that his first name was Albert. Was Albert Einstein the only physician to ever walk the face of this Earth? Was Pablo Picasso the only painter? Jože Plečnik the only Slovene architect? Of course not. All he had to achieve was that journalists, whenever they wanted something from the police, first thought of him. Only him. And apart from journalists also those who made the decisions about jobs and promotions within the police. At forty-four Andrej Kristan had become the youngest-ever General Chief of Police and one of the rare people whose ambitions aimed much higher. In order to fulfil these he needed to continue to gain the positive attention of the media, of television. This attention was reciprocal, he admitted to himself. He loved performing.

"Who are we after today?" the journalist asked, slightly annoyed that Kristan was still smiling at his female colleagues and not him.

"Matej Verbič, a former researcher at the Biotechnical Faculty who had an argument with the Dean and, as far as we know, visited him at his weekend house in Trenta yesterday and..."

As he spoke he observed the female journalists, two girls, must be what... twenty-five? he wondered. They keep sending ever younger ones out on assignments and sometimes he got the impression they must be choosing them like bar owners choose their waitresses – for the cute smile and long legs. Not that he was complaining.

"...basically, the person we're after is dangerous and as far as we know armed with a high calibre weapon, meaning that you should stay at a safe distance until we have secured the place."

"Come on, Andrej, we're not kids," the journalist protested and turned towards his colleagues. "I don't know about you, but I need to get some shots to Ljubljana which we can edit over your boring statement at the end of all of this."

He laughed and was satisfied when the girls also laughed.

"Well, as you said... at the end," Kristan said. "This is not child's play."

Once they have the man they will let him know and he will personally enter the building and bring him in to the cameras. Then...

He produced a smart phone and typed in their target's address. A map of the area came up and he showed the journalists and his colleagues the spot where they should wait with the cameras in order to do business, as he called it. He picked the location himself. A nice tree-lined alley with the corner of the suspect's house visible in the background. The light was right and wouldn't shine straight into his face when he would make a statement, so he would not have to squint. They could zoom into the suspect's house during the conversation. Perhaps he should speak to the cameraman too, he thought.

"Ladies, gentleman..."

He bowed slightly and sat in the passenger's seat in the white van where the specialist unit was already waiting. They drove past the location. There were a number of cars parked outside the house, including the dark green Hyundai Tucson, spotlessly new and clean. He observed the windows on the first floor with the curtains drawn. Then he ordered them to drop him off in the parking lot in front of the hotel across the road from where he could watch the operation. He quickly opened the van door and moved to a police car parked in a corner of the parking area that the suspect could not see from his flat. He was annoyed to see that one of the TV crew vehicles was parked right in the middle of the parking. Could they not for once stick to the arrangements?

The leader of the specialist unit was a tall, dark haired man in his mid thirties who was happy to be rid of Kristan. He saw no point in parading up and down in front of the house three times before the attack. Half an hour before Kristan's arrival in Ajdovščina he and his assistant walked up to the address in plain clothing and visited the tile fitter and enquired about the price of fitting a square metre of tiles, complaining that they could not park outside the workshop because someone with a green Hyundai parked across two spaces...

"Oh, that'll be Verbič," the tile fitter nodded. "Just don't mention him to me. I'm just glad when he's not at home..."

"Oh?"

"Yes, he's a madman," the tile fitter said. "Ask anyone you want. He's had fights with everyone and even threatened to kill us. You saw the car? The idiot changes his car every year because he has a fixed idea that we're destroying them. If you as much as touch his car he goes crazy. And the parking spaces outside are so narrow anyway, you can't even walk past the car without accidentally touching it. He has already reported me to the police twice, accusing me that I scratched the paint. The police came here both times to check the damage I was supposed to have caused. And I approached the two policemen who were near the car, otherwise I would not have dared to get even close to it, and I tell him, 'Come on, show me then what I've damaged!'

'Here, here,' he pointed to a spot where there was nothing at all. The policemen told him that next time they would fine him for… I can't remember what they said. But he just won't give up, the crazy schizophrenic."

He stopped and sighed loudly.

"Sorry, every time I think of this man I lose it…"

He made a spinning gesture above his head with his finger.

"Now, what was it you were interested in?"

So he was at home. Ever since he had been dismissed he was often at home. If he had a guilty conscience for killing someone a short time ago, as he clearly would have, he could glance out of his window occasionally and wonder why a van with tinted windows drove past his flat three times in such a short period of time. And might also wonder why this was the only car in the last ten minutes to drive down an otherwise busy road. Unlikely, but he might have.

They parked in the street which in the summer with the thick leaves of the row of lime trees lining it would have been hidden from view from the house. Now that the branches were bare, less so, but Zupan, the head of the specialist unit, decided that it would still be the best location for them to start their operation and stealthily and swiftly reach the building on Gorica Road. Roadblocks half a kilometre either side of the address meant the road was empty. They ran the last few metres to the wall of the building from where they were not visible from upstairs and then crept to the entrance. Two of them remained there, the other four sneaked up the stairs to the first and only floor of the building and took their places around the door with Dr Matej Verbič written on it. Zupan pressed his ear against the door and indicated to his team to settle and stay quiet. He held his breath and tried, in as much as it was possible, to calm the beating of his heart, in order to hear whether his target was at home, when there was a huge blast from the inside, which almost made him bounce off the door. In reflex he threw himself to the ground and rolled away from the door.

Kristan was sitting in the car with the engine running so as not to be cold, and the police radio link switched on. If all goes well, in five minutes time, their target would be secured or neutralized, just enough action caught on camera to show the number of police involved, though not their faces, with his own face representing them all in the next shot, when he would step before the cameras and inform TV audiences with a slightly tired expression – as if to say, another job done which someone has to do – that the arrested person is a dangerous criminal, suspected of the murder of an internationally renowned scientist on the verge of a striking scientific breakthrough… Well, perhaps he didn't need to use the word 'striking'.

He had great plans for himself and knew that this was most important. Most people have no plans because they don't have ambitions or mistakenly assume that success will come if they are good at what they studied for or what they were employed to do. Tactics without strategy. He smiled. Such fools. If you want to be a good criminal investigator you need to work on being a criminal investigator, but do not expect to have a career from it. If you want a career you need to work on your career. Taras, for example, was the best criminal investigator they had, but he was still stuck in some local police department, he had not even moved up to the General Police Directorate. What for, when he was more useful in the position he was in now. He worked on the most difficult cases and the most and all he receives in exchange are more cases and more difficult cases, and a boss like Drvarič, who was, in some ways a little like himself, just with a terrible lack of elegance and no talent. Did Taras not care because it emerged that his Cinderella is in fact a princess? Was he naïve in this way, even stupid? Could he just not be bothered?

He could not understand people, clever people, who could not see where a lack of this kind of broader view was taking them. Was it possible, he often wondered, that they did not care for the feeling of power a better position brought with it? There is certainly more of the good things and less of the unpleasant stuff. More money, less work. More bonuses, fewer responsibilities. If anything goes wrong with this case it will all be blamed on Taras. If things unfolded successfully – and it looks as if they will – he will play his role as Kristan. He will appear as the one who solved the case, not Taras the ant. Why would one not strive for this, work towards it, especially since these efforts are not really efforts at all, merely a slightly different use of energy? A step to the right instead of a step to the left.

He had it all planned. He was fifty-two. He had been in charge of the federal police for eight years and would continue in his post for another two. But when everyone will expect him to put in his candidacy for another term, one he could easily achieve, he will extend his tentacles into politics, choose the most suitable party, depending on their ratings, and then take up the post of Interior Minister in the government. And then... Anything was possible, even the premiership, especially with all these refugees at the borders. Who else will people vote for if not a policeman who never forgets to add that the police force would not have any problems solving the matter or that the police force knows the solution, if only... and similar. In the meantime Taras will still be up to his neck in this kind of human shit, trying to make sense of some splattered human brain.

He checked his watch. Another minute. He hoped they would be on time.

"Another minute," he said to the driver, not because he wanted to talk to him. He was just checking his own voice, doing a sound rehearsal.

The driver checked the time and nodded.

Did he have a guilty conscience because of people such as Taras? Did he ever have the slightest qualm about being photographed when the hard work was done by others? About appropriating someone else's work? He scratched his chin and cleared his throat so the driver next to him gave him a puzzled look.

"Just a little longer and we're done," said Kristan and the driver nodded.

No, he didn't have a guilty conscience at all. This was his job.

"Shit!" he said to himself in a low voice but not low enough for the patient creature next to him not to hear him and understand.

"Sorry?"

He did not reply to him. Something was happening beyond the driver's shoulder in the TV crew van in the middle of the parking area. The door opened and out jumped the journalist and the cameraman, ready for reporting. The driver followed his gaze and when he saw the scene he swore and began opening the door. Kristan tapped him on the shoulder.

"Leave it, leave it. Let them do their stuff."

Just as he finished the sentence there was a bang and a flash which reached them as a bright flare through the branches of the trees and bushes between the parking in front of the hotel and the house on the other side of the road. But the bang happened some thirty metres away and sounded like a distant firecracker, annoying but not dangerous, so it was so much more unusual, almost funny, that the journalist grabbed his head from which something came flying in their direction, and fell to the ground.

A second shot, but not at them, not at the door, but somewhere else. Zupan beckoned to his colleague on the other side of the door and he came forward and kicked down the door with his heavy police boots. Made of thin white painted wood it shattered instantly. Two of them, Zupan and his partner to the right leapt into the flat. From the door they could already see someone beyond the short hallway who was half turning from the window and trying to point a huge revolver at them. He did not manage to extend his arm to shoot. They hit him when he was some twenty degrees short. Two brief bursts of fire from their Hecklers ended up in his stomach and chest and thrust him onto the windowsill and across it, straight through the half open window.

"Who was he shooting at?" Zupan wondered and stepped to the window to check whether his colleagues waiting outside the building were all right.

Chapter 28.

Wednesday, 10 January

"A black coffee?"

Tina nodded.

Silva disappeared behind the bar and returned with the usual, a coffee, a cappuccino, a mint tea, and clearly from now on, another coffee. She did not need much, two visits were enough for her to put her guests' drinking habits into her memory box. From now on Tina will have to tell her if she wanted something else, but she could handle that as well. A greeting and a barely noticeable questioning look when the customer entered and if a regular didn't respond but merely returned the greeting, then she pulled their card from her memory. It was one of the reasons that Pisker, despite its not ideal location, had so many visitors. People like many things but being made to feel at home is common to everyone. And at sixty she might have difficulties charming them with a pair of tight leggings.

"Anyone seen yesterday's news" Taras asked.

"I thought I was going to die laughing. The idiot... what's his name? The jabbering fool on the TV... well, who cares. He got his ear shot off. Talk about fucking crazy."

Brajc was in a good mood. Like most policemen he didn't like journalists with good reason. They were like moths gathering around a light and Brajc's light and those of ones like him were not particularly bright. All he gets from them if he gets his thirty seconds in front of the camera are accusations and unpleasant questions. An appearance on some weekly chat show where they will discuss police brutality against innocent junkies or something similar.

The shot by one of the two commercial channels, which the national TV station also somehow got a copy of, showed the journalist grabbing his ear and in a slow motion shot shown in multiple repeats with a circle and arrow pointing where to look, and the 45 calibre bullet blowing off his left ear so there was nothing left for any plastic surgeon, however good, to reattach, stitch or reconstruct. The camera then followed him as he was being lifted into the ambulance and also visited him at the hospital where the doctors bandaged his head and fed him extra sedatives and painkillers. All he was capable of when his colleagues thrust a microphone in front of him was a lame cry.

"And then they go and show the shitty fool squealing in hospital. Do you know him Taras?"

"I do."

"And?"

"A shitty fool."

They both laughed. Osterc was dunking his teabag and probably thinking about whether it was already time to wind it around his spoon, and Tina, slightly surprised it seemed, was listening to her colleagues' conversation.

"Puf, and the ear was gone," Brajc continued, pulling at his own ear and smiling at Tina. "Don't worry, they'll print one for him. I read about this the other day, someone in Croatia had it done on a 3D printer..."

Tina gave Taras an almost horrified look.

"He was unlucky," he said. "With a better shot he'd have got it right in the middle of his forehead..."

"An empty shot," Brajc squealed, "an empty shot. He wouldn't even notice it."

"If what happened to Kristan would have happened to us," Taras said and looked at Tina – and with 'us' he meant himself – "you'd understand why we are with Verbič on this one. Did you know," he turned to Brajc and Osterc, "that Hleb reported Verbič's threats to the GPD?"

"So that's why they're dilly-dallying," said Osterc. "I thought it was taking them a long time. And? Did they just bin the report?"

"No, they issued a restraining order. A pity Verbič seems not to have taken any notice of it."

This time Kristan earned himself a visit to the studio, not just giving a statement on site. He wore an elegant grey suit that matched the silvery highlights in his hair.

"This afternoon Ajdovščina was the setting for scenes we are not normally used to in our part of the world..." the news anchor began. Instead of a report from the scene, with their own reporter having been shot, she had to make do with shots from rival stations for which their producer had to grovel before a private rival. But at least they had Kristan in the studio. He faced a difficult choice of whether to appear on the national TV channel or on the private ones. The female journalists from the private channels were younger and their ratings higher, but the police was still a state institution.

"So tell us, Sir, Director of the General Police Department, what exactly happened in Ajdovščina? Who was the marksman who injured our reporter? Was it really the same man who murdered the Dean of the Biotechnical Faculty..."

Had it been Taras who had lead the action in which a passer-by had been injured, in this case the TV reporter, everyone, including himself, would know that he had messed things up. Even if nobody else knew, Taras' face would instantly betray that things were not alright. Kristan on the other hand, was a paradigm of calm and tranquillity which on the TV screen appeared as professional restraint.

There was a moment when Kristan had panicked. It was the instant when the journalist fell to the ground and whatever it was that the bullet had shot from his head came flying right up to the driver's open door... That was the moment. And in fact it was not just a moment. It extended into a few long seconds when he had stayed sitting in the car while the driver jumped out and ran towards the fallen, writhing journalist at whom the shooter sent a second bullet which hit the asphalt and ended up in the glass wall of the hotel lobby. To the half minute later when his driver was pulling back the kicking and entirely crazed wounded man who was trying to find his ear on the ground,

"My ear, my ear... Where's my ear?" he had shouted so the policeman needed to use a special grip to calm him and forcibly drag him to safety which by then was not really necessary since the second bullet was also the last. While the policeman was pulling the journalist to safety, Zupan and his team had already opened fire on the attacker. He was lying by the wall of a the building on Gorica Street number 12 and, for the few moments of life he had left after eight bullets from two German machine guns had savaged and torn his aorta and some of the main veins in his lungs, as Taras could read in Cvilak's report, stared at two barrels of the same kind of guns.

It took about a minute for everything to calm down, a minute in which the blood stopped gurgling from the mouth of the shot man and the birds startled by the shots to settle down again. The only noise that could be heard after that minute by the road to Gorica was the shouting of the man whose ear had been shot off and who had in the meantime managed to get a glimpse of himself in the tinted glass of the police car and clearly didn't like what he saw. Kristan sat motionless in the car and his brain was motionless too. He saw what was happening around him, comprehended it, but it was as if the connection between the sensory centre and the one responsible for responding had been severed.

"Sir, is everything alright?" the driver asked despite having plenty on his hands with the journalist.

Kristan winced, looked at his subordinate as if he was seeing him for the first time, stood up, ran out of the car into the hotel, ran past the receptionist who peered from behind the counter, terrified, went straight to the toilets and locked himself in the cubicle. He sat on the plastic seat and stared at the inside surface of the door, signed with some sharp object by some Emir from Tuzla who happened to be passing through here on 21 Nov 2015, but Kristan was in no state to make any sense of these scrawls. If he was to be asked what he did there in that cubicle, what he thought about, he would not know what to say, but nobody asked. He came back out of the hotel ten minutes later when the ambulance nurses had already managed to bandage the journalist's wound and pumped him with tranquilizers. Calmly, as if nothing had happened, he walked to the car, picked up the radio transmitter from the floor under the passenger seat, pressed the button and spoke into the microphone,

"Swallow one, swallow one, report your status."

The shots broadcast on the national TV station, explained by Kristan's professional voice, showed blood on the asphalt in the parking space, a few drops, the journalist with his head bandaged and an absent gaze as he was being taken away by ambulance, a long distance shot of the covered body with a figure in the dark clothes of special forces leaning over it, squatting by it, and then getting up, turning, like some Clint Eastwood, Dirty Harry, towards the camera. Kristan. What in the moment of panic when the shooting occurred seemed like a disaster, was now turning into his great victory. He really did look good in the special unit uniform, his helmet under his arm like some air force pilot in some American film. In fact Kristan had taken this from Top Gun.

"I thank you very much for coming to our studio and giving us the details," the charmed newsreader said. "And what can I say..." she added. "Can we wish people of your calibre good luck, or what?"

"One cannot rely on luck," Kristan responded reservedly and then smiled. "Though we would all prefer it on our side at the right moment."

"I never would have thought this Kristan would get involved in anything like this. He always seemed a kind of armchair person, a bit of a kitten," Alenka had said when she saw the news item.

"He wasn't part of the action at all."

"What do you mean?"

Taras told her what Kristan had been doing while Zupan and his team were killing Verbič.

"And the journalists don't know this?"

"They do or they don't... If they wanted to know they could, it's not that difficult, after all they were there."

"I can't believe it!"

"You better had. Why do you think she never asked him how the Chief of Police might explain that a civilian was almost killed during a police operation?"

"And they didn't even mention you. After all it was you who brought them to this Verbič guy."

In fact it was their new young colleague. Taras would not know how to even switch on Hleb's computer. Besides, it clearly wasn't such a difficult case, we were just unlucky that with the first murder everything went smoothly for Verbič.

"And how does our young colleague feel about her first solved case?" Brajc drooled.

Tina picked up her coffee and took a sip, as if she had to think about it before answering.

"Disappointed," Taras replied instead of her.

"Disappointed?"

Osterc stretched up above his tea, reminding Taras of meerkats as they extend up on their hind legs above their burrows.

"Disappointed? But we solved the case?"

Tina shrugged her shoulders.

"She believes we didn't do anything extraordinary," Taras said. "She thinks that even a trained monkey could have found Verbič after the second murder."

She smiled,

"Thank you Taras for a very graphic description of my thoughts which is also pretty accurate. I don't know... Perhaps I expected that we would first find out who the headless girl is and then arrive at the murderer who would not be some lunatic fighting for the wounds of Christ."

"God, aren't we picky," Osterc said.

"And beside this," Tina added. "We still haven't discovered who the girl without the head is."

Chapter 29.

Tuesday, 9 January

Taras let the secretary's tears run dry for a second time, let her pour out her anger on him, then, as if he had not heard at all what she had been saying, calmly and in as much detail as he could, explained how his investigations brought him and his colleague to Dr Hleb, unfortunately too late. The secretary listened with an angry expression on her face, but she listened and when Taras finished, all three of them sat in silence for a moment.

"This is why we're wondering, of course, who the woman who Dr Hleb talked to on either the twenty-second or twenty-third of December at the Hotel Jezero in Bohinj might have been."

He carefully observed her face. Nothing, no change. Was she really so good at containing her knowledge, pretending, or did she in fact not understand the question.

"We also need to understand why Dr Hleb had not spoken about the threats when we spoke to him about the body we had found in the Sava Bohinjka."

"I don't understand..."

"Dr Hleb was married, wasn't he?"

"Two kids," the secretary said and Taras waited to see whether she would burst into tears again, but she didn't.

"Can you help us?"

"Help you? With what? How?"

"Do you have any idea who this woman might have been?"

She shook her head.

"This will sound nasty, but you have to understand..."

She flinched.

"...we had a hint worth considering that she might have

been a lover..."

"You bring me," she said, almost clenching her teeth and her face grimacing, "bring me the person who gave you this hint worth considering and I'll tell them straight to their face what I think of them."

"So you think this isn't a possibility?"

"Dr Hleb lived for this here and for his family. He never went anywhere without his wife. She was supposed to go to Bohinj with him but I had to cancel her reservation the last minute because one of their children fell ill."

Taras leaned back in the chair and scratched his head,

"Look, I too am happily married," he said. "I too have two children, but if some beautiful girl twenty years my junior were to cross my path I could find myself in trouble. There aren't many men who could..."

"I don't know what you would do Inspector, and I'm not interested. What I know is that Dr Hleb was not such a man."

Taras put his elbows on the table, entwined his fingers and supported his chin with his thumbs. He sighed and looked into the secretary's eyes. It did not unsettle her.

"And if you want I can put it in writing."

"No need," he said. "I'll do that."

An hour later he and Tina were at Hleb's wife. She lived in Lavrica on the south-eastern outskirts of Ljubljana in a terraced house with a wooden fence and a small garden which probably had flowers growing in it in the summer but was now covered in snow. Taras was glad not to have to be the person to inform her that her husband was dead. As a criminal investigator who was in charge of the case and of course had to participate in inspecting the scene of the crime, he was usually spared this part, though Penca did almost force him some years ago to go on a course for it. It was not worth the money that this extra qualification brought. Now, as he was pressing the bell, he tried to subdue all that was human in him and turn into a machine, a police machine that had to do what a human one could not. The door was opened by a woman who looked too old to be the deceased man's wife and when Taras introduced himself she nodded and invited him inside.

"I'm her mother," she said.

The wife sat on the sofa in the living room, staring with a calm but absent face into the emptiness somewhere beyond the TV which was switched on and showing the National Geographic programme. She gave no indication, either with a gesture or a glance, that she had even noticed them. There was no other noise. The children clearly were not in the house. With unease they sat on the divan opposite her. Taras introduced himself and Tina and expressed his condolences.

"I would like to ask you if you know who could have done something so terrible."

She looked at him for the first time since they had stepped into the room, and this gaze from beyond all the tranquilizers she had been given that day, was in combination with the words she uttered so terrible that Taras only now really regretted that he had not then, in that snowstorm on that last day of the year, just driven past the police vehicle he came across in the middle of the road.

"We knew he was crazy, that he'd do something, but not even we expected something like this."

Her voice was not accusing, just endlessly sad. Taras swallowed his saliva and tried to speak, his first attempt getting lost in a kind of cough before he was able to ask,

"Matej Verbič? Are you talking about him?"

She did not reply, but tears came rolling from her eyes. She did not sob, she did not cry, the tears just ran, dripping onto the off-white sofa.

"Matej Verbič was shot today during a police operation..." Taras continued and carefully observed her face, hoping that he would come across a trace of satisfaction, contentment, but there was none. It was as if he had not said it at all. "Do you know what your husband was doing in Bohinj? Did he inform you of this?"

She gulped and as if speaking was causing her physical pain, uttered,

"I do know... Some arrangement with one of the pharmaceutical companies... He couldn't tell me much more..."

"Is it possible," Taras continued as if he was afraid she might soon run out of energy to continue the conversation, "that what happened to your husband is in any way connected with this?"

"We reported him and they did nothing..."

Taras looked at Tina who picked up a tissue from the table and offered it to the woman. She absently took it and held it in her hand, her tears still dripping unabated onto her knees.

"I don't know whether you know," Taras continued, hating every word he was saying, "but around New Year we found another victim in Bohinj, the body of a young woman... According to the data we have been able to gather, during the meeting in Bohinj, your husband had spoken to an unknown woman who fits the description of the victim. Do you perhaps have any idea who this woman could have been?"

She did not respond, she showed no sign that she had even heard the question. She continued to sit on the sofa, tears still streaming down her cheeks, and when Taras managed to overcome the last drop of humanity in him and was about to repeat the question, she said,

"Woman? He never spoke to me of any woman."

She fell silent again. Taras sat and waited for a while, then looked at Tina who was sitting pale and staring at the floor in front of her, nudged her with his elbow and pointed towards the door.

"Thank you Ma'am, and sorry to have disturbed you. Once again, our deepest sympathies."

"Our deepest sympathies," Tina repeated after him in a voice that sounded like the wife's, on the verge of tears.

He had to hold back not to run outside. When Tina and he stepped out of the house, he beckoned to the elderly lady who had escorted them and she stepped out into the garden. She was wearing just a light cardigan but did not appear to shiver in the cold and it didn't seem as if she noticed the snow and cold around her.

"Look, I need to ask..."

He explained what had brought them to the discovery of Dr Hleb's murder, about the dead girl in the Sava Bohinjka and the meeting with the pharmacists right at the same time, the receptionist...

"...and we would of course like to find out if the murders are related."

He gave her a questioning look.

"And how should I know that?"

"We're interested in what kind of relationship your deceased son-in-law might have had with the girl whom he spoke to at the hotel in December."

The old lady kept looking at him, clearly awaiting a question.

"I'm not alluding at anything, but I'd like to know whether it was possible that they were..."

He stopped and waited to see if she would help him. She didn't. She stared at him expectantly.

"Is it possible that they were lovers?" Tina asked in a tired voice.

The murdered man's mother-in-law slowly but decisively shook her head.

"No."

"You sound very certain," Tina said. "But these are not things that mothers-in-law usually know. Is it possible..."

The old lady smiled with the sad smile of people whose lives have changed forever, who know that things will never be as they used to be, and that the most they can expect from now until their grave is a calm resignation. Questions such as those with which Taras and Tina appeared could not affect her, they were just an incredible nuisance. Had her son-in-law cheated on her daughter...? Even if he had...

"I'm divorced, you see. My husband cheated on me and we split up. If anything, I learnt how to recognize the signs then..."

She shook her head again.

"No, I didn't sense any now."

*

"What if we still don't find out who the first victim was? Tina asked.

Taras looked at his two male colleagues; Brajc rolled his eyes, Osterc shrugged his shoulders.

"You're asking me if I think or assume that Verbič also killed the girl from the lake, aren't you?"

"Yes. We have no proof, do we? In the mails he sent Hleb, in the letters of threats, Verbič never mentions any lover. Would it not have been the most natural thing to do to threaten to tell his wife, before killing him? For a family man such as Hleb is supposed to have been, this would have been a real catastrophe. I checked all his other mail. No personal correspondence with any woman in it at all."

"Perhaps Hleb simply deleted the mails in which Verbič mentioned any lover. Can you check and see if there's any gap in the sequence of the emails we have?"

Tina checked and didn't find any gap at all,

"Thirty letters in thirty days. Pedantic, one a day."

No, of course they had no evidence. Not a single piece. All they had was the receptionist's statement that their second victim had spoken to some woman. This was all. Hleb who could have told them who the woman was is dead. Verbič also.

Brajc, as if he had entirely missed Tina's question turned to Taras and asked,

"Should we, in light of everything, call off tomorrow's exhumation in Jesenice?"

"At Blejska Dobrava[11]," Osterc corrected him.

"Yes, yes, Blejska whatever. We probably don't need to do all this now."

Taras shook his head,

"No. You took it this far, you can go through with it as a reward. If we call it off now, we'll never get permission again. And as far as your apparent concern about Tina; I don't know what's connected to what and what isn't. I hope that it is and perhaps now when we know where to look, it won't be that difficult to prove that Verbič was also somewhere behind the first murder."

As Penca used to say, if you know what to look for you will find it.

"Perhaps it was only in Bohinj that he discovered that Hleb was having a better time than he was and he thought that taking the time to reveal it all to the wife was not enough. Anyway, we will contact Telekom and ask for a printout from their databases

11 Blejska Dobrava, a village to the south-east of Jesenice is where the municipal cemetery is located.

and check all his calls for the last three months. If he was in Bohinj in December then he's the one we are looking for."

"And if he wasn't?"

"If he wasn't then people responsible for making the decisions will tell us what next."

Which probably means that the case of the girl without the head will remain with them until it can be moved to the archive where it will, unless something dramatic happens, remain forever. Basically, for them it will be as if it had all been solved and case closed.

"And anyway, over the weekend I'm going on a skiing trip, no matter what happens, to..." and he made a dramatic pause, "to Bad Kleinkr... Kleink..."

"Bad Kleinkirchheim," Osterc helped him.

Where he would ski the white slopes of Austrian Carinthia and spent the evenings by the fire, taking a dip in the Jacuzzi with a view of the piste-bashers at work and sipping fruit tea.

Chapter 30.

Thursday, 11 January

Klara Hafner, head of the Jesenice Funerary Services sat in her office next to the cemetery in Blejska Dobrava, staring at some papers on her desk. She was trying to solve a curious riddle that was more of a nuisance than interesting. On the hill behind her above the funerary chapels there were about five thousand graves and, especially because of the Muslim migrant workers who came to the industrial town of Jesenice to work, the cemetery was expanding along a former grassy field towards the west. It was not only that Muslims, like the Orthodox Christians, never cremated their dead, it was also that they only buried a single deceased person in each grave.

"Why don't they just tell us what they want," she had complained to her colleagues a little earlier and this thought was still on her mind now that she was sitting alone. Her job was to coordinate these people, the municipality and the old people's home in town where many of the deceased they were obliged to deal with came from.

"Obliged, yes, this is the correct and appropriate phrase."

By law they had to take charge of the deceased from the old people's home and deal with them, which in their case meant bury them. The actual burial was the easy part, before that all the legal matters needed to be sorted out, including finding someone who would pay for the burial. They had to wait for two months with the deceased person in refrigeration before they could bury them or, more often, cremate them, placing their ashes in an urn, and only if within this time period no other option became apparent, did the municipality cover all the costs.

"We can't keep people in refrigeration for two months," she had said at the meeting. "It is not respectful."

The people from the town hall nodded, but nothing changed.

And now she had these criminal investigators around. Through the window of her office she saw the car with the NFL logo on its side stop in the empty parking lot.

Two days earlier Taras had called Golob.

"If we had to exhume the body of a baby to get a DNA sample, would that be possible?" he asked him.

"It depends..." said Golob and Taras explained the background.

"Tut, tut, tut..." he heard down the line.

"Meaning?"

"Meaning it's highly unlikely. You see, a baby's bones are very soft at birth, and contain very small amounts of calcium so under normal circumstances they would disintegrate in thirty years, just as all other soft tissue. You'd need extraordinary circumstances."

"What kind of extraordinary circumstances?"

"For example if the body was waterlogged. Some boggy area or even a broken pipe in a cemetery or something like that. In such circumstances there might be a chance that something was preserved."

"So there is a chance?"

"Theoretically yes, a very small one."

He put down the receiver and called Doles.

"I need an exhumation order."

"An order?"

"Two in fact, two exhumation orders."

Brajc placed both exhumation orders on Klara Hafner's desk, glanced at them and then pushed one closer towards her.

"Sort this out for us."

The Head of Funerary Services picked up the page and read what it said. She looked up and smiled at Brajc,

"Is this how this thing goes?"

He took an instant liking to her.

"I've only been here two years and during this time we've not had an exhumation. If we didn't have it on the price list I wouldn't even know about it. I have a husband at home who's mad about crime investigation series. CSI, NUMB3RS, and especially Bones. And I keep telling him, give me a break, I have plenty of bones to think about at work."

She looked at the page again and the turned to the three men, looking at each one of them individually...

"He's the boss," said Brajc and pointed at Golob.

"Oh, I see," she said and turned towards him. "This will be a difficult one."

"Why?"

"Because," she began. "Come here..."

Golob stepped behind her desk as she typed away in the computer. It took about half a minute for her to find what she wanted.

"Thought so. You see..." she pointed to the screen with her finger. "The child you mention was indeed buried here. There's no name, for the poor kid didn't have one, we do have a date..."

"So?"

"The problem is that there's no record of *where* he was buried.

She glanced across her shoulder towards Golob.

"I'll have the card index checked as well. There might be a note in there, though I doubt it."

Twenty minutes later a small excavator with a container for earth stood next to a double grave. One of the gravediggers was at its wheel and standing next to it were Golob, Brajc, Osterc and the Head of Funerary Services.

"If he's anywhere he'll be in here," she said and pointed to an unkept double grave at the northern most edge of the cemetery. "This is the municipal grave in which we bury the homeless and others without relatives or funds. Or rather we did until we began cremating them. But I don't know how many are buried in here."

Golob shrugged his shoulders and indicated to the gravedigger with the machine to begin.

"I assume you won't need us for a while?" Brajc asked.

Golob shook his head.

"Well, then," Brajc hummed and turned towards Klara

Hafner. "Then you can tell us where we can get a cup of coffee around here and perhaps something spicy with it."

"There's a pub over there in the village," she said. "But you don't need to go there. I can make you a coffee and I know how to spice it up too."

Brajc nodded with even greater satisfaction, looking proudly at Osterc.

Ten minutes later they both had cups of coffee in front of them – even Osterc accepted one this time – as well as a bottle of brandy and a glass in front of Brajc.

"I don't drink," said the Director, "but I know that at a cemetery it comes in useful sometimes."

Golob extended the legs on the fishing stool he always took out in the field with him, sat on it and beckoned to the worker in the miniature excavator. He switched on the engine and the large metal bucket dug into the ground.

"How many are buried in these two graves?" he asked a second worker who came and stood next to him, leaning on the spade, waiting for the excavator to do its part.

"Wouldn't know. Twen'y or so. But none of 'em are very fresh. The last one was buried before I came 'ere."

"In plain wooden coffins?"

"In the ones we 'ave 'ere, yes."

"Then they have probably rotted, haven't they?"

"For sure. These chipboard boxes we sell as caskets are long dust."

Golob turned to the machine about a metre away from him, piling the earth from the grave. For now there were no bones in it. He did not expect to find an entire skeleton, but then he didn't need one. A single tiny bone of the child would do. He smiled. This was much better than lecturing at the university.

A policeman in uniform stepped into the office, glancing at the men sitting at the table and the bottle in front of them.

"I'm looking for two criminal investigators from Ljubljana," he said.

"That'll be us," Brajc said over his glass. "What's up?"

"My commander has sent me. Apparently you're here because of the woman they pulled from the lake."

"From the river running out of the lake," Osterc corrected him.

"Yes, that one. We've just received a message that they've found another in the lake."

"Another what?" Brajc uttered.

"Another body."

Brajc and Osterc looked at each other. Then Brajc slowly raised his glass as if making a toast and drank is slowly before putting it down on the table and looking for his phone in the pocket of his coat.

"God, Taras will be happy to hear this. But he's on his way to Bad Kleinkirchheim."

He said it smoothly without stuttering between the *klein* and *kirchheim*.

Chapter 31.

Thursday, 11 January

The night had been dark, foggy, just what he needed. He stood up at four, stepped out of the house and did not have to look up at the sky to know there were no stars. The dampness saturating the air almost instantly clung to his thick beard.

He turned back into the house, grabbed his old pear-shaped rucksack of light grey canvas which used to be green, his fishing rod, his net, landing net, as they call it, stepped to the extension he used as a garage and sat in the Lada Niva without number plates. It didn't have them because he didn't really need them to drive through the village and off-road to Vogar. He then drove as silently and invisibly as possible towards the lake. Not quietly enough not to wake up a few dogs, but they began barking even at a slightly stronger gust of wind blowing through the bare branches. He could have gone on foot, but for what he was hoping to do, he needed a car. Because if all went well, he would be back before dawn with one of the giant catfish in the back of the car, one of those he was convinced live at the bottom of Fužinar Bay. The largest ever caught between here and Radovljica.

"No catfish in Bohinj Lake? What nonsense," he muttered into his beard when he turned onto the dirt track leading down to the shore. "So wot's this then?"

He waved his hand through the air as if unveiling the cover from the fish that would make Max the Catfish caught by some Austrian guy in Lake Bled look like some poor premature baby.

"Well, if there's none, where does this kitten come from then? Wot 'bout these whiskers?"

There are none because nobody has ever tried to get them

out of the hole in Fužinar Bay, because nobody has ever been hunting for them like he was going now, not even him, especially not during the breeding period when fishing was banned and the fish become careless.

Not only was he a fisherman; like everyone else he knew, all the neighbours and friends, he had also been a hunter since he was eighteen, at twenty he had his own gun, and now possesses a Czech Zbrojovka combination gun to which he later added a Swarovski scope. It shot slightly to the left, but what could he expect, he had bought it second hand and tried for a long time to fix it, but whatever he did, whatever he tried to straighten out its aim, the damn thing still shot to the left. Then he accepted this, learning how to offset it when he used it and that was the end of the problem. And because he was a hunter he was not scared of walking through the forest at night, even if he was alone, he was used to it. But today, as he untied his boat in this mist and stepped into it, he had a strange feeling within. The water was as black as ink and when he struck it with his oars it echoed miles away. Perhaps he was feeling a bit tense because this was illegal out of season, he thought and quenched his doubts with a swig from his hip flask.

"Fuck it, y' 'ave to make summit of yer life," he said, irritatedly realizing he was whispering for which there was no need. The closest living soul was fast asleep in their bed at least half a kilometre away.

About a hundred metres away from the shore he lifted his oars.

"This should be it," he muttered into his beard, peering over the edge of the boat. Perhaps it was because he knew that he was right above the deepest part of the lake, but the water seemed a touch darker here. How many spires of the Church of St John the Baptist would you need to stack in here to reach the bottom? How tall is the spire anyway? He had lived next to it all his life, and, like everyone else, knew that on its wall was a fresco of two white devils, singing angels with goitres and teeth and a mysterious man with an anvil, but how tall was its spire? Fifteen metres? If that was right then he could fit almost three under the boat.

He undid his rucksack, pulled out a sheet of greaseproof paper, unfolded it and placed his bait, three chicken hearts and some liver, on the wooden seat next to him. Then he extended his fishing rod and fixed his chicken bait onto the treble hook which had cost him three euros apiece. Uttering a prayer he had adapted himself to the needs of fishing, he gently lifted it above the water,

"Angel of God, me guardian dear, get me a fish tonight, bring it right 'ere, ever this day, be at me side, and please show me now, where the best fishes do hide."

He threw the bait into the water.

"Amen!"

Almost without a sound the bait disappeared into the dark depths. Slowly but evenly he unwound the point-six-millimetre, bright, plastic line, the end of which was attached to an even thicker braided string with the hook. He knew that with the tension capacity of the main line a thicker string at the end is not of much use, that the main line would snap before this, but he didn't have it for the tension, he had it because of the catfish's teeth.

"Come, come, kitty..." he whispered as the bait travelled into the depths, "now we'll see how sharp y'r tiny teeth are."

A minute later the line was still, the reel stopped spinning. He adjusted the drag knob, placed the rod inside the boat and took his sandwich, his breakfast, out of his rucksack.

Finding his cigarettes in his pocket, he selected one from the packet and lit it. He inhaled the smoke deeply. And he waited.

*

As much as Taras loved cross-country, he hated alpine skiing. He had nothing against the actual moves, sliding down a snowy slope, even though he was not a good skier. In fact he had learnt the basics through cross-country skiing and anyone who learns how to hold their balance on the matchstick-thin skis used in cross-country will also know how to turn corners on the wider alpine skis, even though it might not be exactly elegant. Everything else got on his nerves. From the queues at the chairlifts in Kranjska Gora where he would take Anja and Mojca, to the people queuing up there. When the girls were old enough he let Alenka look after them on the ski slope, after all she had even completed a skiing instructor course. He would spend the time the girls were on the slopes down in the valley on his cross-country skis.

Well, this was also a way of saving on a day ticket, and he also did not have to produce his police badge every time some spoilt teenage brat tried to jump the queue and would then just laugh off his warnings.

"Fucking get in line or we'll go to the station," he threatened one of them and waved his police badge in front of him.

"Taras..." said Alenka through her clenched teeth as they had sat on the chairlift taking them up to the top of Vitranc. "Do you have to? Did you have to do that?"

He had to, yes, and it clearly had an effect.

"It's only because you've never been on a real ski slope," Alenka kept telling him and, after her father returned into her life, kept promising him they would go skiing abroad. To please her he pretended he was interested and then made sure every time that they didn't go. This time, as he was standing at the car loading their skis, it seemed that he had exhausted all possibilities of getting out of it. Perhaps it will not be that bad, he told himself. Six and three quarter billion people on this planet aren't lucky enough to be able to afford skiing, perhaps this will somehow be above his expectations... If only they were going alone and not with the Balažičes. He couldn't expect much from these two fat people who will tire him every evening by munching away and talking about food and wine. And, for the six hundredth time he will have to explain why he does not drink.

Why don't you have one anyway?

He counted the skis, beside the alpine skis he had also put in his cross-country ones, the ski boots and cross-country boots, and was about to close the boot when Alenka appeared at the door holding his phone.

"It's Brajc," she said with a questioning look.

"How's things?" said Brajc who hoped that phones, however modern and whatever applications they come with, still could not transmit the smell of your breath long distance.

"Tell me!"

*

Two hours later he nervously checked his watch, shining a light on it to see. The hands and markings on the watch face were in fact fluorescent and would glow if there was at least some light on them, but none came through the thick mist. He used his lighter and muttered in annoyance. Ten more minutes, he said to himself, hopeful and disappointed at the same time. Ten more minutes and he would need to pack up, row the boat to the shore, return the car to the garage and go about his business as if there had been no night trip at all. God, I'll be tired today, he said to himself, and more so because it was in vain. At least there was not much to do on the farm during the winter. Then, as if guilty for even thinking it, he immediately corrected himself. There is always plenty to do on the farm.

"There's always work, work is good," he repeated out loud.

The line hadn't even moved since he threw in the bait. It was as if the lake was dead.

Nothing. Ten minutes went by, and as any fisherman, he wanted to give himself another ten but when he looked upwards the sky above was changing from black to grey. He sighed, grabbed the rod and tugged it a couple of times and then let it loose again. He knew this was not the way to do it because the hook could get caught on some branch or something else at the bottom of the lake but at this time it didn't really matter. He spat at the water and began winding the nylon line onto the reel. It barely spun twice or three times when it stopped. So suddenly and with a jerk that instead of the line, the boat moved. Just what I need, he thought when it tightened unexpectedly, the hook was stuck, but what if...

He was overcome with fervent expectation. If it did not move, if it did not budge, it means it is stuck on some thick branch that has been rotting down there for centuries. But if it does... He pulled harder but still gently enough for not it to snap. It stayed taut and when he was about to let go, swear and drop everything, but thought he should try once more and if it didn't work this time he would find his knife and cut the line and go home. Whatever it was that was caught on his line moved and gave him a few centimetres of line, which he quickly wound onto the reel. He pulled again and it gave way again, he wound the reel as quickly as he could and slowly realized with disappointment that what was at the end of the line could not be a fish. If it were, it would resist – what he had caught was heavy and still, goodness knows how long it had been at the bottom of the lake, three steeples under the surface, and now it was being steadily pulled towards him. God knows what it will be. People throw all kinds of stuff into the lake.

He leaned across the side of the boat. It's time you reveal yourself, whatever you are, he said, and placed the net closer, just in case. Perhaps it is some tired old catfish after all. It might not be fit for consumption, but a trophy at least. Then the water stirred and three bubbles of gas broke the surface and reached his nose.

"Yuck!" he almost shouted when the stench of rot reached him. "What kind of a rotting carcass..."

He leaned across the water, held the line and pulled it for the last time. He was already holding the string with the lead weights. Thirty centimetres below hung something heavy. He pulled it closer and screamed in horror.

The Devil himself appeared from the water, covered in algae, the skin beneath them white as lime, one eye wide open, the other eye socket empty, hollow, with the large catfish hook caught in it, still decorated with chicken hearts and liver, as if they had been pulled out of the head of this monster.

He jumped back, fell into his boat which rocked on the water and when, after spending a minute or so lying on the wet floor of the boat he dared look over the edge again, neither the head or what was below it, nor his fishing rod were anywhere to be seen. He rowed madly back to the shore, jumped out of the boat without pulling it out of the water, and ran, straight past the car, all the way home.

Chapter 32.

Four hours later Golob had to admit defeat. There were countless bones on the green military canvas next to which he was squatting, but however he looked at them, and whichever way he turned them, there were none that could belong to a child, a newborn baby. The earth they had been digging also did not give much hope of preserving them, dry, sandy, far too aerated. He stood up and shook his head to Brajc who re-appeared for the first time since they had started. Osterc came to see how things were progressing a number of times.

"If it ain't there, it ain't there," said Brajc. "Even the army can't take if there's nothing to take."

He pulled his mobile phone from his pocket and dialled a number.

"Mission accomplished, unfortunately without success. Do you want to speak to Golob?"

He passed the phone to Golob.

"No luck Taras. If indeed he was in one of the two graves we looked at, he is no more. There's nothing left."

"Ask him whether we still need to go to Srednja Vas or if that is off now? Or give me..."

He almost pulled the phone from Golob's hand and repeated the question.

"Yes, but..."

He rolled his eyes and said goodbye.

"Taras would still like us to excavate the grave in Srednja Vas. We'll waste the whole day..."

He swore and walked off towards the car. A puzzled Golob stared after him and then looked at the worker by the grave.

"And what do we do with this now?" the excavator operator

asked. "Should we re-bury it all?"

"Yes, probably..."

The worker with the spade picked up the four corners of the canvas with the bones and shook the contents back into the open grave. The digger driver switched on the engine and grabbed a load of earth with the bucket. With mixed feelings Golob set off after Brajc and Osterc towards the car.

*

"If you have to, then you have to," she said and sat in the back seat of the Audi Q5.

"I do have to," said Taras. "And I don't really think it's fair for..." but she had already closed the door.

As Balažič's car drove down the street and Taras waved without Alenka waving back, he thought about how this would be the first time since they had had their children that they would spend more than two, perhaps at the most three days apart. He unloaded his gear from his own car, leaving only his usual cross-country skis, then he found his phone and dialled a number.

"What do you want, Taras, it's Friday?" came from the speaker.

"Another body has surfaced in Bohinj and I was wondering whether you'd be interested."

"You know I don't go out into the field any more," Cvilak said.

"One last time before retirement?"

Silence.

"In fact I'm going there accompanied by a young woman and need a chaperone in case she succumbs to my charms."

He had to wait a few more seconds for an answer.

"Give me half an hour to get ready. What's this about?"

Taras told him what he knew and as he said goodbye to Cvilak and searched for Tina's number he had a silly thought. This will be quite a party, he said to himself.

Stara Fužina does not have a cemetery of its own. It belongs to the parish of Srednja Vas and the Church of St Martin which lies, with its adjoining cemetery, on a steep hill above the village. Its location makes it look larger than it actually is. The burial ground is very different from the Jesenice one in Blejska Dobrava.

Only neat Catholic graves with tombstones or wooden crosses, full of flowers, and near the fence a stone obelisk overlooking the village, dedicated to those who had fallen in the Great War, listing the names and dates of birth of all who had died.

"Don't tell me they're having a funeral?" said Osterc when they approached the church up a steep road through some houses. There were so many people walking up the hill that they could move only slowly through the crowd.

"They seem to be giving us some angry looks," said Brajc.

They stopped their vehicle outside the small parking lot on the terrace to the right of the entrance where a small excavator was waiting, similar to the one in Jesenice. Outside because the entrance to the parking lot was blocked with a wooden bar. Golob opened the window and addressed the men who were standing by it,

"Can you move this out of the way please?"

They didn't respond, just stared at them, even more angrily than before.

"We're from the police..." Golob tried but to no effect.

Brajc opened the door and stepped outside.

"What is it?" he shouted at them. "Are you deaf? We're here on official business and anyone who tries to make thing difficult for us is fucked."

The men at the horizontal wooden barrier looked at each other. One of them stepped forward and stood in front of Brajc. He was around forty years old, perhaps a year or two older, dressed in green hunting gear and a matching hat.

"Don't care if you're cops, you're not diggin' up our graveyard."

He looked familiar to Brajc, though he could not quite place him.

"And you are?"

"You know damn well who I am."

Then it dawned on him. A day earlier they had talked on the phone. Although talk is perhaps a too optimistic way of describing their conversation.

"Hello," Brajc had said then. "I'd like to talk to Mr Janez Baloh."

Silence down the line.

"I'm from the police and I'd like to talk to him, talk to you if you're him..."

"And what would y' like to talk to me about?" a mistrustful voice at the end of the line asked.

"About the death of your sister Diana Baloh..."

"That's not summit I'm gonna talk about."

"Listen," Brajc tried, "I would only..."

But he was already talking into the beeping indication that the phone had been put down.

"You're not gonna go disturbin' me sister!" the man shouted and as he shouted the crowd which had been approaching the church gathered around them. "Desecrators!" he howled. "Grave robbers!"

"This is what I wanted to talk to you about," Brajc tried again. "If you agreed to a DNA test..."

"I'm not givin' ya anything!" he shouted. "You're not gonna be doin' tests on anything 'ere!"

Brajc pulled his police badge from his pocket and held it furiously in front of him.

"See this?!" he shouted but had to pull it back to avoid it being spat on by the man in the hunting gear. The spit landed on Brajc's jacket.

"Fucking hell!" he shouted and took a step towards Baloh. The crowd behind them stood still and silent as if not knowing whether to continue to support him or wait and see what would happen. After all, these people were some kind of police, even if they weren't in uniform, and spitting at the police...

"Hang on! Stop this!" Golob stepped in front of Brajc with his hands up. "Perhaps you're right. It's not right to be digging up such a neat graveyard."

The crowd stared at him. He turned towards Brajc and used a tissue to wipe the spit off his jacket.

"We'll sort this out another way. There's no need to get upset."

He went to the driver's seat, indicating to Brajc to follow him into the car. Brajc gazed around at the glaring hateful eyes and said out loud, "Why am I bloody well even bothering..." opened the door and sat on the back seat.

"What's the deal here, Golob?" he asked but Golob didn't reply because he was using a cotton bud to stuff the tissue into a test tube.

*

Taras, Tina and Cvilak reached Ribčev Laz in the afternoon when the sun was already setting behind Vogel and the temperature had dropped below zero. They parked on the parking lot at Hotel Jezero, much fuller than during their first visit, and cleared of all snow down to the dry asphalt. Already parked there was the car belonging to Golob's team with the National Forensic Laboratory logo on its side. Taras found Golob at the hotel bar where he was waiting in the company of two colleagues, together with Doles and another man he did not know. Taras checked the time. Four o'clock. He would have been somewhere past Villach by now, less than an hour away from Bad Kleinkirchheim, if the Michelin Route Planner was anything to go by. He felt relieved.

Cvilak and Tina hit it off instantly. Tina was charming and responded politely to all of Cvilak's questions which were similar to Taras' when they first met, then she enquired about his beginnings and heard the same story Taras had heard, though she was treated to it a decade or so earlier in her career than Taras had been. Then they talked about Milčinski, Cvilak's mentor and giant of Slovene pathology with Tina mentioning two of his cases and asking for Cvilak's opinion on things Taras had never heard of, so that somewhere as they passed the exit towards Tržič the old man nodded with satisfaction towards the driver, and said out loud,

"You did well here, dear Taras!"

By the time they reached Radovljica and Taras checked his rear-view mirror, Cvilak was already fast asleep. Tina smiled and winked at him. He didn't know why, but it felt good that she had passed this test.

"We won't be doing any more today," Golob said instead of a greeting. "The valve on one of the cylinders has gone. We'll get a new one tomorrow morning and the divers can go back into the water. It won't be easy because... Well, the gentleman will tell you himself."

He pointed to the man with a thick, bushy, slightly greying beard who was sitting next to him, looking somewhat remorseful. He was wearing a hunting jacket with a thick grey jumper beneath. He wore hunting knickerbockers with thick socks and some kind of heavy boots on his feet. Sticking out of his pocket was a hat or maybe his gloves, the same colour as the jumper. Taras stepped to the table and shook his hand. The man emitted a mixture of smells of which the one stinking of stables was the least obtrusive.

"Štefe," he introduced himself. "My name is Anton, but people call me Tona."

Tina offered him her hand as well and he shook it the same way as Taras' without any particular enthusiasm. Taras looked around the bar and pointed at an empty table in the far corner,

"Let's go over there."

They sat down and as the waiter approached their table Taras dismissed him with a resolute wave of the hand. He pulled his notebook and pen from his pocket.

"Well then Tona, what is it you're saying happened?"

The man coughed, his embarrassment clearly increasing.

"Well, this is how it was... I was out on the lake, right. I wanted to try out some equipment, and..."

He stopped and cautiously looked at Taras.

"Even though there's a fishing ban," Taras helped him.

The man began fidgeting with embarrassment...

"Well, in fact I went for the catfish, right, and they say there ain't any catfish 'ere anyway..."

He stopped again and stared at the tablecloth, waiting for Taras to either save him or condemn him. Taras allowed him to smoulder in silence for a while.

"That's an offence," Taras then continued as if he had not heard the last part about the catfish, "but my colleague here and those over there..." he pointed towards the table where Golob's team and Cvilak were sitting, "are not here to catch offenders. We're here about something else and if you'll make the effort to help us we'll be happy to forget all about why you were out on the lake."

The man was visibly relieved.

"I could 'ave just not told ya 'bout it, right," he said far too courageously for Taras' liking.

"In which case you would be committing a criminal act, not just an offence. And criminal acts cannot just be forgotten.

When he finished Taras had three sentences in his notebook.

"Was it a male or female head?" he asked.

"I dunno... I think it was a man."

"Just the head?"

"What d' ya mean?"

"Was what you pulled out of the water just a head or was there anything attached to it?"

"Oh, course there was. Me first thought was I wouldn't even be able to pull it out."

Taras looked at his notes again. Nothing, that was it.

"And what do you think about the whole thing?"

The man gave him a puzzled look.

"What d' ya mean the 'ole thing?"

"You've probably heard that this is not the first body from the lake we're dealing with?"

The fisherman shrugged his shoulders.

"I dunno. That woman ain't one of us, cos..."

"You would have known?"

"Yes. And this one too. There's no one missing in the village."

Taras nodded. In a small place everyone knows everything about everyone. And all stay silent if needed.

"Was it you who told my colleague about a woman who was pregnant and then there was no child. Was that all you knew about it?"

He carefully observed the bearded face as he asked the question and it was just as well he did, otherwise he would have missed the brief moment when the man's pupils widened. A second later he was back in control, perhaps his eyes a touch narrower than they had been.

"Yes, the poor Bučar girl, she jumped into the water. What else is there to know? Even that's too much."

Taras tried again with the question about who had got her pregnant and how come the police never looked into the matter at the time, and what people had said about it, what happened to the child... All he got was,

"Wouldn't know that."

Taras sighed and turned towards Tina who seemed to be waiting for him to do so.

"Were you the father of this child?"

Tona flinched, straightened the top part of his body as if wanting to push away from the table, and almost shouted,

"No, no, course not! No way! How could I..."

He stared at Tina in horror. She shrugged her shoulders.

"I thought you'd also respond to this with, wouldn't know that."

Taras sighed and looked at his notes again as if to check whether what he had noted was useful in any way and when he decided it wasn't turned to Tona and said,

"So this is all you can tell us?"

The man shook his head, stroked his beard, swayed in the chair as if struggling with his conscience, then conspiratorially leaned towards Taras. Taras also moved closer and his nostrils caught a new stench of stables, stale sweat and alcohol.

"You know, those cat fish, they really are down there, at the bottom of Fužinar Bay, you just remember that."

"So we've finished for today?" Taras asked when they returned to Golob, his team and Cvilak.

"We would have even without the problems with the valve. Do you know how deep that part of the lake is? Not to mention that the water is barely a degree or two above freezing. They went down once, more than that wouldn't even be by the book."

"And what now?" Cvilak asked.

Taras had turned to him for help. When Brajc had called him he had thought that there was a body waiting for them in Bohinj, not that they would need to find the body first.

"So we go back and come again tomorrow or what?"

Taras shrugged his shoulders.

"When will you lot be here?" Cvilak asked Golob.

"Six, half past. So they can go down as soon as it gets light. Even though I must admit, I could do with a long sleep. I've been rushing around since morning. Two cemeteries and now this. Do you know what happened to us in Srednja Vas?"

Taras nodded. Brajc had told him the entire story.

Cvilak cleared his throat and looked at Taras.

"Then, my dear, you will book two rooms at the hotel. One for us and one for the young lady here. I'm too old for this kind of stuff."

Taras scratched his head. It was not that he too wasn't too old, he just wasn't sure that Drvarič would sign for the expense. He checked his notes for the phone number of the director of the hotel. Perhaps he could arrange some kind of exchange. A couple of rooms in return for discretion.

Chapter 33.

The night was the entire opposite of the morning, clear and light with a moon so bright, also because of the snow, that Taras wondered whether he even needed to switch on his head torch or just ski along without it, though in the end he did use it. The snow was fantastic, old and compact, it had melted slightly during the day and frozen again in the evening, so it was smooth and gentle on Taras' skis which he could never be bothered to wax. Even if he did wax them he barely noticed the difference. He probably would were his technique better, but this way… He wasn't after any records anyway.

"And you're going now?" Cvilak asked and looked at his wristwatch. He was one of the few people Taras knew who still wore a watch. Well, apart from Kristan and Drvarič. "Do you know what time it is?"

"Mustn't get fat."

Cvilak looked at him in pity.

"You, get fat?"

It is interesting how quite clever people, people of science, mix up the cause with the result as soon as they veer away from their own field. Taras was slim because he exercised, he did not exercise because he was slim. He often smiled when people said things like, lucky you, you can eat all you want. He could only do so because he sweated it all off afterwards.

"Well, then so that I can enjoy the beer at the bar more when I come back."

Cvilak smiled,

"You mean your coke? Well, I'll enjoy mine without the effort."

"It's not the same," said Taras. "Believe me, after some

physical work it really is satisfying."

Taras knew the cross-country *loipe* from Ribčev Laz to Bohinjska Bistrica or rather the landscape through which it ran and when there was enough snow on the ground he considered it one of the nicest in Slovenia, diverse throughout, but without any steep hills. It was set out as set of circular runs, the longest about ten kilometres in length and was usually not as crowded as other cross-country runs in better known ski centres. He could ski along without having to move out of the way of frustrated enthusiasts who had not made it to competition level and used people like him to build their ego. Added to that there was no great danger of coming across dog walkers who would make holes in the track with their shoes in which you could easily break a ski pole or you could get flung over the tips of your skis when you skidded on dog shit. In any case he was the only one on the track at this time.

He liked cross-country skiing more than any other sport. Firstly, all parts of the body were involved. Leg muscles, of course, from the calf muscles to the glutes, abdominal muscles, back and shoulders, and hands. And the heart, the lungs, the veins... it was this muscular-cardiovascular combination which made sliding along the compact snow for half an hour a kind of meditation. All irrelevant thoughts faded away, stress hormones disappeared in a wave of endorphins if people who studied the process scientifically were to believed, and all that was left was the rhythm, the alternate lifting of the left, then the right ski, pushing on the left, then the right, right pole, then left, breathing, droplets of sweat... He could forget about everything when cross-country skiing. There were times when he could not sleep, when he had stomach cramps because of the stress, and if he hadn't been able to exercise then, and cross-country was his preferred exercise in winter, his own gastric acids would have burnt through his intestines. After an hour, an hour and a half, he would neutralize it and be fine. It took him a while to realize that this was what was keeping him going and he stopped worrying about not doing something more useful in his spare time. Building an extension or washing the car. Anyway, what can be more useful than preventing your own ruin?

It was cold but when he warmed up it was quite bearable. Minus six, minus seven. He thought about the dead girl, the dead Hleb, the dead stranger in the lake and it took a kilometre of so for these thoughts to go away and be replaced by emptiness, *samādhi*. He was old enough not to train according to some kind of programme, in fact he never did. He knew that the more one tried, the more one can get from running or whatever one is doing, but also that not every day was appropriate for racing around until you drop. So he let the feet and his lungs decide. Was today a day he could push them to the end, or just a day for simply sliding along.

He set off slowly, getting a feel for the ground, and revving up the heart, muscles and ligaments and, when he felt he could, he would push harder. He was doing so well that he had to hold himself back not to exaggerate, not to build up his lactic acid too much on an upwards slope, so well he enjoyed his descents and wasn't even concerned he might be thrown off some blind curve, so well he wasn't even aware of the surroundings when he realized that he was already coming to the finish line and past it, and went on go round the circuit a second time. So well that on his second round, without needing to, he slowed dropped his tempo, switched off his head torch and enjoyed gliding through the nocturnal landscape.

"*Is it getting better, or do you feel the same*..." floated into his thoughts. "*...will it make it easier on you now*..."

They were listening to the radio in the car. Cvilak was snoozing on the seat next to him and Taras who knew the lyrics was humming them silently. At his favourite verse he looked in the rear view mirror and saw Tina, also singing along quietly. She realized he was watching her and smiled with embarrassment.

"*...have you come here for forgiveness, have you come to raise the dead*..."

How old was she then, at some point in the early nineties, when U2 came out with this album. Five, six?

"*...have you come here to play Jesus to the lepers in your head*..."

Interesting... How could he at first have thought her face was somewhat imbalanced? He would see her again in half an hour's time and must remember to ask her how come she knows the song.

"And where into this story does the new corpse fit in?"

It went through his head so suddenly that he shook irritatedly as if in doing so the thought would go away.

"Where does this new corpse fit in?"

Not only did the thought not go away, it brought with it two further images, a shot of the white female torso his hand is pulling out of the water and where the head should have been he sees the clean cut stump of the neck and what was left of the face of the Dean of the Biotechnical Faculty which, alternating with the previous image of Tina's face smiling with embarrassment but still repeating the words of the song, seemed like some PowerPoint projection inside his head. He tried to make it go away, think only of Tina singing the lyrics to the song playing on the radio, but it didn't work. He swore and almost stopped, then sighed and continued, no longer trying to rid his thoughts of the images which had intruded into them, there was no way of making them go away.

So let us, he said to himself, look at this thing from a distance instead, get a satellite image, as Penca used to say, look, think, and try to establish if the two images are related. Is Dr Hleb's murderer also the killer of the girl without a head? What does intuition say about this? And what about the person who killed the unknown man at the bottom of the lake?

He reached the curve where the track touched Bohinjska Bistrica and turned back. In front of him as a longish, slightly steeper hill which on this run meant about two hundred metres in length of more intensive effort. With the gradient the two images vanished, all that remained was the ribbed groomed snow and the uneven ski tracks left by other skiers during the day when the snow was softer. Push with the left leg, push with the right, left pole, right, the warm and humid air he breathed out appearing like a cloud of steam in front of him, fogging his view, droplets of sweat gathering on the edges of his hat, freezing into glass tears at the tips of his hair, and as soon as the track levelled out once more, the image of the first corpse appeared again, then the second... And nothing... He found nothing and the images didn't take him anywhere. They alternated at a slower pace and slowly began to disperse. When he had almost stopped thinking about them, when they had faded away, another image appeared before him, that of Hleb's mother-in-law, looking at Tina...

"Is it possible that they were lovers?"

And the eyes asking him in return, is this relevant? What is important anyway? The man is dead, just as he would be dead some day... Prelc, from somewhere Prelc appeared, the face, trying to tell him something, tense, trying to speak... What? Only a few days ago he sat with him on the terrace at his weekend house on the dark side of the lake, watching the snow fall. Prelc was smoking dope, drinking wine and explaining how he had slept with all the women in the house except for the fat Balažič woman... And now he too has died, though he does still breathe and his heart still beats... The image of Alenka, driving off in someone else's car without even looking back...

Had he also slept with Alenka?

The stump, the eye hanging from the socket, Tina's eyes, Alenka's question, "Hmmm, so Irena actually hasn't?", Prelc's grunt and his eyes gazing at him from his ash-grey face... All this rolled through his mind into the emptiness.

Was that "absolutely every one of them" something vague or did he say it deliberately? Was it a slip of the tongue? Had Alenka's father planted Prelc on him? Was this the old man's doing?

Before him was a series of short uphill slopes which brought him to the highest point on the loipe. He pushed towards it, rushed, jumped from his leisurely pace to the fastest he could, pushing himself to the end, right to the end... and when he reached the point from which the rest of the track went only downhill, he collapsed. He fell to his knees and rolled over onto his side, curled up with his face in the snow.

When he looked up again and his heartbeat had calmed enough that his irregular painful gasping for air became a deep steady breathing, he turned onto his back and saw the billions of stars visible in such a place where they are not obscured by artificial light or polluted air. Like that time, a long time ago, at base camp under Dhaulagiri when he had gone out of his tent for a piss in the middle of the night and could not make himself to go back for a long time. He had stood under the monumental white mass which rose almost four kilometres above him and stared at the stars above it, listened to the wind which streamed from the Hidden Valley towards the French Pass, discovering how enlighteningly unimportant everything is. He, his fellow climber sleeping in the tent, the others in other tents, the people down in the valley, the billion in India towards the south, all and everything in the world.

He stood up and was about to ski down the hill, his hands still on his thighs, when he caught sight of the silver reflection on the lake in the distance. Was that a light on its surface? He stopped and looked. The light flickered and split in a straight line into a number of smaller sparkles... No, it was not a light, only the reflection of the moon. He waited for a moment for the beating of his heart to settle and could feel the silence around him. From where he stood he saw a large part of the lake and not a sign of human presence. Stara Fužina was hidden behind one hill, the hotel by the lake behind another. At the far western end of the lake, in Ukanc, a milky mass lingered, the mist that will probably cover the entire lake by morning but was not moving for now, held around the weekend houses of Ljubljana doctors. No light anywhere apart from the sky, no car, not even a barking dog. In the meantime the barely noticeable wind had also abated and in the stillness the lake reflected the moon and the stars that seemed no longer to twinkle, and it was almost impossible to distinguish between what was the lake and what the sky. If anything like a body was to float to the surface now, he would notice it, see the waves spread in concentric circles with a tiny dot in the middle. He was sorry that he has spoilt the image for himself in this way.

Where was all this coming from, why these thoughts? Was he more resistant? Would cross-country skiing not be enough from now on? Was his last antibiotic becoming ineffective?

What's the point, he said to himself, why bother yourself with this? Give Alenka a break. What does it matter what happened... no point at all. Leave things that are buried where they are.

He felt cold and skied down the slope.

Chapter 34.

There was nobody in the room. For a while he thought about lying down on the floor but he touched the fitted carpet and decided it was too hard, so he went to take a shower. He felt a pleasant tiredness, pleasant also at the thought that for today he had finished with all obligations. All. That the only other thing he would do today was be social with people whom he in some way or other found likeable. He called Cvilak and found out that he and Tina were sitting in the hotel bar.

"So we've had our run, have we?" Cvilak asked.

"Indeed."

"I must admit I admire you, Taras."

Taras shrugged his shoulders,

"That's the most common reaction I provoke. Admiration."

Tina laughed and Cvilak looked at her from under his brow.

"Clearly the case with your colleague here. She was asking me about you but I was unable to enlighten her."

Tina blushed.

"What was it that you were interested in?"

"Just asking in general..." she managed to mutter and stared blankly ahead.

"Well, take your time," said Cvilak and pushed away from the table. "I'll go and make use of our apartment being empty."

"Won't you have something to drink with us?"

Cvilak shook his head,

"I've already had a drink, and if I have more, I'll feel like shit tomorrow. I'm old enough to know when to stop. Unfortunately. And by the way, I snore. So just wake me up when you come in and I'll try and move to make it less irritating."

He beckoned to the waiter and dismissed Taras' attempt at

suggesting he would settle the bill.

"Do you have alcohol-free beer?"

The waiter shook his head, "We do have light beer."

He ordered a sandwich, a coke and a glass of water. The waiter looked at Tina and the empty coffee cup in front of her.

"Will you have anything else?"

Tina looked at her cup and then at Taras who also looked at her cup. She smiled – she had an interesting smile, her slightly prominent canines rendered it the smile of a cute female vampire. When he was a boy he had had a cat with fangs that grew so large they stuck out of its snout even when its mouth was closed. Not that Tina's teeth did.

"In fact yes, I'd like a beer now."

The waiter walked off to the counter and Taras watched him for a second or two. How long had it been since he last had a beer… Did he even remember the taste?

"Is it fine for me to have a beer?" she asked like some schoolgirl.

"Gastroesophageal reflux."

"Sorry?"

"I have an upset stomach syndrome, and react badly to alcohol."

"What?"

"That's what people usually ask me. That's why I don't drink."

He explained the story in three sentences. He was happy that she did not ask further questions or try the usual, how do you know you still have the problem if you haven't had anything to drink for so long? He just does.

"What I meant was if you mind if I have one?" she asked.

"No, I'm used to watching others drink."

She laughed.

"I mean in view of the fact that you're my boss."

"I don't know whether you'll get any travel allowance for this today so, technically speaking, you're no longer at work."

They both laughed.

The waiter brought the sandwich, the coke and the beer and forgot about the water. It was one of those places where beer, as a supposed sign of finesse, was only served in small bottles.

When he used to still drink he found this terribly annoying. Now he had a bottle of dark sweetened liquid with some caffeine in it anyway, and his cells yearned for both the sugar and the caffeine. Tina poured her beer into the glass and took a sip. He had trained himself not to think about it, but occasionally couldn't help himself. Like now, for example. He envied her that beer so much. He began eating his sandwich.

"Do you regularly go cross-country skiing?"

"Oh, that? I thought you would be asking more difficult questions."

"Those come later."

This was the third time in the last two years. No, he didn't go cross-country skiing often because there was rarely enough snow. He used to go more regularly when winters were still proper winters.

"Now I do more running than skiing. Rožnik, the Polhov Gradec Hills, sometimes a night run up Šmarna Gora. A kind of running walk."

She was wearing a tight green jumper and Taras had to consciously not stare at her breasts. If he did he then he had to make himself remember that he was twenty or so years older than her and that neither Mihelič nor Prelc would have any such problems. He wanted to believe that it was because he was better than them but what if it was just a case of not having the opportunity? What if this was about him not being born a winner, not having their inbred disregard? What if this was a case of sour grapes morals? How many women could he have as a criminal investigator, even if he wanted to? How many compared to a doctor-surgeon at the medical faculty? Compared to the director of the largest pharmaceutical company in the country? So few that the idea of her taking off the tight green jumper in front of him, because of him, taking off her bra... seemed tempting and at the same time so unfeasible that it was harmless. A beer would undoubtedly help him see it in a more relaxed way, that much he remembered, and thought that perhaps she too had ordered it because of similar restraints.

"That thing the other day was a bit childish of me."

"Which thing?"

She lowered her eyes as if embarrassed to confess.

"The thing about... Disappointment, that the murderer is a plain old madman, and similar teenage stuff like that... that I'm not Miss Marple... When we got to the wife, I... sobered up."

She looked at him.

"You know... realized this is not some crime novel or film, that the dead are not just corpses."

"I thought it was seeing Hleb's face which got to you."

She thought for a moment and shook her head,

"No, it wasn't that. Really not. It wasn't pleasant, especially for the stomach, but I don't know... It was worse seeing the wife. That's one thing I would not want to repeat."

"Nobody would."

She picked up her glass and took a long sip. Taras finished off his coke. The problem with abstinence is that there is no meaningful alternative to alcohol. Especially if there is no non-alcoholic beer available which at least seems similar in volume.

She spilt her beer onto her jumper.

"Don't tell me I'm already tipsy?"

She used a napkin to start wiping away the few drops.

"And besides, with the new guy in the lake you got back your CSI."

When she stretched the jumper the view was even more pleasant. For a moment he wondered whether she had done it deliberately. At least slightly deliberately.

"Do you watch any of these series?"

He nodded.

"Even after all these years and all these cases?"

"When I do watch them, I don't watch them in this way. It's about relationships, with a framework... Just a framework. It could be a police setting, a hospital setting, whatever. In the end it's all about whether or not they'll get hitched."

He told her the joke about the grandma who was caught watching porn at one o'clock in the morning by her grandson...

Besides, recently he didn't watch much other than sports on TV. Champion's League, the Paris Masters, Wimbledon, the Tour de France... He has not watched the news for a long time, any films just from DVDs.

Another sip. She filled her glass. There was only just a tiny amount of beer left in her bottle.

"Why did you join the police, Taras?"

"And now come the real questions?"

He smiled. She didn't join in.

"Yes."

"So, why did I join the police?"

He picked up his bottle as if there was still something in it, when he realized there wasn't he put it down on the table again.

"Now there's a boring story."

"I like boring stories," she said and leaned back in the sofa. "If, of course, you can be bothered to talk about it. Cvilak warned me that you might not."

Taras looked for the waiter who was propped up on the counter trying not to notice anyone.

"No you don't. Nobody likes boring stories, that's why films and crime series are the way they are. Because..."

He pointed at her almost empty bottle and she nodded. He waved at the waiter and showed him with his finger and raised thumb that they wanted another round. He brought is and picked up Tina's empty bottle.

"In fact... bring me a coffee instead," said Taras.

"So coffee doesn't affect you?" she asked.

"No, but I don't drink that many anyway. Two a day."

He waited for the waiter to bring him his third coffee of the day. She waited patiently for him to move it from the tray onto the table and take a sip.

"That was not what I asked, Taras, but alright... And why not?"

"Because the perpetrators are usually as dumb as hell. All the series you watch are based around psychologically fucked up investigators. And crime novels. There's no such thing as a genius perpetrator in these things. Most of the time they're criminals by chance, sloppy.... But do you know how we catch most burglars?"

She shrugged her shoulders.

"We catch the common burglar because they usually take a pair of pliers, hit something or cut through it, and then forget the pliers there. They forget the tools they used to break in. Always, almost always. Or, while on the job, they light a cigarette and leave the butt on site. When I lose my job I'll go into crime, I'll pick up cigarette butts in bars and leave them lying around at the scene of a crime as a diversion."

Had he been drinking beer now he could have used it as an excuse.

"You're a beautiful woman," he said. "I don't like to admit it, but for once in his life Drvarič was actually right."

"I'm not having a beer so I would sleep with you, Taras."

"What for then?"

"The taste."

They laughed and Taras wondered whether her response should be met with regret or relief.

"The problem is when you can't find any logic, when you don't know why someone did something. Some chance perpetrator who has never done anything and then suddenly loses it. That's the problem. Although they will, sooner or later, spill the beans themselves."

Tina's phone rang, she found it in her jacket pocket, looked at the number and silenced it,

"Go ahead..."

She shook her head.

"I remember some guy who had forged eight hundred and fifty cheques and they tried to make him write something in order to compare his handwriting, but he refused. Then Penca thought of a way and showed him some other writing, 'You wrote this though, didn't you!' 'No, I didn't' 'Of course you did!' 'I didn't!' 'Then will you write something so we can compare it?' 'Yes, I will.' And he did. Or we had an inspector who went to interrogations with a magnifying glass, pointed it to the suspect, and said, 'I can see into your head, admit what you have done.' And they did."

She laughed and he laughed as well.

"Basically, don't expect much. I've been in the police force for twenty years and don't know if they could make two watchable episodes from all the stuff I have seen. This could well be the most interesting case in my career."

She picked up her glass and took a sip without taking her eyes off him. Some women, Taras thought to himself, drink beer like men, others as if it was castor oil. Tina didn't belong to either of these categories. Cutely was the word that came to his mind.

"You're not from Ljubljana, Taras, are you?"

He shook his head,

"No."

"Am I pestering you?"

He shook his head again.

"Maribor… or there about. Then to Ljubljana for Secondary Police School, because there was no money for anything else and the State funded schooling there. That's why I joined the police force. Then at the station in Moste for a while, and then the Criminal Justice and Security College so I could go on a course and get rid of my uniform… And that's more or less it."

She looked at him as if she was waiting for some more, as if she wanted to ask more but was not sure whether she could.

"Is Taras your real name? Taras Birsa?"

"Why?"

"Because Taras is a very rare name and Birsa is a surname from the Littoral, not from Styria?"

He stayed silent a few moments, picked up the coffee cup as if he was about to start reading the future from it.

"It's my only name," he said eventually.

She nodded.

"What about you?"

"Me? Well, that really is a boring story… Ljubljana, father a language professor, mother a librarian, secondary school, computers, psychology. That's it… Was that a smile… are you laughing at what I said?"

"Sorry, it wasn't intentional."

"No, no… Perhaps we agree. What part?"

"Well, both the last two, if I'm honest."

"Why?"

"Well, if you think about it… A computer is a working machine, a tractor. We need it but I don't see any reason to get excited about it. I don't see why I should take it for a spin around town when it's made for ploughing."

"That's not the point. Computing is a new world, an entire new world in which we spend more and more time. The virtual which we talk about all the time is no longer virtual."

"I don't."

She laughed.

"OK, and the psychology?"

"Because it isn't useful. It's like football experts in a studio before some important match. Do you watch them?"

"Occasionally."

"Then you know. Their predictions are about as useful as those of an octopus in an aquarium. If it swims left it will be Germany, if it swims right, France. It's clever in retrospect."

She laughed.

"Who was it who called? Before..."

She pouted and it appeared very flirtatious. Especially for a woman who was supposed not to be raising any expectations in the man sitting at the opposite side of the table.

"You're a policeman. You'll find out."

"Boyfriend? Why didn't you take it?"

She gave him a much more serious look than before.

"Is that your way of telling people that they're asking you too personal questions?"

He looked at the waiter who was leaning over the counter on his elbows, reading a newspaper.

"I was a foster child with an elderly couple. There were always about three of us. Then the older ones left and new ones came... They would get some money from social services for each of us and this helped them make ends meet and we had somewhere we could call home."

He smiled and nodded towards the phone on the table.

"I couldn't be bothered to take it. He can sometimes go on and on... I'll speak to him tomorrow."

They sat in silence for a while, then she looked at him with her large eyes.

"What about...?"

"Father, mother? When I was put in foster care I was too young to remember them. I only found out their names when I enrolled in the police school. They were both dead by then and..."

She watched him motionless from behind her glass.

"Has it occurred to you that I might be telling you all this because I want you to feel sorry for me?"

"What happened to them?"

"Nothing. I don't know... I never knew them."

She put her elbows onto the table and supported her head with her hands and lowered her face to the height of her chin behind the glass.

"And there was no need for it. And no traumas at all, I can tell you... I mean if there were any they have gone. I have no problem talking about it, it's just that there is nothing to say."

"Does Cvilak know?"

He shook his head.

"And Brajc and Osterc?"

"Nobody has ever asked me. Men don't talk about these things."

The waiter came to the table next to them and took off the tablecloth. She waited for him to disappear into his trenches.

"Firstly... I don't doubt for a second that you want to get into my knickers, Taras. Just like Brajc or Osterc..."

"Damn the comparison."

It really did hurt.

"And besides, Osterc probably wouldn't. He would get you an exhaust pipe, that would be his way."

They both laughed.

"And anyway," she said. "I also graduated in a useless science called psychology and know that humour functions as an indirect fulfilment of forbidden stimuli or desires. According to Freud, of course. Based on this realization other psychology loafers came to the conclusion that those who like aggressive jokes are mostly people with suppressed aggression and those who find sexual joked funny, people with..."

She stopped and gave him a meaningful look with those large eyes.

"Quite possible," he said, "but was it me or the grandma who watched porn?"

Taras finished his second coffee and had long eaten his sandwich. Why had God, or whoever it was who was in charge of these things, not punished him with an oversensitivity to caffeine?

"Was it tough?"

One of the best things about drinking, a mild state of drunkenness, is that it transfers a person from the digital to the analogue, from the rational to the intuitive. How can a sober person know when is the right moment to stroke a girl's hand?

"I don't know. At the time I though it wasn't but later, looking back... In Ljubljana, in Tacen, at the Police Academy, I had various problems... Perhaps this was also one of the reasons."

He had received a written reprimand before expulsion because he was caught drunk. He kept getting caught drunk.

"I thought it was normal, but then you see that not everyone has this need for..."

"Love?"

He smiled,

"...drawing attention to themselves."

"Was that why you began climbing, mountaineering?"

"I don't know. Perhaps. You know how it is, it's never just one thing."

He had thought a lot about this before. There must have been something which drove him into those rock faces.

"It's never one thing," he repeated. "And as a psychologist you know anyway that there's always something libidinal in the background, isn't there?"

"Yes, usually."

"Do you know what a rock face reminds me of? Used to remind me of... Any rock face?"

She shook her head.

"Remind might not be the right word. What I thought of when I found myself in front of a rock face. And I'm not telling you this in order to get into your knickers, as you call it..."

She blushed; at least the part of her face visible above the glass...

"...although, I don't know, that is perhaps the normal reaction to your..."

She blushed even more.

"My what, Taras?"

"I don't know why, but the German word *Ausrüstung* keeps coming to mind.

"Equipment?"

"I was hoping you didn't speak German."

They laughed.

"Image, let's say image."

She topped her glass and took a sip.

"What image is this?"

She put her glass back on the table and looked at him with expectation.

"Are you not interested in what I think when I see some rock face in the mountains?"

"Perhaps," she said.

"Well, when I stand in front of a rock face, looking at it from the bottom or from the other side of the valley... I feel the same awe I have when I look at a woman's naked body. Don't laugh..."

She already was, though this time this really was not his intention.

"I don't know why, I don't know how to explain it. I know it's silly, but that's what I think of."

"And which one does the North Face of Triglav remind you of?"

She laughed and Taras also smiled.

"No one specific. There is nothing specific in it. All I'm saying is that before a rock face and a woman's naked body, I'm in awe of... It's hard to explain."

"What about my... body? What rock face?"

"I'd need to see it first."

She became serious and picked up the glass again, holding it in front of her. Now she probably was a little inebriated.

"Don't you miss mountaineering?"

"It's not the only thing I miss. After forty there's a whole load of things, from vinyl records onwards, I don't see why climbing would be any different."

He missed the times he thought he would live forever, he and all those around him, when he could drink without having a guilty conscience, when a woman sitting at the opposite side of the table brought him joy and a goal, and not like now when there were also a thousand hurdles which between her and him, hurdles which were probably always there, but now also came with a thousand reservations.

"But it's fine. Everything is great."

He grinned. It was probably true. He has everything. Unlike his colleagues who are no longer, his peers who look like corpses, unlike Brajc, unlike the girl and the man from the lake. Unlike a whole bunch of people. He would not change places with anyone.

"Now you tell something about yourself?"

She put the glass back on the table. Empty.

"I'm afraid I don't feel like talking any more."

She stood up. Taras did too, surprised. Now what was this about? He went to the waiter who was waiting for them to leave. After he settled the bill, he walked up the stairs after her to the apartment they were all given for the night. Tina walked in front of him, almost angrily he though, until she slipped slightly on the narrow staircase and caught Taras' hand, giggling drunkenly. Then they walked on tiptoes to the apartment, opened the door and found Cvilak sleeping in the first room with a double bed. They could not see him in the dark but heard him snoring. Taras rolled his eyes. Tina went past the bed to reach the door to the second room, opened the door and a little while later found a bedside lamp she could switch on. Taras, despairing, sat on the sofa and watched the sleeping Cvilak. This was not how he imagined it would end. In fact he hadn't thought or known how it would end at all, but this was definitely not it.

What should he do? Wake him up? He could hear clothes rustling and then saw the outline of Tina's head appear at the door.

"Good night, Taras."

She left the door slightly ajar and switched off the light. Taras was left sitting in the dark. This would be a long night. Like those in the mountains sometimes. He got undressed, leaving only his underwear and T-shirt and lay down on his end of the double bed. He tried covering his head but it didn't help, Cvilak's regular wheezing and crackling which was every now and then supplemented with a king of gasping gulp, as if something accumulated in his throat and he had to push it down before catching his regular rhythm again. Taras despaired and pulled the blanket from his head. He turned onto his back and stared at the ceiling for a while, then got up, squatted and felt the carpeted floor. It was as hard as concrete, but better than lying awake next to Cvilak all night. He picked up his pillow and blanket and tip-toed to Tina's room. Carefully he opened the door and in the half-light noticed the outline of her face peeping from under the blanket.

"Sorry, but can I lie on your floor? It's impossible to go to sleep there. Hear that?"

She didn't say anything, just uncovered her blanket. She was naked.

There was something else. Shaking, in fear and in fervid expectation at the same time. In awe of a rock face before ascent, in awe of a naked woman, waiting.

Chapter 35.

Friday, 12 January

There was a sausage, scrambled egg and two slices of white bread on Cvilak's plate and after lingering at the breakfast buffet for a long time, Taras ended up with the same. The only difference was that Taras had put only mustard next to the sausage whereas Cvilak had both mustard and mayonnaise. Cvilak raised his brow when Taras put the plate down on the table. They were the only people in the dining room, which was officially not yet open. An extra benefit for knowing the director.

"I thought you were vegetarian," Cvilak said.

"Why did you think that?"

Cvilak scratched his head.

"You aren't?"

Taras sighed and dipped the sausage in the mustard.

"Well, I thought that you might be."

Cvilak was someone who enjoyed his food and that was obvious. He picked up the miniature sausage with three fingers, brought it to his nose and smelt it as if he was smelling a cigar, then dipped it first into the mustard and then the mayonnaise, biting off half of it and adding a piece of white bread to the bite. Taras could not understand the pleasure that many people get from food. It was not a question of physiology, his taste buds worked fine, he distinguished between food he liked more and food he liked less; what he didn't understand was how taste alone can bring so much pleasure to some people. So much that they can waste an entire day in a restaurant where waiters with absent gazes bring them oversized plates with miniscule cannelloni stuffed with foie gras and decorated with squid ink.

What's the fun in that? Any hotdog you eat after a hundred-kilometre bike ride is infinitely better.

"And how did you sleep?" said Osterc.

"On the floor in the room next door."

"On the floor?"

He bit into the sausage again and Taras tried to figure from the tone of his voice whether his questions were merely rhetorical.

"And I was wondering where you were. I went to the toilet in the middle of the night and couldn't see you."

He could not be sure.

"You snored like a chainsaw," said Taras rubbing the back of his neck.

He had set the alarm on his phone for six o'clock. Early enough to wake up before Cvilak, get to the bathroom before the old man opened his eyes. He switched off the alarm and rolled out from under the blanket where Tina was still lying, naked, just like him. For a moment he stared at her bottom thinking how nice it would be to crawl back, fall asleep again and wake up together. Or not go back to sleep at all.

Instead he, like some teenager with an erection almost to his navel, tried to find his underpants and T-shirt on the sofa and by the bed, so he could cover up his problems if Cvilak was to turn round in his bed just as he was walking past. He listened at the door. At first he could not hear anything and worried that he might be too late, then he sensed the light snoring, nothing as loud as it had been the previous night.

He quietly opened the door and took a peek into the darkness of the room. He could not see whether Cvilak was lying with his face towards him and could thus not know whether his eyes were open. Chancing it, he tiptoed past the bed to the bathroom. If Cvilak was to open his eyes now or if he had them open, things could not be more obvious. But he didn't. He didn't move.

Taras sat on the toilet seat and breathed a sigh of relief.

"We got pissed as if we were students," Brajc had once commented on some session he had had.

Taras switched on the light above the mirror and stared at his face. He will give poor old Cvilak another ten minutes before he would wake him up by taking a shower.

"So then, Taras..." he said to himself. "So then, you old fool..."

His face had the dumb smirk of a man who had been lucky the night before and now nothing seemed impossible. He knew that this would not last so he stopped looking at his lips and began considering other parts of his face. He had stared a million times at faces across the interrogation table, trying to figure out what they were thinking, what character they hide, and especially whether they were lying. What could he say about his own? What was his face like?

He was not handsome, he knew that and had over the years stopped thinking about it, in as much as that is possible. Until someone stuck a photo of himself under his nose that was fine. He appeared on very few holiday photos and Alenka had to force him to occasionally step in front of the camera. His nose was twice broken but he could not use that as an excuse because it was barely noticeable, only the shape was somehow irregular, but it had been like that from the start. Alenka had once said jokingly that he had the most beautiful face from the tip of his nose downwards, including the scar he had diagonally across the upper lip to the bottom of his nose. A memento of the piece of ice in a frozen waterfall he himself hit with his ice axe, fortunately above his front teeth. He knew what she was trying to say. His nose was no better. His eyes an indeterminate shade of brown-green, closer together than they perhaps should be, his forehead just the right height and his brown hair also good for his age. His ears neatly close to his head, so he had nothing to complain about there.

Was it at leas an interesting face? Interesting like Niki Lauda's, who in some interview said that his burns gave his face character; if Taras had understood him correctly since the interview was in German. Is it possible to separate the face from character? The pot from its contents? Clearly enough for an almost twenty years younger and beautiful woman to pull back the bed covers.

The corners of his mouth turned up again. So be it, he said to himself, you've earned it, Tarzan.

He could hear movement in the bedroom and quickly took

off his underpants and stepped into the shower. He smelt the fingers of his right hand before he washed it with soap and sighed.

Someone knocked on the bathroom door.

"Yes?" he asked.

"Taras, I need to take a piss."

"Just a minute."

He washed off the shampoo, stepped out of the shower, dried himself off, wore his underpants and left the bathroom to the fretting Cvilak.

"Age, you know, prostate..."

As he listened to Cvilak's trickle in the bathroom he peeped into Tina's room. He felt an unstoppable desire to see her naked again. When she will wake up she would be ashamed about last night as he will be in an hour or two. They will gaze past each other and in a couple of days' time have a talk and agree it is never to be repeated.

No luck. She was covered with the blanket up to her ears and looking the other way, still fast asleep, it seemed.

"Is Tina still asleep?" Cvilak asked looking gloomily at his plate and then at the buffet as if unable to decide whether to get himself a second helping or not.

Taras shrugged his shoulders.

"Did you stay up late last night?"

"Not really, about an hour..."

He spotted her at the entrance to the dining room. She searched for them with her gaze and when she spotted them she smiled and waved, and then went to the food buffet.

"There she is," said Taras pointing her out to Cvilak.

She came laughing with a tray on which she had a bowl of muesli with milk and a glass of orange juice.

"Vegetarian?" Cvilak asked.

"No, why do you ask?"

"Sleep well?" asked Cvilak.

"Like a baby," she said. "What about you?"

"Likewise, just a little louder, as you probably heard?"

Tina took a spoonful of her oats and Cvilak followed it with his gaze as she brought it to her mouth.

"Why did you think I was vegetarian?"

"He asked me the same thing," said Taras.

"I thought you were both the kind of people who might be vegetarian, that's all," Cvilak said. "I could have started talking about the weather, but this seemed more original."

They laughed and as Cvilak was wiping the last grease from his plate with some bread, Taras looked into Tina's eyes. She did not look away. He shuddered, as probably any teenager would shudder.

The divers, Golja and the other guy he only knew vaguely, were already in the boat, checking their gear, when they arrived. Golob was also there with his team and Doles was among them also. The darkness of the morning was slowly, barely noticeably turning from a clear night into a grey, cloudy day. There wasn't a single colour around them that did not have a tinge of grey in it apart from the bright yellow of the rubber dinghy and the yellow dive tanks,. And the silence, around them and in the distance. There are no birds, Taras thought, there are no birds in winter and just as he was about to point it out to the others, a harsh caw of a lone crow was heard in the distance. He had forgotten to check the weather forecast and could only hope there would not be any heavy rainfall. That was all they needed. Though forty metres below the surface of the lake, it probably didn't make much of a difference.

Doles approached Taras. He fidgeted with his feet.

"What do you think about all this?" he asked, pointing at the lake with his hand.

Taras shrugged his shoulders,

"No idea."

"When we arrested... well, dealt with Verbič, I thought we were onto something. Now I don't know where we stand," Doles smiled with embarrassment. "You don't realize how many people I have breathing down my neck. Sometimes I think that they've mixed things up a little and have started blaming me for every new body that appears."

"Are they after you?" Taras asked. "Is anyone lining up for your job?"

Doles nodded. He was not stupid, just young, and it was just a question of time before he would regret he hadn't studied property law instead. He turned to Cvilak and Tina,

"In fact, you two can wait at the hotel."

Tina shook her head whereas Cvilak looked first at the boat and then Taras,

"Know what," he said, "I'll take this general offer. You only get rheumatism once in your life; the only problem is that you can never get rid of it."

"In fact we can all wait at the hotel," said Golob. "We won't be any use to them out on the lake."

"No," said Taras. He didn't really know why, but he wanted to be there when they pulled the body out of the water. If indeed they find it.

When the boat pushed away from the shore, Taras was glad that Cvilak and the had others decided not to come. The dinghy looked big, but with the two divers and all the equipment they had put in it, there was barely any space left for him and Tina on a narrow hard wooden seat. And the cold that seemed to be bearable on shore began to bite to the bone with the damper air out on the water. Tina wrapped herself in her winter jacket and Taras thought this was one of those days when any man would need to wear something warm under his trousers, which would ensure him at least a trace of dignity.

They reached the buoys. Golja switched off the engine and tied the boat to one of them. He turned towards Taras and pointed with his hand towards the west, towards Stara Fužina, but still along the surface of the lake.

"Considering that we didn't find him yesterday in the quadrants we have marked here, we will go today where we didn't want to go, but will clearly have to. To the middle of Fužinar bay. Do you know what that means Taras?"

Taras shook his head,

"I have no idea, and don't want to. Diving always seemed a kind of gay sport to me."

"Gay?" Golja snorted. "And I suppose you with your lederhosen and edelweiss on your chest are more fuckworthy, or what?"

"That's the mountaineers. We climbers have long switched

to GoreTex."

"Gay?!" Golja repeated and got ready for the dive. "It's four degrees at the bottom of this fucking lake. Does the police even have the money for splashing around down there?"

"Was money ever a problem?" Taras asked and they both laughed.

A minute later both divers were in the water. Of course they jumped in so that a wave of cold water splashed over Taras. He looked at the drops clinging to the twenty year old GoreTex. It might have been waterproof when it was new but that was clearly no longer the case and perhaps it really was time he bought himself a new one. He followed the two figures slowly disappearing into the depths below them and for a long time also the air bubbles rising to the surface. When these moved further away from the boat he had to look at Tina. She too was staring at them and it seemed as if she had been all along. She smiled and he returned the smile. For a while they sat in silence. Taras looked at the shore as if he was searching for something.

"Are you already feeling guilty?" she asked after a while when nothing happened.

"Not yet. You?"

"No," she said and looked at him with a nerve he would not have expected from her. "In fact I don't think I will at all."

He gave her a questioning look.

"Because we are alone and..." she looked around, "just off the record... No, I wasn't drunk..."

Taras picked a small stone from the sole of his shoe and threw it in the water. Plonk. He watched the tiny concentric waves merge with the surface of the lake before they reached the boat. He turned towards Tina,

"A little tipsy perhaps?"

"Just enough."

"Whatever... it helped."

"It was nice, if that is what you were thinking," she said.

He nodded. He ran his hand along the icy surface and looked towards the shore.

What a difference between this lake in the winter and in the summer. The boat was tied to the buoys at the lake's western, most touristy end, about one hundred and fifty metres away from the beach which was packed full in the summer months, with the lake full of canoes, dinghies and surfboards… The same distance from the hotel and from Stara Fužina. When the girls were still young they often came here in the summer like many others as a kind of alternative to a seaside holiday. Of course at the time he didn't know, , that when he swam a little further out from the shore, he was swimming above such great depths. He sighed to himself. It wasn't true that there was no guilty conscience.

It had not just been nice. It had been very nice and it was wrong and thus exciting and new and it would have been nice even if it was worse, but it wasn't. Taras had got undressed, dropping his underpants and T-shirt on the floor. He climbed onto her slender body, shivering on the bed in the same way his own was shivering, not because it was cold but with excited expectation. He had stroked the raised nipples and then kissed them with his tongue, holding back not to dive into her too soon and, finding it difficult to resist, not long after, attempted to tune into the rhythm, her rhythm, his rhythm, the rhythm of the creaking bed, not to wake up Cvilak, listening to her muffled sighs…

"It was very nice," he said, and she nodded.

When they had finished, they lay next to each other on their backs for a while, staring at the ceiling. Then Tina extended her left hand to the nightstand next to the bed where she had left her clothes, found a packet of paper tissues in her pocket, pulled one out and wiped away the pool of semen from her belly.

"An admirable balancing act," said Taras. "Not a drop spilt."

They muted their giggle.

Then they lay like that for a while until she turned to him, gave him a mischievous laugh, brushed her hand against her groin and then brought her middle finger to Taras' lips.

"Can I sit next to you?" Tina asked after a while.

"You can."

She moved across the boat and cuddled up next to him…

"I'm freezing," she said as if in an excuse.

Taras put his right hand over her shoulder and rubbed

her left shoulder and back. He thought that someone might be watching from the shore. They would need binoculars to see anything but for some strange reason he didn't care. He smiled at the thought of the scene such a voyeur would see. Two people in love in a boat in the middle of Lake Bohinj in January. In the middle of the January emptiness, and what was more, the couple were waiting for a fresh corpse which would have already been on the shore and all this would not have been necessary, had the panicking fisherman not dropped his rod into the water... Then he corrected his thought – the corpse was not fresh.

"One of us will have to speak first," she said so quietly that Taras barely heard her.

"What about?"

"That this was the first and last time. That we're not single, that you have a family, that we're colleagues and that this won't work... That it was just about sex."

Taras didn't say anything but not because he didn't agree. He was silent because it went without saying.

"It's always just about sex," he said.

She glanced at him suspiciously from under his wing.

He could have said that it was never just about sex and it would have been just as true. Whatever he would say would be both right and the wrong at the same time.

"Not yet today, right?"

She smiled and snuggled even closer to him. There was nobody on the shore at this time but he could not get rid of the feeling that they were being watched, that sitting in the boat was as if they were sitting in the spotlight on a stage in front of an invisible audience.

They waited for about half an hour and Taras suggested to Tina that if she was too cold he could drop her off on the shore and she could walk to the hotel which was only a ten minute walk away, but she refused. He would get to the shore and back in fifteen minutes and the divers could wait that long if they happened to surface in the meantime. Why did he come out onto the lake at all? Who did he want to prove what to? Did he just want to be alone?

Then there was a ripple in the water next to the boat and

a large bubble of air emerged, broke through the surface. He pushed her slightly aside and leaned across the darkness underneath them. All was calm for a second, then another bubble, and immediately after it another and another.

"They're coming out," said Taras, happy that this would soon be over.

They leaned across the rubber side of the boat and watched the increasing flow of air.

"There's one of them," said Taras and extended his hand to show a figure moving rapidly towards the surface...

Decompression? It was not a diver. It couldn't be a diver; the thought rushed through his brain before it registered the stench that reached them with the air pockets, and before the pear-shaped balloon popped out of the water. When the balloon settled, Taras saw that below it was a rope attached to something larger, floating about a metre below the surface. He reached out to the balloon, grabbed hold of the rope underneath it and slowly pulled it towards the boat. Tina also reached out to help him.

"Do you know what we're pulling out?" he asked her.

She gave him a surprised look, surprised just for a brief moment, then she gulped and nodded. Taras pulled the rope upwards and the thing underneath swung and began moving to the surface. Tine let out a shriek but managed to still hold onto the rope. Had he been in the boat alone, Taras would have probably let go and allowed the thing at the end of the rope to disappear again under the buoy, but now he briefly looked away and then tightened the rope on which, barely half a metre from his wrist, half above and half under the surface, hung the body of a man. The divers had tied the fishing rod into his lap and it looked grotesque. Like some kind of fisherman from Hell who had poked his eye out with his own fishhook.

"Good morning there," said Taras when the body hit the boat and added, perhaps because of Tina or perhaps because he just needed to say something, "We need to have a little discussion about parking your car in the Triglav National Park."

Chapter 36.

The sight of poor Robi Lap was so much worse because he rose to the surface in a stinking cloud of decay. Bloated insides were rotting away and he would probably have floated to the surface even without the help of the divers had it not been for his winter jacket which had taken on so much water it acted as a counterweight. Apart from the gouged out eye the body seemed undamaged, green and slimy from the algae, but in one piece. Taras tried to lift it out of the water with the rope, but gave up. He used a clove hitch knot to tie the rope between the balloon and the body to the rowlock. The boat leaned to one side and Taras indicated to Tina to sit on the other side.

"We'll wait for the other two," he said to Tina who had calmed down after the initial shriek and tried to help him raise the body. "No throwing up this time?"

She gave him a sour smile and propped her elbows on her knees.

He looked at the dead man who had sunk back into the water, only half a metre under the surface this time. They could pull him out and get soaked in doing so and at least under the water the stench was bearable. He found his mobile in the inside pocket of his anorak and dialled a number.

"We have him..."

He waited for a while and then said,

"You'll get to see him. We just need to wait for Golja and the other guy to come out of the water and we will come."

Then he dialled another number and repeated, virtually repeated what he had said, and then a third time.

"Well," he said when he put the phone back into his pocket. "Soon the entire flock will assemble."

It took ages for the bubbles from the divers to begin to appear on the surface and eventually their black neoprene diving hoods appeared. Taras and Tina waited in silence during this time, each on their own side of the boat, Tina resting on her knees and Taras watching her. She looked… he was looking for the right expression and, to his horror, found it. Even now, she looked cute. As she had been cute when he was on top of her, moaning with her eyes closed… Had it really happened? Now, with the dead body floating just under the surface at the side of the boat it seemed quite impossible that it had. Cute as she was when she was drinking coffee, or humming to a tune in the car, or… Had he really, only a few hours ago grazed on her body as she had grazed on his? In this boat, on this lake, and with these floating gassy remnants of a body next to them, the memory of it seemed like a crazy dream.

Golja grabbed the side of the dinghy and spat out the regulator.

"Home delivery," he said. The second diver surfaced next to him.

"Goodness, Taras, you tied him to the boat. A good job there aren't any sharks here."

Taras smiled.

"Have you read Hemingway's *Old Man and the Sea*?" Golja asked him. "Did you think it was a gay novel?"

"I never said anything about fishermen."

"If you two feel like it, then perhaps we could get this thing into the boat," the other diver said. "Because I'm as cold as hell here."

Taras spread the black body bag on the bottom of the dinghy, put on some latex gloves and, with the help of the divers, pulled the dead man into the boat. He tried not to get totally wet, but it was unavoidable. He tried to hold the slimy cadaver as far away from him as possible but it just made things more difficult and he twice almost fell onto it. Tina wanted to help but he told her to stay where she was. The boat was rocking badly enough anyway. The stench was unbearable.

"Just imagine this rotten guy in the summer," Golja said.

They were a strange company as they returned to the shore.

A girl in a red down jacket, a soaked Taras, two divers in their black suits and a black bag on the bottom of the boat. Tina was silent, Taras also, in fact only Golja was talking, apparently in a good mood and Taras could see why. For him this really was like going out picking mushrooms and the prize mushroom was right there on the bottom of their boat. Had they not found him now they would need to spend another day diving in the freezing water.

"Down there it's dark as a cun... sorry, dark as a tunnel," he corrected himself when he looked at Tina. "These lights are pretty useless. I swam along the bottom, touching it with my hands, not too much in order not to raise the silt... There's a kind of fine silty shit, like a glaze over the stones... then my hand got caught in what I thought was a wire. I pulled on it and brought it up to my eyes and realized it was a fishing line. Shit! But I didn't want to get my hopes up, because Taras, damn it, I can admit this to you now, I never thought we would find him so quickly. Not even in smaller ponds. There's loads of these fishing ropes and similar stuff down there anyway. Well, I pulled on the rope and a fishing rod comes floating towards me and by then I was already in a cloud of silt, but I could almost smell him. I swam up a metre or so and slowly wound the reel as if I was fishing, and that took me to this guy here. Do we have any idea who he is?"

Taras told him about the car parked near the shore whose owner has been missing for a while.

Golja listened and then touched the body bag with his foot.

"Really, who'd have thought that we'd do this so quickly."

They had reached so close to the shore that Taras could recognize Cvilak among the crowd of people waiting for them. It wasn't difficult to, he was the only one with a white coat over his other clothes. There were also two uniformed policemen who had come from the blue and white police car parked behind them and behind that was a white car with some kind of markings which did not belong to the police.

Cvilak waved at them as they approached the shore. It looked odd, considering the circumstances, as if he was waving to a group of tourists returning from a boat ride on the lake. Despite this Taras waved back. The markings on the white car turned out to be the logo if the state TV station.

"Did you too go diving?" Cvilak asked when Taras jumped out of the boat.

He helped the divers lift the bodybag out of the boat onto the gravel beach which had been cordoned off with a police cordon to a radius of around fifty metres. Beyond it stood a few nosey bystanders. Taras glanced at them. A younger couple, a family with two children who didn't understand what was going on and, fed up of waiting, wanted to walk on, and an elderly man with a dog. The dog was on a lead and squealed and fidgeted like the two children, looking at its master. The two uniformed policemen ran along to help them but Taras told them to stay back. It was bad enough that he was wet and besides, the policemen were not wearing gloves, and Taras didn't want a lecture about correct handling of evidence from Golob, the most pedantic person in the world. He smiled when he recognized the same two young men who had found the body on New Year's Eve.

"This one have its head?" the one who had helped Taras pull the girl out of the water asked.

"This gentlemen over here will tell us," said Taras and moved out of the way for Cvilak who was already bending over the bodybag with his latex gloves, unzipping it along its entire length. Taras thought about moving further away. Out on the lake it had at least been slightly breezy, here on the shore, without the air flow to carry the smell away, the stench of rotting flesh burnt the nostrils. So much that he asked Tina to stick two pieces of paper tissue into his nose. He would have done so himself but he was still wearing the gloves with which he had pulled the body out of the water and did not want them anywhere close to his face, let alone his nose.

Cvilak spent a long time examining the face. He felt with his finger along the eye socked where the eye had been gauged out but left the fishhook in it. He felt across the entire skull, front and back, paying particular attention to the back, then he stood above the body and looked at it, before unzipping the winter coat the dead man had been wearing and asked Taras to help him turn the body round.

"Right," he said and took a step back, taking off his gloves. "I have seen what I needed to see. Golob, my dear, the patient is yours."

He turned to Taras.

"It's hard to say because he's been in the water for a long time, but if I had to bet on it, I'd say that when we'll check under the microscope we'll find what is known as acute over-inflating which occurs when the alveolar walls rupture."

"He drowned?" Taras asked.

"At first glance and after all this time and the changes caused by decomposition – yes."

Taras turned to the body which was now once again in the bodybag, and then gazed across the lake…

"Did you notice the stones in the pockets?"

"Yes, even as we were lifting him into the boat."

"Disappointed?" Cvilak asked.

"No, no…" Taras shook his head and looked at Cvilak. "I was just thinking from where he could have, weighed down by all those stones, jumped into the middle of the lake."

He walked off towards the police cordon and realized he was about to be confronted by a female journalist and a cameraman who was even from this distance trying to take shots of anything interesting and had now turned his lens on him. He knew that he would not be able to avoid her, so he didn't try. He lifted up the cordon and stopped just beyond it.

"Hello," said a girl in her late twenties offering him her hand.

"Probably not a good idea until I wash them…"

She did not understand.

"Oh, well… whatever. I'm from RTV Slovenia…"

She introduced herself and asked him for a minute of his time. She was polite and Taras decided he would be too. He told them who he was and said that they had found a body of a man around thirty years of age in the lake and that they were still verifying his identity. The cause of death was probably drowning.

"Is this death connected to the body you found at the New Year not far from here?"

"We don't know that."

"And the death of Professor Hleb which, if I'm not mistaken, you are also investigating?"

"This too I am unfortunately unable to answer. We do not know yet."

"Alright," she said and surprisingly didn't sound disappointed. "We would like you to appear on our news programme *Reactions* tonight. Can you do that?"

He smiled.

"That's not something I decide about."

He told her to call the Ljubljana Police Directorate, ask for Bojan Drvarič who is his superior and would undoubtedly be delighted to call in at the studio.

"But we would like you to come," she said.

"As I said, that's not something I decide about."

*

He spent a long time scrubbing his hands. He had never actually touched the body but despite this had a feeling that the stench had stuck to them. Was it possible it had stuck to his clothes as well? He smelt the sleeve of his jacket. He was unsure. It seemed as if the whole world stank. Can an unbearable smell stay in your memory, in your brain, a bit like the outline of the sun if you look at it for too long? He went to the car and found his cross-country skiing trousers and changed right there in the parking area. They too were still slightly wet, damp from the sweat, but still better than the jeans which had been soaked to well above the knees.

He found Tina over a cup of coffee. Literarily. She was holding it under her nose, smelling it. Cvilak was having a tea with rum, but when Taras arrived it was on the table in front of him. Clearly some people get used to anything. He ordered a coffee as well and also held it under his nose. Was it the poor guy from the lake's fault or was the coffee rubbish? It smelt sour.

"What? Are you off skiing again?" Cvilak asked him when he saw him.

Rubbish or not, the coffee was what he needed. For a minute he didn't have to talk because clearly nobody was in talking mood. They sat in silence, sipping their drinks until Cvilak sighed, a sign that he had had enough of this. He turned to Tina and asked her how she was feeling.

"Fine, apart from the smell..."

"And after two weeks on the job, does this work seem to be as you thought it would be," Cvilak asked.

She smiled,

"Taras threatened me with delirious drunken sons killing their fathers and grandfathers..."

She was wearing the same green jumper she had been wearing yesterday, but nothing was the same. Yesterday he had been wondering how he would undress her, today he knew. Yesterday he could not have imagined that it could have happened, today it was hard to not think that it could happen another time.

*

"Did you have many girlfriends like this?" she asked when they were already lying in bed, covered with the blanket.

Her voice had lost its previous self-consciousness, its joyousness. Suddenly she was a girl who worried that she had said yes too soon.

"Tonnes."

She was silent for a while. He hadn't expected her to bite the bait.

"I'm being serious."

"Have you ever walked around our station?"

"In general."

"No, but they were all, every last one of them, beautiful and clever."

That was the best response he could think of.

"Liar," she said, but sounded calm.

"...but I came across Hollywood. Enough stuff for ten series, though I'm not sure I like it."

She looked at Cvilak with her large eyes similar to how Gwyneth Paltrow looked at Morgan Feeeman in *Seven*.

"Do *you* like *your* work?"

"Me?" Cvilak seemed surprised as if nobody had ever asked him anything like that before. "Bah... Are you asking me whether I like working with corpses?"

"Yes. It's probably not what you wanted to do when you

were..."

She tried to find the right word.

"I know, I know what you're saying. No, as a student of medicine this really isn't what I had in mind. How could someone want to become someone who cuts up dead people?"

She nodded.

"Do you know what I wanted to become? A surgeon, because that was something the girls went for. Well, things turned out differently."

"As usual," said Tina and looked at Taras.

"As to whether I like this work?"

Cvilak fell silent and thought for a few seconds,

"I don't know. Sometimes I hate it. When I get young people onto my table, or even children. On the other hand it is interesting and, after all, someone has to do it. I'm retiring this year anyway."

He lifted his cup of tea with rum and held it in front of his mouth,

"What I'll do after that, I really do not know." He looked at Taras. "Perhaps I'll take up cross-country skiing."

Taras chuckled,

"I'd like to see that."

"And what do you think about our Taras?" Cvilak turned to Tina again.

"What do you mean?"

Cvilak shrugged his shoulders and pointed at Taras.

"Interesting," she said after thinking about it for a while.

Cvilak raised his eyebrows and looked at both of them.

"He certainly keeps well, doesn't he? Did you know that he's almost fifty?"

Tina blushed.

"Thank you," said Taras. "I wanted to show her my ID card anyway, now I won't have to."

He knows, he thought, he knows everything.

They had to wait for two hours for Golob to appear at the hotel bar. He ordered himself a coffee as he walked in and joined them.

"So?" Taras asked when Golob didn't show any desire to talk.

"His pockets were full of stones, large gravel stones, such as can be found all round the lake. I'd like to know where the boat from which he jumped into the water is."

"Jumped?"

"There are no visible injuries apart from the gouged out eye, no sign of self-defence, no rope marks to indicate he'd been tied up, nothing. Of course he might have been asleep for some reason or other when he was put in the water. This is something Cvilak will be able to tell us when he opens him up."

Cvilak nodded.

"And this is more or less all for now," Golob said, gratefully grabbing the coffee that had been brought to the table.

"This is what we had to wait for for two hours?" Taras groaned.

"If you drain the lake for me we can stay here for another two days," said Golob.

Taras dismissively waved his hand and turned to Cvilak. After all, it was the time when normal people with normal jobs go home and start thinking about the weekend. Has Golob even noticed that it was getting dark and that it was Friday.

"When do you think we can have it?"

"Urgent?"

Taras nodded. Cvilak glanced at the investigating magistrate and then looked at Taras again,

"Is Monday morning too late?"

Taras nodded again.

"Then tonight, if I get everyone together. I'll call them and see how we can arrange it and let you know. Right?"

"Right," said both Taras and the investigating magistrate.

Cvilak sat on the passenger seat, Tina in the back. Taras set the radio to Val 202 and listened to the coverage of the ski jumping. Cvilak tried to talk to Tina who wasn't really following his questions and he had to keep repeating them. He doesn't know when to stop, Taras thought.

"Do you know what surprises me?" she said suddenly when it seemed that even Cvilak was bored talking and began staring at the road in front of them. "And this is the difference between TV series and real life. We got the new body and Taras, who clearly knew who the body would belong to and who expected it, didn't once mention how the body fitted into the contexts, nothing about what it meant for our investigation, what it has to do with the dead girl… and you didn't even ask him."

Taras and Cvilak looked at each other.

"What is he supposed to have said?" Cvilak asked. Taras looked at her in the rear view mirror. She looked tired and agitated.

"Because I still need to think it all through." He pointed at his forehead, "the little grey cells and all that…"

By the time they reached the motorway Cvilak was already asleep. Taras glanced in the mirror and met her gaze. She looked so serious that he could not help himself. He extended his right hand and between the seats reached for her knee. She moved it away. He reached for it again and once again she moved it away. When he did so a third time she didn't. He stroked her knee and thigh, then she placed her hand on his and he drove like that for the next few kilometres, all the way to the toll station in Torovo where he had to slow down and use the gear stick.

Chapter 37.

When Taras arrived at the Institute everyone was already there. The police-medical-judiciary proletariat was hanging around the corridor between refrigeration and dissection, talking languidly, resigned to the fact they had to all still be at work, despite the late hour.

"Here we are again, Taras," Cvilak greeted him. "Managed to change clothes and everything?"

"And eat something and everything," said Taras. "Has Golob finished?"

"About an hour ago. He said he'd call you when he knows anything. Shall we go in?"

Tina didn't come. She asked him whether he would like her to come and he told her she didn't have to.

"There's no need that after all this, this one becomes your first autopsy."

"Need a mask?" Cvilak asked Taras who nodded.

"I think all the rest of you will also need masks, won't you?"

He handed out the masks used by doctors at autopsies. They are coated on the inside with a gelatinous substance which is supposed not to let the smell through but when the stench was as bad as this one, it was pretty ineffective. Fortunately the nasal membrane gets used to even these smells after a few minutes and after some time the human nose no longer registers a continuous stench.

With Kisovec, his helper, some ten years younger than himself, Cvilak pulled the now naked body onto the trolley and moved it the few metres from refrigeration, across the corridor, to the dissection table where they simply attached the metal base on which the body lay to the sink construction used for this purpose. Kisovec moved the bottom part of the body trolley out into the corridor and then closed the door. There were five people around the body on the table and Majda the typist was sitting with an expressionless face at a computer about two metres away, waiting. Taras stood next to her.

"Body of a man, age around thirty..." Cvilak began in a monotonous voice. His voice and the clicking of the keys on the computer were the only noise in the room until they were joined by the clicking of the camera. Even though the view of the body was not best from there, or perhaps because of that, Taras remained standing next to Majda who sat straight and motionless at the keyboard, moving only her fingers. The sight of the now white body, covered in a green patina, everything shrivelled up, with a bloated stomach which made it look as if he had a huge balloon inside him, was revolting. Taras wondered in horror what would happen when Cvilak made his incision from the neck to the groin and unavoidably also cuts this bulge. Why did criminal investigators have to be present in cutting up dead bodies? What was it that he might notice that the pathologist wouldn't?

They were not there yet. For about ten minutes Cvilak listed external characteristics and then, without any noticeable pause after the full stop Majda had typed, gave Kisovec the sign. He used the scalpel to cut across skin on the top of head, pulled half of it back towards the occiput and the other half forward towards the face, peeling it and preparing it for the Cvilak who used a saw to circle the skullcap or calvaria as they call it, placing this lid onto the metal tray. He returned to the open skull, reached into it with both hands but then winced and pulled them out again. Taras thought the reason might be some technical problem, damage due to the extended exposure to water. That Cvilak could have come across something new, something unexpected, seemed almost impossible.

"Taras, can you come a little closer..." Cvilak said and beckoned to him with his bloody glove.

Taras stepped to the scalped and opened head and looked into its grey interior covered with a reddish mucus. For the second time in three days he was looking at a human brain and both times it looked to him like brawn covered in raspberry syrup.

"What is it?" he asked.

"This."

Cvilak stuck two fingers into the grey gelatinous brain, pressing onto it with his fingers two centimetres apart. The brain yielded to the pressure and from the elastic surface something smooth and metallic appeared.

"Forceps!" Cvilak cried out.

He pushed the tweezers against both fingers and used them to get hold of this foreign object in the human flesh, slowly and steadily pulling it out. He held it up in front of his eyes and turned it so that the two-centimetre-long cylindrical object, pointed on one side, was also visible to Taras.

"Do you know what this is, Taras?"

"I do. So he didn't drown after all."

Cvilak placed the bullet on the metal tray and put the tweezers next to it and used both hands to check the brain, turning towards Taras,

"Don't rush. When we get to the lungs you'll see that technically the guy drowned. When he fell into the water he was still alive."

The bottle was half empty. Cvilak pulled a glass from the drawer.

"You won't have one, of course," he said to Taras who didn't even try to shake his head.

He poured himself out a glass, drank half and put the glass back on the desk.

"I've taken to having a drink or two after each autopsy; I mean since that girl without the head. Perhaps I shouldn't but sometimes it is better for your health to have a drink than not to have one. I can't wait to retire."

"Are you sure?" Taras asked.

"What about?"

"About retiring?"

Cvilak shrugged his shoulders and stared for a while at the label on the bottle before speaking as if addressing the bottle,

"Must be. Do you know how many people in this country dream about retiring? Why would I be any different?"

He looked at Taras.

"What about you?"

"What about me?" Taras asked.

"What do you think about the whole thing?"

"Someone shot him, dragged him into the boat and threw him into the lake, if I understand correctly?" Taras asked.

"The thing about the boat is your addition. All I'm saying is that he had the bullet in his head before he hit the water and that he was still breathing."

"Could he have swum out there?"

"Oh, come on!"

"Is there any way of telling how long he was alive with the bullet in his head before he drowned?"

Cvilak shrugged his shoulders.

"Judging by the blood which accumulated under the skull, quite a while."

"It means someone could have shot him on the shore, put him into the boat and thrown him into the lake? Where we found him, he could not exactly have fallen from the shore, especially not with his pockets full of stones."

"As I said, it is a possible scenario. An hour, perhaps and hour and a half, that's the time I would give him."

"Would he have died anyway, if he hadn't drowned?"

"How many people do you know who walk around with a bullet in their head?" Cvilak asked sarcastically and finished his whisky. "You know, it's not bad at all," he said and poured himself out another. "I do admire you Taras, how you can live such an ascetic, rational life? Without spice..."

Taras smiled. He now knew for sure that Cvilak not been asleep when he and Tina were having fun.

He put his hand on the table to get up and get out on time.

"Do you know what you're doing, Taras?"

He looked at him like a father might look at a son who was getting himself into trouble. At least that was how Taras imagined a father.

"You weren't asleep, were you?"

"I mean, the girl is as cute as hell. Don't think that you're immune just because you're thirty years older."

"Twenty," said Taras.

"Whatever," Cvilak whispered. "A couple of more nights like that and you'll be begging on your knees to be with her."

Taras smiled and looked at the grey-haired man by his side. He liked him, like someone might like a father.

"It was just about sex. Once and never to be repeated."

"Oh yes..."

"I didn't initiate it. What would you have done in my shoes? Would you refuse?"

Cvilak shook his head,

"No, you're not tricking me this way. No your shoes and my shoes stuff, and I don't need to answer questions like that. I'm sixty and, unlike you, I look my age. It's only right and fair to do so."

Taras patted him on the shoulder,

"You see. I'll be your age soon and this was my last chance. Can you blame me? Besides, you were the one who suggested something like this anyway."

"Me?" Cvilak jumped up.

"You, going on about how nobody can get through life without something... to help them."

Cvilak gave him a prolonged stare and then finished off his drink.

"All that I said was that life is shit hard if you don't muck it up now and then. I didn't mean it in this way. That was all. Well, if you had to jump you could have chosen some desperate forty-year-old housewife with a couple of grown up children. That would have been more or less acceptable, but this..." he shook his finger, "this, Taras, is not fair to her or to Alenka. If you think you'll get through it with a tick in your book of achievements and some nice memories, you're wrong. Just remember that! You're not the first to get yourself into shit this way."

Taras sat meekly in his chair and because he was not objecting, Cvilak's anger was slowly abating. He poured himself out another half a glass and smelt it.

"It does get rid of the smell, that it does."

He emptied the glass and somewhat indecisively put the bottle back into the drawer.

"It's about time we went home, isn't it?"

"You're shit scared of retiring, aren't you?"

Cvilak nodded.

"Shit, yes. It's not about not knowing what to do with myself. I'll manage that somehow. But as I leave the dissection room for the last time I know that I'll only be back once and that then I will have Kisovec messing around with my entrails. Can you imagine, the dilettante? Every time I lock the office door I think about it. If I go now, the next time I'll be here is on the table with Kisovec's sharpened claws above me."

Chapter 38.

As briefly as possible, he explained to Drvarič about the new body in Lake Bohinj.

"What does this mean for our case?"

"I don't know," Taras said. "We're looking for a connection between Hleb and the girl, and now we will add this Lap guy as well."

The phone was silent for a while.

"Well, find one…" he finally said. Clearly there was something else Drvarič wanted to get off his chest.

"Anything else?" Taras asked.

"You'll have to go on TV this evening. Be there at a quarter to ten."

"Why me? I thought that was your thing."

Or Kristan's he thought. How come none of the posers took the opportunity?

"They want you."

"Since when can the TV say who they want from the police?"

Silence again and then,

"The decision isn't mine, if that helps."

"Oh," said Taras, "and which minister was it this time?"

"Ours, the Minister of the Interior."

Taras laughed. He wasn't even being serious when he mentioned the minister.

"Well, if it has to be, it has to be…"

He said goodbye. It was nine o'clock which meant that he barely had enough time to take a quick shower, brush his teeth and get dressed. He was as tired as hell.

*

The woman took him into makeup where he sat on the chair

and closed his eyes while the make-up girl put foundation on his face.

"Fluid?" she asked.

"I don't know."

He smiled. How should he know?

"Will you stay in the studio for a long time?"

"Probably not."

"Well, then we'll use powder."

The same girl took him to the office where he caught the news headlines announcing what was to come. He was the second item, immediately after the meeting of the Prime Minister with Angela Merkel.

"...and in the meanwhile the bodies in the Bohinj area seem to be piling up, the police are still in the dark, desperately attempting to reach the truth."

He looked at the woman who gave him an embarrassed smile and he smiled back.

During the report on the meeting with Mrs Merkel he was taken to the studio where the newsreader shook his hand and let the technician place a microphone under his shirt while he shuffled some papers on his desk. Taras was old enough to know what that meant.

Once Frau Merkel was over and the newsreader stepped out in front of the camera, he put on an accusing look even before he said a single word. He more or less repeated what was said before about the bodies piling up while the police..."

Then they ran the report about the discovery of the new body in Lake Bohinj, shots of their arrival on the shore, focusing on the people next to the dead Lap, him, Golob, Cvilak, Tina... and his three '*we don't know*'s with which the report ended.

"Well," the presenter finally turned towards him." So do tell us, what is it that you *do* know?"

"Quite a lot, in fact," Taras said slowly. He would not allow himself to be provoked. "Can you be a little more specific?"

"Have you found out yet who the headless woman who has been lying for two weeks at the Institute for Forensic Medicine is?"

Taras flinched.

"You mean the woman whose body was badly damaged... No, we don't know yet."

"Why don't we call a spade a spade Mr Birsa? The body found in the river is missing its head."

"That's what you say. I'm saying that the body is badly damaged which has made identification..."

"Well, let's have a look."

On the screen in front of them appeared the same journalist who had also stood outside the Medical Faculty where the IMF is and where...

"...there is a big secret which the Slovenian Police has been keeping from the public. Let's find out."

A camera shot – as if it was an amateur camera – went down the corridor, turned towards refrigeration, briefly showed a hand opening the door, pulling the handle on the refrigeration compartment and pulling out...

Surely they won't? Taras thought...

They did.

"Tell us, Mr Birsa – why all this conspiracy? What are you trying to hide from us? Don't you think that the public has a right to know?"

"This was not very nice," Taras said. "Simply not nice."

"You didn't answer my question."

"And I have no intention of doing so."

"Really?..." The presenter of the news programme sat back in his chair. "Do you often fly into a rage like this, Inspector?"

"What rage?"

"Spot please..."

"And with the police still in the dark..." the same journalist was telling the camera, this time outside the University Hospital...

They didn't need to go far, Taras thought.

"...individual policemen are becoming ever more nervous and their moves clearly verging on the desperate."

They showed a much lower quality shot with a sign saying –mobile phone footage. It showed the events at the graveyard in Srednja Vas and statements of the agitated villagers, focusing for about five second on Brajc who stood next to the small excavator in the idyllic graveyard in Srednja Vas with a crowd of people with flowers in their hands.

"...and when the police are nervous it is the innocent bystanders who have the misfortune to be in the wrong place at the wrong time who pay the price."

The camera, the TV camera again, followed the journalist as she was walking down the corridor of the country's largest hospital, knocked on the door and entered. The man lying in the bed was the guy whose face Taras had stuck in the snow.

"Tell us what happened on the second of January when you met Inspector Taras Birsa in Bohinj."

"This is the kind of rage I was talking about, Mr Birsa," the presenter said over the shot of the man in bed telling his story in a weak voice. "This kind of rage – does it often affect you?"

Taras stayed silent. Had he been younger, he would have made the mistake of speaking, but now he was finding the whole thing funny.

"Well, if..."

"Are you even interested in what actually happened or do you know anyway?"

"Unfortunately we don't have the time to..."

"Are you even interested in what actually happened?"

*

It had been five years since Taras had last tried alcohol. At home, in front of the TV, he had poured himself a glass of white wine, carefully choosing one with a low acidity. He had drunk it and spent the night in A&E. It had been perhaps his twentieth attempt, and every time the results were worse.

"Taras," Prelc had said when he had conducted all the tests he could have conducted himself and gathered all the others his multidisciplinary colleagues had sent him, and spread them out on his desk in his office in Alenka's clinic, some kind of proof of the attention he had given to the matter. "I think this is psychological. There's no reason for you to have such intestinal problems. All the right flora and fauna in there, no ulcers, nothing. Basically, I'm sorry to say that I'm unable to help you."

"But it's painful."

"I'm not saying it isn't. All I'm telling you is that I'm sorry and that you are probably crazy. I'd like to have a drink with you sometime, but... Go and see a psychiatrist. I know a good one. Do you want me to arrange an appointment?"

His abstinence too was also ever harder to handle.

*

He switched on the TV and surfed the programmes. He thought about opening a book. When was the last time he had read a book and which one was it? The summer holidays? Half a year ago? He went to the bookshelf and looked through the books there, picking out three he had bought at the book fair in November. He placed them on the table in front of him. The choice was a mixture of prices and expectations. Of course, since Alenka's clinic, he could ignore the price factor, but you cannot rid yourself of old habits that easily. Or stomach pain. Michal Viewegh, *The Creative Writing Lesson*, a thin booklet; then *The Dying Animal* by Philp Roth of a similar thickness, and a much thicker volume, *Neverwhere* by Neil Gaiman. The first two he knew about, not the third one, and he picked out all of them because he liked the titles. He opened the third book and began reading.

*

The night before he went to London, Richard Mayhew was not enjoying himself.

He had begun the evening by enjoying himself: he had enjoyed reading the goodbye cards, and receiving the hugs from several not entirely unattractive young ladies of his acquaintance; he had enjoyed the warnings about the evils and dangers of London, and the gift of the white umbrella with the map of the London Underground on it that his friends had chipped in money to buy; he had enjoyed the first few pints of ale...

*

He put the book down. This Richard May... whatever, enjoyed his ale. Well, let him, he said to himself and lay back on the sofa with a view of the ceiling.

*

When Cvilak picked up the scalpel to cut into the bloated belly, Taras moved as far away as he could from the dissecting table, and turned towards the corner. Despite this, the whizzing sound, almost as if someone had punctured a bicycle tyre, and the stench of rotten eggs reached him almost simultaneously.

"Not having any tonight, are we?" Cvilak said, waiting for the wheezing sound to abate before continuing to cut towards the navel.

"The intestinal flora is alive and decomposes the food we eat," Cvilak explained as he was cutting into the body, almost as if he wanted to place what he was doing into the context of safe academics. "As it does so, it communicates with the host and in return produces vitamins and fatty acids which act as signals for the cells, colonocytes, the liver... When a person dies these processes in the host stop, the concentration of oxygen in the digestive tract falls and because there is no more immune system which would prevent the microbes from invading the host's tissues, there is no more mucus production – that is a mixture of polysaccharides and proteins..." he said and opened up the dead body in front of him, "in which the microbes are caught and can be neatly removed with stools so with the mucus membrane we thus prevent the direct contact of the microbe products and our own products of decomposition. And when all this – oxygen and mucus – is no more, the microbes discover there is no food left and start eating away at whatever is available. They attack the host's tissues and begin metabolizing it. They eat you up from the inside, which suddenly means that gasses are formed from all the proteins which form the tissues of the body, CO_2 from fermentation, methane from the sulphur and nitrogen which are a composite part of proteins, ammoniac which stinks and H_2S which also stinks. Ammoniac of four day old piss – by the way they used to use it for cleaning the fat off sheep skins – and H_2S of rotten eggs. That starts accumulating in the diaphragm, in the human intestine and it all inflates. That's why bodies come floating to the surface after a while. You die, sink, ferment – and float to the surface."

He stopped for a moment and half turned towards Taras and the others, as if to check whether they were still following him.

"In cold water, of course, this process is slower, roughly it means that with every ten degrees that the water temperature is lower, the rate of decomposition is halved. This means that the quantity of gasses found in the body can help us determine when the person died. With this we also need to account for various microbes which begin to enter the body from the outside, through the skin etc. etc..."

He put down his scalpel onto the tray and picked up something larger which Taras could not name. When he turned his back to them, leaning over Lap, there was a crunching sound.

"The belief that at four degrees centigrade nothing happens is wrong. Things are happening, just slower. Microbes are alive and happy even at minus twenty, surviving inside the pores created when the ice forces the salts out of the cells. Between this grid of crystals you get hypersaturated surfaces made up of tiny tubes where all the nutrients which the microbes feed and develop on, albeit slowly, are concentrated. This is also why, when drilling for samples on the subglacial Lake Vostok on the Antarctic, they found and managed to revive organisms some tens of thousands of years old. There are no limits with microbes."

Doles pointed to the corpse,

"I hope this one too leads to Verbič. I don't want to think that it might turn out that he wasn't responsible for this one either."

Is he? Would the case be taken from him after last night's TV debacle? Would he be sent on leave? Would they wait for the Virgin Mary to appear to him?

"It will," Taras said.

The good thing about bodies piling up is that the information also piles up. Especially with bodies that still have a head and an ID in their pocket.

"It's just a matter of time."

The investigating magistrate nodded gratefully.

"Just another body or two and we'll get there."

Doles' eyes bulged.

"I'm joking," said Taras who felt sorry for the young investigating magistrate. Taras can at least try and do something while Doles can only wait.

*

"Should we tell each other who has slept with whom or should we not talk about that?"

When was that? Twenty years ago? Twenty-two...

"I don't want to know. Don't tell me even if I ever do ask."

"Alright," Alenka had said. Why does he now think it was with relief?

*

He reached for his phone on the shelf behind his head. He called Tina and waited. It rang. He counted to ten and put the phone back on the shelf. He stared at the ceiling for a while and his head was buzzing. Once more he reached out with his hand and pressed redial. Tina answered after three rings,

"Hello?"

"Hi," he said. "I'm ringing you because of this Lap guy of ours..."

"Yes?"

"He didn't drown. Well, he did, but before that he got a bullet in his head."

"He was shot?" came from the phone like an echo.

"Yes. Well, I just wanted you to know."

He expected her to say thank you or something like that and then say goodbye, but she was just silent for a while.

"That was quite a thrashing on TV," she said.

*

The presenter gave him a pitying look,

"Wouldn't it be better if you concentrate on doing your work and let me do mine?"

"He absolutely dismantled this mentor of yours," Tina's boyfriend had said with satisfaction. "That's the end of him..."

*

"I don't know, I didn't watch it."

Still, he wasn't unaffected.

"Should I come to the station?" she asked.

Now it was Taras who was silent for a while.

"Koper Street 14," he said. "I'd like to see you."

He barely had enough time to take a shower and the bell rang. She was wearing a winter jacket and a tight jumper and tracksuit bottoms under it and as soon as she entered he leapt at her, embraced her and pushed his hands into her trousers, kissed her and pulled her along to the sofa in the living room where he had already drawn the Venetian blinds and switched on a floor lamp with dim lighting. She gently but firmly pushed him away. He gave her a puzzled look.

"You will, Taras... after this."

She reached for the pocket of her jacket and produced a hand-rolled cigarette.

"A joint?" he asked.

Tina nodded.

"I don't smoke."

"You will now."

She gave him a serious look as if everything depended on this joint.

"I don't understand..."

She smiled. She found a lighter in the same pocket and lit the joint. She took a draw, held it inside her for so long she coughed slightly and passed the joint to Taras.

"Tonight I'd like to hear you laugh. I've never seen you laugh. Really laugh. And I'd like to."

He didn't take it.

"If you don't take it, I swear I will go home where my boyfriend is waiting for me. He thinks I'm watching over the body with a bullet in its head and water in its lungs."

"OK," said Taras. "Only if you take your clothes off."

She smiled and once again offered him the joint. This time he took it and took a quick draw as it was about to extinguish. She pulled her jumper over her head, undid her bra, stood up, took off her tracksuit bottoms, her socks and her panties. Elegantly, swiftly but not in a hurry. She sat on the sofa, lifted her legs onto it and turned towards Taras with her head on her knees.

Taras took another draw, inhaling deeper this time, but it made him cough even more than Tina. He returned the joint and tried to calm the twitching in his windpipe. When was it he last smoked? When he was still climbing? Probably never after that.

He stroked her knees and moved his hand to the inside of her thigh. She did not spread her legs but passed the joint.

"Your turn."

*

They lay in silence for a long time. Five minutes, ten, more?

Time disappeared and Taras still had a numb feeling in his head and a dry mouth. She snuggled up against him with her head on his chest and stroked his nipple. His hand rested on her bottom, gently stroking it.

"When does your wife come back?" she eventually asked and he wanted to scream in anger.

"Tuesday, Tuesday evening. That's... the day after tomorrow."

They were silent again for a while.

"And what now?"

Taras ran his hand, his middle finger, along her spine, from the neck down to the lower part of her back and the beginning of the cleft between her buttocks.

"I don't know."

"What do you mean, you don't know? It's not the first time, is it?"

He didn't reply straight away.

"It doesn't matter if it isn't. I was just wondering. It is mine, if you want to know."

"Why do you think it isn't the first time?"

She smiled, turned around and pushed herself up in her elbows, looking at him from close by, ten centimetres from his eyes.

"As I said. It is the first time for me, and I see that it isn't for you."

She stared at him and waited; when he didn't say anything, she smiled and stroked his hair,

"It doesn't matter."

Then she pushed herself away from him, sat on the edge of the sofa and began collecting her clothes.

"If you want you can stay over."

"Would you really want that?"

She looked him in the eyes, still with the same smile as before when she had passed him the joint or when she had tugged on his belt.

He nodded.

"And what am I supposed to tell my boyfriend? That I slept over at Forensics?"

*

When she left he sat on the sofa and stayed there for a while, naked and numb. Then he stood up, opened the tilting windows to get rid of the smell of the joint and went to have a shower. He disposed of the remnants of the joint in the toilet and made sure they were all flushed away. He stood under the hot water for a long time, and as he was drying himself he thought he heard the sound of a car outside the house. The doorbell rang and Taras, wrapped in the towel, ran to the door. Had he not still been stoned, he would have probably registered that the car which had driven to the house had also driven away.

"Hi," said Alenka smiling. "The only woman who has still not tired of her husband after twenty years is remorsefully returning home."

She stepped into the hallway and hugged him. He flinched when her cold jacket touched his skin.

"I missed you, my Sherlock Holmes. How did you know it was me?"

He gave her a hug as his still absent brain was trying in panic to search for the right answer.

"Or do you now open the door with a towel round your bum?"

"I recognized the sound of the car," he said and thought that his speech was slurred as if he had just had sixteen beers. What car, she didn't come with her car anyway?

She didn't pick up on that point. She looked at him and tugged on his towel,

"I'll go and have a shower too and join you."

While Alenka was in the bathroom he checked the living room. He even smelt the sofa to make sure there were no traces of Tina's perfume or any stains, then he sat down and tried to concentrate. He switched his phone to silent mode, so he would not have to answer if she called him and would not have to explain any messages received at midnight on Sunday, then he switched on the TV as if worried that he would be betrayed by the silence.

Chapter 39.

Monday, 15 January

He walked past the porter at five to nine when everyone should be in the office already, Brajc and Osterc, as well as Tina. He did not want to come across her alone. In fact he should try and find her alone, so he could take her for a coffee and tell her what he needed to tell her.

When he had opened the door and seen Alenka with her suitcase and skis in a canvas bag, he felt sick with surprise and the horror of what might have happened had she arrived five minutes earlier. How could he ever look her in the eyes again? No, he would clean up after himself and this will not happen again. He will not hurt her, he will not destroy everything they had built over these twenty plus years. And also, he said to himself, just as the situation appeared to become manageable, he was not moving back into a one bedroom flat. He was too old for these things and the next kids he will hold in his arms, change nappies and rush around looking for emergency medical assistance for will at best be his grandchildren.

He walked past the porter who noticed him at the last moment and almost shouted after him that Drvarič was looking for him. Taras went down the long corridor to the office, sighed, almost with some kind of stage fright, and opened the door. There was nobody there, the room was empty. He went to his desk and found a note in Tina's handwriting. It must have been hers because it certainly wasn't Brajc's or Osterc's.

"We are at Kristan's office. Called you but unavailable."

He took his phone from his pocket, set the ringing profile to normal, found forty cents from his wallet and went out to the corridor where the drinks machine stood. He waited for his coffee – he wasn't going anywhere without a coffee.

*

Walking slowly, it took ten minutes to get to Kristan's office and he sipped on the coffee along the way. It was a clear, fresh morning, and in the distance, when he turned the corner he could see the snow on the distant Kamnik Alps. Had the avalanche danger level already dropped to below orange?

He stepped into the lobby of the building close to the famous Nebotičnik, waved his ID at the porter who nodded disinterestedly and continued up the stairs to the third floor and the door which had Chief Commissioner written on it with the name Andrej Kristan, MA under it. He knocked on the door, greeted the secretary who smiled and gestured to him to continue through to Kristan's office. She met him half way and escorted him to the door, knocked, and announced him,

"Mr Birsa is here..."

The police hero of our time sat at the end of a long black table with Drvarič to his left and his three colleagues on his right. When Taras entered someone who was talking stopped, he thought it was Brajc, and they waited for him to sit down. He sat next to Osterc and didn't look at Tina even though he could sense her eyes on him as he entered and greeted them all as nonchalantly as he could.

"We'd better just go over it all briefly," said Kristan, surprising Taras who had a ready response which he didn't need.

"A whole day in Bohinj and the IFM all evening..." he had intended to say and when he thought about it he was embarrassed that after thirty years he still triggered his servile reflex. Why should he explain to Drvarič and Kristan why he was fifteen minutes late?

"Taras..." Drvarič began with Kristan by his side, silent as usual, as if observing how well Drvarič will transfer his thoughts to his subordinates, "how can I say this so I'm not misinterpreted. We don't want things to become more complicated now that they are clear."

They had thrown him to the lions and now they had a guilty conscience. And no, they would not take the case away from him.

Drvarič looked at Kristan who remained motionless but clearly this was perceived as some kind of an invisible sign.

"Things were complicated from the very beginning," said Taras. "But I don't know who this we are, or which things are now clear?"

Kristan and Drvarič looked at each other, very obviously this time.

"We are all of us," Drvarič replied. "Which things are clear? It is clear who the murderer is in this story."

"Which story?"

Kristan cleared his throat and all five of them turned towards him.

"Let's leave that… for now. Drvarič, why don't you just tell us what you wanted to say?"

"We have a printout of Verbič's calls…" Drvarič said and then fell silent, looking at Taras.

"And?" Taras asked.

"Brajc, will you?" Drvarič turned to Brajc who nodded.

"Well, we have the list of calls and there are two things. Firstly, that he was not in Bohinj last December, in fact he was not in Bohinj at all. Not once."

"Which of course does not prove that he was in fact not there. In principle it says that his phone wasn't there, but…" Drvarič unnecessarily explained.

"Did he have it with him when he killed Hleb?" Taras asked.

"He did," said Brajc. "And, one more thing – just before Christmas, on 23rd December, he called someone in Bohinj."

Taras smiled.

"And this someone wasn't Hleb?"

"What?" Drvarič was surprised. "Do *you know* who he called?"

"If he called someone in Bohinj and if things are becoming more complicated," Taras said scornfully, "then it could only have been Mr Mihelič."

He didn't miss the barely noticeable glance Drvarič and Kristan gave each other.

"You two can tell me what that means."

Once again brief eye contact and then Drvarič. Like two

telepaths, Taras thought.

"Last time Mihelič complained about you, you don't know this, do you?"

Taras shrugged his shoulders.

"Last time we talked he seemed enthusiastic. He even gave me a bag of glucosamine supplements."

"He called the GPD," Kristan finally spoke. "He threatened to – and I quote – make a fuss if we – and I quote again – do not remove this inspector from before my eyes. That was more or less what he said. I promised him that he would not hear any more from him, meaning you.

"Well, whatever," said Taras and snorted disdainfully, "why didn't he say that from the beginning and we would both have been spared the joy of meeting each other?"

"Taras, you will have to understand certain things." The tone of voice Kristan chose had now changed, become more official and a few ranks above what it had been previously.

"What will I have to understand?" Taras asked, clearly ignoring the distance Kristan was trying to establish.

"That there is something we call public interest, and also that here we have something we in the police call hierarchy."

His face acquired a threatening expression, his grey eyes staring at Taras who was briefly stunned, shuffled in his chair, and smiled,

"And there is also something," Taras said after a moment of uneasy silence, "we call the Organisation and Work of the Police Act which ensures protection to anyone whose supervisors try to force them into something which breaches this very act. I'm convinced that, according to this same act, after these telephone conversations I should go and find Mihelič or even call him in for an investigative interview, and if he refuses..."

"We did that," Kristan interrupted him.

"Did what?"

"You'll find out everything, but first about the law, rights etc. Taras, if I were to dismiss you tomorrow and indicate to your dear friends at RTV Slovenia that I did so because it was impossible to work with you any longer, do you think many people would stand by you?"

He looked at him as if expecting and answer. Of course Taras didn't even try to give him one.

"Not one. So stop strutting about and listen. We're all in the same boat. Well, yesterday Drvarič and I drove to Slovenske Konjice... and yes, you're not the only one to work on Sundays... and we conducted what was the friendliest interview in the history of the Slovenian Police. Right now the secretary is typing up the conversation and you'll have it on your table in twenty minutes. Will that be alright?"

Taras observed him for a second or two, staring impertinently straight at him. He certainly managed to keep cool, that he had to admit. Only seconds ago he was threatening him.

"This typed up report will inform you that he had spoken to Verbič because Verbič had called him and tried to convince him that he was the one who should be credited for some medicine they had apparently discovered. Apparently you know all about it."

Taras didn't respond.

"We checked. Indeed it was only Verbič who called."

"Why must I..." Taras began and then corrected himself, "Why must it be my team who is handling this case?"

Kristan smiled, as if to say, wasn't it obvious.

"Because we thought, and still do, that this is the best we can give this case. And if we have to change our minds, then fuck you, Taras."

Well, done. A word of praise, a kind of friendly one, substantiated with a swear word. Clearly he would have been told off at home if his grandchildren were left without a paediatrician.

"No, I really would like to know," Taras continued, ignoring the friendly tone Kristan had switched to. "Over this last fortnight I've often had the feeling that it's only the three of us, sorry, the four of us..." he smiled at Tina for the first time since he entered the room and when he looked at her she seemed somewhat distracted, "well, that only we care about finding out who killed our girl."

"Taras, how could you think something..." Drvarič began but Kristan interrupted him.

"Surely you don't think the police would be in some kind of cahoots with Mihelič? Surely you don't think that he killed her or had her killed, or whatever?"

"Why would he be someone who's beyond suspicion of killing or having someone killed?"

"Because," said Kristan, "for fuck's sake, he's in a business worth billions which could pull this entire country out of the shit it's in and ensure it had money to pay for the salaries of the likes of us. We don't all have rich wives like you so we don't need to care."

"Sorry," he said after a few seconds of silence. "I got carried away."

Taras stood up and went towards the door.

"Taras, fuck it..." Drvarič jumped after him and Taras had to laugh. This swear word was the first genuine thing which came out of Drvarič's mouth in a long time.

"I'll wait for the report, alright? And add to it a list of untouchables, so I don't waste my time."

He closed the door and took a deep breath. Rich wife... What about the twenty years when she wasn't rich?

The others came into the office about five minutes after him and sat silently at their desks. Taras sat at his computer reading the headlines. A few minutes passed before Brajc was the first to speak,

"Why are you bothered by all this?"

Taras lifted his head from behind the screen. Brajc, Osterc and Tina all observed him.

"Just let Kristan and Drvarič go out and do the fieldwork instead of us. Do you think they'll tell us any more than they tell them? I think it's great."

Brajc opened his arms to substantiate what he had said and looked towards Osterc and Tina, as if wanting their confirmation. Osterc even nodded.

"You're right, let's go for a coffee."

Tina sat opposite him and observed him. Unlike him, she did not look away when their eyes met and made Taras feel embarrassed, hoping that neither Brajc nor Osterc would notice, and if they did, that they would assume it was because of the previous meeting. He lifted his cup of coffee, his second that morning if the one from the machine counts.

"So what's with those phone logs?"

"Oh, yes!" Brajc jumped in, hitting his forehead. "You don't even know the main thing. We didn't only get the madman Verbič's list of phone calls..."

He looked at Taras triumphantly.

"You also got Lap's. And?"

Brajc's face showed his disappointment,

"Now tell me that you also know who he called the day before his supposed death?"

"The supposed day before his death, not the day before his supposed death..."

"What?"

"Nothing, forget it... Tell me then, who did he call?"

"Zidar..."

He stopped and watched Taras and because Brajc clearly didn't intend to finish his sentence, Taras had to ask,

"That Zidar?"

"The Zidar," Brajc continued slowly, "who will remain in jail for the next seven years, well, five in fact; he has already been in for two."

Taras scratched his chin, then took a sip of his coffee. The gesture was subconscious but everyone, even Taras himself, knew it. He needed two seconds to process the information and place it in the right place. The problem was that this time there was no right place. From the very beginning this case seemed to defy logical explanation. Just as he thought he had a lead, a pattern, a piece of the puzzle which might get him somewhere, get him to the other pieces and, as he liked to say, the unveiling of the Mona Lisa, everything fell apart. He was now holding this new piece of the puzzle in his head, finding a slot to fit it in, but there was none.

"Is this the Zidar who was convicted over some financial embezzlement?" Tina asked.

Taras shook his head and finally looked at her. His feelings as he did so were mixed. On the one hand he wished she wasn't there, on the other that he would be alone with her and they would both be naked. He left home in the morning determined he would tell her what he had to tell her, now this resolve was melting away like April snow.

"No, you're thinking of the banker Zidar, who was convicted but has appealed and will probably never go to jail, believe me. The guy we're talking about is the true king of the drugs scene in Ljubljana, probably in the whole of Slovenia," Brajc explained. "The man who seized the crime scene in our country from the Serbian and Albanian mafia, more or less gained independence. Hats off to him! At the GPD they have a list of people who they know he has had killed, but they can't prove anything. They were unable to convict him of anything until they caught him for possession of cocaine on the basis of having bugged his phone and ... Seven years for, if I'm not mistaken, just as many kilos."

"We never dealt with him," Taras said and put his coffee cup on the table. "And, to be honest, I'm glad of that."

It was not just that it was very hard to prove anything with Zidar because those in contact with him didn't talk, what disturbed Taras was that, as an outside observer of the case against him, he repeatedly felt that Zidar was always a step in front of the investigations. He could not explain some of these things in any other way but that Zidar had his own man within the police force, and not among the operatives, higher up. In the way that Mihelič had Kristan who put a wall around him. Taras, the main investigator in charge of the case, cannot get to the man whose name crops up every time something new appears.

"Well, clearly we will have to now, if Zidar won't be on the list of untouchables."

"You don't believe that Mihelič has anything to do with our girl, do you?" Tina asked.

She was wearing jeans and a red jumper with a white Norwegian pattern, very retro, and Taras though that she was probably not even born when jumpers like that were first popular. Her hair in a ponytail made her look even younger than she did usually. Like some first year student.

"Why do you think I don't believe Mihelič is behind all this?"

"Would you otherwise let Kristan cut you from him like this?"

Taras smiled and thought she blushed. So here we are, he said to himself. Pretty, clever and naïve.

"Nice that you have such an opinion of me..."

She blushed even more and in her embarrassment hid behind her cup of coffee. The more she was embarrassed, the less he wanted to talk to her today.

"...and no, I don't believe he is."

"Because?" she asked from behind her cup and Taras wondered if Brajc and Osterc had picked up that they were not talking only about the case here. He gave them an almost sneaky glance and Brajc who was clearly clueless and in front of whom in the last fifteen years no woman, let alone a beautiful one, has taken off her clothes, lifted his hands above the table and showed his palms.

"What need would the old man have for that?"

He looked at Osterc. He too would solve a thirty-year-old infanticide before he figures out that his boss has slept with the intern. He was sitting up straight in his chair, holding his tea in his lap. After the ten minutes they had already been in the shop, he was getting ready to take his first sip.

"But what if he is guilty?"

Taras nodded. Osterc was thoughtful for the next five to six seconds, holding onto his cup with both hands.

"I don't think he is."

He looked at the three of them as if trying to see if anyone else wanted to say anything. Clearly none of them did.

"I don't believe he is."

Tina waited for a continuation, an explanation, but Taras clearly did not intend to give them one.

"You don't believe it? He *is* the only person who had contact with all the people involved so far."

The three men at the table looked at each other and Taras smiled.

"Tina, where do you think you are? The police are barely any better than the army. When the General says jump, the soldier jumps, that's how it works. The General said that he conducted the interview with another general – as Mihelič is in his field of work – and the soldier, meaning me, because we aren't the army, gets a little pissed off, and that's it. But is Mihelič because of this, because he's an idiot, guilty? I think he isn't. I think he isn't the one who cut our girls' head off."

"Who then? Zidar?"

Taras put his empty cup on the table, picked up the plastic-wrapped biscuit with two fingers and then put it back down on the saucer.

"Zidar could have sent Lap after her, but as far as we know Lap is a small-time dealer, not some kind of contract killer. And who killed him then?"

He looked at them all again.

"I don't know, but that's not even important right now... You two finish with Stara Fužina or Jesenice, and we'll see whether that takes us anywhere. I'll go and see Zidar."

"What about me? Am I coming with you," Tina asked.

Taras shook his head.

"No, you'll do something else. Call the newspaper Delo and ask them for any documentation they have on Zidar. Tell them to e-mail it to you and if they have anything older, go there and check that too."

She gave him a puzzled look.

"The last ten years or so are in digital form, earlier things are still on paper, but they probably don't have anything on Zidar older than ten years anyway."

She listened to him and if she was disappointed she didn't show it. He did not want her with him. It was bad enough as it was.

"What should I look for?"

He shrugged his shoulders.

"Look for our victim. That's what we've been doing all along anyway... Until we're told to do something else."

Chapter 40.

It was the Illicit Drugs Section of the Organized Crime Division at the GPD which was responsible for Zidar, though with the lively secondary activities usually involved, it could easily have been included in the Homicide and Sexual Offences Section, though in this tugging between two services and two levels, the rights of the strongest won. There was a period in Taras' life when he would have taken on this work as a challenge, as his contribution to a better society. This period had long passed. In as far as organized crime was concerned, his opinion was in line with that of the average Slovene – find a rope and hang them. He had enough police experience behind him to know that this was not workable in practice and that it would probably be enough if the police had broader powers when it came to control, proof of source of wealth, seizing assets and things like that, though Zidar undoubtedly deserved no less than hanging. He was caught when his phone was bugged, despite the fact that he himself changed mobile phones more often that Taras did his underwear, but his associates didn't. Were the four bodies that had been linked to him revenged? Had justice been served? Did anyone care?

Five, in fact if we now add to them the inflated Lap, Taras thought as he stepped into the room where Zidar was sitting behind the table with a blank expression on his face, a bull-like face under a shaved head which, because of his thick, short neck, appeared to grow straight out of his torso. Tattooed hands, muscles bursting from the turned-up sleeves. It made Taras think about what state his liver might be in with all the steroids. He also attributed the prominent cheekbones and lower jaw to these. Taras greeted him and sat on the chair opposite him.

"You don't have to talk to me," he said. "This is just an investigative interview."

Nothing.

"Just so you know."

He didn't need to explain this because Zidar undoubtedly knew already. He placed the folder on the table, opened it and found a photograph of Lap taken during the autopsy, a photo of his face before Cvilak began working on it. He showed it to Zidar.

He only glanced at it.

"Basically what this is about is that we found a certain Robi Lap in Lake Bohinj with a bullet in his head. Quite by chance, he was pulled from the bottom by a fisherman. The guy had been convicted and given a suspended sentence of two years in prison about a year ago, thanks – so our inquiries have shown – largely to the fact that he occasionally worked for you."

Nothing.

"Before this, we found in the same lake, well, in the river not far from it, a woman's body with her head cut off..."

He carefully observed Zidar's face. No change.

"No?"

Nothing.

"To be honest, between the two of us. I doubt you have anything to do with all this, but if you won't help, I'll have to consider that possibility as well. Besides, the transcript of this conversation of ours will go on file and when in five year's time you will ask for conditional release, it will say – uncooperative."

He was wasting his time. Zidar knew he was bluffing and that he would be released in five years' time no matter what. He sat on his chair with his hands resting on each other, bent at right angles at the elbows, his vacant gaze never meeting Taras' eyes, however much Taras was trying to get him to look him in the eye. How come he even agreed to this conversation?

Taras pushed his chair away from the table and turned towards the door. He grabbed the handle...

"Inspector..."

Taras turned round.

Zidar turned his head in his direction. He was looking straight at him.

"Was she dead when...?"

Taras returned to the table and sat on the chair.

"Are we going to trade?"

His phone in the pocket of his jacket rang. He swore to himself, pulled it out of his pocket and rejected the call without looking who was calling. He placed it on the table in front of him.

"Was she dead before her head was cut off?" Zidar repeated and this time didn't even bother looking at Taras. He was staring blankly into the emptiness beyond him.

Taras supported his chin with one hand and spent a while blatantly staring straight at Zidar's face. Zidar didn't move. As if he had all the time in the world and indeed he had. At least a few more years. Then Taras reached into the folder again and pulled out another photograph. He looked at it again, as if wanting to check something on it, then, as he did with the one or Robi Lap, placed it on the table and turned it towards Zidar.

He took another page from the folder, a copy of the autopsy report of the girl without a head and swiftly and impersonally read out the summary. He tried to speak clearly and at the same time with his peripheral vision observe Zidar. He waited to be interrupted or show some sign that he would stop him, but he didn't. He thus read through the entire report which took him about five minutes. Then he looked up at Zidar. Was his face a touch gloomier than it had been, or was it just Taras' imagination?

"Basically," he sighed and shook his head, "the poor girl was alive..."

A small lie is a gift from the gods and Zidar was not a person he would feel any qualms about lying to.

"So, now you know what I know. Would you be so kind and tell me anything in return?"

How silly, he was asking a multiple murderer, someone who orders people to be killed, to be kind.

"Who, for a start, was this woman?"

Nothing.

"Well, thank you very much."

He could have saved himself the trip here. He picked up the photos and the report, stuck them back into the envelope, stood up and went to the door. Once more he held the handle…

"In fact I do have an offer for you Inspector."

Taras turned around.

"You're probably not short of money, no, but still."

How does he know he is not short of money?

"Am I not?"

A minimal smile appeared on Zidar's face."

"I'm not thinking about your pay, but your wife's clinic…"

Taras knew that, in interviews like this, controlling yourself was half the game and he was good at doing so, but this time he could not stop his jaw from dropping.

"Didn't you know?" Zidar now smiled more obviously and if Taras had ever as a policeman felt uncomfortable, it was now. How could he not have known? How come this piece of shit had…

"My son. He's in first year at primary school, I want to say he's been going to Alenka's… It is Alenka isn't it? Well, he's been going there for six, almost seven years."

"And?" Taras said, not even trying to hide his surprise. He sat back on the chair, pulled out his phone and checked the screen, as someone who was in a hurry might do, then left it on the table.

"I know that you're financially… settled, nevertheless I'll still make you an offer…"

He stopped and waited for Taras who had in the meantime regained his usual expression and had decided that no matter what might come flying at him, he would retain it.

"I can promise you one-hundred-thousand euros in a shopping bag, tax-free…" he paused and stared into Taras' eyes, "and I'm being quite serious about this…"

"If?"

"If you find out the name of this person, this shit of a person…"

His face momentarily turned from a controlled greyness to a raging purple.

"…and if you keep his name for me. One-hundred-thousand euros for you to tell me first who the bastard…"

His voice stopped in a kind of rasp, as if he was choking on something he had swallowed. Taras watched him calmly as he gasped, gulped and clenched his teeth…

"It would help if I knew what all this was about."

Zidar stood up suddenly and Taras jumped back from his chair. But Zidar didn't attack him. He took a step backwards and, as if not sure where to direct his rage, grabbed his chair, lifted it up above his head and smashed it against the table. It fell apart and, like Taras' phone, flew towards the door. With what was left of it Zidar hit the table another two times, threw the two wooden stumps he was left holding at the wall, then fell to his knees, pressed his hands against the floor and when the warder jumped into the room behind Taras, began throwing up among the wreckage of the table and chair.

"Thanks for your concern, but I think we'll manage ourselves," Taras sent away the guard who gave him a doubtful look and only left when Taras went to the door to close it.

He could just as well not have. During the next fifteen minutes which Taras spent in the interrogation room, Zidar did not speak again. He sank into silence and there was no indication that he would break it again. That he intended to do anything else. He kneeled on the floor with his forehead in his own vomit.

Out in the corridor he reassembled his phone which with Zidar's rage had fallen into three pieces, the casing and the battery. He entered his PIN. It worked. He had dropped it a thousand times, it had been bashed on all sides and still worked. Clearly not smart enough to stop working.

Five minutes later he was in the administrator's office. He vaguely knew him and hoped he too would remember him.

"Have you found out anything?" the administrator asked.

"I found out he knows who the first victim in Bohinj is," Taras told him.

"The girl without the head?"

"Yes, and now we've pulled another corpse out of the lake, a man, Zidar's helper, small fish. He had his head."

"And you are convinced Zidar also knew the first victim?"

Taras nodded.

"He knows her well. That seems to be why he agreed to see me. He wanted to know what we know..."

"And he found out?" the administrator asked.

Taras smiled uneasily.

"Not really, because we don't know much. Can you find out who this woman is?"

The administrator rocked in his chair and furrowed his brow.

"I can try. But, whatever way I manage to obtain this information, you won't be able to use it anywhere. In court I mean."

Taras shook his head.

"As long as we find out."

The administrator shrugged his shoulders.

"I can try," he repeated. "But Zidar is well aware that in here walls talk and I'm certain that after his experience with the phones he won't mention anything for a while that he doesn't want us to know about."

Perhaps he will, Taras though. They were after the same person.

*

Once back in the car, he remembered the phone call. It was Tina. He fastened his seatbelt, switched on the engine, and when, a few minutes later he left Slovenska Vas on the road from Mokronog to Trebnje, he first called Brajc then Tina.

*

Tina had called Delo's archive and asked the kind secretary who spoke with a Carinthian accent for everything they had on Zidar. She was in the office alone, Brajc and Osterc had followed their lead to wherever it took them.

"I don't believe there's anything on him in the paper archive," the woman said.

Tina sat at the computer for a while, staring at the screen, in fact staring emptily before her, rather than at the screen.

"What are you doing, girl?" she said to herself. "After just two weeks on the job you go and sleep with the married boss. Are you nuts? What kind of an excuse can you find for yourself, silly cow?"

Had she been drunk in Bohinj? Not enough to use that an excuse. Was she madly in love? She thought about it… and when she did she was horrified… but no, she was not madly in love. A little perhaps.

She had forgotten to ask how long it would take them to send the articles, but surely it would not take that long, or would it? She found it annoying that she was alone in the office. Not only that she could not ask anyone anything. She didn't want to be alone with herself.

How can you be a little in love? "Come on, don't be stupid, you're not in love," she said and her own voice startled her.

"You just wanted to fuck," she said out loudly and deliberately roughly. "And now stop making a drama out of it. Nobody will find out and it won't happen again..."

Again... Taras had got what he wanted, she too, she had to admit to herself, and he would not risk his wife finding out. End of story.

Perhaps she could call the archives again and ask them how long it would take. What would Taras do? He would probably yell at them from the start.

Did she have a guilty conscience because of Aleksander? Not really, if she was honest. Before this she could never have imagined that she would do anything like this and go home as if nothing had happened, but now... Was sex with Taras better? Certainly different, and different usually means better, at least at the beginning... So yes, it was different and better, but who cares... But that wasn't it. At least it wasn't just that.

She pressed redial on the phone.

Because, she said to herself and angrily thought that she was repeating the "Because?" which Taras used. Because Taras was... she was looking for the right word. Grateful? Was that the right word? Because when he had seen her naked, he barely noticeably, perhaps even without being aware of it himself, shook his head, as if to say, wow, what a sight? Because Aleksander took it for granted, not because he was used to it, from the very beginning? For granted that he could graze on her body. Was this the difference between the digital and analogue generation? Was this the difference between a criminal investigator and a marketing expert or just the difference between some Taras and some Aleksander?

Something appeared on screen. A new mail and at the same time the Carinthian accent on the phone.

"How can I help you?"

Tina apologized.

"No problem," the voice at the end of the line said. "With computers things are more or less instant."

Tina put down the phone and clicked on the mail attachment. Perhaps that was part of the answer, she thought. Things are more or less instant with computers, but not necessarily better.

Half an hour later she had gone through what there was to go through. There were not many articles. Most of them were about Zidar's trial and called him the King of Narcomafia; there were two short interviews with him in which he claimed that the police were after him because of personal grudges – one was that he had supposedly slept with a woman who later became the wife of one of the criminal investigators – and there were a few articles, more like reports from the period before his trial, social events where Zidar appeared in the company of his wife who was, according to the photographs and dates of the articles too old to be their victim and, as Tina added wickedly, also too fat. There were no other women in the photographs, and only one of the captions from the time before the tabloid press must have noticed that they were dealing with a criminal, had a caption saying: Mitja Zidar, lover of expensive cars and beautiful women. Next to him was some starlet, half singer, half mannequin and with the third half probably something else as well, but she was, as far as Tina knew, still alive. Just in case she searched her name on the Internet and the first thing that came up were photographs of her New Year performance.

Had Taras given her this task just to get rid of her?

She looked through the articles again and stopped at the one discussing the trial, the day of the verdict. It had a photograph which had the cameraman in it and a microphone held by a hand – it wasn't clear whose – and the courthouse in the background. The caption said, 'The trial which gave the media much to talk about recently is over. Zidar to go to prison.'

Her phone rang. Taras.

"Hello," she said, realising with horror that her voice was trembling.

"Hi," he said, "what's up?"

"I called the archives..." she told him. His voice didn't tremble, she thought disappointedly. "What about you?"

She didn't want it, but this 'what about you?' sounded so personal, so unprofessional, that she wanted to add something to correct it. 'How was the interview with Zidar,' or something like that, but he was already telling her and had clearly not picked up on the timbre of her voice.

"...that's why I told Brajc that Osterc and he should enquire out in the street who this woman might be for whom Zidar is smashing up tables in jail, and you can contact a few journalists who wrote about it at the time and ask them if they have any ideas. Someone will know something."

"It wasn't the wife," said Tina. "I checked."

There was a moment of silence at the end of the line.

"Perhaps I'm doing him an injustice," she then heard Taras say, "but what I saw was an attack of rage. I didn't think..."

She allowed him to find the right word.

"...if it had been the wife, we would have known for some time," he then said. "I'll explain when I get to the office."

"See you," she said and hung up.

She spent the next half an hour calling the names that appeared under the articles and realized that finding journalists is not as easy as one might think. Most of the editorial offices she tried to find only existed at Internet addresses, and there were no secretaries, and until she found one of them who gave her the phone numbers of two of the others, she was searching blindly. What she got from these conversations was unfortunately also not of much use. She did get some names, starlets as the one mentioned in the article, but they were all still alive and participated at various popular events.

"What do I get in exchange for giving you this information?" one of the journalists had asked.

"The satisfaction of having helped the course of justice?" she tried.

"Let's make a deal here," he went on as if she hadn't said anything. "If you tell me why you want to know, I might be able to help you."

"Unfortunately I can't..."

"Then I too, unfortunately can't," he said and put down the phone.

She sat for a minute staring at the page on which she had noted what she thought was of interest from the newspaper article, slowly crossing out point after point. There was nothing left. Then she blindly entered Zidar's name into the browser and checked the hits, which took her to the sites of two TV channels, a private one and the state-owned one. She looked at all the articles reporting on Zidar's trial. Neither said anything she didn't know about. She carefully checked the video coverage of their reports, trying to see whether she would see any woman of around thirty, but there was none. The only woman the camera lingered briefly on was his wife, and Tina was once more able to verify that she didn't fit the description of the girl in refrigeration at the Institute of Forensic Medicine. Once again she wickedly thought that she also didn't look like a woman someone would fly into a rage over.

She picked up her pencil and crossed out the entire page. Nothing. She had barely drawn the second line of her cross when the door opened and Osterc and Brajc walked in and then Taras immediately after them.

Chapter 41.

Dr Aleksander Golob, essentially a microbiologist with a PhD, the title of which covered three lines and would cause radio or TV presenters insurmountable troubles if they had to read it out aloud, sat at the desk in his office on Vodovodna 95, angrily staring at the piece of paper in front of him. After finishing his doctorate where he, if we want to simplify things, dealt with bacteria in the digestive tracts of wild animals and possible ways of utilizing them in biogas production from all kinds of things – because these all kinds of things are in their diet unlike domesticated cows and similar ruminants – his scientific career was predicted to have a brilliant future until he, for reasons he himself was not sure of, one day, out of curiosity enrolled on a course in forensics, and ended up at the National Forensic Laboratory of which he has been, for the past few years, also the head.

"So?!" he muttered tight-lipped.

He took a green marker pen and highlighted a sentence on a memo he had received from the Ministry. Your financial report is not complete in… this and this paragraph… and we request additional information. It was impossible that any report he had sent, financial or any other kind, would not be complete and until now he had asked the ministry to check their records three times, and three times received this letter. They will have to check again. The laboratory had received the money anyway, so he could wait.

When Brajc and Osterc knocked on his door, he was just finishing his reply which he concluded with… I once more attach forms JPF 23 and ZKM 76 as proof of my claims. With regards…

"Hello," his visitors said almost in synch.

Golob nodded, signed the letter and put the page into a green folder he then placed on the far right corner of his otherwise empty desk. Then he opened his drawer and took out a blue folder, opened it and with an almost ceremonial move took out a page from it.

"Sit down," he said and showed them the chairs waiting on the opposite side of the desk.

"You want the DNA report, don't you?" he asked, and Brajc ummed and Osterc nodded. He turned round for them to see the document, a piece of paper with a few numbers and lines on it. Then he fell silent.

Brajc and Osterc leaned over the page on the desk and stared at it for a second.

"Well, what do you think?" Golob asked.

Brajc was about to say something but Osterc got in first,

"I've often looked at these DNA reports but still don't understand..."

He was unable to explain what he didn't understand because after a kick in the shin, Brajc's kick in the shin, it took quite an effort not to cry out loud. But it was too late anyway.

Golob smiled, looked at his visitors, leaned back in his chair and joined his fingers. He loved the work as a forensic but there was one thing he missed from his previous life, his university career – lecturing, passing on knowledge. He rather fancied himself having a talent for this.

"So are they or are they not uncle and niece?" Brajc still thought it was worth a try.

"I will explain this clearly to you. The way things work is..."

As he spoke he stared somewhere above the visitors.

"When we get a biological sample of a hair follicle – because a hair alone is not enough, you should know that – so, a hair follicle, or sperm, or mouth swabs, or, as in our case, saliva... we come across our cells everywhere. Your cells have forty-six chromosomes, twenty-three from your father, twenty-three from your mother," he began his lecture which was usually intended for Taras who, if he had the time, enjoyed listening to it. But Taras had heard all this before, these two not.

Perhaps Golob indeed had a gift for passing on knowledge,

but he should have refined this a little more. Not really given an opportunity to do so, as with many who know a great deal, this knowledge leaps in all directions when he tries to convey it to someone else. In nature everything is connected to everything and this was what Golob's explanations were like.

"This does not mean that as the father you just give half of your DNA, no, these cells mix a little in the process," he continued.

Brajc kicked Osterc again and tried to sit in as comfortable a position as possible. He knew that this would last.

"So the half of the chromosomes a child inherits from you are not identical to your chromosomes because the cells mix. Certain parts cross over, and this is why each child is unique. Imagine having two books that you tear apart by chapters and then randomly create a new one, in which the chapters have a random sequence. But in this kind of sequence you get some genes which mix more, and other which mix less. Those that mix less are those essential for survival, are blood groups, genes for eye colour... These genes are relatively well preserved and by looking at them, by seeing the portion of these genes preserved, you are able to find out whether we are looking at your father, your grandfather etc. You have half of your father's genes, only a quarter from your grandfather. With brothers and sisters these variations are even smaller."

Osterc nodded. Brajc decided he deliberately wouldn't and after a few questioning looks towards Brajc where he got no response, Golob decided to concentrate on Osterc. He wouldn't cast pearls before swine.

When you pick a sample and extract the DNA... You of course cannot sequence the entire genome, but use certain ones... Well, now I need to explain a little molecular biology to you...

"I don't think that's really our..." Osterc tried.

"You don't? It is a wonderful science. Especially when you go into details..."

Brajc gave Osterc a look full of contempt.

"You must realize that the DNA consists of two strands," Golob went on, now with his eyes half closed, looking up at the ceiling. "One strand is organized with in a five prime end to three prime end direction, the other in the opposite direction. Now, if you want to analyze this, you need to use short segments of DNA which in high temperature align to entirely complementary points on the..."

Blah, blah, blah... Brajc repeated in his head. Blah, blah, blah...

"...if you get the sample from the sister you would get small shifts in certain segments. These shifts, however, are far smaller than they would be if we compare the DNA to a sample from a cousin. Some genes are full in one direction and full in the other... Are you getting an idea here?"

He pointed with his finger on the page in front of them. Osterc nodded, Brajc stared blankly ahead.

"All this relates to the father's line. With the mother there's another catch. During fertilization the sperm cell merely sticks to the egg and injects its DNA into it. This DNA then travels to the nucleus of the egg cell where it mixes with the mother's DNA. These are the eukaryotic cells whereas bacteria and archaea are prokaryotic cells, and viruses are not even on the map because they cannot reproduce on their own. Eukaryots have another characteristic that... Our cells need another apparatus, which is called the mitochondria, and it is this that generates energy. If we go back into history, it was once a prokaryot, an archaea that swallowed a bacterium and basically worked in symbiosis from then onwards and developed into animal cells. When the archaea swallowed a photosynthetic, phototrophic bacterium, it became a chloroplast and that was the starting point of the development path of plants."

His gaze descended from the ceiling and gave Osterc an enthusiastic look.

"It means that if your mother gave you her egg she gave you her genetic material but with it also her mitochondria. And because the mitochondrion originates from bacteria it also still partly has its own genome. This means that through this mitochondrial genome you can trace your grandmothers."

"Grandmothers?" Osterc asked.

"Yes, you can trace the female lineage entirely. This mitochondrial genome was also used when they created a phylogenetic tree of all races, sub-races, all anthropoids, and were able to calculate who Eve was almost twenty thousand years ago which was a narrow point for humans when there were apparently only around five thousand people left on Earth..."

Blah, blah, blah... Brajc repeated and was now also moving his lips. Silently, but they were moving and he looked like some inert fish, a carp or something. Osterc glanced at him a couple of times in embarrassment, but it seemed Golob didn't notice.

"...so it then utilizes the other genes in the small genome which I told you about before, and it means you get similar lines."

He tapped on the page on the desk three times with his index finger and stared at Osterc,

"So, what can we tell about our case? Are our man and woman uncle and niece or not?"

"They are?" Osterc tried.

"They aren't," said Golob giving Osterc a disappointed, accusing look.

How was this possible if he put so much effort into it?

Brajc gave them both a pitying look then looked at the page in front of them as if wanting to verify the accuracy of Golob's claims, brushed his hand through his thinning hair, scratched his head and looked at Osterc.

"I hope that will settle it for him."

*

They were laughing as they walked in and for a moment Tina thought they might have been talking about her. They weren't but she could imagine men taking about their conquests. Do they change over the years? She doubted they did. Would she be able to not speak about Taras with her friends? Probably. It would certainly not sound very commendable – I slept with my much older boss. This boss seemed to be in a good mood right now, he was laughing with her other colleagues and she felt somewhat stupid when she remembered,

I have never seen you laugh. Blah, blah... And I would like to... Blah, blah... Clearly he knows how to.

"Right, let's all talk things over here," said Taras and began telling them about his visit to Zidar at the prison in Dob.

"The guy offered you a hundred thousand euros if you tell

him in time who killed this poor woman of ours?" Brajc asked.

"Well, well..." said Osterc.

"And you declined?" Brajc asked somewhat miffed.

"The room is wired," said Osterc.

Taras smiled. Any clever person who has no need for money would not think twice about declining. It was not that the room was wired – it wasn't – it was just that you can never get rid of a mafioso who gives you money. This would be less easy for someone like Brajc who lived in his former wife's flat with her silent consent but only until the markets pick up and when they will get around two hundred and fifty thousand euros for it, of which Brajc should get around a hundred thousand after he pays all the taxes. With that amount, all you can buy in Ljubljana is a small studio apartment. And much less easy for Osterc who lives with his family in a metal prefab next to the dug out foundation pit for a proper house of bricks and mortar, the building of which has been waiting to progress for so long that the pit has filled up with water.

"It means that the guy knows who this woman is," said Osterc.

"Yes, but not who killed her. Even he doesn't seem to have an idea about who did it."

"And Lap?" Tina asked. "What does he have to do with all this?"

"If Lap is Zidar's man, he was in Bohinj because he sent him there. Why? I don't know."

"Like some kind of bodyguard for our girl?" Tina suggested.

"Lap was a small-time dealer and also a drug user himself. He does not seem to me to be a person you would entrust with protecting someone close to your heart."

Taras looked at Brajc.

"How did you two do?"

Brajc told them about their visit to the National Forensic Laboratory and concluded with a summary,

"So we have two children, a boy and a girl, whom someone left outside the door of the Jesenice Social Services Centre. After the death of the boy the woman, the alleged mother, commits suicide, I'm almost certain of this, thought everyone in the village will insist that it was an accident and the official report from the time also says it was an accident. She drowned in the lake. Based on the DNA analysis of the younger brother of this woman..." he looked up from the page he was holding, "the fucker who offered us his DNA by spitting at us, and the DNA from our woman without the head, shows that there is no relationship link between the two."

Taras nodded.

"It seems to me quite clear and conclusive," Brajc added. "A sad story but old and nothing to do with us."

"Very clear and very conclusive," Osterc repeated.

"And as such we can hand over this case to the people in Kranj and they can decide whether to take it further or not. Right?"

He looked at Taras and then Osterc who was still nodding when Brajc looked at him and didn't stop even when they both turned towards Taras.

"You won't hand this over to Kranj, will you?" Brajc asked with a voice which only half indicated this was a question. The other half revealed a bitter realization.

"Look for the sister. Tina?"

Tina briefly summarized her search through the archives, phone calls to journalists and looking through TV reports..."

"All names, all the girls I found out about are alive."

When she finished there was a silence in the room and Taras took on his contemplative position. Was he thinking or just putting us through the works? Tina wondered and glanced at Brajc and Osterc. They clearly were not thinking about the case at all, just waiting for their boss to mull it over.

Taras smiled, almost with embarrassment,

"I needed fourteen days to get a feeling... Clearly I'm getting older. None of you have?"

The three of them looked at each other.

"In fact, Tina, you had done. On your first day."

If I blush once more, she swore to herself, I will go off and hit my head against the...

"Had done what?"

"You twice pointed out this... detail. When we first drove to

Bohinj and I asked you what newest profession would say about a body without a head..."

He stopped and waited for her.

"Am I supposed to repeat it?"

He nodded.

"I think I said something about an organized person..."

"No, no, the other thing."

She shrugged her shoulders.

"I don't know. I can't remember."

"You said, specific hatred. And then again, with Hleb. 'How much hatred must have driven someone to do such a thing?'"

"So you think despite everything that it is the same murderer who killed all three?" Osterc asked. "That it was Verbič after all? Kristan would be overjoyed."

"Verbič hated Hleb, and we're pretty sure of that, and he also killed him. He could also have hated his..." he wanted to say lover but changed his mind. "His female acquaintance if he saw her in Bohinj when the receptionist at the hotel also saw her. But I'm afraid we will soon have to accept that Verbič was not in Bohinj last December and neither was his phone. And that he also did not possess a low calibre gun."

"Then it was Zidar," said Osterc. "The woman had been his lover but when he was put in jail she went her own way and he had her killed. It would not be the first body left in his trail."

"He threw up, when I told him that..." he stopped and was a little embarrassed when he finished the sentence. "I told him that she was still alive when she had her head cut off."

"You what?" Tina asked.

Taras shrugged his shoulders.

"And why would he also get rid of Lap?"

He scratched his head and stared at an indeterminate spot among the files in the wall cupboard in front of him and thought for a few seconds.

"Hatred is always specific..." he muttered.

Then, with a flinch, he took his phone from his pocket, checked the time, stood up, and reached for his coat that hung on the hanger in place of his usual winter jacket.

"I'd love to stay with you and chatter about this into the late afternoon, but I'm afraid I can't."

"Are you going to the funeral?" Brajc asked.

Taras nodded.

"Isn't it sad?" Brajc went on to say. "A man, a doctor, loaded with money and everything, and now... Poof, and he is no more!"

"Would it have been less sad if he wasn't loaded with money?" Osterc asked.

"Of course it would..." said Brajc and that was the last thing Taras heard when he closed the door behind him.

Chapter 42.

Funerals were the next thing on Taras' list of things without which he would be much happier. It was not only about the loss, it was also the fear of who might be next. Would it be him? When he began climbing, the mountaineering community was relatively small, everyone knew everyone and anyone who had a fatal accident was someone he knew, and whose funeral he had to attend. Over time it had been his closer friends who began dying and the name on the temporary wooden grave marker was often that of someone he had travelled with to France, to Chamonix, with whom he had spent a night freezing on some shelf high up on the rock face, waiting for dawn, or with whom he had turned off at some rest stop on some Italian motorway on the way home and had as many as five beers and a coke before he needed to go for a piss. He so hated funerals that he for a while didn't even notice the people who don't. Surprisingly, but there were quite a number of people who seemed to go to funerals as some kind of social event. An opportunity for some food and drink and meeting old acquaintances. For the living to gloat over those who were no longer alive.

The day was sunny and relatively warm. The cleared pathways were already dry with only the occasional patch of melting snow. Taras was clearly among the last to arrive at the funeral chapel because there was a crowd of people outside among which he, even before he spotted Alenka, recognized a few faces, some of the ones from the New Year's Eve party in Bohinj, and Cvilak. Alenka stood at the entrance to the chapel with one of the women from the party who compassionately said to him,

"You two were friends, weren't you?"

"Yes," said Taras.

Alenka had hoped they would become and would, if they weren't at the funeral, comment on any similar question with,

"Taras has no friends."

He used to have, and they are no more, so what? Is he supposed to become friends with someone just because they cycled up to Vršič together, or what?

"Yes, precisely that," Alenka would say. "Normal people become friends by having a coffee together. You don't need to climb Mount Everest for them to qualify."

The highlight of their socializing was cycling across Vršič in Trenta where Prelc had such cramps that Taras had to go across Predel to Kranjska Gora to get the car. When he returned he found him in a bar next to the River Soča in the company of two thirty-year olds and Prelc was extremely upset when Taras didn't have the time to go to some party in the evening and 'take things from there.'

"This is Monika. She works in the hospital in Šempeter..."

"I'm a nurse," Monika giggled. Her face was pretty and her body nice and rounded, as Prelc said about her later when they were on their way back to Ljubljana.

"The two of us have many nice things to talk about, as we are both in the same business," Prelc prattled away, and Taras nodded.

"...and this is Anastasia, who is in trade."

"I work in a grocer's in Solkan," Anastasia said, a tall, slim woman who could not decide whether to show the same kind of enthusiasm over a criminal investigator as her friend had shown over a surgeon doctor.

He had had to sit there for two hours, listening to Prelc' mating dance, before his phone rang, giving him the excuse that he had to urgently return to Ljubljana.

"If I had to study again, I would choose medicine and surgery all over again. You can't imagine how soft they become when they find out," Prelc complained with regret over a lost chance, on the way back somewhere before Martuljek, and then fell asleep.

Taras had not mentioned this part of the socializing to

Alenka although he later often wondered why. What would have happened if he had done?

"Oh well, that's what our dear Rajc is like," Alenka would have said. "If he wasn't running after some skirt I'd start worrying something was wrong."

Some people possess the charm and charisma which mean they are forgiven for everything.

"Will you go to say goodbye?" she asked him, pointing towards the door to the funerary chapel and he nodded.

He couldn't even stand the smell of chrysanthemums, let alone the wreaths and candles and coffins and all that, or the crazy thoughts that go through one's head as they stand by the dead person with a broken being by their side, a wife, a mother, a son or a daughter. Their suffering could not even be compared to his own feelings and thoughts at the time. Had he stayed for long enough at the coffin or urn, had he put on a sad enough face, had he expressed his condolences in a convincing manner?

He stood in the dwindling queue into the chapel where there were some five more people waiting and slowly moving to the door. Poor Rajc had not been cremated as he had hoped he would be. The coffin in front of him, hidden from view by those standing in front of him, was open, the lid propped up against the wall. Similar to the funeral of Taras' friend who had lain in front of them, his face in a grimace he acquired when an ice shelf broke under his feet and he realized that he was about to fall fifty metres into the foot of an icy waterfall. Like a run-over cat, Taras thought at the time. When Taras had reached the place he found a pile of something soft lying before him and when he had tried to massage his heart and give him mouth-to-mouth, blood had gushed out at him.

He stepped up to Prelc and looked at him. He was sixty if he remembered rightly, perhaps sixty-one. This Prelc in the coffin looked around eighty with dull, withered hair and a grotesque mask which bore little resemblance to the face of the man he had known. With one eye slightly ajar… Why was it necessary to display him like this?

"Sincerest condolences," he muttered to the old woman standing by the coffin, looking almost as withered as her husband since he had last seen her. Her eyes were crying but the tears had dried out, she absently shook his hand, as if she was not entirely certain who the man shaking her hand was or what was happening around her.

With relief he left the chapel and bumped into Cvilak outside.

"And then this..." the old man said, pointing with his hand behind Taras' back. "It almost makes me feel guilty."

Taras gave him a puzzled look. Prelc and Cvilak were not friends, barely acquaintances.

"Did you know that he had his attack when he was with me?" he said. "Well, the next time he visited me he was my patient. Ain't that fucking life!"

Flowers were brought from the chapel and piled onto a cart and Taras patted Cvilak on the shoulder. He turned round to find Alenka who was still where he had left her, just that there was now another woman next to her who gave Taras her hand and introduced herself, but he instantly forgot her name.

"Have you learnt your speech?" he asked Alenka.

"I'll read it," she said with an unusual calm, unusual for anyone who didn't know her. Taras knew that she could, when needed, be as cold as ice. When her father died she had cried only once, the day before the funeral at the time he was being cremated. She didn't cry at the funeral, not during the speeches, not when the choir sang or when they placed the urn into the square hole. She had stood at the graveside with the then schoolgirls Anja and Mojca both crying next to her, stroking their hair. With her own blonde hair reaching almost down to her black coat, she was incredibly beautiful.

"Are you OK?" Taras had asked when he, last in the line, threw a flower onto the urn.

She had nodded and even smiled slightly.

"As long as I have the three of you..."

Two workers of the Žale cemetery, in ridiculous purple uniforms and hats to match, brought the coffin covered in wreaths from the chapel. Karin walked behind the cart and Taras would preferred to have waited until the end of the line, but Alenka pulled him into the procession immediately after Karin. They slowly walked the fifty metres along the gravel path to the area where speeches were given. Three singers stepped out of the crowd and sang *On a Lake Near Triglav*.

"I'm first," Alenka whispered into Taras' ear and went off to the speaker's stand. The Slovenian flag hung behind her and despite attending countless funerals, Taras still could not get used to the idea that it was compulsory. Did the State really need to show its presence here as well?

"I have not known many people who loved life as much as you did, dear Rajko..." Alenka began and for a moment he thought that her voice was, despite appearances, trembling slightly. "We met when I was still a student, you were my professor, but you had the rare quality that in conversation and treatment, these boundaries spontaneously blurred. Your students loved you because with you we acquired the feeling that we were not merely material from which nothing promising will ever emerge, semi-finished products or even worse, as some of your colleagues at the time tried to make out, we comprehended that being a doctor is not merely a matter of technique, of learning things, but is also or essentially about a person's attitude, stance and conviction. What help is it to a doctor, however good, if the patient doesn't trust you, you'd often say although..." she paused briefly, "those who knew you also know that not exactly in those words."

A few people smiled.

"Then we ended up being colleagues. The medical profession is a strenuous one, stressful and sometimes thankless. With all this one has to struggle and take great care not to grow old too soon, not to allow your face – as you used to say yourself – turn into that of a sad joker. After all, you used to say, we have never cured anyone entirely, everyone leaves this world in the end. You managed to stay sane with humour. And although your jokes were sometimes rough and too sharp for many, I don't know a single woman who would not prefer to go to a charming doctor rather than anyone else, even if this doctor's response to them listing their ailments was, 'Well, dear, we're old, what do you expect?'"

Again a few people smiled.

"The world is as we make it for ourselves, you would often

say, and although you were not spared bitterness in your life, you lived by this. I cannot recall you ever complaining and this is how we will remember you. We liked you Rajc, and we'll miss you."

Bitterness, Taras thought. What could have been bitter in the life of Rajko Prelc apart from his end?

There were two more speeches, the Head of the University Hospital and, bizarrely, the president of the Dobova Hunting Association, of which Prelc was apparently a member, though Taras hadn't known this. The singers sang two more songs, both traditional Slovene songs, *The Linden Green* and another the title of which Taras didn't know. The procession then set off for the gravesite.

"You said that nicely," Taras whispered to Alenka.

Her eyes were damp and she tried to wipe them with her handkerchief, taking care not to smudge her makeup.

"I am glad," she said so quietly Taras barely heard her, "that it's all over. That he didn't suffer. Did you see what he was like in the hospital?"

Taras thought of those troubled eyes, as if they wanted to scream out.

Whatever it was he wanted to say, you were the last person to hear his voice.

"How did Karin take it? I mean, how is she taking it?"

Alenka shook her head.

"She was always tough, but..." she shook her head. "Rajko was all she had, regardless of what he was like."

After Alenka's speech Balažič approached him, nodded and offered him his hand which Taras absently shook.

"How things turn, don't they. And if I think that he always teased me about this."

And he patted his stomach which even his loose coat couldn't hide.

Taras nodded and Balažič uttered a few more polite sentences such as about how we are today and aren't tomorrow; then he asked,

"Oh, and what about that thing in Bohinj? The murder? Have you solved it yet?"

Taras shook his head,

"We're working on it."

"Any suspects?"

"A few, these are always easy to find."

"Well, at least we, all of us who were at that party at Rajc's place are safe."

Taras smiled,

"Of course the murder happened a week before that."

Balažič smiled as if what he was saying was pointing to something Taras should know.

"That's not what I meant. Most of us have our weekend houses there anyway. They called us for... What was it called?"

"An investigative interview?"

"Yes, some woman. But you said at the time that you would know if there was a murderer in the room. That's what I was referring to."

The first notes of the funeral march were already playing and Balažič quickly said his goodbyes.

"You will come to the meal afterwards?" he asked.

They walked along the central path and then turned to the first side path and then along a smaller path to the open grave. Taras held Alenka by the hand throughout, staring at the gravel path in front of them. He did not want to see the dates on the gravestones, years of birth and years of death. Lying in the graves were not only those whose time had ran out, there were graves of children, graves of his peers who had died of cancer or were run over by a drunken driver or whatever, soon the girl without the head will also lie in a grave like this with her name and year of birth and year of death, from which anyone passing by will be able to see that she was too young to die. Buried to the left or right of someone who died in the nineteenth century. In a cemetery one becomes aware of their own transience which many see as some kind of final justice. Perhaps some see it as consolation, Taras certainly didn't perceive transience this way, even though it affected everyone, and he certainly didn't see it as just.

On the sides of the pile the earth was black, in the middle and on the top a light brown clay soil. The gravestone was hidden behind wreaths and when the carriage with Prelc's coffin arrived, the two workers in purple began moving the flower arrangements in order to make enough room for all the others they had brought with the carriage. Taras, not sure what to do with himself, helped them a little. He picked up one of the wreaths from the cart and moved it onto the grave, moving one that was already there slightly out of the way. He was surprised to see the inscription on the gravestone. He looked at Alenka and pointed at it with his eyes.

"Later..." she whispered.

It said Rajko Prelc, 1980 – 1987.

Chapter 43.

"Well, let's get this over with as well," Alenka said, hanging her handbag on the backrest of a massive wooden chair in Kmečki Hram, a traditional inn where many of the customary post funeral feasts from the nearby Žale cemetery were organized. We humans are programmed beings, Taras thought, little less than animals, and when things get complicated we act instinctively. In this case, death – funeral – feast – traditional inn… Something like this. He knew that they would be served beef soup, sautéed meat, sautéed potatoes, a mixed salad, and two types of wine, red and white, and for him an apple or orange juice as a kind of extension of the ceremony. He could not imagine people going off for some sushi after a funeral, it would not be decent. Whenever something crucial happens, something fateful, people resort to a pre-determined plan.

He knew everything that would come next, as an abstinent he was forced to passive observation. Even as they walked into the inn, people seemed relieved, though still a little reserved. And hungry. Waiting outside the chapel, talking to others, the funerary procession, the speeches, *The Linden Green*… At least two hours, enough for anyone to start feeling hungry and thirsty of course, thirsty for alcohol. It's much easier to drink with 'we all die' in your head. And with alcohol comes a morbid joy of life, the joy of being alive while the deceased person is no longer. When they had buried Peter after that stupid waterfall in Tamar, everyone got drunk, dead drunk, including Taras who was still able to drink at the time.

It will take until the soup for everyone to relax, and until the first refill of the litre pitchers of wine for them to let go. And in the end, there will be two sober, distant people in the room.

Karin and Taras who will have to watch how all these overweight and scruffy doctors can pour into themselves everything from *Cviček* to Riesling, whereas he got stomach cramps at the mere thought of wine or beer or anything alcoholic.

"What have you found instead? Nobody can handle this life the way it is… " Cvilak had said.

Had he found it?

"It's not the first time, is it?"

"Have you not thought that the differences in response could be ascribed to the age difference?" he had asked her as he travelled along her back towards her buttocks and back.

"Wisdom?" she asked, stressing the irony.

"Yes," he had said quite seriously.

She was silent for a while and then asked,

"Well, and what does wisdom have to say about all this?"

Now it was his turn to be silent for a while.

"The problem with wisdom is," he eventually spoke, "that it is entirely useless to anyone, especially to others. After the age of forty, providing you're not an idiot, everything becomes clear, nothing can surprise you, but knowing this does not help you at all. You know… and that's it."

What could he have said? That people are programmed beings, barely less than animals? That they had ended up together because she saw in him something she cannot find in her advertising jerk and he the last opportunity to have sex with a younger woman? That every decision we make is the result of our minor and sometimes not so minor unscrupulousness?

"The shallowest truths are the most banal."

"You mean the deepest?"

"No," he said, "the shallowest. Life is always in the shallow waters, in the depths there is little else but darkness."

She had raised her head and looked at him with her big eyes.

"Oh, so the wise old man still has a sense of humour. Had I known that before…"

And of course, when she looked at him, he knew, as a wise person, that it is never just about sex. That would be too easy.

*

"Let's wait until the first people start leaving, then we too can go," Alenka leaned towards him, wrongly interpreting his smile.

He had sat at the end of a long table, Alenka next to him, but after five minutes she stood up and went to sit next to Karin who was sitting in the middle – to look after her, as she said herself. Balažič with his rounded wife sat next to Taras to his right. Whenever he looked at her he remembered how she was the only one among all the women in Bohinj with whom the dearly departed had not slept. She soon followed Alenka to Karin. Prelc could have said anything and Taras would have probably forgotten, but this stupidity stuck. Balažič's wife stood with Alenka next to Karin, patting her on the shoulder.

There must have been around thirty people sitting around the table along the longest wall in the main area of the inn. There were people at two other tables but clearly not part of their company. Taras knew many of those there from Bohinj. The loudest of them all was sitting next to him anyway.

"Well, as long as that's done and over," Balažič said as he ladled some already slightly cold mushroom soup into his plate from a large porcelain dish, having already finished a plate of beef soup before that.

"Is it?"

"It is," said Balažič with a surprising determination and conviction. "Such ceremonies, burials or weddings, whatever, exist so that we don't feel alone."

He offered Taras the ladle. Taras declined.

"Although ultimately, every one of us is alone on this shitty planet. If you're lucky, you only realize that at events like this."

Taras gave him a surprised look. He would not have thought that a shitty planet was something Balažič would say.

"I wanted to study philosophy," Balažič continued, slightly embarrassed as if he had guessed what Taras was thinking. "But my mother wanted me to become a doctor, and I did."

He leaned closer to Taras.

"It's not that much of a deal. Everyone thinks it is but it isn't. Especially not now with the Internet. If you don't know what's wrong, you send the patient out of the room and ask Google."

Taras smiled and glanced towards Karin.

"What about you, Inspector? What did you want to become and couldn't? Don't get me wrong, but I think you must be a bit like me."

His talking was not annoying because everyone else was also already lively. New pitchers of wine appeared on the table, red right in front of Taras. Balažič stood up and filled his own and his absent wife's glasses.

"You don't drink, I know. Our deceased friend explained it all to me. Also about your parents, or foster-parents. That's why I'm asking. Am I being nosey?"

Taras smiled.

"I didn't really have a choice. I think that was the basis of it all. I never asked myself what I would have wanted to be, but even if I had done, I doubt philosophy would have been my choice."

Primary school next to the church in his home village, then either the local metalwork school and the police secondary school. So much for choice.

"Yes, but it is a charming science," Balažič continued. "Charming if you have a sponsor to pay for your theorizing." He laughed. "Altho' filosofie iz of course not chust about theorizing..." he tried to put on a Slavoj Žižek voice. "So. Well, you're one of the few among us here..." he indicated the crowd gathered in the room, "because all of us knew two generations in advance what we would be. And our children also know. You have two daughters don't you?"

Taras nodded.

"I doubt that they will join the police?"

"No."

"Well, you see, but my son and daughter will become doctors. Family business, that's what it's about. Doctors are tops at this. Even better than architects. It's funny how we don't stop complaining how bad we have it, isn't it?"

He looked towards the far end of the table where the main course was just being served. Taras was right, meat, various kinds of it, and sautéed potatoes.

"How well did you know Rajc?"

Taras shrugged his shoulders.

"Over the last few years, since Alenka and he have the clinic..." He sighed. "Since they *had* it, we met occasionally and went cycling together a few times."

"And then he'd have a drink or two, and you not. How did that look? I mean how does it work for you? You sit and wait for him to stop?"

Taras smiled.

"Basically, yes."

"And then Rajc must have certainly told you," Balažič continued after he finished his glass of wine, "that he had slept with all the women who were in the room at the time, if you were in a room at the time."

Taras looked at him. Balažič smiled, but his smile was an uneasy contrast to his red-face which could not have been the result of a single glass of wine.

"He did mention something along those lines," Taras said and tried to keep a light tone, "at that party at New Year in Bohinj..."

Balažič poured himself out another glass, nodding as he did so.

"...but, if it helps that you know, he did mention he hadn't with your wife."

Balažič pulled a face and drunk half the glass.

"And what did he say about why not?"

He looked at him from behind the glass he was holding up to his mouth, as if worried that something fatal might happen if he was not in constant readiness.

"He didn't mention that," said Taras.

Balažič gave him a smile of disbelief.

"Come on. He must have explained something like that."

"I got the feeling that he would have had Alenka not appeared."

"I see," Balažič said and finished his second glass. He placed it on the table, looked at it for a second or two, then refilled it.

"Well, had Alenka not appeared, he would have told you that it was because my wife is fat."

He stared into Taras' eyes as if not wanting to lose contact with them.

"I don't know..."

"But, you know something, my wife was not always fat."

Where is this going? Taras wondered. Was it this which put him off socializing with drunken Slovenes? No, not that they drank and were merry, what annoyed him was that they drank and then tired him with all their traumas.

"It doesn't matter," he said. "The man's dead."

"That's right," Balažič almost shouted so a few people around the table turned to look at them. Balažič waved his glass at them, "And that's why I'm here, drinking to his eternal health."

He raised his glass towards Taras who raised his own apple juice and clinked.

"But," Balažič went on once he put the glass down, "I didn't want to bore you, I apologize. I wanted to ask you something else. Do you remember how I asked you in Bohinj if you would know if there was anyone there who was a murderer, and you said you would?"

Taras nodded.

"How would you know that?"

"It was just something to say."

Balažič burst our laughing but with the atmosphere similar all around the table, nobody paid attention to him.

"Really? You just said it like that?"

"Really."

"Then you also could not have known who among us would become a murderer, if any of us had intended to become one?"

Taras smiled but did not answer.

"Do you know what dawned on me? Well, what I thought of when this happened to Rajc... There were... How many of us were there? Men whose women Rajc had slept with?"

"I don't know, I didn't count," said Taras, no longer hiding the fact that he was not enjoying the conversation. Balažič paid no attention.

"Eleven. There was eleven of us, twelve with you. And do you know of any instance where twelve people each have something against the main character?"

"The last supper?" Taras said. "And in that case eleven, not twelve. Why would I have anything against Prelc?"

Balažič ignored the question, nor did he move his eyes off

Taras.

"Shit, you know, I'd never even thought about that association. No, I'm not talking about Jesus and Judas. I was thinking about Agatha Christie, and the *Murder on the Orient Express*. You know the story?"

"I do."

"A murder and twelve stabbing wounds and twelve passengers on a train between Vinkovci and Belgrade, etc., etc… Do you think the old lady got the idea of the twelve murderers from the apostles?"

"I don't know," Taras said. "But Prelc wasn't murdered by anyone, if I am not mistaken."

"And by the way," Balažič went on, "have you ever guessed half way through any of Agatha Christie's books who the murderer is?"

"No, I haven't, but you were talking about Prelc as a victim of murder."

"Well, you know how it is… A stroke can also be staged. Don't you think that eleven doctors would know how to swap anticoagulants for something with the opposite effect? Rajc had high blood pressure and took…"

"Medication against blood clotting. I do know what anticoagulants are. But there was an autopsy…"

"Which found nothing unusual, did it? How could it have done? They found that a blood clot caused a brain haemorrhage but not what had caused the brain clot, because that was not what they were looking for. His anamnesis was enough."

Taras now looked at Balažič seriously for the first time. Staring at him was a round red face with blue veins visible under the skin above his cheekbones. There was a kind of dedication in his gaze, a commitment to a task he had set himself a long time ago and was only now finding the courage to complete.

"You do know I'm a police officer?"

"Exactly."

"And you've just told me that you suspect that Prelc was murdered by someone. Am I right?"

"No, no…" Balažič said hurriedly. "I said that if someone had wanted to, they could have murdered him. And that there are a number of us here who would have a motive to do such a thing."

"Eleven apostles whose wives Prelc had been involved with?"

Balažič stared straight into his eyes, the light-hearted tone with which he had begun this conversation had vanished.

"There were not eleven apostles, Inspector."

Taras pushed away from the table, picked up his glass of apple juice, lifted it to his mouth and, as if changing his mind, put it back down onto the table.

"What is it that you're trying to tell me?"

Balažič was confused, pulled his head between his shoulders and stuttered,

"Me... Nothing, nothing, I was just..."

"What have you two been up to?" Alenka asked, returning to their end of the table with Balažič's wife.

*

"Karin, if you need anything, you have my phone number. If you want, you can come and stay with us tonight."

Karin smiled and then slowly, as if it was incredibly hard to do so, shook her head,

"I'm going straight to Bohinj after this."

Alenka stopped, waiting for an explanation but none was forthcoming. She kissed Karin on the cheeks and went towards the door. Taras followed her and when they got to the corner where Balažič now sat with his wife, Balažič stood up and held Taras back slightly.

"I'm sorry of I was too... aggressive. I watch all these TV series, crime movies and such, and get carried away. I forgot about what I actually wanted to tell you. Can I now, or should I call you tomorrow morning?"

"Go ahead."

"Well, I don't know if you know. In that investigative interview or whatever you call it, your colleague asked me about the boat which had disappeared and was then returned, and so on?"

"Yes?"

"Well, I reported the theft, then the boat appeared back at my mooring..."

"And?"

"Basically, that was not my boat. My wife saw it when it was brought back and she can't tell one boat..."

He looked towards her carefully.

"...from another. I wanted to call the police, but I said to myself you had your hands full of things more important to do than looking for mixed up boats. Someone else has mine and I have theirs, and we're even. Was I right?"

The look Taras gave him would have drilled a tunnel through him but then his gaze moved away from him into an indeterminate point in the middle of the inn, and waited for a brief moment.

"So it's not the same boat?"

"No, and that's why, how can I put it, I had a slight guilty conscience for not letting the police know. The one that was brought back was much better than the one we had. Do you think that I should call the police in Bohinjska Bistrica? That was where I had reported the theft."

"No need, I'll do it," Taras said.

Balažič offered him his hand.

"And forget about all that before. When I have a few drinks I get carried away and babble on."

Chapter 44.

"What's up with him today?" Tina asked when Taras closed the door behind him.

"What do you mean?"

Brajc gave her a surprised look while Osterc waited for his failed programs to re-load on his computer.

Tina waved her hand in the air with embarrassment.

"Oh, I don't know..."

"We're used to him," said Osterc from behind his box. "These silences of his where he thinks something will just appear to him."

"Why doesn't he share it with us?"

Brajc grinned.

"Because he doesn't know what to. Well, he did anyway. Didn't he say something about hatred?"

Tina gave him a disappointed look. It was obvious you had to hate someone to cut off their head. At least it was to her.

"What's bothering you?" Brajc asked her.

She shook her head. What did he mean by that specific hatred? Was there any other kind?

"Nothing, forget about it."

She had her own work to do, of however little importance it might be. She put *RTV Slovenia* into the browser and into the search field entered *Zidar*. Twenty-three reports came up, and she opened the most recent one about Zidar's arrival at the prison in Dob. She noted the name of the journalists who reported from outside the prison. Then she found the phone number of the TV station's secretary and called it from her landline.

"Hello, can I speak to Tanja Kolenc please?" she asked and

the voice at the end of the line said,

"Just a moment, I'm putting you through."

It rang for a while and she persisted until the same voice appeared again,

"Just a moment, I'm putting you through."

After three rings someone picked up the phone. A man's voice. She introduced herself and asked to speak to the journalist Tanja Kolenc.

"Just a moment," the man said and in the background she could hear,

"Tanja, it's the police, for you..."

"Tanja Kolenc, how can I help you?" the journalist eventually appeared on the phone and Tina felt disappointed and a simultaneous shame. It is not very nice to hope that someone will not come to the phone because they are dead. She hoped she was not indicating such and introduced herself again...

"And because we would like to clarify a few details in the Zidar case, I'm calling anyone who had anything to do with it."

"Please," she said, "go ahead."

What was she supposed to ask her? Sorry, do you know a girl of your age and probably appearance who might be missing?

"In fact it would be better to meet, if possible?"

"Of course it's possible. Were you thinking of today?"

They arranged to meet at eight, after the evening news.

Why had she even suggested this? What could she possibly come up with by the evening? She looked around the office. Brajc and Osterc existed in it with the calmness of those to whom after twenty years a space is so familiar that they could sit there without doing anything particularly useful and feel quite relaxed about it. Osterc was clicking with his mouse, staring at the screen and she wanted to stand behind him and see what he was clicking on; Brajc sat there, spread out on his chair, reading a two-day-old newspaper which had somehow found its way into their office. It was as if they were both waiting for Taras and his nose. In fact it seemed they were all three waiting for it.

*

"What were you and Balažič talking about?" Alenka asked as they drove back home in the darkness of the evening.

"About how it was not true that Prelc hadn't slept with his wife."

She stayed silent. Taras repeated the sentence.

"Does that really bug you?" she asked after a while. "Whether I had anything going with Prelc or not?"

"Clearly not only me," said Taras and looked at her. She was staring out of the front windscreen. They drove on in silence for a further kilometre.

"It wasn't I who brought up the matter. I just listened. Balažič even believes that Prelc was killed by one of the eleven, or twelve, men who were in Bohinj at that party, because Prelc cuckolded them or rather claimed his *jus primae noctis*."

"Prelc died of a stroke. Ask Cvilak."

"Balažič thinks someone caused him the stroke."

"Oh..."

They arrived at the house and Taras used the remote to unlock the garage door and drive into it. He climbed out of the car and waited for Alenka to do the same, then locked it. They went into their flat and Taras stood in front of the TV, picked up the remote control, changed his mind and put it back in the table."

"In fact I would want to know about it."

"About what?"

He stayed silent.

"Even if you won't like it?"

Alenka sat on the sofa and he sat in a chair by the table.

"OK, so you did," he said. "In fact you can spare me the details."

He stood up and left... Someone who doesn't drink has a limited choice of reactions in such situations. He stood up and went to the cupboard above the kitchen sink, stared at the bottles of alcohol, a variety of stuff from vodka to whisky and home made brandy he had acquired as gifts over the years and had not been able to pass on. He closed the cupboard and checked the fridge. A bottle of wine for any chance guests.

"After the second or third year we went on some trip together," she said, as if she had not heard him. "At the time he had already been eyeing me up for a while, I knew that, and admit that I didn't mind..."

"You don't have to, please."

"...and that evening we danced and I had a few drinks, and you know, I can't handle my drinks, and then we went to his room..."

He wanted to shout at her to stop but he couldn't. As if he hoped until the last moment that she would say, I was drunk and I fell asleep...

"...and as you put it, we fucked."

She fell silent and looked at him, waiting to see if he would ask, say, anything.

"So now you know."

"Prelc said fucked, not me."

He pressed the remote and some match appeared on screen.

"And then?" he heard himself say.

"Then we continued to be together in this way for a while."

He tried to follow the men in blue and the men in green running around the pitch but he couldn't even read which teams they belonged to.

"And your friend Karin? They were together then, weren't they?"

She was silent. He switched channels.

"You said she knew about Prelc's conquests."

He switched again.

"Well?"

"She knew. Don't force me to go on, please."

She was crying.

"Aha..."

He switched off the TV and switched it back on again immediately.

"So now you know," she said.

"Just one question..."

"Tell me," she said when there was no sign that he intended to continue.

"Did you know... Of course you knew that Prelc was womaniser par excellence, one of the worst in this world. Did that not bother you?"

She was silent.

"Did you do a threesome?"

He didn't look at her but could hear her sob. He sat, elbows on the kitchen table, supporting his head.

"Do you know how I feel right now? As if I had just blown the last twenty years."

She began crying again and as she did so cried out,

"Have you not made any mistakes in your life?!"

He looked up at her,

"I no longer know whether it was a mistake or not."

*

He put the bottle of wine on the table in front of him and stared at it for a while, then found an opener and screwed it into the cork.

"What are you doing?" she asked. In the long minutes they had sat alone, she on the sofa and he at the kitchen table, she had stopped crying. With dried up tear marks across her cheeks she watched him pour out two glasses of wine.

"Your ex lover, not to use a word which would be more in his style, said that this abstinence shit of mine is psychological. It's time we get rid of this problem. Want some?"

He offered her a glass. She didn't take it.

"Right then, let's see..."

He tilted the glass and took a sip, swigged it through between his teeth and tongue, and emptied the entire glass of red wine. Five years had passed since the last time he had tried drinking. Not enough to forget the sensation of the drink running down the throat almost at the same time it was reaching the brain.

"Now, that *is* it, not running!"

He looked at Alenka. She looked tired and when she looked tired nobody in the canteen asked her for her student coupons. They hadn't asked him for well over a decade. He poured out another glass, but could have spared himself that.

The pain was so sudden and, despite his previous experiences, so intense that he doubled over in the chair and barely managed to push himself away from the table enough for him not to hit it with his forehead. Not again, he managed to think in disappointment when the pain in the stomach was accentuated by something new. It was as if he unexpectedly received a punch in the stomach, so quickly he didn't even have time to call out for help, so quickly that rather than being afraid, it brought him a sense of surprise. He gasped for air two or three times, rasped and fell from the chair into the darkness.

*

Tina showed her police ID and acquired a visitor's badge that she put in her pocket. She waited for the journalist who came smiling from the other side of a glass partition and opened it from the inside with her pass.

"Can we go to the house bar for a coffee, or is this something more official?"

"Coffee will be fine," said Tina and followed her into the elevator.

In the elevator she listened and observed her while the journalist explained about the thousands of coffees she had already had on that day and how she would now just have to have another one.

"Half of this work is waiting..." she said.

She was... Well, she wasn't as beautiful as she appeared in the reports that didn't show that her head is not quite in proportion with her bottom and where makeup covered her acne. She spoke with a slight Styrian melodic accent that, for some reason, also seemed to get lost in the reports, and she liked talking, non-stop in the slow elevator to the fourth floor.

"So what is it you're interested in..." she continued in a chatty manner as if they met for coffee every day.

"I'd like to know how you followed the case against Zidar. I want to know about the people who were around him, those who came to the court sittings, especially women, his women..."

She thought for a while, then began talking. It was like a shower, a summer storm which, just as you think it is about to end, starts pouring again. Tina listened somewhat tiredly and tried to tie the threads together. But there really were none, just lots of words about the difficulties of working as a journalist, about unsupportive courts who don't realize we are all in the same boat and put up a thousand and one obstacles for selfless journalists, especially those from TV channels who only want to report genuinely and objectively from the court room and bring their viewers the essence of events. About editors who demand a live report for the news even when nothing happened at the court or it all happened behind closed doors...

"...then, after you've waited for four hours in a room without air conditioning, you try and step out in front of the camera fresh and blooming for a two minute report. Can you imagine? Then your mother calls you and asks you what's wrong with you, that you seemed all wrinkled on the TV..."

...about how the accused also do not understand the work of journalists and how journalists are basically the last guarantee that they are not stood in front of a wall and...

"...we, the journalists, not the judges or their lawyers..."

...and how she had problems with their statements, most of all with Zidar himself.

"I offered this criminal the chance to say something in his defence at least ten times and he never stepped in front of the camera.

Tina wasn't sure whether it was the way she babbled on or simply a lack of sleep which made her barely able to follow what she was saying, but this last point didn't escape her,

"But how, if I saw you talking to Zidar in the reports?"

Not only talking, their conversation was rather relaxed.

"Oh, no, that wasn't me. A lot of people get that mixed up."

Tina gave her a puzzled look.

"It's true that it says Kolenc like me, but it's not Tanja but Tjaša. And we're not even related. Funny isn't it? Well, I took her place somewhere half way through the trial."

"And where did she go?"

"Uff," she said and rolled her eyes at the ceiling. "If I'm not mistaken she was moved to science and technology and stuff like that. Making documentaries. There was talk of something going on between her and this Zidar, and I..."

She leaned across to Tina and whispered,

"...am pretty certain there is something there. Why else would she have gotten his statements and I got none?"

Tina stared at her in shock and Tanja responded with a meaningful raise of the eyebrows.

Was it possible that people this stupid worked in this

building? Tina wondered. This is what I've been asking about all along!

*

After a famotadine injection and two hours on a hospital bed in the corridor at the A&E department Taras recovered enough for the doctor to see him. He looked just as exhausted as Taras and there was a sea of people outside in the corridor, had it not been for Alenka he would probably not have given him this minute of his time.

"You have your wife to thank," he said without greeting. "Had she not immediately given you a dose of antihistamines, you would now be in another department."

Alenka stood by the wall. Taras didn't even twitch.

"Wine?"

Taras nodded.

"People usually get blotches on their skin and that's it. Panic attacks..."

"It wasn't panic. I could not breathe."

"Yes, well," the doctor smiled. "That's one of the apparent forms of panic, what did you think? You'll stay here tonight, just in case, and tomorrow, if all is well, we'll send you home."

"Won't do," said Taras.

The doctor gave Alenka a questioning look. She nodded tiredly.

*

He was pale and exhausted, as if he had just run the marathon. Alenka wanted to hold his arm when he stepped out of the car, but he moved it away. At home he crawled onto the sofa, she sat on a chair by the table.

"How is it?" she asked.

He didn't answer.

"Can I come and sit next to you?"

He didn't reply and she stayed at the table. His head was empty. As if it had been emptied... What a pity it isn't like a computer and you can restart it if needed.

"Come," he made a space next to him on the sofa. She sat down and leaned her head on his shoulder. The sat like that in silence, then Taras lifted his hand and stroked her hair. She raised her head to look at him in the eyes.

"The world is as it is, Taras. You won't change it, even if you kill yourself, you won't prove anything to anyone, even if you rip yourself apart. Nothing will change if you continue to live as if you don't have five euros in your wallet and think about who I slept with thirty years ago. Even war crimes are obsolete after all this time."

"War crimes are never obsolete."

She wanted to say something but he interrupted her,

"I don't want to talk about this."

They both remained silent for a while.

"Cvilak mentioned at the funeral that he felt responsible for his death," Taras said, deliberately not mentioning Prelc's name.

"Clearly he was borderline." She too avoided it. "This just pushed him across the edge. It would have happened sooner or later."

"What pushed him across the edge?"

Taras pushed her away and looked straight at her.

"He asked Cvilak whether he could see the body of the girl from Bohinj. He showed it to him and that was where it happened."

"He died, because he had a stroke at work, in the hospital, didn't he?"

"No, he had a stroke in hospital, but not at work. He had it when your colleague Dr Cvilak took him to see the body that you've been dealing with over the past weeks."

He stared at her as if he had seen a ghost.

"You didn't know?"

He stood up and went to the shelf where they had the phone. He looked through the numbers, got to the letter C, found the number and dialled.

*

"Hello Cvilak," said a voice which was unmistakably Prelc's.

"What's up? What can our slaughter house offer yours?"

"Apparently you have the body from Bohinj on ice at your place. Could I take a look?"

"What for?" Cvilak asked more or less as a courtesy. Cases which appeared in the media had various colleagues interested and similar visits were not rare.

"Taras asked me to take a look," Prelc said and Cvilak told him that if that was the case, he could come round any time, but was slightly offended. What could Prelc tell Taras about the body which he could not have done?

They went to the mortuary and Cvilak showed him the slot where the body was and himself sat at the desk to read the report on an autopsy of a younger man who had been found dead a few days earlier in the attic of a house in the old part of town.

"Heroin," he had predicted when he was brought in, and heroin it was.

Just as he was about to put down the papers, almost with satisfaction, he heard a cry behind him and a sound of sliding metal. He turned round and saw Prelc, clinging onto the side of the drawer and – before Cvilak could reach him – falling onto the floor.

When Taras put down the phone, his expression was a huge question mark. He sat on the sofa as if Alenka wasn't there. He sat like that for two minutes, staring at the blank TV screen.

"Who was the Rajko Pelc on the gravestone? His son?"

"Yes," said Alenka. "Their son."

They had met at medical school, she too was a promising surgeon but soon after graduation she fell pregnant. The child was born with a heart condition and the doctors predicted he would die before the age of two, three at the most, but they hadn't reckoned on Karin. She went to all the possible clinics in the world, made sure he had all the possible treatments and extended his life to seven years.

"A year after he died they discovered a method of correcting the condition. With a device which now costs just over fifty cents," Alenka told him. "Those who knew her then said that Karin died with their son. You wouldn't believe me if I told you she used to be quite a beauty, would you?"

"I would," he said caustically.

She fell silent.

"She never worked as a doctor, a surgeon?"

Alenka shook her head.

"And watched unaffected as her Prelc played around as if on

heat?"

She blushed.

What had Prelc told him in Bohinj? That he would settle down, or what?

"Did he have anyone on the side recently?"

Alenka was silent.

"Someone more serious than usual?"

"I don't know."

What was he talking about then with that joint in his mouth? That he would settle down, that his wife had been a gymnast at the Olympic Games in Montreal, that he might need his help...

"And Karin was a gymnast?"

"Karin? We used to go to yoga together, and believe me, she, for one was never a gymnast. You'd be hard to find a less supple woman."

"What then? Prelc mentioned that she had participated at the Olympics in Montreal like Nadia Comăneci or in the same place as Nadia Comăneci... You don't know anything about this?"

"No, she never mentioned anything like that to me."

"That she competed or almost competed, like Jackie Stewart in Rome, but three Olympics earlier? Nothing?"

"Who?"

She shook her head. He went to the computer, switched it on and typed in the password, clicked on Google and waited impatiently for the window to open. He typed in Jackie Stewart wiki... Read what came up and when he looked up from the computer, his face was even greyer than before. His phone rang and he was still sitting at the computer in disbelief, looking over what had come up. Alenka went to the phone and looked at the screen.

"Your colleague is calling," she said and passed him the phone.

"Taras," he could hear a voice out of breath at the end of the line. "Taras, sorry to call you, but I think I know who our girl is."

He listened as if he wasn't listening and only responded when she repeated what she had said.

"Thank you Tina. You will explain it to me in half an hour's time at the station. Call Brajc and Osterc and tell them that we'll meet there. They should bring their guns with them, you too."

"Where are we going?" she asked.

"We're going to pick up the person we've been looking for," he said. "We're going after our murderer."

When he hung up he noticed the ash-grey face of his wife. He got dressed and went to get his car from the garage.

Chapter 45.

"Why don't we leave it to special forces?" Brajc asked, trying awkwardly to strap his gun to him. The strap was too short.

Taras shook his head,

"Not this time."

"And where are we going anyway?"

Taras had picked them up at the police station. Brajc was sitting next to him, Tina and Osterc in the back. It was a quarter to ten in the evening and if one had to describe the expressions on their faces, the best word would be – confusion. Tina's least of all.

"Tina, you first," he said as he turned from Celovška Street onto the motorway.

She told them about her visit to the TV station, her conversation with Tanja Kolenc who had covered the crime section since Tjaša, also Kolenc, was removed from that section after getting involved with Zidar, and was moved to the science section...

"That's why she knew Hleb," Taras said. "And that was why the receptionist at the hotel said she seemed familiar."

"In early November Tjaša Kolenc resigned and nobody knew why. I enquired about her phone number which is unavailable, and her family..."

She met Taras' eyes in the mirror.

"She didn't have one. She came from a foster family with which she did not maintain contact."

"Is she our victim?" Brajc asked.

Taras nodded.

"And we are going?"

"To Bohinj."

He changed the radio station and then switched off the radio.

"It wasn't Zidar who killed her or ordered her murder, they did not kill her to send him a message and our pharmaceutical tycoon is innocent. Verbič also in as far as the bodies in Bohinj are concerned, and your digging in the past brought up a tragic death of a baby and the mother, and nothing else..."

"Who then?" Brajc asked.

"Funny," Taras sighed. "Last autumn, towards the end of September, at my wife's clinic, the part of it run by Dr Prelc, they introduced some new method into the treatment of something or other I can't remember. A TV crew from RTV Slovenia visited them and I happened to be there at the time and I recall a young girl… About your age, Tina. She stood in front of Dr Prelc with a microphone asking him about this latest treatment."

What had surprised Taras at the time was that Dr Prelc appeared quite normal. He didn't neigh and stamp his hooves, if we can call it that, he didn't set all the guns of an ageing playboy onto the girl, he didn't use expressions like 'young colleague' or give compliments, or drool over her so that everyone else around would be embarrassed. No, the only thing he did was to invite her for a coffee after the shoot.

"Look, if you have the time and can join me for a coffee, I can explain the significance of this new method," he had said. "These things are complicated even for scientists."

Even Alenka, who Taras had been waiting for at the clinic to take out for a meal, commented that Prelc was becoming strangely normal.

"Must be getting old," she had decided.

"I sat with this man on the terrace of his weekend house in Ukanc where we are going now, when he tried to tell me something before he was interrupted, something about how he needed to settle down, that was what he said… I didn't know why he was telling me, because we were not friends… At least I didn't think we were… Prelc then also mentioned that he might need my professional help. Now I know why."

He explained to them about the funeral, about the gravestone, the son who had died aged seven, the wife who due to his illness had abandoned her career, who with his death lost a son but in a way also her husband...

"At the time he mentioned that his wife, meaning Karin, had performed or almost performed at the Olympic Games in Montreal in 1976. And because he mentioned Nadia Comăneci with her perfect ten at these games... If I remember correctly on uneven bars."

He looked at Tina in the mirror. She smiled and despite everything Taras could not avoid thinking how cute she was.

"Some of you in this car weren't even born then."

She rolled her eyes, covered her mouth with her hand so Osterc wouldn't see and sent him a kiss.

"Well, because he mentioned her, I also assumed that she was a gymnast. I missed that he also mentioned someone else, Jackie Stewart, who had a story similar to Karin. I googled this and found out that Jackie Stewart, before becoming a racing driver, had also tried to qualify for the Olympics in Rome..."

"And?" Brajc asked impatiently.

"...in shooting, not gymnastics."

"So..." Bajc could not take this much longer.

"Karin Prelc, then still Podlesnik, was the national champion between 1974 and 1979 – in shooting with low calibre arms. The only woman, so I was told by a man from the National Shooting Association whom I managed to find half an hour ago, who was equally as good with a rifle and a pistol. Had it not been for Yugoslav Olympic machinations, she would have participated at Montreal, but in the end she was sent only as a reserve."

They drove along in silence for a while until Osterc spoke from the back seat.

"Is she not your wife's friend?"

"Yes."

"And Lap?" Tina asked.

"I don't know. I can just assume that he was sent by Zidar who clearly sensed that something was happening to his Tjaša. He came across Mrs Prelc dealing with her rival and got a shot in the eye."

The road to the weekend house was cleared and Taras didn't try to hide their arrival. He parked next to the Volvo crossover and looked at his team.

"She already has two on her conscience," he said and tapped his gun.

He knocked with the ancient knocker because there was no bell and waited. Once again, to no response, so he quickly and forcefully opened the door and looked into the room from the side. The door which would have obscured the view from the hallway into the main room of this residential weekend house was open and he spotted Karin. He stepped towards her, wiping off the snow from his shoes in the hallway.

"Hello Karin."

She sat on the sofa, still dressed as she had been at the funeral, with the black veil hiding half her face. She had a glass of red wine in front of her and watched Taras. He walked towards her so that his three colleagues were also able to come inside, but he indicated to them that they should wait at the door.

"Can I sit down?"

"Please."

Her face was calm, calm as it had been at the funeral and at the feast afterwards. A kind of determination emanated from it and there seemed to be no weapons around.

"Would you like a drink, Taras?" she asked as if she hadn't noticed the others. "Oh, of course, you don't drink."

"You know why we're here, Karin?"

She smiled.

"To be honest, I thought you'd have come earlier."

Her gaze was almost accusatory.

"What kept you?"

What had kept him? When he went to collect his trio from the station, he had thought about that himself.

"A number of things. That you threw the body in the water, that you removed its head... Water removed all traces and without a head it's difficult to establish the identity... Was that deliberate?"

She smiled again.

"Beginners luck. Don't overestimate me, Taras. As far as these things go I'm a complete amateur. Why did I throw her in the water? What else could I do with her if I live by the lake? The head? I wanted to give it as a gift to my dear husband, but, well, in the end I could not muster that much evil."

"Do you still have it?"

She pointed beyond his back with her finger.

"In the shed. It was there all the time."

Taras turned around and looked at Brajc who nodded.

"And why did you do that Karin?"

She pulled a face and shook her head.

"You know what, I don't even know any more, Taras. It is all… strange. Did you notice my son, the gravestone…? I saw you."

Taras nodded.

"I was in love with him, madly. Rajko… You know what a beautiful person he was? Slim, handsome, wavy hair turning silver even then. Richard Gere, they called him. Did you know that they were born on the same day? Rajko senior and Rajko junior. Everyone loved him… You would have liked him. Didn't you want a son? Alenka told me."

"No, I didn't. She just thinks I did."

She straightened her veil, then lifted it back from her face. Taras could see her eyes for the first time. They were dry but with her mascara smudged all around then.

"I was a student when became pregnant, graduated when I was eight months pregnant and gave birth to the most beautiful child in the world. A spitting image of his father."

Two tears appeared from her eyes, rolled down her cheeks and fell onto her lap.

"He would have been the age of this girl here now," she said, pointing with her thin finger at Tina.

Two more tears on the same path. She didn't wipe them away, she didn't even move.

"When were you last happy in your life? You don't know, do you? I do. I was last happy five minutes after the birth of my son, before they told me there was something wrong with him. Doctors can be so cruel. 'This one won't make it,' one of them had said in front of me. Do you know what happened to him?"

Taras nodded.

"What is it you climbers say? Alenka once explained it to me. It's better to be born without … how does it go – without a dick than without luck. Isn't it?"

"Something like that," he nodded.

"If you're lucky you might still grow one. Yes, vulgar, but that's what life is like. I don't know Taras, when Rajko told me he was leaving because he had met another woman..."

She closed her eyes and despite this shed two more tears.

"He had loads of women... you know that, don't you Taras?"

"I know."

"I don't now if you know... He had loads of women... Alenka also, did you know?"

"I know," Taras replied coldly.

"You know? And I pretended that I didn't care, but I did care. It hurt..."

She sighed and closed her eyes again.

"As if someone had rewound the film, as if my life was playing out before my eyes... and all you can say after such a projection is that it was miserable. Too much of everything."

She opened her eyes and looked at him. This was a different Karin altogether.

"What would you do if you came home and waiting for you there was some guy, naked, and told you that he was not expecting you, but Alenka? And that she was pregnant by him."

"Pregnant?"

"Yes pregnant with my man. With whom I was unable to have another child."

"She was not pregnant," said Taras and repeated it. "Believe me, she wasn't."

"She said she was."

"When you held the gun to her head. What was she supposed to have done?"

Karin grimaced.

"And you shot her?"

"Yes."

"What about the man we also pulled from the lake?"

"I don't know where he appeared from. He just stood there, watching."

"And you shot him as well."

She nodded.

"Then you stuck them into Balažič's boat and rowed out

towards Stara Fužina where the lake is deepest..."

"I've been coming here for thirty years, Taras. I know more about the lake than the locals."

"And you weighed down the man, but not the woman."

"She was naked. Where was I supposed to stuff the stones?"

"Then you burnt the boat on the shore and took another one to go back."

"It was all bloody," she said apologetically.

"But your didn't tie the boat to Balažič's mooring?"

"I don't know, Taras..."

If only those spoilt brats not taken the boat out onto the lake and unintentionally not 'returned' it to Balažič, if only he had believed the girl who said they found the boat on the shore, and if only Balažič's wife would have noticed that it was not their boat...

Taras brushed his hand through his hair.

"I watched you, the other day, out on the lake."

He looked at her. There was a wicked smile on her face.

"What are you talking about?"

"You," she once again pointed her thin, old woman's finger beyond his back, "and this girl there. You were very friendly with each other out on the lake."

"We were cold," said Taras.

A kind of rasping sigh came from her, almost a growl.

"All you men are the same."

The door behind Taras opened and someone cleared his throat. Taras turned round and saw Brajc whose face showed that what he had found was not pretty.

"As I told you, she was there all the time."

Taras sighed and ran his hand through his hair again. Too much of everything... He looked at her and tried to compose himself. Let's finish this,

"There's one more thing we need to clarify... The death of your husband. Apparently he took blood pressure pills, had anyone switched these pills for ones with the opposite effect, that could have caused a stroke."

Karin laughed.

"Who told you that?"

Taras kept silent.

"Well, that's one thing we won't ever know, will we?"

She gave him an evil look.

"But don't worry, if there is anything you'd find in him it would be excessive quantities of Viagra. It was that which killed him, not me."

She picked up the glass and held it against the light.

"Like blood," she said. "You don't know what you're missing."

"She was a human being, Karin."

"Just like I once was."

She raised her glass as if wanting to toast with it, tilted it and slowly but with determination drank all the wine, then she carefully placed it back onto the table, as if she was afraid it might fall out of her hands at any moment. Taras beckoned to Osterc who pulled some handcuffs from his pocket and approached them, but was stopped by the gurgling sound coming from the woman's mouth. Tina came running up to them and stopped in confusion, looked at the woman who had curled up in a ball and in terrible spasms crawled from the sofa onto the floor, and then at Taras who sat there absently, almost calmly following what was going on. Then he looked at her and turned towards Osterc,

"Call Cvilak."

*

The head of the girl they had pulled out of the river was in a box, wrapped in plastic on the top shelf among the tools and Taras didn't look at it. He handed it over to Cvilak who agreed to be driven to the site two hours later, showed him the body and gave him a description of the death...

"Karin..." Cvilak whispered and stood silently by the body for a while. Then he sighed and kneeled by it. "Cyanide," he said, "I bet it was cyanide." He turned round and his gaze stopped on Tina, "It prevents cells from breathing. It inhibits the enzyme cytochrome c oxidase and essentially what happens is internal suffocation. You call out and...

Epilogue

He stepped outside the house and took a deep breath of air. A southerly breeze which brought warmer air with it and the snow on the roof had begun to melt.

"Case closed," he said to himself half aloud and thought that in the early morning he could jump up to Pokljuka for some cross-country skiing before all the snow melted and before starting all the paperwork and putting the story together for the court, for Drvarič, for the media. With this damn global warming you can never be sure any more whether the January snow might also be the last.

He found his head torch in the glove compartment, switched it on and found the tracks in the snow leading from the far end of the yard down to the lake, some thirty metres away. The water was black, cold, unpleasant and the foehn wind which began blowing from the mountains caused large waves to form on the surface. He found a flat stone and tried skimming it over the surface. It hit a wave and sank without bouncing off the surface. There is a difference between the way waves splash against the coast at the sea and the way the water from the lake splashes against the shore, the waves seem to break in a different way. By the lake you can always smell moss, decay, rot, mud. Even the sound a stone skipping on the surface of the sea or the lake seems different.

The sea heals wounds, the lake opens them.

He stood there for a while until he heard steps behind him and turned round. A silhouette was approaching along the track, carefully finding the steps without a torch. Tina. She stepped from the trail onto the gravel on the shore and stood next to him.

"Has Cvilak finished?"

She nodded. He picked up another stone and threw it at a low angle at the water. It bounced off one wave to sink at the next.

"Is it always this sad?" she asked.

From a nearby fir tree a crow set off in staggering flight across the water. He stared after it until it was simply a silhouette above his head, until it disappeared in the dark. It began to drizzle, initially so lightly that it was not even visible on the lake. Almost as if a slightly thicker mist had descended over the lake. Then tiny dots began to appear on the surface, slowly getting bigger. He'd have to forget about Pokljuka.

"It's different in the summer," he said. "A million people, swimming, rowing, surfing, lots of paragliders, sand volley... it's all alive. As if it was not the same lake."

"That's not what I was thinking about."

Of course she wasn't. He pulled his phone from his pocket and checked the screen. Saturday, 16 January, half past two in the morning. Was the Marche motorway station on the way to Ljubljana open all night? He needed a coffee. At least a coffee.

THE END

Acknowledgements

For the story to remain within the framework of the realistic, I have to thank a number of people, especially the following:

Dr Jože Balažic, Head of the Institute of Forensic Medicine in Ljubljana; Dr Dorijan Keržan, Director of the National Forensic Laboratory; Dr Blaž Stres, Associate Professor at the Biotehnical Faculty in Ljubljana and at the University of Innsbruck; Anita Bregar, Head of the Centre for Social Services, Jesenice; and Dunja Murn and Rok Lehner from the Jesenice municipal cemetery at Blejska Dobrava. Their help was crucial and greatly appreciated.